VAMPIRES
The Recent Undead

Other anthologies edited by Paula Guran

VAMPIRES
The Recent Undead

Edited by Paula Guran

PRIME BOOKS

Vampires: The Recent Undead

Copyright © 2011 by Paula Guran.

Cover art by Szabo Balaz.

Cover design by Stephen H. Segal.

ISBN: 978-1-60701-254-2

All stories are copyrighted to their respective authors,
and used here with their permission.
An extension of this copyright page can be found on pages 429-430.

Publisher's Note:
No portion of this book may be reproduced by any means, mechanical,
electronic, or otherwise, without first obtaining the permission of the
copyright holder.

For more information, contact Prime Books:

www.prime-books.com

To Chelsea Quinn Yarbro:
A woman to whom many who
write (or read) vampire fiction
owe more than they may realize.

Contents

Introduction

"*. . . every age embraces the vampire it needs.*"
—Nina Auerbach

The year 2010 may have marked a new high point in the popularity of the vampire. Although Stephenie Myer's Twilight series (books and film), Charlaine Harris's Southern Vampire Mystery series and its HBO incarnation as *True Blood*, and the *Vampire Diaries* television series (based on L.J. Smith's young adult series of the same name from the nineties) all began earlier in the decade, their popularity hit blood-fever pitch in 2010. Films like *Daybreakers* and *Let Me In* (the American remake of Swedish film *Let the Right One In* based on John Ajvide Lindqvist's novel *Låt den rätte komma*) also made an impact. In the UK, even *Doctor Who* featured vampire-like creatures in an episode titled "Vampires in Venice." The Brits also enjoyed the second *Being Human* series—featuring a vampire living with a ghost and a werewolf—on BBC Three.

As for vampire fiction not (yet) on TV or film, it ranged from the "literary horror" of *The Passage* by Justin Cronin to a bevy of best-selling urban fantasy and paranormal romance titles and series for both adult and young adult readers. There were children's books as well (including *Dick and Jane and Vampires*). The final two books of Gail Carriger's Parasol Protectorate trilogy featured a "Victorian vampire slayer" while Seth Grahame-Smith mashed up the Great Emancipator with fangsters in *Abraham Lincoln: Vampire Hunter*.

Vampires were inescapable.

Hundreds of thousands of words have been written about vampires, our fascination with them, and their meaning and place in our culture. If you want in-depth information, either scholarly or written for popular consumption, there's plenty available. The focus of this anthology is short vampire fiction published 2000-2010, but let's take a quick sip of the bloody background for context.

The idea of the vampire has probably been around since humanity first began to ponder death. In Western culture the vampire has been a pervasive icon for more than two centuries now, but the image of the vampire as something other than a disgusting reanimated corpse was profoundly reshaped in the early nineteenth century by a group of British aristocrats.

Mary Wollstonecraft Godwin, Percy Shelley, Matthew Lewis, Lord Byron, and Byron's physician, Dr. John Polidori, decided to amuse themselves one damp summer 1816 evening in a villa on Lake Geneva by writing ghost stories. Mary Godwin (who later married Shelley) created a modern myth (and science fiction) with *Frankenstein, or Prometheus Unbound*. Polidori picked up a fragment written by Byron and produced a story based on it: "The Vampyre." It featured Lord Ruthven, a seductive refined noble as well as a blood-sucking monster who preyed on others. The character was obviously based on the already notorious Byron himself.

"The Vampyre" became wildly popular, particularly in Germany and France. The theatres of Paris were filled by the early 1820s with vampire-themed plays. Some of these returned to England in translated form.

As Brian Stableford has written, "The Vampyre" was the "most widely read vampire story of its era . . . To say that it was influential is something of an under-statement; there was probably no one in England or France who attempted to write a vampire story in the nineteenth century who was not familiar with it, one way or another." Poldori's story was certainly the inspiration for the serialized "penny dreadful" *Varney the Vampire or, The Feast of Blood* (1845-47) by (most likely) James Malcolm Rhymer. *Varney* appealed to the masses, but was of even less literary merit than the short story to which it owed so much.

It took Sheridan le Fanu to craft a true literary gem with his novella "Carmilla," published in 1872. The tale of a lonely girl and a beautiful aristo-cratic female vampire in an isolated castle also brought steamy (albeit lesbian) sexuality into the vampire mythos.

But it was Bram Stoker's novel *Dracula* (1897) that became the basis of modern vampire lore: Dracula was a vampire "king" of indefinite lifespan who could not be seen in mirrors, had an affinity to bats and aversions to crucifixes and garlic. He had superhuman strength, could shapeshift and control human minds. Stoker's vampires needed their native soil and the best way to kill one was with a stake through the heart followed by decapitation. There were humans who, like Abraham Van Helsing, hunted vampires . . . etc.

Not that Stoker's Count Dracula was originally all that he came to be. Stoker described him as a tall old man with "a long white moustache, and clad in black from head to foot, without a single speck of colour about him anywhere." The Count's "eyebrows were very massive, almost meeting over the nose" and there were hairs in the center of his palms. He also had bad breath.

True cultural permeation—and refinement of the Dracula archetype—came through later stage and screen adaptations. The silent film *Nosferau* (1922), for instance, took Dracula's nocturnal nature and turned it into the inability to survive sunlight. Bela Lugosi's portrayal (first on stage then, in 1931, on screen) of a suave foreign aristocrat in evening attire who seduced beautiful young women and slept in a coffin had much to do with the popular image of the count.

Various vampiric attributes and powers were added or subtracted in films and short stories in the decades thereafter. (Along with other innovations, Christopher Lee's Dracula "showed fang" for the first time in 1958.) But although the vampire thrived in those two media, no truly notable vampire novels were published until 1954 when Richard Matheson contributed the idea of vampirism as an infectious disease with apocalyptic consequence in his novel *I Am Legend*.

Other novels from the 1960s also added embellishments to the icon, but in the 1970s the image of the vampire changed radically. Fred Saberhagen's *The Dracula Tape* (1975) presented a sympathetic Dracula telling his own story. Stephen King downplayed vampiric eroticism, upped the level of terror, and focused on the vampire as a metaphor of corrupt power in his 1975 vampire novel *'Salem's Lot* (1975). Anne Rice introduced a vampire with a conscience who needed others of his kind, in *Interview With the Vampire* (1976). King and Rice brought the vampire fully into the cultural mainstream.

Less well-known to the public, but highly influential, Chelsea Quinn Yarbro began her series featuring the first truly romantic and heroic vampire, the Count Saint-Germain, with *Hôtel Transylvania* in 1978.

Meanwhile, millions had watched Jonathan Frid portray Barnabas Collins on television's Gothic soap opera *Dark Shadows* (1966-1971) as he transformed from an evil villain to a vampire seeking redemption and his long-lost love. Dracula was again portrayed (beginning in 1977 on Broadway and followed by a 1979 film) by Frank Langella, who de-emphasized the violence and stressed the supremely seductive.

Throughout the 1980s and 1990s vampires came in all varieties in literature and other media: traditional monsters, heroes, detectives, aliens, rock stars, psychic predators, loners, tribal, erotic, sexless, violent, placed in alternate histories, present in contemporary settings . . . the vampire became a malleable metaphor of great diversity in many forms, even—first in Lori Herter's *Obsession* (1991)—in the romance marketing category. A number of notable vampire novels were published in the eighties and nineties, but Anne Rice continued to make the firmest impression on the masses as the best-selling queen of vampire novelists. The vampire also became graphically sexual in the mid-nineties as well.

The 1990s also saw a number of vampire-themed anthologies of original stories and, consequently, more opportunities for short form vampire fiction. Among these were Ellen Datlow's *Blood Is Not Enough: 17 Stories of Vampirism* (1990) and *A Whisper of Blood* (1995); *Love In Vein: 20 Original Tales of Vampire Erotica* (1994) and *Love In Vein II: 18 More Tales of Vampiric Erotica* (1997) edited by Poppy Z. Brite and Martin H. Greenberg; and *100 Vicious Little Vampire Stories* (1995) edited by Stefan Dziemianowicz, Robert Weinberg, and Martin H. Greenberg. Marking the centenary of the publication of *Dracula*, the mostly original *The Mammoth Book of Dracula: Vampire Tales for the New Millennium*, edited by Stephen Jones, was published in 1997. For the very adult there were highly eroticized vampires in anthologies like *Love Bites* (1994), edited by "Amarantha Knight" (aka Nancy Kilpatrick). For younger readers there was *Vampires: A Collection of Original Stories* (1991) edited by Jane Yolen and Martin H. Greenberg (1991). Genre magazines and anthologies provided other venues for short vampire fiction, even if they had no specific connection to the icon.

Toward the end of the last century—sometime after the release of Laurell K. Hamilton's fourth Anita Blake Vampire Hunter fantasy novel, *The Lunatic Cafe* (1996), perhaps during the second (1997-1998) or third (1998-1999) season of television series *Buffy the Vampire Slayer*, and just before the first of Christine Feehan's romance *Dark Prince*, the first of her Dark series (1999)—vampires started getting "hot."

The "good guy" vampire—usually sexy, often romantic, sometimes redeemed or redeemable, sometimes ever-heroic—started to dominate pop culture. So did sexy-but-empowered female vamps and kick-ass vampire hunters.

The frightening vamp was most definitely still around, however, and making an impact. A few examples: films *28 Days Later* (2002), *I Am Legend* (2007) *Van Helsing* (2004), and *30 Days of Night* (2009), based on the 2002 comic book mini-series written by Steve Niles and illustrated by Ben Templesmith. The novel *Fangland* by John Marks (2007) was an *homage* to Stoker-type scares.

The high literary metaphorical vampire (*The Historian*, Elizabeth Kostova, 2005) was still in our group psyche too, along with the viral/apocalyptic vamp (*The Passage*, Justin Cronin, 2010), the comedic vampire (*You Suck: A Love Story*, Christopher Moore, 2007), the science fictional/sociological vampire (*The Fledgling*, Octavia Butler, 2007), and just about every other variety—new or old.

But the popularity of paranormal romance and urban fantasy vampires soared and at least *seemed* to be the *numero uno* vampire of the decade. Numerous best-selling series featured vampires and then *Twilight*, a vampire fantasy/romance for teens by Stephenie Meyer was released in 2005. It and the other three books of Meyer's saga were immensely popular, but the films based on the series propelled the romantic vampire hero to stratospheric levels of popularity. The *True Blood* TV series (based on Charlaine Harris's novels) helped fuel the bloodlust.

What does all this mean? Pop culturists, scholars, pundits, various experts, and those who really have no idea but think they do will continue to weigh in. We'll leave the analyses to them.

In practical terms, for short vampire fiction it has meant a boom in anthology opportunities for original urban and paranormal romance stories and, increasingly, for both types of fiction written for the young adult market. Vamps also crept into many urban fantasy, paranormal romance, supernatural mystery, and cross-genre original anthologies without a specifically fanged theme. Even funny vampires found their way into anthologies in the oughts.

There seem to have been fewer occasions, however, for writers with other vampiric ideas to show their talents. But new stories still found their way into periodicals, non-vamp anthologies, and compilations of reprinted stories that included a limited number of original stories. (See page 427 for a list of vampire anthologies published 2000-2010.)

The stories of *Vampires: The Recent Undead* were published from 2000 into early 2010. If you are an avid vampirist, you are sure to have come across some of them previously—this is, after all, a retrospective—but I think you'll also make some new discoveries. You will certainly find a wide variety of vampire stories herein. It is so diverse, I'm fairly sure not every selection will please every reader. But that is to be expected. This first decade of the twenty-first century seems to have been marked by division more than cohesion. The world of 2011 is not the same as that of the year 2000, nor even the world of 2007. New threats and, consequently, new terrors have arisen. How we face those fears—or escape them—has a lot to do with our preferences in vampires.

Maybe we "needed" to embrace vampire heterogeneity in the past ten years.

As we enter a new decade, what kind of vampire will we embrace? Nancy Kilpatrick edited a 2010 anthology *Evolve: Vampire Stories of the New Undead*. Its stories (none of which could appear here due to contractual necessity) may show a glimpse of the future of the vampire. *Evolve²: Vampire Stories of the Future Undead* is slated for this year. If you are looking for a glimpse of the Next Vampire, you might get some clues there.

Meanwhile I hope you enjoy exploring these examples of the myth of the vampire as written—so far—for the New Millennium.

Paula Guran, January 2011

The Coldest Girl in Cold Town
Holly Black

I chose "The Coldest Girl in Coldtown" for The Year's Best Dark Fantasy and Horror: 2010. *Since then I've come to feel even more strongly that it has the makings of a classic. Black's irony-rich tale has more characterization, world building, social commentary, and emotion than many novels can manage with a dozen times as many words.*

Black is a best-selling author of contemporary fantasy novels for teens and children. Her first book, Tithe: A Modern Faerie Tale *(2002) was included in the American Library Association's Best Books for Young Adults. She has since written two other books in the same universe,* Valiant *(2005), and* Ironside *(2007). Valiant was a finalist for the Mythopoeic Award for Young Readers and the recipient of the Andre Norton Award for Excellence in Young Adult Literature. Black collaborated with artist Tony DiTerlizzi, to create the Spiderwick Chronicles. The Spiderwick Chronicles were adapted into a film and released in February 2008. Black has co-edited three anthologies:* Geektastic *(with Cecil Castellucci, 2009),* Zombies vs. Unicorns *(with Justine Larbalestier, 2010), and* Bordertown *(with Ellen Kushner, 2011). Her first collection of short fiction,* The Poison Eaters and Other Stories, *came out in 2010. She has just finished the third book in her Eisner-nominated graphic novel series,* The Good Neighbors, *and is working on* Red Glove, *the second novel in* The Curse Workers *series, which will be released in April 2011.* White Cat, *the first in the series, was published in May 2010. The author lives in Massachusetts with her husband, Theo, in a house with a secret library.*

MATILDA WAS drunk, but then she was always drunk anymore. Dizzy drunk. Stumbling drunk. Stupid drunk. Whatever kind of drunk she could get.

The man she stood with snaked his hand around her back, warm fingers digging into her side as he pulled her closer. He and his friend with the open-necked shirt grinned down at her like underage equaled dumb, and dumb equaled gullible enough to sleep with them.

She thought they might just be right.

"You want to have a party back at my place?" the man asked. He'd told her his name was Mark, but his friend kept slipping up and calling him by a name that started with a D. Maybe Dan or Dave. They had been smuggling her drinks from the bar whenever they went outside to smoke—drinks mixed sickly sweet that dripped down her throat like candy.

"Sure," she said, grinding her cigarette against the brick wall. She missed the hot ash in her hand, but concentrated on the alcoholic numbness turning her limbs to lead. Smiled. "Can we pick up more beer?"

They exchanged an obnoxious glance she pretended not to notice. The friend—he called himself Ben—looked at her glassy eyes and her cold-flushed cheeks. Her sloppy hair. He probably made guesses about a troubled home life. She hoped so.

"You're not going to get sick on us?" he asked. Just out of the hot bar, beads of sweat had collected in the hollow of his throat. The skin shimmered with each swallow.

She shook her head to stop staring. "I'm barely tipsy," she lied.

"I've got plenty of stuff back at my place," said MarkDanDave. *Mardave*, Matilda thought and giggled.

"Buy me a 40," she said. She knew it was stupid to go with them, but it was even stupider if she sobered up. "One of those wine coolers. They have them at the bodega on the corner. Otherwise, no party."

Both of the guys laughed. She tried to laugh with them even though she knew she wasn't included in the joke. She was the joke. The trashy little slut. The girl who can be bought for a big fat wine cooler and three cranberry-and-vodkas.

"Okay, okay," said Mardave.

They walked down the street and she found herself leaning easily into the heat of their bodies, inhaling the sweat and iron scent. It would be easy for her to close her eyes and pretend Mardave was someone else, someone she wanted to be touched by, but she wouldn't let herself soil her memories of Julian.

They passed by a store with flat-screens in the window, each one showing different channels. One streamed video from Coldtown—a girl who went by the name Demonia made some kind of deal with one of the stations to show what it was really like behind the gates. She filmed the Eternal Ball, a party that started in 1998 and had gone on ceaselessly ever since. In the background, girls and boys in rubber harnesses swung through the air. They stopped occasionally, opening what looked like a modded hospital tube stuck on the inside of their arms just below the crook of the elbow. They twisted a knob and spilled blood into little paper cups for the partygoers. A boy who looked to be about nine, wearing a string of glowing beads around his neck, gulped down the contents of one of the cups and then licked the paper with a tongue as red as his eyes. The camera angle changed suddenly, veering up, and the viewers saw the domed top of the hall, full of cracked windows through which you could glimpse the stars.

"I know where they are," Mardave said. "I can see that building from my apartment."

"Aren't you scared of living so close to the vampires?" she asked, a small smile pulling at the corners of her mouth.

"We'll protect you," said Ben, smiling back at her.

"We should do what other countries do and blow those corpses sky high," Mardave said.

Matilda bit her tongue not to point out that Europe's vampire hunting led to the highest levels of infection in the world. So many of Belgium's citizens were vampires that shops barely opened their doors until nightfall. The truce with Coldtown worked. Mostly.

She didn't care if Mardave hated vampires. She hated them too.

When they got to the store, she waited outside to avoid getting carded and lit another cigarette with Julian's silver lighter—the one she was going to give back to him in thirty-one days. Sitting down on the curb, she let the chill of the pavement deaden the backs of her thighs. Let it freeze her belly and frost her throat with ice that even liquor couldn't melt.

Hunger turned her stomach. She couldn't remember the last time she'd eaten anything solid without throwing it back up. Her mouth hungered for dark, rich feasts; her skin felt tight, like a seed thirsting to bloom. All she could trust herself to eat was smoke.

When she was a little girl, vampires had been costumes for Halloween. They were the bad guys in movies, plastic fangs and polyester capes. They were Muppets on television, endlessly counting.

Now she was the one who was counting. Fifty-seven days. Eighty-eight days. Eighty-eight nights.

"Matilda?"

She looked up and saw Dante saunter up to her, earbuds dangling out of his ears like he needed a soundtrack for everything he did. He wore a pair of skin-tight jeans and smoked a cigarette out of one of those long, movie-star holders. He looked pretentious as hell. "I'd almost given up on finding you."

"You should have started with the gutter," she said, gesturing to the wet, clogged tide beneath her feet. "I take my gutter-dwelling very seriously."

"*Seriously.*" He pointed at her with the cigarette holder. "Even your mother thinks you're dead. Julian's crying over you."

Maltilda looked down and picked at the thread of her jeans. It hurt to think about Julian while waiting for Mardave and Ben. She was disgusted with herself, and she could only guess how disgusted he'd be. "I got Cold," she said. "One of them bit me."

Dante nodded his head.

That's what they'd started calling it when the infection kicked in—Cold— because of how cold people's skin became after they were bitten. And because of the way the poison in their veins caused them to crave heat and blood. One taste of human blood and the infection mutated. It killed the host and then raised it back up again, colder than before. Cold through and through, forever and ever.

"I didn't think you'd be alive," he said.

She hadn't thought she'd make it this long either without giving in. But going it alone on the street was better than forcing her mother to choose between chaining her up in the basement or shipping her off to Coldtown. It was better, too, than taking the chance Matilda might get loose from the chains and attack people she loved. Stories like that were in the news all the time; almost as frequent as the ones about people who let vampires into their homes because they seemed so nice and clean-cut.

"Then what are you doing looking for me?" she asked. Dante had lived down the street from her family for years, but they didn't hang out. She'd wave to him as she mowed the lawn while he loaded his panel van with DJ equipment. He shouldn't have been here.

She looked back at the store window. Mardave and Ben were at the counter with a case of beer and her wine cooler. They were getting change from a clerk.

"I was hoping you, er, *wouldn't* be alive," Dante said. "You'd be more help if you were dead."

She stood up, stumbling slightly. "Well, screw you too."

It took eighty-eight days for the venom to sweat out a person's pores. She only had thirty-seven to go. Thirty-seven days to stay so drunk that she could ignore the buzz in her head that made her want to bite, rend, devour.

"That came out wrong," he said, taking a step toward her. Close enough that she felt the warmth of him radiating off him like licking tongues of flame. She shivered. Her veins sang with need.

"I can't help you," said Matilda. "Look, I can barely help myself. Whatever it is, I'm sorry. I can't. You have to get out of here."

"My sister Lydia and your boyfriend Julian are gone," Dante said. "Together. She's looking to get bitten. I don't know what he's looking for . . . but he's going to get hurt."

Matilda gaped at him as Mardave and Ben walked out of the store. Ben carried a box on his shoulder and a bag on his arm. "That guy bothering you?" he asked her.

"No," she said, then turned to Dante. "You better go."

"Wait," said Dante.

Matilda's stomach hurt. She was sobering up. The smell of blood seemed to float up from underneath their skin.

She reached into Ben's bag and grabbed a beer. She popped the top, licked off the foam. If she didn't get a lot drunker, she was going to attack someone.

"Jesus," Mardave said. "Slow down. What if someone sees you?"

She drank it in huge gulps, right there on the street. Ben laughed, but it wasn't a good laugh. He was laughing at the drunk.

"She's infected," Dante said.

Matilda whirled toward him, chucking the mostly empty can in his direction automatically. "Shut up, asshole."

"Feel her skin," Dante said. "Cold. She ran away from home when it happened, and no one's seen her since."

"I'm cold because it's cold out," she said.

She saw Ben's evaluation of her change from *damaged enough to sleep with strangers to dangerous enough to attack strangers.*

Mardave touched his hand gently to her arm. "Hey," he said.

She almost hissed with delight at the press of his hot fingers. She smiled up at him and hoped her eyes weren't as hungry as her skin. "I really like you."

He flinched. "Look, it's late. Maybe we could meet up another time." Then he backed away, which made her so angry that she bit the inside of her own cheek.

Her mouth flooded with the taste of copper and a red haze floated in front of her eyes.

Fifty-seven days ago, Matilda had been sober. She'd had a boyfriend named Julian, and they would dress up together in her bedroom. He liked to wear skinny ties and glittery eye shadow. She liked to wear vintage rock T-shirts and boots that laced up so high that they would constantly be late because they were busy tying them.

Matilda and Julian would dress up and prowl the streets and party at lockdown clubs that barred the doors from dusk to dawn. Matilda wasn't particularly careless; she was just careless enough.

She'd been at a friend's party. It had been stiflingly hot, and she was mad because Julian and Lydia were doing some dance thing from the musical they were in at school. Matilda just wanted to get some air. She opened a window and climbed out under the bobbing garland of garlic.

Another girl was already on the lawn. Matilda should have noticed that the girl's breath didn't crystallize in the air, but she didn't.

"Do you have a light?" the girl had asked.

Matilda did. She reached for Julian's lighter when the girl caught her arm and bent her backwards. Matilda's scream turned into a shocked cry when she felt the girl's cold mouth against her neck, the girl's cold fingers holding her off balance.

Then it was as though someone slid two shards of ice into her skin.

The spread of vampirism could be traced to one person—Caspar Morales. Films and books and television had started romanticizing vampires, and maybe it was only a matter of time before a vampire started romanticizing *himself*.

Crazy, romantic Caspar decided that he wouldn't kill his victims. He'd just drink a little blood and then move on, city to city. By the time other vampires caught up with him and ripped him to pieces, he'd infected hundreds of people. And those new vampires, with no idea how to prevent the spread, infected thousands.

When the first outbreak happened in Tokyo, it seemed like a journalist's prank. Then there was another outbreak in Hong Kong and another in San Francisco.

The military put up barricades around the area where the infection broke out. That was the way the first Coldtown was founded.

Matilda's body twitched involuntarily. She could feel the spasm start in the muscles of her back and move to her face. She wrapped her arms around herself to try and stop it, but her hands were shaking pretty hard. "You want my help, you better get me some booze."

"You're killing yourself," Dante said, shaking his head.

"I just need another drink," she said. "Then I'll be fine."

He shook his head. "You can't keep going like this. You can't just stay drunk to avoid your problems. I know, people do. It's a classic move, even, but I didn't figure you for fetishizing your own doom."

She started laughing. "You don't understand. When I'm wasted I don't crave blood. It's the only thing keeping me human."

"What?" He looked at Matilda like he couldn't quite make sense of her words.

"Let me spell it out: if you don't get me some alcohol, I am going to bite you."

"Oh." He fumbled for his wallet. "Oh. Okay."

Matilda had spent all the cash she'd brought with her in the first few weeks, so it'd been a long time since she could simply overpay some homeless guy to go into a liquor store and get her a fifth of vodka. She gulped gratefully from the bottle Dante gave her in a nearby alley.

A few moments later, warmth started to creep up from her belly, and her mouth felt like it was full of needles and Novocain.

"You okay?" he asked her.

"Better now," she said, her words slurring slightly. "But I still don't understand. Why do you need me to help you find Lydia and Julian?

"Lydia got obsessed with becoming a vampire," Dante said, irritably brushing back the stray hair that fell across his face.

"Why?"

He shrugged. "She used to be really scared of vampires. When we were kids, she begged Mom to let her camp in the hallway because she wanted to sleep where there were no windows. But then I guess she started to be fascinated instead. She thinks that human annihilation is coming. She says that we all have to choose sides and she's already chosen."

"I'm not a vampire," Matilda said.

Dante gestured irritably with his cigarette holder. The cigarette had long burned out. He didn't look like his usual contemptuous self; he looked lost. "I know. I thought you would be. And—I don't know—you're on the street. Maybe you know more than the video feeds do about where someone might go to get themselves bitten."

Matilda thought about lying on the floor of Julian's parents' living room. They had been sweaty from dancing and kissed languidly. On the television, a list of missing people flashed. She had closed her eyes and kissed him again.

She nodded slowly. "I know a couple of places. Have you heard from her at all?"

He shook his head. "She won't take any of my calls, but she's been updating her blog. I'll show you."

He loaded it on his phone. The latest entry was titled: *I Need a Vampire.* Matilda scrolled down and read. Basically, it was Lydia's plea to be bitten. She wanted any vampires looking for victims to contact her. In the comments, someone suggested Coldtown and then another person commented in ALL CAPS to say that everyone knew that the vampires in Coldtown were careful to keep their food sources alive.

It was impossible to know which comments Lydia had read and which ones she believed.

Runaways went to Coldtown all the time, along with the sick, the sad, and the maudlin. There was supposed to be a constant party, theirs for the price of blood.

But once they went inside, humans—even human children, even babies born in Coldtown—weren't be allowed to leave. The National Guard patrolled the barbed wire—wrapped and garlic-covered walls to make sure that Coldtown stayed contained.

People said that vampires found ways through the walls to the outside world. Maybe that was just a rumor, although Matilda remembered reading something online about a documentary that proved the truth. She hadn't seen it.

But everyone knew there was only one way to get out of Coldtown if you were still human. Your family had to be rich enough to hire a vampire hunter. Vampire hunters got money from the government for each vampire they put in Coldtown, but they could give up the cash reward in favor of a voucher for a single human's release. One vampire in, one human out.

There was a popular reality television series about one of the hunters, called *Hemlok*. Girls hung posters of him on the insides of their lockers, often right next to pictures of the vampires he hunted.

Most people didn't have the money to outbid the government for a hunter's services. Matilda didn't think that Dante's family did and knew Julian's didn't. Her only chance was to catch Lydia and Julian before they crossed over.

"What's with Julian?" Matilda asked. She'd been avoiding the question for hours as they walked through the alleys that grew progressively more empty the closer they got to the gates.

"What do you mean?" Dante was hunched over against the wind, his long skinny frame offering little protection against the chill. Still, she knew he was warm underneath. Inside.

"Why did Julian go with her?" She tried to keep the hurt out of her voice. She didn't think Dante would understand. He DJed at a club in town and was rumored to see a different boy or girl every day of the week. The only person he actually seemed to care about was his sister.

Dante shrugged slim shoulders. "Maybe he was looking for you."

That was the answer she wanted to hear. She smiled and let herself imagine saving Julian right before he could enter Coldtown. He would tell her that he'd been coming to save her and then they'd laugh and she wouldn't bite him, no matter how warm his skin felt.

Dante snapped his fingers in front of Matilda and she stumbled.

"Hey," she said. "Drunk girl here. No messing with me."

He chuckled.

Melinda and Dante checked all the places she knew, all the places she'd slept on cardboard near runaways and begged for change. Dante had a picture of Lydia in his wallet, but no one who looked at it remembered her.

Finally, outside a bar, they bumped into a girl who said she'd seen Lydia and Julian. Dante traded her the rest of his pack of cigarettes for her story.

"They were headed for Coldtown," she said, lighting up. In the flickering flame of her lighter, Melinda noticed the shallow cuts along her wrists. "Said she was tired of waiting."

"What about the guy?" Matilda asked. She stared at the girl's dried garnet scabs. They looked like crusts of sugar, like the lines of salt left on the beach when the tide goes out. She wanted to lick them.

"He said his girlfriend was a vampire," said the girl, inhaling deeply. She blew out smoke and then started to cough.

"When was that?" Dante asked.

The girl shrugged her shoulders. "Just a couple of hours ago."

Dante took out his phone and pressed some buttons. "Load," he muttered. "Come on, *load*."

"What happened to your arms?" Matilda asked.

The girl shrugged again. "They bought some blood off me. Said that they might need it inside. They had a real professional set-up too. Sharp razor and one of those glass bowls with the plastic lids."

Matilda's stomach clenched with hunger. She turned against the wall and breathed slowly. She needed a drink.

"Is something wrong with her?" the girl asked.

"Matilda," Dante said, and Matilda half-turned. He was holding out his phone. There was a new entry up on Lydia's blog, entitled: *One-Way Ticket to Coldtown.*

"You should post about it," Dante said. "On the message boards."

Matilda was sitting on the ground, picking at the brick wall to give her fingers something to do. Dante had massively overpaid for another bottle of vodka and was cradling it in a crinkled paper bag.

She frowned. "Post about what?"

"About the alcohol. About it helping you keep from turning."

"Where would I post about that?"

Dante twisted off the cap. The heat seemed to radiate off his skin as he swigged from the bottle. "There are forums for people who have to restrain someone for eighty-eight days. They hang out and exchange tips on straps and dealing with the begging for blood. Haven't you seen them?"

She shook her head. "I bet sedation's already a hot topic of discussion. I doubt I'd be telling them anything they don't already know"

He laughed, but it was a bitter laugh. "Then there's all the people who want to be vampires. The websites reminding all the corpsebait out there that being bitten by an infected person isn't enough; it has to be a vampire. The ones listing gimmicks to get vampires to notice you."

"Like what?"

"I dated a girl who cut thin lines on her thighs before she went out dancing so if there was a vampire in the club, it'd be drawn to her scent." Dante didn't look extravagant or affected anymore. He looked defeated.

Matilda smiled at him. "She was probably a better bet than me for getting you into Coldtown."

He returned the smile wanly. "The worst part is that Lydia's not going to get what she wants. She's going become the human servant of some vampire who's going to make her a whole bunch of promises and never turn her. The last thing they need in Coldtown is new vampires."

Matilda imagined Lydia and Julian dancing at the endless Eternal Ball. She pictured them on the streets she'd seen in pictures uploaded to Facebook and Flickr, trying to trade a bowl full of blood for their own deaths.

When Dante passed the bottle to her, she pretended to swig. On the eve of her fifty-eighth day of being infected, Matilda started sobering up.

Crawling over, she straddled Dante's waist before he had a chance to shift positions. His mouth tasted like tobacco. When she pulled back from him, his eyes were wide with surprise, his pupils blown and black even in the dim streetlight.

"Matilda," he said and there was nothing in his voice but longing.

"If you really want your sister, I am going to need one more thing from you," she said.

His blood tasted like tears.

Matilda's skin felt like it had caught fire. She'd turned into lit paper, burning up. Curling into black ash.

She licked his neck over and over and over.

The gates of Coldtown were large and made of consecrated wood, barbed wire covering them like heavy, thorny vines. The guards slouched at their posts, guns over their shoulders, sharing a cigarette. The smell of percolating coffee wafted out of the guardhouse.

"Um, hello," Matilda said. Blood was still sticky where it half-dried around

her mouth and on her neck. It had dribbled down her shirt, stiffening it nearly
to cracking when she moved. Her body felt strange now that she was dying. Hot.
More alive than it had in weeks.

Dante would be all right; she wasn't contagious and she didn't think she'd
hurt him too badly. She hoped she hadn't hurt him too badly. She touched the
phone in her pocket, his phone, the one she'd used to call 911 after she'd left
him.

"Hello," she called to the guards again.

One turned. "Oh my god," he said and reached for his rifle.

"I'm here to turn in a vampire. For a voucher. I want to turn in a vampire in
exchange for letting a human out of Coldtown."

"What vampire?" asked the other guard. He'd dropped the cigarette, but not
stepped on the filter so that it just smoked on the asphalt.

"Me," said Matilda. "I want to turn in me."

They made her wait as her pulse thrummed slower and slower. She wasn't a
vampire yet, and after a few phone calls, they discovered that technically she
could only have the voucher after undeath. They did let her wash her face in the
bathroom of the guardhouse and wring the thin cloth of her shirt until the water
ran down the drain clear, instead of murky with blood.

When she looked into the mirror, her skin had unfamiliar purple shadows,
like bruises. She was still staring at them when she stopped being able to catch her
breath. The hollow feeling in her chest expanded and she found herself panicked,
falling to her knees on the filthy tile floor. She died there, a moment later.

It didn't hurt as much as she'd worried it would. Like most things, the surprise
was the worst part.

The guards released Matilda into Coldtown just a little before dawn. The world
looked strange—everything had taken on a smudgy, silvery cast, like she was
watching an old movie. Sometimes people's heads seemed to blur into black
smears. Only one color was distinct—a pulsing, oozing color that seemed to
glow from beneath skin.

Red.

Her teeth ached to look at it.

There was a silence inside her. No longer did she move to the rhythmic drumming of her heart. Her body felt strange, hard as marble, free of pain. She'd never
realized how many small agonies were alive in the creak of her bones, the pull of
muscle. Now, free of them, she felt like she was floating.

Matilda looked around with her strange new eyes. Everything was beautiful. And the light at the edge of the sky was the most beautiful thing of all.

"What are you doing?" a girl called from a doorway. She had long black hair, but her roots were growing in blond. "Get in here! Are you crazy?"

In a daze, Matilda did as she was told. Everything smeared as she moved, like the world was painted in watercolors. The girl's pinkish-red face swirled along with it.

It was obvious the house had once been grand, but it looked like it'd been abandoned for a long time. Graffiti covered the peeling wallpaper and couches had been pushed up against the walls. A boy wearing jeans but no shirt was painting make-up onto a girl with stiff pink pigtails, while another girl in a retro polka-dotted dress pulled on mesh stockings.

In a corner, another boy—this one with glossy brown hair that fell to his waist—stacked jars of creamed corn into a precarious pyramid.

"What is this place?" Matilda asked.

The boy stacking the jars turned. "Look at her eyes. She's a vampire!" He didn't seem afraid, though; he seemed delighted.

"Get her into the cellar," one of the other girls said.

"Come on," said the black-haired girl and pulled Matilda toward a doorway. "You're fresh-made, right?"

"Yeah," Matilda said. Her tongue swept over her own sharp teeth. "I guess that's pretty obvious."

"Don't you know that vampires can't go outside in the daylight?" the girl asked, shaking her head. "The guards try that trick with every new vampire, but I never saw one almost fall for it."

"Oh, right," Matilda said. They went down the rickety steps to a filthy basement with a mattress on the floor underneath a single bulb. Crates of foodstuffs were shoved against the walls, and the high, small windows had been painted over with a tarry substance that let no light through.

The black-haired girl who'd waved her inside smiled. "We trade with the border guards. Black-market food, clothes, little luxuries like chocolate and cigarettes for some ass. Vampires don't own everything."

"And you're going to owe us for letting you stay the night," the boy said from the top of the stairs.

"I don't have anything," Matilda said. "I didn't bring any cans of food or whatever."

"You have to bite us."

"What?" Matilda asked.

"One of us," the girl said. "How about one of us? You can even pick which one."

"Why would you want me to do that?"

The girl's expression clearly said that Matilda was stupid. "Who doesn't want to live forever?"

I don't, Matilda wanted to say, but she swallowed the words. She could tell they already thought she didn't deserve to be a vampire. Besides, she wanted to taste blood. She wanted to taste the red, throbbing, pulsing insides of the girl in front of her. It wasn't the pain she'd felt when she was infected, the hunger that made her stomach clench, the craving for warmth. It was heady, greedy desire.

"Tomorrow," Matilda said. "When it's night again."

"Okay," the girl said, "but you promise, right? You'll turn one of us?"

"Yeah," said Matilda, numbly. It was hard to even wait that long.

She was relieved when they went upstairs, but less relieved when she heard something heavy slide in front of the basement door. She told herself that didn't matter. The only thing that mattered was getting through the day so that she could find Julian and Lydia.

She shook her head to clear it of thoughts of blood and turned on Dante's phone. Although she didn't expect it, a text message was waiting: *I cant tell if I luv u or if I want to kill u.*

Relief washed over her. Her mouth twisted into a smile and her newly sharp canines cut her lip. She winced. Dante was okay.

She opened up Lydia's blog and posted an anonymous message: *Tell Julian his girlfriend wants to see him ... and you.*

Matilda made herself comfortable on the dirty mattress. She looked up at the rotted boards of the ceiling and thought of Julian. She had a single ticket out of Coldtown and two humans to rescue with it, but it was easy to picture herself saving Lydia as Julian valiantly offered to stay with her, even promised her his eternal devotion.

She licked her lips at the image. When she closed her eyes, all her imaginings drowned in a sea of red.

Waking at dusk, Matilda checked Lydia's blog. Lydia had posted a reply: *Meet us at the Festival of Sinners.*

Five kids sat at the top of the stairs, watching her with liquid eyes.

"Are you awake?" the black-haired girl asked. She seemed to pulse with color. Her moving mouth was hypnotic.

"Come here," Matilda said to her in a voice that seemed so distant that she was surprised to find it was her own. She hadn't meant to speak, hadn't meant to beckon the girl over to her.

"That's not fair," one of the boys called. "I was the one who said she owed us something. It should be me. You should pick me."

Matilda ignored him as the girl knelt down on the dirty mattress and swept aside her hair, baring a long, unmarked neck. She seemed dazzling, this creature of blood and breath, a fragile manikin as brittle as sticks.

Tiny golden hairs tickled Matilda's nose as she bit down.

And gulped.

Blood was heat and heart running-thrumming-beating through the fat roots of veins to drip syrup slow, spurting molten hot across tongue, mouth, teeth, chin.

Dimly, Matilda felt someone shoving her and someone else screaming, but it seemed distant and unimportant. Eventually the words became clearer.

"Stop," someone was screaming. "Stop!"

Hands dragged Matilda off the girl. Her neck was a glistening red mess. Gore stained the mattress and covered Matilda's hands and hair. The girl coughed, blood bubbles frothing on her lip, and then went abruptly silent.

"What did you do?" the boy wailed, cradling the girl's body. "She's dead. She's dead. You killed her."

Matilda backed away from the body. Her hand went automatically to her mouth, covering it. "I didn't mean to," she said.

"Maybe she'll be okay," said the other boy, his voice cracking. "We have to get bandages."

"She's *dead*," the boy holding the girl's body moaned.

A thin wail came from deep inside Matilda as she backed toward the stairs. Her belly felt full, distended. She wanted to be sick.

Another girl grabbed Matilda's arm. "Wait," the girl said, eyes wide and imploring. "You have to bite me next. You're full now so you won't have to hurt me—"

With a cry, Matilda tore herself free and ran up the stairs—if she went fast enough, maybe she could escape from herself.

By the time Matilda got to the Festival of Sinners, her mouth tasted metallic and she was numb with fear. She wasn't human, wasn't good, and wasn't sure what she might do next. She kept pawing at her shirt, as if that much blood could ever be wiped off, as if it hadn't already soaked down into her skin and her soiled insides.

The Festival was easy to find, even as confused as she was. People were happy to give her directions, apparently not bothered that she was drenched in blood.

Their casual demeanor was horrifying, but not as horrifying as how much she already wanted to feed again.

On the way, she passed the Eternal Ball. Strobe lights lit up the remains of the windows along the dome, and a girl with blue hair in a dozen braids held up a video camera to interview three men dressed all in white with gleaming red eyes.

Vampires.

A ripple of fear passed through her. She reminded herself that there was nothing they could do to her. She was already like them. Already dead.

The Festival of Sinners was being held at a church with stained-glass windows painted black on the inside. The door, papered with pink-stenciled posters, was painted the same thick tarry black. Music thrummed from within and a few people sat on the steps, smoking and talking.

Matilda went inside.

A doorman pulled aside a velvet rope for her, letting her past a small line of people waiting to pay the cover charge. The rules were different for vampires, perhaps especially for vampires accessorizing their grungy attire with so much blood.

Matilda scanned the room. She didn't see Julian or Lydia, just a throng of dancers and a bar that served alcohol from vast copper distilling vats. It spilled into mismatched mugs. Then one of the people near the bar moved and Matilda saw Lydia and Julian. He was bending over her, shouting into her ear.

Matilda pushed her way through the crowd, until she was close enough to touch Julian's arm. She reached out, but couldn't quite bring herself to brush his skin with her foulness.

Julian looked up, startled. "Tilda?"

She snatched back her hand like she'd been about to touch fire.

"Tilda," he said. "What happened to you? Are you hurt?"

Matilda flinched, looking down at herself. "I . . . "

Lydia laughed. "She ate someone, moron."

"Tilda?" Julian asked.

"I'm sorry," Matilda said. There was so much she had to be sorry for, but at least he was here now. Julian would tell her what to do and how to turn herself back into something decent again. She would save Lydia and Julian would save her.

He touched her shoulder, let his hand rest gingerly on her blood-stiffened shirt. "We were looking for you everywhere." His gentle expression was tinged with terror; fear pulled his smile into something closer to a grimace.

"I wasn't in Coldtown," Matilda said. "I came here so that Lydia could leave. I have a pass."

"But I don't want to leave," said Lydia. "You understand that, right? I want what you have—eternal life."

"You're not infected," Matilda said. "You have to go. You can still be okay. Please, I need you to go."

"One pass?" Julian said, his eyes going to Lydia. Matilda saw the truth in the weight of that gaze—Julian had not come to Coldtown for Matilda. Even though she knew she didn't deserve him to think of her as anything but a monster, it hurt savagely.

"I'm not leaving," Lydia said, turning to Julian, pouting. "You said she wouldn't be like this."

"I killed a girl," Matilda said. "I killed her. Do you understand that?"

"Who cares about some mortal girl?" Lydia tossed back her hair. In that moment, she reminded Matilda of her brother, pretentious Dante who'd turned out to be an actual nice guy. Just like sweet Lydia had turned out cruel.

"You're a girl," Matilda said. "You're mortal."

"I know that!" Lydia rolled her eyes. "I just mean that we don't care who you killed. Turn us and then we can kill lots of people."

"No," Matilda said, swallowing. She looked down, not wanting to hear what she was about to say. There was still a chance. "Look, I have the pass. If you don't want it, then Julian should take it and go. But I'm not turning you. I'm never turning you, understand."

"Julian doesn't want to leave," Lydia said. Her eyes looked bright and two feverish spots appeared on her cheeks. "Who are you to judge me anyway? You're the murderer."

Matilda took a step back. She desperately wanted Julian to say something in her defense or even to look at her, but his gaze remained steadfastly on Lydia.

"So neither one of you want the pass," Matilda said.

"Fuck you," spat Lydia.

Matilda turned away.

"Wait," Julian said. His voice sounded weak.

Matilda spun, unable to keep the hope off her face, and saw why Julian had called to her. Lydia stood behind him, a long knife to his throat.

"Turn me," Lydia said. "Turn me, or I'm going to kill him."

Julian's eyes were wide. He started to protest or beg or something and Lydia pressed the knife harder, silencing him.

People had stopped dancing nearby, backing away. One girl with red-glazed eyes stared hungrily at the knife.

"Turn me!" Lydia shouted. "I'm tired of waiting! I want my life to begin!"

"You won't be alive—" Matilda started.

"I'll be alive—more alive than ever. Just like you are."

"Okay," Matilda said softly. "Give me your wrist."

The crowd seemed to close in tighter, watching as Lydia held out her arm. Matilda crouched low, bending down over it.

"Take the knife away from his throat," Matilda said.

Lydia, all her attention on Matilda, let Julian go. He stumbled a little and pressed his fingers to his neck.

"I loved you," Julian shouted.

Matilda looked up to see that he wasn't speaking to her. She gave him a glittering smile and bit down on Lydia's wrist.

The girl screamed, but the scream was lost in Matilda's ears. Lost in the pulse of blood, the tide of gluttonous pleasure and the music throbbing around them like Lydia's slowing heartbeat.

Matilda sat on the blood-soaked mattress and turned on the video camera to check that the live feed was working.

Julian was gone. She'd given him the pass after stripping him of all his cash and credit cards; there was no point in trying to force Lydia to leave since she'd just come right back in. He'd made stammering apologies that Matilda ignored; then he fled for the gate. She didn't miss him. Her fantasy of Julian felt as ephemeral as her old life.

"It's working," one of the boys—Michael—said from the stairs, a computer cradled on his lap. Even though she'd killed one of them, they welcomed her back, eager enough for eternal life to risk more deaths. "You're streaming live video."

Matilda set the camera on the stack of crates, pointed toward her and the wall where she'd tied a gagged Lydia. The girl thrashed and kicked, but Matilda ignored her. She stepped in front of the camera and smiled.

My name is Matilda Green. I was born on April 10, 1997. I died on September 3, 2013. Please tell my mother I'm okay. And Dante, if you're watching this, I'm sorry.

You've probably seen lots of video feeds from inside Coldtown. I saw them too. Pictures of girls and boys grinding together in clubs or bleeding elegantly for their celebrity vampire masters. Here's what you never see. What I'm going to show you.

For eighty-eight days you are going to watch someone sweat out the infection. You are going to watch her beg and scream and cry. You're going to watch her throw up food and piss her pants and pass out. You're going to watch me feed her can after can of creamed corn. It's not going to be pretty.

You're going to watch me, too. I'm the kind of vampire that you'd be, one who's new at this and basically out of control. I've already killed someone and I can't guarantee I'm not going to do it again. I'm the one who infected this girl.

This is the real Coldtown.

I'm the real Coldtown.

You still want in?

This Is Now
Michael Marshall Smith

Michael Marshall Smith proves in "This Is Now" that the cultural archetype is so strong that vampires themselves need not necessarily make a full appearance in order for a story to pivot around them. Of course, a great story is about many things—like life itself, for instance.

*Smith is a novelist and screenwriter. As Michael Marshall Smith he has published over seventy short stories and three novels—*Only Forward, Spares, *and* One of Us*—winning the Philip K. Dick, International Horror Guild, and August Derleth awards as well as France's Prix Bob Morane. He has won the British Fantasy Award for Best Short Fiction four times, more than any other author. Writing as Michael Marshall, he has published five best-selling thrillers, including* The Straw Men, The Intruders, *and* Bad Things. The Servants *(2009) was published under the name M.M. Smith. His new Michael Marshall novel,* Killer Move. *will be published in 2011. He lives in North London with his wife, son, and two cats. His website is www.michaelmarshallsmith.com*

"Okay," Henry said. "So now we're here."

He was using his "So entertain me" voice, and he was cold but trying not to show it. Pete and I were cold too. We were trying not to show it either. Being cold is not manly. You look at your condensing breath as if it's a surprise to you, what with it being so balmy and all. Even when you've known each other for over thirty years, you do these things. Why? I don't know.

"Yep," I agreed. It wasn't my job to entertain Henry.

Pete walked up to the thick wire fence. He tilted his head back until he was looking at the top, four feet above his head. A ten-foot wall of tautly criss-crossed wire.

"Who's going to test it?"

"Well, hey, you're closest." Like the others, I was speaking quietly, though we were half a mile from the nearest road or house or person.

This side of the fence, anyhow.

"I did it last time."

"Long while ago."

"Still," he said, stepping back. "Your turn, Dave."

I held up my hands. "These are my tools, man."

Henry sniggered. "*You're* a tool, that's for sure."

Pete laughed too, I had to smile, and for a moment it was like it was the last time. Hey presto: time travel. You don't need a machine, it turns out, you just need a friend to laugh like a teenager. Chronology shivers.

And so—quickly, before I could think about it—I flipped my hand out and touched the fence. My whole arm jolted, as if every bone in it had been tapped with a hammer. Tapped hard, and in different directions.

"Christ," I hissed, spinning away, shaking my hand like I was trying to rid myself of it. "Goddamn *Christ,* that hurts."

Henry nodded sagely. "This stretch got current, then. Also, didn't we use a stick last time?"

"Always been the brains of the operation, right, Hank?"

Pete snickered again. I was annoyed, but the shock had pushed me over a line. It had brought it all back much more strongly.

I nodded up the line of the fence as it marched off into the trees. "Further," I said, and pointed at Henry. "And you're testing the next section, bro."

It was one of those things you do, one of those stupid, drunken things, that afterwards seem hard to understand. You ask yourself why, confused and sad, like the ghost of a man killed though a careless step in front of a car.

We could have not gone to The Junction, for a start, though it was a Thursday and the Thursday session is a winter tradition with us, a way of making January and February seem less like a living death. The two young guys could have given up the pool table, though, instead of bogarting it all night (by being better than us, and efficiently dismissing each of our challenges in turn): in which case we would have played a dozen slow frames and gone home around eleven, like usual—ready to get up the next morning feeling no more than a little fusty. This time of year it hardly matters if Henry yawns over the gas pump, or Pete zones out behind the counter in the Massaqua Mart, and I can sling a morning's home fries and sausage in my sleep. We've been doing these things so long that we barely have to be present. Maybe that's the point. Maybe that's the real problem right there.

By quarter after eight, proven pool-fools, we were sitting at the corner table. We always have, since back when it was Bill's place and beer tasted strange and metallic in our mouths. We were talking back and forth, laughing once in a while, none of us bothered about the pool but yes, a little bit bothered all the same. It wasn't some macho thing. I don't care about being beat by some guys who are passing through. I don't much care about being beat by anyone. Henry and Pete and I tend to win games about equally. If it weren't that way then probably we wouldn't play together. It's never been about winning. It was more that I just wished I was better. Had *assumed* I'd be better, one day, like I expected to wind up being something other than a short order cook. Don't get me wrong: you eat one of my breakfasts you're set up for the day and tomorrow you'll come back and order the same thing. It just wasn't what I had in mind when I was young. Not sure what I *did* have in mind—I used to think maybe I'd go over the mountains to Seattle, be in a band or something, but the thought got vague after that—but it certainly wasn't being first in command at a hot griddle. None of ours are bad jobs, but they're the kind held by people in the background. People who are getting by. People who don't play pool that well.

It struck me, as I watched Pete banter with Nicole when she brought round number four or five, that I was still smoking. I had been assuming I would have given it up by now. Tried, once or twice. Didn't take. Would it happen? Probably not. Would it give me cancer sooner or later? Most likely. Better try again, then. At some point.

Henry watched Nicole's ass as it accompanied her back to the counter. "Cute as hell," he said, approvingly, not for the first time.

Pete and I grunted, in the way we would if he'd observed that the moon was smaller than the earth. Henry's observation was both true and something that had little bearing on our lives. Nicole was twenty-three. We could give her fifteen years each. That's not the kind of gift that cute girls covet.

So we sat and talked, and smoked, and didn't listen to the sound of balls being efficiently slotted into pockets by people who weren't us.

You walk for long enough in the woods at night, you start getting a little jittery. Forests have a way of making civilization seem less inevitable. In sunlight they may make you want to build yourself a cabin and get back to nature, get that whole Davy Crockett vibe going on. In the dark they remind you what a good thing chairs and hot meals and electric light really are, and you thank God you live now instead of then.

Every once in a while we'd test the fence—using a stick now. The current was on each time we tried. So we kept walking. We followed the line of the wire as it cut up the rise, then down into a shallow streambed, then up again steeply on the other side.

If you were seeing the fence for the first time, you'd likely wonder at the straightness of it, the way in which the concrete posts had been planted at ten yard intervals deep into the rock. You might ask yourself if national forests normally went to these lengths, and you'd soon remember they didn't, that for the most part a cheerful little wooden sign by the side of the road was all that was judged to be required. If you kept on walking deeper, intrigued, sooner or later you'd see a notice attached to one of the posts. The notices are small, designed to convey authority rather than draw attention.

"No Trespassing," they say. "Military Land."

That could strike you as a little strange, perhaps, because you might have believed that most of the marked-off areas were down over in the moonscapes of Nevada, rather than up here at the quiet Northeast corner of Washington State. But who knows what the military's up to, right? Apart from protecting us from foreign aggressors, of course, and The Terrorist Threat, and if that means they need a few acres to themselves then that's actually kind of comforting. The army moves in mysterious ways, our freedoms to defend. Good for them, you'd think, and you'd likely turn and head back for town, having had enough of tramping through snow for the day. In the evening you'd come into Ruby's and eat hearty, some of my wings or a burger or the brisket—which, though I say so myself, isn't half bad. Next morning you'd drive back South.

I remember when the fences went up. Thirty years ago. 1985. Our parents knew what they were for. Hell, we were only eight and *we* knew.

There was a danger, and it was getting worse: the last decade had proved that. Four people had disappeared in the last year alone. One came back and was sick for a week, in an odd and dangerous kind of way, and then died. The others were never seen again. My aunt Jean was one of those.

But there's a danger to going in abandoned mine shafts, too, or talking to strangers, or juggling knives when you're drunk. So . . . you don't do it. You walk the town in pairs at night, and you observe the unspoken curfew. You kept an eye out for men who didn't blink, for slim women whose strides were too short—or so people said. There was never that much passing trade in town. Massaqua isn't on the way to anywhere. Massaqua is a single guy who keeps his yard tidy and doesn't bother anyone. The tourist season up here is short and not exactly intense. There is no ski lodge or health spa and the motel frankly isn't up to much. The fence seemed to keep the danger contained and out of town, and within a few years its existence was part of life. It wasn't like it was right there on the doorstep. No big-city reporter heard of it and came up looking to make a sensation—or, if they did, they didn't make it all the way here.

Life went on. Years passed. Sometimes small signs work better than great big ones.

As we climbed deeper into the forest, Pete was in front, I was more-or-less beside him, and Henry lagged a few steps behind. It had been that way the last time, too, but then we hadn't had hip flasks to keep us fuelled in our intentions. We hadn't needed to stop to catch our breath so often either.

"We just going to keep on walking?"

It was Henry asked the question, of course. Pete and I didn't even answer.

At quarter after ten we were still in the bar. The two guys remained at the pool table. When one leaned down, the other stood silently, judiciously sipping from a bottled beer. They weren't talking to each other, just slotting the balls away. Looked like they're having a whale of a time.

We were drinking steadily, and the conversation was often two-way while one or other of us trekked back and forth to empty our bladder. By then we were resigned to sitting around. We were a little too drunk to start playing pool, even when the table became free. There was no news to catch up on. We felt aimless. We already knew that Pete was ten years married, that they had no children and it was likely going to stay that way. His wife is fine, and still pleasant to be with, though her collection of dolls is getting exponentially bigger. We knew that Henry was married once too, had a little boy, and that though the kid and his mother now lived forty miles away, relations between them remained cordial. Neither Pete nor I are much surprised that he has achieved this. Henry can be a royal pain in the ass at times, but he wouldn't still be our friend if that's all he was.

"Same again, boys? You're thirsty tonight."

It was Pete's turn in the gents so it was Henry and I who looked up to see Nicole smiling down at us, thumb hovering over the REPEAT button on her pad. Deprived of Pete's easy manner (partly genetic, also honed over years of chatting while totting and bagging groceries), our response was cluttered and vague.

Quick nods and smiles, I said thanks and Henry got in a "Hell, yes!" that came out a little loud.

Nicole winked at me and went away again, as she has done many times over the last three years. As she got to the bar I saw one of the pool-players looking at her, and felt a strange twist of something in my stomach. It wasn't because they were strangers, or because I suspected they might be something else, something that shouldn't be here.

They were just younger guys, that's all.

Of course they're going to look at her. She's probably going to want them to.

I lit another cigarette and wondered why I still didn't really know how to deal with women. They've always seemed so different to me. So confident, so powerful, so in themselves. Kind of scary, even. Most teenage boys feel that way, I guess, but I had assumed age would help. That being older might make a difference. Apparently not. The opposite, if anything. "Cute just don't really cover it," Henry said, again not for the first time. "Going to have to come up with a whole new word. Supercute, how's that. Hyperhot. Ultra—"

How about just beautiful?

For a horrible moment I thought I'd said this out loud. I guess in a way I did, because what pronouncements are louder than the ones you make in your own head?

Pete returned at the same time as the new beers arrived, and with him around it was easier to come across like grown-ups. He came back looking thoughtful, too.

He waited until the three of us were alone again, and then he reached across and took one of my Marlboro: like he used to, back in the day, when he couldn't afford his own. He didn't seem to be aware he'd done it. He looked pretty drunk, in fact, and I realized that I was too. Henry is generally at least a little drunk.

Pete lit the cigarette, took a long mouthful of beer, and then he said:

"You remember that time we went over the fence?"

The stick touched, and nothing happened.

I did it again. Same result. We stopped walking. My legs ached and I was glad for the break. Pete hesitated a beat, then reached out and brushed the thick black wire with his hand. When we were kids he might have pretended it was charged, and jiggered back and forth, eyes rolling and tongue sticking out.

He didn't now. He just curled his fingers around it, gave it a light tug.

"Power's down," he said, quietly.

Henry and I stepped up close. Even with Pete standing there grasping it, you still had to gird yourself to do the same.

Then all three of us were holding the fence, holding it with both hands, looking in.

That close up, the wire fuzzed out of focus and it was almost as if it wasn't there. You just saw the forest beyond it: moonlit trunks, snow; you heard the quietness. If you stood on the other side and looked out, the view would be exactly the same. With a fence that long, it could be difficult to tell which side was in, which was out.

This, too, was what had happened the previous time, when we were fifteen. We'd heard that sometimes a section went down, and so we went looking. With animals, snow, the random impacts of falling branches and a wind that could blow hard and cold at most times of year, once in a while a cable stopped supplying the juice to one ten yard stretch. The power was never down on for more than a day. There was a computer that kept track, and—somewhere, nobody knew where—a small station from which a couple of military engineers could come to repair the outage. It had happened back then. It had happened now.

We stood, this silent row of older men, and remembered what had happened then.

Pete had gone up first. He shuffled along to one of the concrete posts, so the wire wouldn't bag out, and started pulling himself up. As soon as his feet left the ground I didn't want to be left behind, so I went to the other post and went up just as quickly.

We reached the top at around the same time. Soon as we started down the other side—lowering ourselves at first, then just dropping, Henry started his own climb.

We all landed silently in the snow, with bent knees.

We were the other side, and we stood very still. Far as we knew, no one had ever done this before.

To some people, this might have been enough.

Not to three boys.

Moving very quietly, hearts beating hard—just from the exertion, none of us were scared, not exactly, not enough to admit it anyway—we moved away from the fence. After about twenty yards I stopped and looked back.

"You chickening out?"

"No, Henry," I said. His voice had been quiet and shaky. I took pains that mine sound firm. "Memorizing. We want to be able to find that dead section again."

He'd nodded. "Good thinking, smart boy."

Pete looked back with us. Stand of three trees close together there. Unusually big tree over on the right. Kind of a semi-clearing, on a crest. Shouldn't be hard to find.

We glanced at each other, judged it logged, then turned and headed away, into a place no one had been for nearly ten years.

The forest floor led away gently. There was just enough moonlight to show the ground panning down towards a kind of high valley lined with thick trees.

As we walked, bent over a little with unconscious caution, part of me was already relishing how we'd remember this in the future, leaping over the event into retrospection. Not that we'd talk about it, outside the three of us. It was the kind of thing which might attract attention to the town, including maybe attention from this side of the fence.

There was one person I thought I might mention it to, though. Her name was Lauren and she was very cute, the kind of beautiful that doesn't have to open its mouth to call your name from across the street. I had talked to her a couple times, finding bravery I didn't know I possessed. It was she who had talked about Seattle, said she'd like to go hang out there some day. That sounded good to me, good and exciting and strange. What I didn't know, that night in the forest, was that she would do this, and I would not, and that she would leave without us ever having kissed.

I just assumed . . . I assumed a lot back then.

After a couple of hundred yards we stopped, huddled together, shared one of my cigarettes. Our hearts were beating heavily, even though we'd been coming downhill. The forest is hard work whatever direction it slopes. But it wasn't just that. It felt a little colder here. There was also something about the light. It seemed to hold more shadows. You found your eyes flicking from side to side, checking things out, wanting to be reassured, but not being sure that you had been after all.

I bent down to put the cigarette out in the snow. It was extinguished in a hiss that seemed very loud.

We continued in the direction we'd been heading. We walked maybe another five, six hundred yards.

It was Henry who stopped.

Keyed up as we were, Pete and I stopped immediately too. Henry was leaning forward a little, squinting ahead.

"What?"

He pointed. Down at the bottom of the rocky valley was a shape. A big shape.

After a moment I could make out it was a building. Two wooden storeys high, and slanting. You saw that kind of thing, sometimes. The sagging remnant of some pioneer's attempt to claim an area of this wilderness and pretend it could be a home.

Pete nudged me and pointed in a slightly different direction. There was the remnants of another house further down. A little fancier, with a fallen-down porch.

And thirty yards further, another: smaller, with a false front.

"Cool," Henry said, and briefly I admired him.

We sidled now, a lot more slowly and heading along the rise instead of down it. Ruined houses look real interesting during the day. At night they feel different, especially when lost high up in the forest. Trees grow too close to them, pressing in. The lack of a road, long overgrown, can make the houses look like they were never built but instead made their own way to this forgotten place, in which you have now disturbed them; they sit at angles which do not seem quite right.

I was beginning to wonder if maybe we'd done enough, come far enough, and I doubt I was the only one.

Then we saw the light.

After Pete asked his question in the bar, there was silence for a moment. Of course we remembered that night. It wasn't something you'd forget. It was a dumb question unless you were really asking something else, and we both knew Pete wasn't dumb.

Behind us, on the other side of the room, came the quiet, reproachful sound of pool balls hitting each other, and then one of them going down a pocket.

We could hear each other thinking. Thinking it was a cold evening, and there was thick snow on the ground, as there had been on that other night. That the rest of the town had pretty much gone to bed. That we could get in Henry's truck and be at the head of a hiking trail in twenty minutes, even driving drunkard slow.

I didn't hear anyone thinking a reason, though. I didn't hear anyone think *why* we might do such a thing, or what might happen.

By the time Pete had finished his cigarette our glasses were empty. We put on our coats and left and crunched across the lot to the truck.

Back then, on that long-ago night, suddenly my heart hadn't seemed to be beating at all. When we saw the light in the second house, a faint and curdled glow in one of the downstairs windows, my whole body suddenly felt light and insubstantial.

One of us tried to speak. It came out like a dry click. I realized there was a light in the other house too, faint and golden. Had I missed it before, or had it just come on?

I took a step backwards. The forest was silent but for the sound of my friends breathing. "Oh, no," Pete said. He started moving backwards, stumbling. Then I saw it too.

A figure, standing in front of the first house.

It was tall and slim, like a rake's shadow. It was a hundred yards away but still it seemed as though you could make out an oval shape on its shoulders, the colour of milk diluted with water. It was looking in our direction.

Then another was standing near the other house.

No, two.

Henry moaned softly, we three boys turned as one, and I have never run like that before or since.

The first ten yards were fast but then the slope cut in and our feet slipped, and we were down on hands half the time, scrabbling and pulling—every muscle working together in a headlong attempt to be somewhere else.

I heard a crash behind and flicked my head to see Pete had gone down hard, banging his knee, falling on his side.

Henry kept on going but I made myself turn around and grab Pete's hand, not really helping but just pulling, trying to yank him back to his feet or at least away.

Over his shoulder I glimpsed the valley below and I saw the figures were down at the bottom of the rise, speeding our way in jerky blurred-black movements, like half-seen spiders darting across an icy windowpane.

Pete's face jerked up and I saw there what I felt in myself, and it was not a cold fear but a hot one, a red-hot melt-down as if you were going to rattle and break apart.

Then he was on his feet again, moving past me, and I followed on after him towards the disappearing shape of Henry's back. It seemed so much further than we'd walked. It was uphill and the trees no longer formed a path and even the wind seemed to be pushing us back. We caught up with Henry and passed him, streaking up the last hundred yards towards the fence. None of us turned around. You didn't have to. You could feel them coming, like rocks thrown at your head, rocks glimpsed at the last minute when there is time to flinch but not to turn.

I was sprinting straight at the fence when Henry called out. I was going too fast and didn't want to know what his problem was. I leapt up at the wire.

It was like a truck hit me from the side.

I crashed the ground fizzing, arms sparking and with no idea which way was up. Then two pairs of hands were on me, pulling at my coat, cold hands and strong.

I thought the fingers would be long and pale and milky but then I realized it was my friends and they were pulling along from the wrong section of the fence, dragging me to the side, when they could have just left me where I fell and made their own escape.

The three of us jumped up at the wire at once, scrabbling like monkeys, stretching out for the top. I rolled over wildly, grunting as I scored deep scratches across my back that would earn me a long, hard look from my mother when she happened to glimpse them a week later. We landed heavily on the other side, still moving forward, having realized that we'd just given away the location of a portion of dead fence. But now we had to look back, and what I saw—though my head was still vibrating from the shock I'd received, so I cannot swear to it—was at least three, maybe five, figures on the other side of the fence. Not right up against it, but a few yards back.

Black hair was whipped up around their faces, and they looked like absences ill lit by moonlight.

Then they were gone.

We moved fast. We didn't know why they'd stopped, but we didn't hang around. We didn't stick too close to the fence either, in case they changed their minds.

We half-walked, half-ran, and at first we were quiet but as we got further away, and nothing came, we began to laugh and then to shout, punching the air, boys who had come triumphantly out the other side.

The forest felt like some huge football field, applauding its heroes with whispering leaves. We got back to town a little after two in the morning. We walked down the middle of the deserted main street, slowly, untouchable, knowing the world had changed: that we were not the boys who had started the evening, but men, and that the stars were there to be touched. That was then.

As older men we stood together at the fence for a long time, recalling that night.

Parts of it are fuzzy now, of course, and it comes down to snap-shots: Pete's terrified face when he slipped, the first glimpse of light at the houses, Henry's shout as he tried to warn me, narrow faces the color of moonlight. They most likely remembered other things, defined that night in different ways and were the centre of their recollections. As I looked now through the fence at the other forest I was thinking how long a decade had seemed back then, and how you could learn that it was no time at all.

Henry stepped away first. I wasn't far behind. Pete stayed a moment longer, then took a couple of steps back. Nobody said anything. We just looked at the fence a little longer, and then we turned and walked away.

Took us forty minutes to get back to the truck.

The next Thursday Henry couldn't make it, so it was just me and Pete at the pool table. Late in the evening, with many beers drunk, I mentioned the fence.

Not looking at me, chalking his cue, Pete said that if Henry hadn't stepped back when he did, he'd have climbed it.

"And gone over?"

"Yeah," he said.

This was bullshit, and I knew it. "Really?"

There was a pause. "No," he said, eventually, and I wished I hadn't asked the second time. I could have left him with something, left us with it. Calling an ass cute isn't much, but it's better than just coming right out and admitting you'll never cup it in your hand.

The next week it was the three of us again, and our walk in the woods wasn't even mentioned. We've never brought it up since, and we can't talk about the first time any more either. I think about it sometimes, though.

I know I could go out walking there myself some night, and there have been slow afternoons and dry, sleepless small hours when I think I might do it: when I tell myself such a thing isn't impossible now, that I am still who I once was. But I have learned a little since I was fifteen, and I know now that you don't need to look for things that will suck the life out of you. Time will do that all by itself.

Sisters
Charles de Lint

If you read Charles de Lint (and you should, if you don't) you might be surprised (if delighted) to find one of his stories in this anthology. Widely credited with having pioneered the contemporary fantasy genre, with (so far) thirty-six novels and nineteen books of short fiction—including The Mystery of Grace, The Blue Girl, Moonheart, The Onion Girl, *and* Widdershins—*and known as a master in his field, de Lint has won many honors for his fiction, including the World Fantasy Award and the Aurora. Most of de Lint's fiction has been written for adults, but he's also penned several books for young people. He's not, however, written many vampire stories.*

"Sisters" is one of two stories featuring Apples—a sixteen-year-old vampire who received "the Gift" from a stranger during a Bryan Adams (remember him?) concert—and her younger sister Cassie. The first story, "There's No Such Thing," was published in 1991. "Sisters" first appeared as an original story in de Lint's World Fantasy Award-nominated YA collection Strays and Waifs *in 2002. It has never been published elsewhere. Written while the television series* Buffy the Vampire Slayer *was shaping the pop cultural image of the vampire, "Sisters" offers a different view of adolescence and undeath.*

One: Appoline

It's not like on that TV show, you know where the cute blond cheerleader type stakes all these vampires and they blow away into dust? For one thing, they don't disappear into dust, which would be way more convenient. Outside of life in televisionland, when you stake one, you've got this great big dead corpse to deal with, which is not fun. Beheading works, too, but that's just way too gross for me and you've still got to find some place to stash both a head and a body.

The trick is to not turn your victim in the first place—you know, drain all their blood so that they rise again. When that happens, you have to clean up after yourself, because a vamp is forever, and do you really want these losers you've been feeding on hanging around until the end of time? I don't think so.

The show gets a lot of other things wrong, too, but then most of the movies and books do. Vamps don't have a problem with mirrors (unless they're ugly and don't want to look at themselves, I suppose), crosses (unless they've got issues with Christianity), or garlic (except who likes to smell it on anybody's breath?). They don't have demons riding around inside them (unless they've got some kind of satanic inner child), they can't turn into bats or rats or wolves or mist (I mean, just look at the physics involved, right?) and sunlight doesn't bother them. No spontaneous combustion—they just run the same risk of skin cancer as anybody else.

I figure if the people writing the books and making the movies actually do have any firsthand experience with vampires, they're sugar-coating the information so that people don't freak out. If you're going to accept that they exist in the first place, it's much more comforting to believe that you're safe in the daylight, or that a cross or a fistful of garlic will keep them at bay.

About the only thing they do get right is that it takes a vamp to make a vamp. You do have to die from the bite and then rise again three days later. It's as easy as that. It's also the best time to kill a vamp—they're kind of like ragdolls, all loose and muddy-brained, for the first few hours.

Oh, and you do have to invite us into your house. If it's a public place, we can go in the same as anyone else.

What's that? No, that wasn't a slip of the tongue. I'm one, too. So while I like the TV show as much as the next person, and I know it's fiction, blond cheerleader types still make me twitch a little.

- 2 -

Appoline Smith was raking yellow maple leaves into a pile on the front lawn when the old four-door sedan came to a stop at the curb. She looked up to find the driver staring her. She didn't recognize him. He was just some old guy in his thirties who'd been watching way too many old *Miami Vice* reruns. His look— the dark hair slicked back, silk shirt opened to show off a big gold chain, fancy shades—was so been there it was prehistoric. The pair of dusty red-and-white velour dice hanging from the mirror did nothing to enhance his image.

"Why don't you just take a picture?" she asked him.

"Nobody likes a lippy kid," he said.

"Yeah, nobody likes a pervert either."

"I'm not some perv'."

"Oh really? What do you call a guy cruising a nice neighbourhood like this with his tongue hanging out whenever he sees some teenage girl?"

"I'm looking for A. Smith."

"Well, you found one."

"I mean, the initial 'A,' then 'Smith.'"

"You found that, too. So why don't you check it off on your life list and keep on driving?"

The birder reference went right over his head. All things considered, she supposed most things would go over his head.

"I got something for you," he said.

He reached over to the passenger's side of the car's bench seat, then turned back to her and offered her an envelope. She supposed it had been white once. Looking at the dirt and a couple of greasy fingerprints smeared on it, she made no move to take it. The guy looked at her for a long moment, then shrugged and tossed it onto the lawn.

"Don't call the cops," he said and drove away.

As if they didn't have better things to do than chase after some guy in a car making pathetic attempts to flirt with girls he happened to spy as he drove around. He was one of just too many guys she'd met, thinking he was Lothario when he was just a loser.

She waited until he'd driven down the block and turned the corner before she stepped closer to look at the envelope he'd left on the lawn.

Okay, she thought, when she saw that it actually had "A. Smith" and the name of her street written on it. So maybe it wasn't random. Maybe he was only stalking her.

She picked up the envelope, holding it distastefully between two fingers.

"Who was in the car?"

She turned to see her little sister limping down the driveway towards her and quickly stuck the envelope in her jacket pocket.

"Just some guy," she told Cassie. "How're you doing?"

Cassie'd had a bad asthma attack this morning and was still lying down in the rec room watching videos when Apples had come out to rake leaves.

"I'm okay," Cassie told her. "And besides, I've got my buddy," she added, holding up her bronchodilator. "Can I help?"

"Sure. But only if you promise to take it easy."

It wasn't until a couple of hours later that Apples was able to open the envelope. She took it into the bathroom and slit the seal, pulling out a grimy sheet of paper with handwriting on it that read:

I no yer secret. Meet me tonite at midnite at the cow castle, or they'll be trouble.
I no you got a little sister. Don't call the cops. Don't tell nobody.

Okay, Apples thought, getting angry as she reread the note. The loser in the car just went from annoying pervert to a sick freak who needed to be dealt with.

Nobody threatened her little sister.

By "cow castle" she assumed he meant the Aberdeen Pavilion at Lansdowne Park, commonly known as the Cattle Castle because the cupola on its roof gave it a castle-like appearance. And though it was obviously a trap of some sort, she'd be there all the same. She couldn't begin to guess what he wanted from her, what he hoped to accomplish. It didn't matter. By threatening Cassie, he'd just gone to the head of her "deal with this" list.

- 3 -

Okay, here's the thing. I didn't ask to get turned, but it's not like we sat down and talked out how I felt about it. By the time it's over, I've been three days dead, I rise, and here I am, vamp girl, and I don't mean sexy, though I can play that card if I have to. Anybody can do it. It just needs the right clothes and make-up, with one secret ingredient: attitude.

It's funny. I didn't have too many friends before I got turned. I don't have so many now either, mind you, but now it's by choice. Getting turned gave me this boost of self-confidence, I guess, and that's really what people find attractive. Everybody's intrigued by someone comfortable in their own skin because most of us aren't.

The parents freaked, of course. Not because I'm a vamp—they still don't know that—but because so far as they know, I just did the big disappearing act the night I got turned. Went to a concert and came back home four days later. Trust me, that did not go over well. I was canned for a solid month, which made feeding a real pain—having to sneak out through a window between two a.m., when Dad finally goes to bed, and dawn to find what I can at that time of the night. I never much cared for booze or drugs when I was human and that's carried over to what I am now. I still hate the taste of it in someone's blood.

Yeah, I drink blood. But it's not as gross as it sounds. And it's not as messy as it is in some of the movies.

- 4 -

The Aberdeen Pavilion was a wonderfully eccentric building in the middle of Lansdowne Park where the Central Canadian Exhibition, the oldest agricultural fair in

Canada, was held every year. The pavilion was the largest of the exhibition buildings that dotted the park, an enormous barn-like structure surrounded by parking lots, with an angled roof curved like a half-moon and topped with a cupola. For a city kid like Apples, going inside during the Ex had always been a wonderful experience. The air was redolent of farm smells—cattle, sheep, horses, hogs—and she'd loved to walk along the stalls to look at the livestock, or sit with Cassie on the wooden seats in the huge arena and watch the animals vying for first place ribbons.

Though she still took Cassie to the midway every August, she hadn't gone inside the pavilion for a couple of years now.

As she walked across a parking lot towards the Cattle Castle, Apples wondered if this was part of the freak's plan, if he knew that this was where she'd gotten turned. It had been right here, between the Cattle Castle and the Coliseum when she'd come to see a Bryan Adams concert a few years ago.

She didn't have to close her eyes to be able to visualize the woman, that first sight of her coming out from between the parked cars. Tall and svelte, with a loose walk that lay somewhere between the grace of a panther and a runway model. Golden blond hair fountained over her shoulders and down her back in a spill of ringlets and she was dressed all in black: short velvet skirt, low cut T-shirt and high-heeled ankle boots. Apples remembered two conflicting sensations: that this woman was so unbelievably gorgeous, and that no one else seemed to notice her.

"Come with me a moment," the woman said and without a word to her friends, Apples had left them to follow the stranger into a darker part of the parking lot.

And nothing was the same for Apples, not ever again.

I no your secret.

Maybe he did.

The area around the Cattle Castle appeared to be deserted, though there were a handful of cars in the parking lot. Apples recognized the sedan that had come by her house earlier in the day and walked in its direction. There was no one seated in it, but Apples could smell the driver. She assumed her semi-literate pervert was lying across the seat, waiting until she'd walked by so that he could jump out and take her by surprise.

That was okay. She had a surprise of her own. But first she wanted to know how he'd gotten her name and address. With her luck, somebody had put up a directory of known vamps website on the Internet and every would-be Van Helsing and Buffy was looking for her now.

She walked by the car and pretended to be shocked when he opened the door and confronted her, a gun in hand.

I hope you've got wooden bullets for that thing, she wanted to tell him, but she kept silent.

"Get in the car," he told her, waving the gun. "Not there," he added as she started to walk around to the passenger's side. "Behind the wheel. You can drive, right?"

To some remote location, Apples supposed. Where he'd have his nasty way with her. Or kill her. Probably, he planned to do both, hopefully in that order. Though technically, any physical relationship with her had to be classified as necrophilia. Euew.

This whole business was so clichéd that she could only sigh. Still, a remote location would work for her, too.

She came back around to the driver's side and got in.

"Where to, gun boy?" she asked.

His face reddened and she watched the veins lift on his brow.

"This isn't some joke," he told her, waving the barrel of the gun in her face. "You're in way over your head now, kid."

Apples looked at him for a long beat.

"You still haven't said where to."

He frowned. "Just drive. I'll tell you where."

"Okay. You're the boss."

She started the car and put it in drive.

"Turn right after the gate," he told her.

She did as he told her, pulling out of the parking lot and turning right onto the Queen Elizabeth Driveway.

"So what's your deal?" she asked as they went under the Lansdowne Bridge at Bank Street and continued west.

"Shut up."

"Why? Are you going to shoot me? I'm driving the car, moron."

"Just shut up."

"Where'd you get my name and address?"

"I told you, just—"

"Shut up. Yeah, yeah. Except I'm not going to. So why don't you stop sounding like a skipping CD and tell me what your problem is?"

"You're the problem," he said. "End of story."

"Maybe. Except where does it begin?"

They'd driven under the bridge at Bronson now and the Rideau Canal on their right became Dows Lake. She noticed that they'd started draining the water in the canal in preparation for winter.

"Take a right at the lights," he said, "and then a left on Carling."

"Not unless you start talking, I won't."

"I've got two words for you: *Randall Gage*."

"Those aren't words, they're a name. And they don't mean anything to me."

"You killed him."

Apples made the right onto Preston Street and stopped at the red light waiting for them at Carling Avenue. She turned to look at her captor.

"I'm not saying I did," she told him, "but how would you know anyway?"

She was always careful. There were never any witnesses.

"He told me you would."

"It's still not ringing any bells," she said.

The light went to green and she made the left turn onto Carling. She could smell the first telltale hint of nervousness coming from her captor, could almost read his mind:

Why's she so calm? Why isn't she scared?

Because I'm already dead, moron.

"Well?" Apples asked.

"Randall was about five-eight, a hundred-and-sixty pounds. Blond, good looking guy. He used to come into the coffee shop where you work."

A face rose up in Apples's mind, sharp and sudden. She remembered Randall Gage now, remembered him all too well, though she hadn't known his name. After the first time he'd seen her at the Second Cup where she worked, he seemed to come in every time she had a shift. "A. Smith," he'd always read from her name tag, fishing for the first name, which she never gave him. Then he'd made the mistake of grabbing her after a late shift and forcing her into the back of his van. He'd bragged to her about other girls he'd snatched, how the last one hadn't survived, so if she wanted to live, she'd better just lie back and enjoy it, but no problem there, sweetcakes, because this he guaranteed, she was going to enjoy it.

Rather than find out, she'd drained him.

And then not been able to get back to where she'd stashed his body when his three days were up and he rose from the dead. She'd had to track him for most of the night before she finally found him trying to hide from the dawn in some-body's garden shed, the idiot. Like the sun was going to burn him.

"You still haven't explained how you got my address," she said.

"Legwork," her captor said.

"Or what you plan to do to me."

"Same as you did to Randall. Take the Queensway on-ramp," he added as they passed Kirkwood Avenue.

Apples felt like driving the car into the nearest lamp post, but then she reminded herself that whatever remote location he was directing her to would benefit her as well.

"He raped and killed a twelve-year-old girl," she said, her voice gone hard and cold.

Her captor shook his head. "He was never connected to anything."

"He *told* me he did, you moron."

"Don't matter. You still had no right to kill him."

"I never said I did."

"He told me you were coming for him—called me up, told me your name, where you worked, what you looked like."

Apples supposed that Gage hadn't bothered to explain that he was already dead by that point.

"So what's it to you?" she asked.

"He was my brother."

Now, that, Apples could understand.

- 5 -

Who turned me? I never learned her name. She just said she liked the look of me—the inside look of me. She drained me, took me away and watched over me for the three days until I rose as a vamp. Then she cut me loose.

Yeah, of course we talked before I went home to face the music. She filled me in on the rules and regs. I don't mean there's vamp police, running around handing out tickets if you do something wrong. There's just things you can do and things you can't and she straightened me on them. Gave me the lowdown on all the mythology. Useful stuff. She never did get into why she turned me besides what I've already told you, so your guess is as good as mine.

No, I never saw her again.

- 6 -

"How did I kill him?"

"What?"

"Your brother. How am I supposed to have killed him?"

They were on the Queensway now, the multiple lane divided highway that bisected the city from east to west. Apples kept to the speed limit—100 kilometers—but they were already passing Bayshore Shopping Centre and about to leave the city. The last few kilometers they'd ridden in silence. The surviving Gage sibling rested his gun on his thigh and stared out the front windshield. He turned to Apples.

"That's one of the things I need to know."

"Have you ever killed anybody?" she asked.

He shrugged. "A couple of guys. Once was in the middle of a holdup, the other time in jail. I never got connected to either one."

"How did it feel?"

"What the hell kind of a question is that?"

Apples shot him a glance. "Did it feel good? Did it feel righteous? Did you feel sad? Did it give you a hard-on?"

"How did it feel for you?"

"Like a waste."

"So you did kill Randall."

"I never said that."

"Anybody looks at you, they see this sweet little kid—what are you, sixteen?"

I was when I died, she thought. And she hadn't aged a day since. That wasn't causing problems yet, but it would soon. Still, she only had to wait one more year. That was when Cassie turned sixteen and she planned to turn her. The thing about vamps is, they don't get sick. And if you've got something wrong with you, it's gone once you're turned. Goodbye leg brace and asthma. Cassie didn't know it, but Apples planned for them to be sixteen together. Forever.

"I'm nineteen," she told Gage.

He nodded. "But everybody looks at you and just sees this sweet little kid. Nobody knows the monster hiding under your skin."

Apples shot him another look. That was about as good a way to put it as any. How much did he know? And how many people, if any, had he told?

"I guess you'd know all about monsters," she said. "Seeing how your little brother grew up to be one and you're not exactly an angel yourself."

Anger flickered in his eyes and the gun rose to point at her.

"You shoot me now," she reminded him, "and you're killing yourself as well."

"Just shut up and drive."

"I think we've already played that song."

- 7 -

So what are my weaknesses? You mean, beyond getting staked or beheaded? Hey, how stupid do I look? Figure it out for yourself.

Just kidding.

Apparently, the way it works is that whatever meant the most to you when you were alive, becomes anathema to you when you're dead. Not people, but things and ideas. So I guess if you did worship the sun, then it could fry you as a vamp. Same if you loved eating Italian, with all that garlic in the sauces. Or maybe you were way serious about church.

Here's a funny fact: pretty much any vampire turned in the past few decades can be warded off with chocolate. And if not chocolate, then some kind of junk food, not to mention cigarettes, coffee or beer. Junkies are probably the biggest problem for normal people since you can only ward them off with needles and drugs. There's not much by way of sacred icons anymore.

- 8 -

Apples kept following her captor's directions. Eventually they exited the Queensway and drove down increasingly small back roads in the rural area west of the city. When they finally reached a bumpy track that was only two ruts on the ground with branches raking the sides of the car, he had her stop.

"Get out," he said.

She did, stretching her back muscles and looking around her with interest. She didn't get out of the city much, but ever since she'd been turned, she'd had this real yearning to just run in the woods.

Gage slid across the bench seat and joined her on her side of the car, the gun leveled at her once more.

"So you killed Randall because he told you some B.S. story about boffing some twelve-year-old."

"Not to mention killing her."

"So how was that your business?"

"Well, call me crazy, but I take offence to misogynist morons hurting kids."

"So you're just some do-gooder."

"Not to mention his intention to do the same to me."

Gage gave a slow nod. "But I still don't get how you killed him. You're just some—"

"Slip of a girl. I know."

"With a big mouth."

He frowned at her. His nervousness was a stronger scent now, some animal part of his brain already registering what the rest of him hadn't worked out yet.

"I just don't get it," he said.

"And that's where you made your mistake," she told him. "That's the question you should have asked yourself before you ever came by my house with your little party invitation and threatening my little sister."

The gun rose, muzzle pointing at her head.

"You're way out of your league, kid."

"I don't know." She grinned, showing him a pair of fangs. "See, I'm faster than you."

Her hand moved in a blur of motion, plucking the gun from his hand and flinging it a half dozen feet away.

"I'm stronger than you."

She grabbed his hand and twisted it, bending it up around his back, exerting pressure so that he couldn't move.

"And I'm hungry."

She bit his neck and the hollowed fangs sank deep. He began to jerk as she drew the blood up from his veins, but it was no use.

It never was.

Afterwards, she sat down by his body and began to talk, conversing with the corpse as though it was asking her questions. She took her time in responding. After all, they had three days to wait.

Normally she would have simply stashed the body and come back when it was time for it to rise, but considering the problems she'd already had with his brother, she didn't feel like tempting fate a second time with one of these Gage boys. She called home on her cell phone and luckily got the answering machine, which let her leave a message without having to explain too much. Her parents would still be mad when she got home, but hey, she was nineteen now, no matter how young she might look.

When she stashed the phone back in the pocket of her jacket, she went and found a good-sized branch that she could carve into a stake while she talked and waited.

- 9 -

Do I have any regrets? Sure. I can't have babies, for one thing. Well, yeah, I can still have sex. I just can't have a baby and that sucks. I always figured when I got old—you know, like in my twenties—I'd get married and have kids.

I miss eating, too. I mean, I can eat and drink the same as you, but I can't process it, so afterwards I have to go throw it up like some bulimic. It's so gross. Annalee—she works at the coffee shop with me—caught me doing it one time and it was really awkward. She's all, "Don't do this to yourself. Trust me, you're not fat. You need help to deal with it. It's nothing to be ashamed of."

"It's not what you think," I tell her. "I've just got a touch of stomach flu."

"Every time you eat you throw up," she says, and I'm thinking, what? Are you keeping tabs on me? How weird is that? But I know she just means well.

I guess the other thing I'm going to miss is growing old. I'll always look sixteen, but inside I age the same as you. What happens when I'm all old and ancient? The only guys that'll be my age—you know, in their thirties and forties—interested in being with me then are going to be these pedophile freaks. And who wants to hang out with sixteen-year-old boys forever?

But I didn't choose it and I'm not the kind to get all weepy and do myself in. I figure, if this is what I am, then I might as well make myself useful getting rid of losers like you and your brother. I guess I read too many superhero comics when I was a kid or something.

And I really want this chance to give Cassie a shot at a better life. Well, a different one, anyway. She deserves to see what it's like to walk around without her leg brace and bronchodilator.

Maybe she'll join me in this little crusade of mine, but it'll have to be her choice. Just like getting turned has to be her choice. I'll give her the skinny, the bad and the good, and she can decide. And it's not like we *have* to kill anybody. I only do it when losers like you don't leave me any choice. Most times, I just feed on someone until they get so weak they just can't hurt anybody for a long time. I check up on them from time to time—a girl gets hungry, after all—and if they've gone back to their evil ways, I turn them into these anemics again. They usually figure it out. When they don't . . . well, that's what stakes are for, right?

My weakness? I guess I can tell you that. It's anything to do with Easter. I used to be an Easter maniac—I loved every bit of it. I guess because it's like Halloween, a serious candy holiday, but without the costumes. I was never one for dressing up and scary stuff never turned me on. Good thing, the way things worked out. Imagine if the very thought of vamps and ghouls was my nemesis. I'd be long gone by now. But Easter's tough. I have to avoid the stores—which is not easy, but better than trying to avoid Christmas—and play sick on the day itself.

- 10 -

Apples saw Gage's eyes move under his lids. She didn't get up from where she was kneeling on the ground beside his shoulder, just reached over for her now-sharpened stake and lifted it. Gage's eyes opened.

"How . . . how do you live with yourself . . . ?" he asked.

Apples shivered. She'd never stopped to think that he could actually hear everything she'd been saying. She'd only talked to pass the time. Because there was no one else she could talk to about it.

"The only other choice is where you're going," she said.

"I welcome it."

When he said that, forgotten memories returned to her. The nightmare she'd had to undergo through her own three days of change from dead human to what she was now. It was like swimming through mud, trying to escape the clinging knowledge of the worst that people were capable of doing to each other, but drowning in it at the same time. Not for three days, but for what felt like an eternity. It had been such a horrifying experience that the only way she'd managed to deal with it was by simply blocking it away.

How had she forgotten?

Better yet, how could she forget it again? The sooner the better.

"That's because you're a loser," she said.

"And you're going to do this to your sister."

"You don't know anything about me or my sister!"

She brought the stake down harder than necessary. Long after he was dead, she was still leaning over him, pressing the stake down.

Finally, she let it go and rocked back onto her ankles. She got up and dragged his body back into the car, wiped the vehicle down for any fingerprints she might have left in it. She soaked a rag in gas, stuck it in the gas tank, and lit it.

She was out of sight of the car and walking fast when the explosion came. She didn't turn to look, but only kept walking. Her mind was in that dark place Gage had called back into existence.

How could she put Cassie through that?

But how could she go on, forever, alone?

For the first time since she'd been turned, she didn't know what to do.

Two: Cassandra

Apples has a secret and I know what it is.

Her real name's Appoline, but everybody calls her Apples, just like they call me Cassie instead of Cassandra, except for Mom. She always calls us by our given names. But that's not the secret. It's way bigger than having some weird name.

My sister is so cool—not like I could ever be.

I was born with a congenital birth defect that left me with one leg shorter than the other so I have to wear this Frankenstein monster leg brace all the time. At least that's what the kids call it. "Here comes the bride of Frankenstein," they used to say when I came out for recess—I was always last to get outside. I'm glad Apples doesn't know, because she'd beat the crap out of them and you can't do that just 'cause people call you names.

I've also got asthma real bad, so I always have to carry my puffer around with me. Even if I didn't have the leg brace and could run, the asthma wouldn't let me. I get short of breath whenever I try to do anything too strenuous, but I'm lucky 'cause I've only had to go the hospital a few times when an attack got too severe.

I know you shouldn't judge people by their physical attributes, but we all do, don't we? And if you just aren't capable of simple things like walking or breathing properly, you're not even in the running so far as most people are concerned. People see any kind of a disability and they immediately think your brain's disabled as well. They talk to me slower and never really listen to what I'm saying.

Oh, I'm not feeling sorry for myself. Honest. I'm just being pragmatic. I'm always going to be this dorky kid with the bum leg who can't breathe. I could live to be eighty years old, with a whole life behind me, but inside, that's who I'll always be.

But Apples has never seen or treated me that way, not even when we have a fight, which isn't that often anyway. I know that sounds odd, because siblings are just naturally supposed to argue and fight, but we don't. We get along and share pretty much everything. Or at least we did up until the night of that Bryan Adams concert. She went with a bunch of friends and then didn't come back from until four days later. Boy, were Mom and Dad mad. I was just really worried, and then I guess I felt hurt because she wouldn't tell me where she'd been.

"It's not that I won't," she'd tell me. "It's that I can't. That chunk of time is just like this big black hole in my head."

But I know she remembers something from it. She just doesn't think I can handle whatever it was.

And that was when she changed. Not slowly, over time, like everybody does, you get older, you stop playing with Barbies, start listening to real music. But bang, all of a sudden. She was always fun, but after that four-day-long night out, she became this breezy, confident person that I still adored, but felt I had to get to know all over again.

That wouldn't be a problem, but she also got all *X-Files*, too. All mysterious about simple things. Like I'll never forget her face when I announced just before dinner one day that I was now a vegetarian. I simply couldn't condone the slaughter of innocent animals just so that I could live. "You are what you eat," I told them, not understanding Apples's anguished expression until much later.

And Easter was particularly weird when it came around the following year. Used to be her favorite holiday, bar none, but that year she claimed she'd developed a phobia towards it and wouldn't have anything to do with any of it. When Dad asked why, she said with more exasperation than usual, "That's why they call it a phobia, Dad. It's an *unreasonable* fear."

Okay, maybe those aren't the best examples, but when you add everything together. Like there was this period when I thought she was bulimic, but although she was throwing up a lot after meals, she didn't have any of the other symptoms. She never seems overly concerned about her weight, she doesn't lose weight. In fact, she just seems to keep getting stronger and healthier all the time. So I couldn't figure out what and where she was eating.

She also stopped having a period. I caught her throwing out unused tampons one day around the time she was usually menstruating, so I watched out for it the next month, but she threw them out then, too, like she didn't want anyone to know that she wasn't still using them. It seemed unlikely that she was pregnant—and as the months went by, it was obvious she wasn't—and she sure couldn't be hitting menopause.

By now you're thinking I'm this creepy kid, always spying on my sister, but it's not like that. I came across all these things by accident. The only reason I looked further into them was that I was worried. Wouldn't you have been, if it was happening to your sister? And the worst was I had no one to talk to about it. I couldn't bring it up with my parents, I sure wasn't going to talk about it to anyone outside of the family, and I couldn't begin to think of a way to ask Apples herself. I couldn't follow her around either, not with my leg brace and having to catch my breath all the time. So while I know she snuck out at night, I could never follow to see where she was going, what she was doing.

I got to thinking, maybe I should write one of those anonymous letters to an advice columnist. The only reason I thought of that is that I'm just this help column junkie—Dear Abby, Ann Landers, the "Sex & Body" and "Hard Questions" columns in *Seventeen*. My favorite is Dan Savage's "Savage Love" which runs in *Xpress,* our local alternative weekly, though Mom and Dad'd probably kill me if they knew I was reading it. I mean, it's all about sex and gay stuff and I know I'm never going to have a boyfriend—who wants the Frankenstein monster on their arm?—but I still figure it's stuff I should know.

Imagine writing in to one of them with my problem. I'd try Dan first.

Dear Dan,

My sister doesn't eat or menstruate anymore, but she's not losing weight, nor is she pregnant. She has a phobia about Easter and sneaks out of the house late at night, going I don't know where.

I'm not trying to butt into her life, but I'm really worried. What do you think is wrong with her? What can I do?

Confused in Ottawa

What's wrong with her? I started to think that the answer lay in one of those cheesy old sci-fi or horror movies that they run late at night. That she'd become a pod person or a secret monster of some kind. Except not in a bad way. She's not mean to me, or anyone else that I can see. She's just . . . weird.

And then on my sixteenth birthday, I find out. It's after the big dinner and presents and everything. I'm lying on my bed, looking up at the ceiling and trying to figure out why I don't feel different—I mean, turning sixteen's supposed to be a big deal, right?—when Apples comes in and closes the door behind her. I scoot up so that I'm leaning against a pillow propped up at my headboard. She props the other pillow up and lies down beside me. We've done this a thousand times, but tonight it feels different.

"I've got something to tell you," she says and my head fills up with worry and questions that only gets worse when she goes on to add, "I'm a vampire."

I turn to look at her.

"Oh, please."

"No, really," she says.

As she starts to explain how it all began after that concert when she did her four-day mystery jaunt, all the oddities and weirdnesses of the past few years start to make sense—or at least they make sense if I'm willing to accept the basic premise that my sister's turned into a teenage Draculetta.

"Why didn't you ever tell me before?" I ask.

"I wanted to wait until you were the same age as I was when I . . . got turned."

"But *why*?"

"Because I want to turn you."

She's sitting cross-legged on the bed now, facing me, her face so earnest.

"If you get changed," she goes on, "you can get rid of both your leg brace and your puffer."

"Really?"

I can't imagine life without them. The chance to be normal. Then I catch myself. Normal, but dead.

But Apples is nodding, a big grin stretching her lips. She holds out her right hand, pointer finger extended.

"Remember when I lost my nail in volleyball practice?" she asks. "The whole thing came right off."

I nod. It was so gross.

"Well, look," she says, still waving her finger in front of my face. "It's all healed."

"Apples," I say. "That was four years ago. Of *course* it's healed."

"I mean it healed when I changed. I had no fingernail the night I went to the concert, but there it was when I came back four days later. The . . . woman who changed me, she said the change heals anything."

"So you're just going to bite me or something and I become like you?"

She nods. "But we have to work this out just right. It takes three days before you're changed, so we'll have to figure out how and where we can do that so that no one gets suspicious. But don't worry. I'll be there for you the whole time, watching over you."

"And then we'll live forever?"

"Forever sixteen."

"What about Mom and Dad?"

"We can't tell them," she says. "How could we even begin to explain this to them?"

"You're explaining it to me."

But she shakes her head. "They wouldn't understand—how could they?"

"The same way you think I can."

"It's not the same."

"So we live forever, but Mom and Dad just get old and die?"

She gets this look on her face that tells me she never thought it out that far.

"We can't change everybody," she says after a long moment.

"Why not?"

"Because then there'd be no one left for us to . . . "

"What?" I ask when her voice trails off.

She doesn't say anything for a long moment, won't meet my gaze.

"To feed on," she says finally. I guess I pull a face, because she quickly adds, "It's not as bad as it sounds."

She's already told me a whole lot of things about the differences between real vamps and the ones in the books and movies, but drinking blood's still part of the deal and I'm sorry, but it still sounds gross.

Apples gets up from the bed. She looks—I don't know. Embarrassed. Sad. Confused.

"I guess you need some time to process all of this stuff I've been telling you," she says.

I give her a slow nod. I'd say something, but I don't know what. I feel kind of overloaded.

"Okay, then," she says and she leaves me in my bedroom.

I slouch back down on the bed and stare at the ceiling again, thinking about everything she's told me.

My sister's a vampire. How weird is that?

Does she still have a soul?

I guess that's a bizarre question in some ways. I mean, do any of us have souls? It's like asking, Who is God?, I guess. The best answer I've heard to that is when Deepak Chopra says, "Who is asking?" It makes sense that God would be different to different people, but also different to you, depending on who you are at the time you're asking.

I guess I believe we have souls. And when we die, they go on. But what that means for Apples, I don't know. She's dead, but she's still here.

She's different now—but she's still the big sister I knew growing up. There's just more to her now. Maybe it's like asking "Who is God?" She's who she is depending on who I am when I'm wondering about her.

Sometimes I think it's only kids that wonder about existential stuff like this. Grown-ups always seem to be worried about money, or politics, or just stuff that has physical presence. It's like somewhere along the way they lost the ability to think about what's inside them.

Here's a story I like: one day Ramakrishna, this big-time spiritual leader back in the nineteenth century, is praying, when he suddenly has this flash that what he's doing is meaningless. He's looking for God, but already everything is God—the rituals he's using, the idols, the floor under him, the walls, *everything*. Wherever he looks, he sees God. And he's just so blown away by this, he can't find the words to express it. All he can do is dance, like, for hours. This joyful Snoopy whirling and dervishing and spinning.

I just love the image of that—some old wise man in flowing robes, just getting up and dancing.

I'd love to be able to dance. I love music. I love the way I can feel it in every pore of my body. When your body's moving to the music, it's like you're part of the music. You're not just dancing to it any more, you're somehow helping to create it at the same time.

But the most I can do is sort of shuffle around until I get all out of breath and I never let anyone see me trying to do it. Not even Apples.

Boy, can she dance. Every movement she makes is just so liquid and smooth. She's graceful just getting up from a chair or crossing a room. And I don't say this because of the contrast between us.

But none of this helps with what she's told me. All I can do is feel the weight of the door that she closed behind her and stare at the ceiling, my head full of a bewildering confusion.

Normally when I have something I can't work out, Apples is the one who helps me deal. But now she's the problem . . .

Did you ever play the game of if you could only have one wish, what would you wish for? It's so hard to decide, isn't it? But I know what I would do. I would wish that all my wishes come true.

But real life isn't like that. And too often you find that the things you think you really, really want, are the last things in the world that you should get.

I've always wanted to be able to walk without my leg brace, to run and jump and dance and just be normal. And breathing. Everybody takes it for granted. Well, I wish I could. And here's my chance. Except it comes with a price, just like in all those old fairy tales I used to read as a kid.

I have to choose. Go on like I am, a defect, a loser—at least in other people's eyes. Or be like Apples, full of life and vigor, and live forever. Except to do that I've got to drink other people's blood and everybody else I care about will eventually get old and die.

What kind of a choice is that?

This is the hardest thing I've ever had to try to work out.

I get Mom to drive me to the mall the next day. I know she worries about me being out on my own, but she's good about it. She reminds me not to overexert myself and we arrange what door she'll meet me at in a couple of hours, and then I'm on my own.

I don't want to go shopping. I just want to sit someplace on my own and there's no better place to do that than in the middle of a bunch of strangers like in the concourse of this mall.

I watch the people go by and find myself staring at their throats. I can't imagine drinking their blood. And then there's this whole business that Apples explained about how she only feeds on bad people. That just makes me feel sicker. When she told me that, all I could think about was that time at dinner when I announced I was becoming a vegetarian and the look on her face when I told them why.

You are what you eat.

I don't want the blood of some freak serial killer nourishing me. I don't even want the blood of a jaywalker in me.

After awhile I make myself stop thinking. I do the people-watching thing, enjoying the way all these people are hurrying by my little island bench seat. But of course, as soon as I start to relax a little, some middle-aged freak in a trench coat has to sit down beside me, putting his lame moves on me. He walks by, once, twice, checks out the leg brace, sees I'm alone, and then he's on the bench and it's "That's such a beautiful blouse—what kind of material is it made of?" and he's reaching over and rubbing the sleeve between his fingers . . .

If I was Apples, with this vamp strength she was telling me about, I could probably knock him on his ass before he even knew what was happening. Or I could at least run away. But all I can do is shrink away from him, feeling scared, until I see one of the mall's rent-a-cops coming.

"Officer!" I yell. They're all wanna-be-cops and love it when you act like they're real policemen.

The pervert beside me jumps up from the bench and bolts down the hall before the security guard even looks in my direction. But that's okay. I don't want a scene. I just want to be left alone.

"Was he bothering you?" the guard asks.

I see him take it in. The leg brace. Me, so obviously helpless—and damn it, it's true. And he's all solicitous and pretty nice, actually. He asks if I'm on my own and when I tell him I'm meeting my mom later, offers to walk me to the door where I'm supposed to meet her.

I take him up on it, but I'm thinking, it doesn't have to be this way. If I let Apples change me, nobody will ever bother me again. It'd be like my own private human genome project. Only maybe I'm not supposed to be healthy. I keep thinking that maybe my asthma and bad leg are compensating for some other talent that just hasn't shown up yet.

I think of people throughout history who've overcome their handicaps to give us things that no one but they could have. Stephen Hawking. Vincent van Gogh with his depressions. Terry Fox. Teddy Roosevelt. Stevie Wonder. Helen Keller.

I'm not saying that they had to be handicapped to share their gifts with us, but if they hadn't been handicapped, maybe they would have gone on to be other people and not become the inspirations or creative people they came to be.

And I'm not saying I'm super smart or talented, or that I'm going to grow up and change the world. But it doesn't seem right to just become something else. I won't have earned it. It's just too . . . too easy, I guess.

"There's a reason why I am the way I am," I tell Apples later.

We're sitting in the rec room, the TV turned to *MuchMusic*, but neither of us are really watching the Christina Aguilera video that's playing. Dad's in the kitchen, making dinner. Mom's out in the garden, planting tulip and crocus bulbs.

"You mean like it's all part of God's plan?" Apples asks.

"No. I don't know that I believe in God. But I believe everything has a purpose."

Apples shakes her head. "You can't tell me you believe your asthma and your leg are a good thing."

"It might seem like they weaken me, but they actually make me strong. Maybe not physically, but in my heart and spirit."

Apples sighs and pulls me close to her. "You always were a space case," she says into my hair. "But I guess that's part of the reason I love you as much as I do."

I pull back so that we can look at each other.

"I don't want you to change me," I say.

Apples has always been good at hiding what she's feeling, but she can't hide the disappointment from me.

"I'm sorry," I tell her.

"Don't be," she says. "You need to do what's right for you."

"I feel like I'm letting you down."

"Cassie," she says. "You could never let me down."

But she moved out of the house the next day.

Three: Appoline

Life sucks.

Or maybe I should say, death sucks, since I'm not really alive—but everybody thinks death sucks because for them it's the big end. So that doesn't work either.

Okay. How about this: undeath sucks.

Or at least mine does.

I had to move out of the house. After four years of waiting to be able to change Cassie, I just couldn't live there any more once she turned me down. I can't believe how much I miss her. I miss the parents, too, but it's not the same. I've never been as close to them as Cassie is. But I adore her and talking on the phone and seeing her a couple of times a week just isn't enough.

Trouble is, when I do see her or talk to her, that hurts, too. Everything just seems to hurt these days.

I've been thinking a lot about Sandy Browning, my best friend in grade school. We were inseparable until we got into junior high. That's when she starting getting into these black moods. Half the time you couldn't see them coming. It was like these black clouds would drift in from nowhere and just envelop her. When I discovered she was cutting herself—her arms and stomach were crisscrossed with dozens of little scars—I couldn't deal with it and we sort of drifted apart.

There's two reasons people become cutters, she told me once, trying to explain. There's those that can't feel anything—the cutting makes them feels alive. And then there are the ones like her, who have this great weight of darkness and despair inside them. The cutting lets it out.

I couldn't really get it at the time—I couldn't imagine having that kind of a bleak shadow swelling inside me—but I understand her now. Ever since Cassie turned me down, I've got this pressure inside me that won't ease and I feel like the only way I can release it is to open a hole to let it out. But it doesn't work for me. The one time I ran a razor blade along the inside of my forearm, it hardly bled at all and the cut immediately started to seal up. Within half an hour, there wasn't a mark on my skin.

Sandy had been completely addicted to it. Her family moved away the year before I became a vamp and I don't know what ever happened to her. I wish I'd been a better friend. I wish a lot of things these days.

I wish I'd never talked to Cassie about my wanting to turn her.

Sometimes I wonder: did I want to do it for her, so that she could finally put aside the limitations of her physical ailments, or did I do it for me, so I wouldn't have to be alone?

I guess it doesn't matter.

I'm sure alone now.

I live in a tiny apartment above the Herb and Spice Natural Foods shop on Bank Street. I like the area. During the day, it's like a normal neighborhood with shops along Bank Street—video store, comic book shop, gay bookstore, restaurants—and mostly residential buildings in behind on the side streets. But come the night, the blocks up north around the clubs like Barrymore's become prime hunting grounds for someone like me. All the would-be toughs, the scavengers and the hunters, come out of the woodwork, hoping to prey on the people who come to check out the bands and the scene.

And I prey on them.

But even stopping them from having their wicked way doesn't really mean all that much anymore. I'm too lonely. It's not that I can't make friends. Ever since I got turned, that's the least of my problems. It's that I don't have a foundation of normalcy to return to anymore. I don't have a home and family. I just have my apartment. My job at the coffee shop. My hunting. I can't seem to get close to anyone because as soon as I do, I remember that I'm going to be like I am forever, while they age and die. Sometimes I imagine I can see them aging, that I can see the cells dying. It's even worse when I'm back home, seeing it happen to Cassie and my parents, so it's not like I can move back there again either.

That's when I decide it's time to track down the woman who turned me.

It's harder than I think. I don't really know where to start. Because she found me outside a concert at the Civic Centre, I spend most of December and January going to the clubs and concerts, thinking it's my best chance. Zaphod Beeblebrox 2 closes down at the end of November, but Barrymore's is still just up the street from where I live, so I drop in there almost every night, sliding past the doorman like I'm not even there. I can almost be invisible if I don't want to be noticed—don't ask me how that works. That's probably why I can't find the woman, but I don't give up trying.

I frequent the Market area, checking out the Rainbow and the Mercury Lounge, the original Zaphod's and places like that. Cool places where I think she might hang out. I go to the National Arts Centre for classical recitals and the Anti-Land Mines concert in early December. To Centrepoint Theatre in Nepean. Further west to the Corel Centre. I even catch a ride up to Wakefield, to the Black Sheep Inn, for a few concerts.

This calls for more serious cash than I can get from my salary at the coffee shop and the meager tips we share there, so I take to lifting the wallets of my victims, leaving them with less cash as well as less blood. My self esteem's taking a nose dive, what with already being depressed, making no headway on finding the woman, and having become this petty criminal as well as the occasional murderer—I ended up having to kill another guy when I discovered he was raping his little sister and I got so mad, I just drained him.

It's weird. I exude confidence—I know I do from other people's reactions to me, and it's not like I'm unaware of how well I can take care of myself. But my internal life's such a mess that sometimes I can't figure out how I make it through the day with my mind still in one piece. I feel like such a loser.

I have this to look forward to forever?

Cassie's the only one who picks up on it.

"What's the matter?" she asks when I stop by for a visit during her Christmas holidays.

"Nothing," I tell her.

"Right. That's why you're so mopey whenever I see you." She doesn't look at me for a moment. When she does look back, she has this little wrinkle between her eyes. "It's because of me, isn't it? Because I didn't want to become a . . . to be like . . . "

"Me," I say, filling in for her. "A monster."

"You're not a monster."

"So what am I? Nothing anybody else'd ever choose to be."

"You didn't choose to be it either," she says.

"No kidding. And I don't blame you. Who'd ever *want* to be like this?"

She doesn't have an answer and neither do I.

Then one frosty January evening I'm walking home from the coffee shop and I see her sitting at a window table of the Royal Oak. I stop and look at her through the glass, struck again by how gorgeous she is, how no one else seems to be aware of it, of her. I go inside when she beckons to me. Today she's casual chic: jeans, a black cotton sweater, cowboy boots. Like me, she probably doesn't feel the cold anymore, but she has a winter coat draped over the back of her chair. There's a pint glass in front of her, half full of amber beer.

"Have a seat," she says, indicating the empty chair across from her.

I do. I don't know what to do with my hands. I don't know where to look. I want to stare at her. I want to pretend I'm cool, that this is no big deal. But it is.

"I've been looking for you," I finally say.

"Have you now."

I nod. Ignoring the hint of amusement in her eyes, I start to ask, "I need to know—"

"No, don't tell me," she says, interrupting. "Let me guess. First you tried to turn . . . oh, your best friend, or maybe a brother or a sister, and they turned you down and made you feel like a monster even though you only feed on the wicked. But somehow, even that doesn't feel right anymore. So now you want to end it all. Or at least get an explanation as to why I turned you."

I find myself nodding.

"We all go through this," she says. "But sooner or later—if we survive—we learn to leave all the old ties behind: friends, family, ideas of right and wrong. We become what we are meant to be. Predators."

I think of how I wanted to turn Cassie and start to feel a little sick. Up until this moment, her refusing to be turned had seemed such a personal blow. Now I'm just grateful that of the two of us, she, at least, had some common sense. Bad enough that one of us is a monster.

"What if I don't want to be a predator?" I ask.

The woman shrugs. "Then you die."

"I thought we couldn't die."

"To all intents and purposes," she says. "But we're not invincible. Yes, we heal fast, but it's genetic healing. We can deal with illnesses and broken bones, torn tissues and birth defects. But if a car hits us, if we take a bullet or a stake in the heart or head, if we're hurt in such a way that our accelerated healing facilities don't have the chance to help us, we can still die. We don't need Van Helsings or chipper cheerleaders in short skirts to do us in. Crossing the street at the wrong time can be just as effective."

"Why did you turn me?"

"Why not?"

All I can do is stare at her.

"Oh, don't take it so dramatically," she says. "I know you'd like a better reason than that—how I saw something special in you, how you have some destiny. But the truth is, it was for my own amusement."

"So it was just a . . . whim."

"You need to stop being so serious about everything," she tells me. "We're a different species. The old rules don't apply to us."

"So you just do whatever you want?"

She smiles, a predatory smile. "If I can get away with it."

"I'm not going to be like that."

"Of course you won't," she says. "You're different. You're special."

I shake my head. "No, I'm just stronger. I'm going to hold onto my ideals."

"Tell me that again in a hundred years," she says. "Tell me how strong you feel when anything you ever cared about, when everybody you love is long dead and gone."

I get up to leave, to walk out on her, but she beats me to it. She stands over me, and touches my hair with her long cool fingers. For a moment I imagine I see a kind of tenderness in her eyes, but then the mockery is back.

"You'll see," she says.

I stay at the table and watch her step outside. Watch her back as she walks on up Bank Street. Watch until she's long gone and there are only strangers passing by the windows of the Royal Oak.

The thing that scares me the most is that maybe she's right.

I realize leaving home wasn't the answer. I'm still too close to the people I love. I have to go a lot farther than I have so far. I have to keep moving and not make friends. Forget I have family. If I don't have to watch the people I love age and die, then maybe I won't become as cynical and bitter as the woman who made me what I am.

But the more I think of it, the more I feel that I'd be a lot better off just dying for real.

Four: Cassandra

In the end, I did it for Apples, though she doesn't know that. I don't think I can ever tell her that. She thinks I did it to be able to run and breathe and be as normal as an undead person can be. But I could see how being what she is and all alone was tearing her apart and I started to think, who do I love the best in the world? Who's always been there for me? Who stayed in with her weak kid sister when she could have been out having fun? Who never complained about taking me anywhere? Who always, *genuinely* enjoyed the time she spent with me?

She never said anything to me about what she was going through, but I could see the loneliness tearing at her and I couldn't let her be on her own anymore. I started to get scared that she might take off for good, or do something to herself, and how could I live with that?

Besides, maybe this is my destiny. Maybe with our enhanced abilities we can be some kind of dynamic duo superhero team, out rescuing the world, or at least little human pieces of the world.

The funny thing is, when I told her I wanted her to turn me, she was the one who argued against it. But I wouldn't take no and she finally gave in.

And it's not so bad. Even the blood-sucking's not so bad, though I do miss eating and drinking. I guess the worst part was those three days I was dead. You're aware, but not aware, floating in some kind of goopy muck that feels like it's made up of all the bad things people have ever done or thought.

But you get over it.

What's my fear? Fuzzy animal slippers. I used to adore them, back when I was alive. Even at sixteen-years-old, I was still wearing them around the house. Now I break into a cold sweat just thinking about them.

Pretty lame, huh? But I guess it's a better weakness than some you can have. Because, really. How often do you unexpectedly run into someone wearing fuzzy animal slippers?

I still have this idea that we should turn Mom and Dad, too, but I'm going to wait awhile before I bring it up again. I think I understand Apples's nervousness better after she told me what she learned the last time she saw the woman who turned her. I don't think it's that she doesn't love our parents. She's just nervous that they won't make the transition well. That they'll be more like the woman than us.

"Let's give it a year or two," she said, "'till we see how we do ourselves."

Mom and Dad sure weren't happy about me moving out and into Apples's apartment. I wish I could at least tell them that I'm not sick anymore, but I'm kind of stuck having a secret identity whenever we go back home for a visit. I have to carry around my puffer and pretend to use it. I have to put the leg brace on again, though we had to adjust it since my leg's all healed.

What's going to happen to us? I don't know. I just know that we'll be together. Always. And I guess, for now, that's enough.

The Screaming
J.A. Konrath

Joseph Andrew Konrath's first novel, Whiskey Sour *(2004), introduced Lt. Jacqueline "Jack" Daniels. The eighth in the series,* Stirred, *will be published this year. Joe is also the editor of the Hitman anthology* These Guns For Hire *(2006). Under the name Jack Kilborn, Konrath has written four horror novels. His short stories have appeared in more than sixty magazines and compilations, and his work has been translated into ten languages. His blog,* A Newbie's Guide to Publishing *(jakonrath.blogspot.com), gets over a million hits a year.*

Konrath's "The Screaming" was originally published in The Many Faces of Van Helsing, *edited by Jeanne Cavelos. This excellent anthology featured new stories of literature's first vampire hunter: Bram Stoker's Dr. Abraham Van Helsing. In "The Screaming," we find the hunter and the hunted creepily combined.*

"Three stinking quid?"

Colin wanted to reach over the counter and throttle the old bugger. The radio he brought in was brand new and worth at least twenty pounds.

Of course, it was also hot. Delaney's was the last pawnbroker in Liverpool that didn't ask questions. Colin dealt with them frequently because of this. But each and every time, he left the shop feeling ripped off.

"Look, this is state of the art. The latest model. You could at least go six."

As expected, the old wank didn't budge. Colin took the three coins and left, muttering curses under his breath.

Where the hell was he going to get more money?

Colin rubbed his hand, fingers trailing over dirty scabs. His eyes itched. His throat felt like he'd been swallowing gravel. His stomach was a tight fist that he couldn't unclench.

If he didn't score soon, the shakes would start.

Colin tried to work up enough saliva to spit, and only half-managed. The radio had been an easy snatch; stupid bird left it on the window ledge of her flat, plugged in and wailing a new Beatles tune. Gifts like that don't come around that often.

He used to do okay robbing houses, but the last job he pulled left him with three broken ribs and a mashed nose when the owner came home early. And Colin'd been in pretty good shape back then. Now—frail and wasted and brittle as he was—a good beating would kill him.

Not that Colin was afraid to die. He just wanted to score first. And three pounds wouldn't even buy him a taste.

Colin hunkered down on the walk, pulled up the collar on his wool coat. The coat had been nice once, bought when Colin was a straighty, making good wage. He'd almost sold it many times, but always held out. English winters bit at a man's bones. There was already a winter-warning chill in the air, even though autumn had barely started.

Still, if he could have gotten five pounds for it, he'd have shucked it in an instant. But with the rips, the stains, the piss smell, he'd be lucky to get fifty p.

"'Ello, Colin."

Colin didn't bother looking up. He recognized the sound of Butts's raspy drone, and couldn't bear to tolerate him right now.

"I said, 'ello, Colin."

"I heard you, Butts."

"No need to be rude, then."

Butts plopped next to him without an invite, smelling like a loo set ablaze. His small eyes darted this way and that along the sidewalk, searching for half spent fags. That's how he'd earned his nickname.

"Oh, lucky day!"

Butts grinned and reached into the street, plucking up something with filthy fingers. There was a lipstick stain on the filter, and it had been stamped flat.

"Good for a puff or two, eh?"

"I'm in no mood today, Butts."

"Strung out again, are we?"

Butts lit the butt with some pub matches, drew hard.

"I need a few more quid for a nickle bag."

"You could pull a job."

"Look at me, Butts. I weigh ten stone, and half that is the coat. A small child could beat my arse."

"Just make sure there's no one home, mate."

Easier said, Colin thought.

"You know"—Butts closed his eyes, smoke curling from his nostrils—"I'm short on scratch myself right now. Maybe we could team up for something. You go in, I could be lookout, we split the take."

Colin almost laughed. He didn't trust Butts as far as he could chuck him.

"How about I be the lookout?"

"Sorry, mate. You'll run at the first sign of trouble."

"And you wouldn't?"

Butts shrugged. His fag went out. He made two more attempts at lighting it, and then flicked it back into the street.

"Sod it, then. Let's do a job where we don't need no lookout."

"Such as?"

Butts scratched his beard, removed a twig.

"There's this house, see? In Heysham, near where I grew up. Been abandoned for a long time. Loaded with bounty, I bet. That antiquey stuff fetches quite a lot in the district."

"It's probably all been jacked a long time ago."

"I don't think so. When I was a pup, the road leading up to it was practically invisible. All growed over by woods, you see. Only the kids knew about it. And we all stayed far away."

"Why?"

"Stories. Supposed to have goblins. Bollocks like that. I went up to it once, on a dare. Got within ten yards. Then I heard the screaming."

Colin rolled his eyes. He needed to quit wasting time with Butts and think of some way to get money. It would be dark soon.

"You think I'm joshing? I swear on the head of my lovely, sainted mother. I got within a stone's throw, and a god-fearful scream comes out of the house. Sounded like the devil his self was torturing some poor soul. Wet my kecks, I did."

"It was probably one of your stupid mates, Butts. Having a giggle at your expense."

"Wasn't a mate, Colin. I'm telling you, no kid in town went near that house. Nobody did. And I've been thinking about it a lot, lately. I bet there's some fine stuff to nick in there."

"Why haven't you gone back then, eh? If this place is full of stealables, why haven't you made a run?"

Butts's roving eyes locked onto another prize. He lit up, inhaled.

"It's about fifteen miles from here. Every so often I save up the rail money, but I always seem to spend the dough on something else. Hey, you said you have a few quid, right? Maybe we can take the train and—"

"No way, Butts."

Colin got up, his thin bones creaking. He could feel the onset of tremors in his hands, and jammed them into his pockets.

"Heysham Port is only a two-hour ride. Then only a wee walk to the house."

"I don't want to spend my loot on train tics, and I don't want to spend the night in bloody Heysham. Piss-ant little town."

Colin looked left, then right, realizing it didn't matter what direction he went. He began walking, Butts nipping at his heels.

"I got old buds in Heysham. They'll put us up. Plus I got a contact there. He could set us up with some smack, right off. Wouldn't even need quid; we can barter with the pretties we nick."

"No."

Butts put his dirty hand on Colin's shoulder, squeezed. His fingernails resembled a coal miner's.

"Come on, mate. We could be hooked up in three hours. Maybe less. You got something better to do? Find a hole somewhere, curl up until the puking stops? You recall how long it takes to stop, Colin?"

Colin paused. He hadn't eaten in a few days, so there was nothing to throw up but his own stomach lining. He'd done that, once. Hurt something terrible, all bloody and foul.

But Heysham? Colin didn't believe there was anything valuable in that armpit of a town. Let alone some treasure-filled house Butts'd seen thirty years back.

Colin rubbed his temple. It throbbed, in a familiar way. As the night dragged on, the throbbing would get worse.

He could take his quid, buy a tin of aspirin and some seltzer, and hope the withdrawal wouldn't be too bad this time.

But he knew the truth.

As far as bad decisions went, Colin was king. One more wouldn't make a dif.

"Fine, Butts. We'll go to Heysham. But if there's nothing there, you owe me. Big."

Butts smiled. The three teeth he had left were as brown as his shoes.

"You got it, mate! And you'll see! Old Butts has got a feeling about this one. We're going to score, and score big. You'll see."

By the time the rail spit them out at Heysham Port, Colin was well into the vomiting.

He'd spent most of the ride in the loo, retching his guts out. With each purge, he forced himself to drink water, so as not to do any permanent damage to his gullet. It didn't help. When the water came back up, it was tinged pink.

"Hang in there, Colin. It isn't far."

Bollocks it wasn't far. They walked for over three hours. The night air was a meat locker, and the ground was all slope and hill. Wooded country, overgrown with trees and high grass, dotted with freezing bogs. Colin noticed the full moon, through a sliver in the canopy, then the forest swallowed it up.

They walked by torchlight; Butts had swaddled an old undershirt around a stick. Colin stopped vomiting, but the shivering got so bad he fell several times. It didn't help that Butts kept getting his reference points mixed up and changed directions constantly.

"Don't got much left, Butts."

"Stay strong, mate. Almost there. See? We're on the road."

Colin looked down, saw only weeds and rocks.

"Road?"

"Cobblestone. You can still see bits of curbing."

Colin's hopes fell. If the road was in such disrepair, the house was probably worse off.

Stinking Heysham. Stinking Butts.

"There it is, mate! What did I tell you?"

Colin stared ahead and viewed nothing but trees. Slowly, gradually, he saw the house shape. The place was entirely obscured, the land so overgrown it appeared to be swallowing the frame.

"Seems like the house is part of the trees," Colin said.

"Was like that years ago, too. Worse now, of course. And lookit that. Windows still intact. No one's been inside here in fifty years, I bet."

Colin straightened up. Butts was right. As rundown as it was, the house looked untouched by humans since the turn of the century.

"We don't have to take everything at once. Just find something small and pricey to nick now, and then we can come back and—"

The scream paralyzed Colin. It was a force, high pitched thunder, ripping through him like needles. Unmistakably human, yet unlike any human voice Colin had ever heard.

And it was coming from the house.

Butts gripped him with both hands, the color fleeing his ruddy face.

"Jesus Christ! Did you hear that? Just like when I was a kid! What do we do, Colin?"

A spasm shook Colin's guts, and he dry-heaved onto some scrub brush. He wiped his mouth on his coat sleeve.

"We go in."

"Go in? I just pissed myself."

"What are you afraid of, Butts? Dying? Look at yourself. Death would be a blessing."

"My life isn't a good one, Colin, but it's the only one I've got."

Colin pushed past. The scream was chilling, yes. But there was nothing in that house worse than what Colin had seen on the street. Plus, he needed to get fixed up, bad. He'd crawl inside the devil's arse to get some cash.

"Hold up for me!"

Butts attached himself to Colin's arm. They crept towards the front door.

Another scream rattled the night, even louder than the first. It vibrated through Colin's body, making every nerve jangle.

"I just pissed myself again!"

"Quiet, Butts! Did you catch that?"

"Catch what?"

"It wasn't just a scream. I think it was a word."

Colin held his breath, waiting for the horrible sound to come again. The woods stayed silent around them, the wind and animals still.

The scream cut him to the marrow.

"There! Sounded like *hell*."

Butts's eyes widened, the yellows showing.

"Let's leave, Colin. My trousers can't hold anymore."

Colin shook off Butts and continued creeping towards the house.

Though naive about architecture, Colin had grown up viewing enough castles and manors to recognize this building was very old. The masonry was concealed by climbing vines, but the wrought iron adorning the windows was magnificent. Even decades of rust couldn't obscure the intricate, flowing curves and swirls.

As they neared, the house seemed to become larger, jutting dormers threatening to drop down on their heads, heavy walls stretching off and blending into the trees. Colin stopped at the door, nearly nine feet high, hinges big as a man's arm.

"Butts! The torch!"

Butts slunk over, waving the flame at the door.

The knob was antique, solid brass, and glinted in the torchlight. At chest level hung a grimy knocker. Colin licked his thumb and rubbed away the patina.

"Silver."

"Silver? That's great, Colin! Let's yank it and get out of here."

But Colin wouldn't budge. If just the door knocker was worth this much, what treasures lay inside?

He put his hand on the cold knob. Turned.

It opened.

As a youth, Colin often spent time with his grandparents, who owned a dairy farm in Shincliffe. That's how the inside of this house smelled; like the musk and manure of wild beats. A feral smell, his grandmum had often called it.

Taking the torch from Butts, he stepped into the foyer, eyes scanning for booty. Decades of dust had settled on the furnishings, motes swirling into a thick fog wherever the duo stepped. Beneath the grime, Colin could recognize the quality of the furniture, the value of the wall hangings.

They'd hit it big.

It was way beyond a simple, quick score. If they did this right, went through the proper channels, he and Butts could get rich off of this.

Another scream shook the house.

Butts jumped back, his sudden movement sending clouds of dust into the air. Colin coughed, trying to wave the filth out of his face.

"It came from down there!" Butts pointed at the floor, his quivering hand casting erratic shadows in the torchlight. "It's a ghost, I tell you! Come to take us to hell!"

Colin's heart was a hummingbird in his chest, trying to find a way out. He was scared, but even more than that, he was concerned.

"Not *hell*, Butts. It sounded more like *help*."

Colin stepped back, out of the dust cloud. He thrust the torch at the floor, looking for a way down.

"'Ello! Anyone down there?"

He tapped at the wood slats with the torch, listening for a hollow sound.'

"'Ello!"

The voice exploded up through the floorboards, cracking like thunder.

"PRAISE GOD, HELP ME!"

Butts grabbed Colin's shoulders, his foul breath assaulting his ear.

"Christ, Colin! There's a wraith down there!"

"Don't be stupid, Butts. It's a man. Would a ghost be praising God?"

Colin bent down, peered at the floor.

"What's a man doing under the house, Colin?"

"Bugger if I know. But we have to find him."

Butts nodded, eager.

"Right! If we rescue the poor sap, maybe we'll get a reward, eh?"

Colin grabbed Butts by the collar, pulled him close.

"This place is a gold mine. We can't let anyone else know it exists."

Butts gazed at him stupidly.

"We have to snuff him," Colin said.

"Snuff him? Colin, I don't think—"

Colin clamped his hand over Butts's mouth.

"I'll do it, when the time comes. Just shut up and follow my lead, got it?"

Butts nodded. Colin released him and went back to searching the floor.

"'Ello! How'd you get down there!"

"There is a trap door, in the kitchen!"

Colin located the kitchen off to the right. An ancient, wood burning stove stood vigil in one corner, and there was an icebox by the window. On the kitchen table, slathered with dust, lay a table setting for one. Colin wondered, fleetingly, what price the antique china and crystal would fetch, and then turned his attention to the floor.

"Where!"

"The corner! Next to the stove!"

Colin looked around for something to sweep away the dust. He reached for the curtains, figured they might be worth something, and then found a closet on the other side of the room. There was a broom inside.

He gave Butts the torch and swept slowly, trying not to stir up the motes. After a minute, he could make out a seam in the floorboards. The seam extended into a man-sized square, complete with a recessed iron latch.

When Colin pulled up on the handle, he was bathed in a foul odor a hundred times worse than anything on his grandparent's farm. The source of the feral smell. And it was horrible.

Mixed in with the scent of beasts was decay; rotting, stinking, flesh. Colin knelt down, gagging. It took several minutes for the contractions to stop.

"There's a ladder." Butts thrust the torch into the hole. His free hand covered his nose and mouth.

"How far down?" Colin managed.

"Not very. I can make out the bottom."

"Hey! You still down there!"

"Yes. But before you come down, you must prepare yourselves, gentlemen."

"Prepare ourselves? What for?"

"I am afraid my appearance may pose a bit of a shock. However, you must not be afraid. I promise I shall not hurt you."

Butts eyed Colin, intense. "I'm getting seriously freaked out. Let's just nick the silver knocker and—"

"Give me the torch."

Butts handed it over. Colin dropped the burning stick into the passage, illuminating the floor.

A moan, sharp and strong, welled up from the hole.

"You okay down there, mate?"

"The light is painful. I have not born witness to light for a considerable amount of time."

Butts dug a finger into his ear, scratching. "Bloke sure talks fancy."

"He won't for long." Colin sat on the floor, found the rungs with his feet, and began to descend.

The smell doubled with every step down; a viscous odor that had heat and weight and sat on Colin's tongue like a dead cat. In the flickering flame, Colin could make out the shape of the room. It was a root cellar, cold and foul. The dirt walls were rounded, and when Colin touched ground he sent plums of dust into the air. He picked up the torch to locate the source of the voice. In the corner, standing next to the wall, was . . .

"Sweet Lord Jesus Christ!"

"I must not be much to look at."

That was the understatement of the century. The man, if he could be called that, was excruciatingly thin. His bare chest resembled a skeleton with a thin sheet of white skin wrapped tight around, and his waist was so reduced it had the breadth of Colin's thigh.

A pair of tattered trousers hung loosely on the unfortunate man's pelvis, and remnants of shoes clung to his feet, several filthy toes protruding through the leather.

And the face, *the face*! A hideous skull topped with limp, white hair, thin features stretched across cheekbones, eyes sunken deep into bulging sockets.

"Please, do not flee."

The old man held up a bony arm, the elbow knobby and ball-shaped. Around his wrist coiled a heavy, rusted chain, leading to a massive steel ball on the ground.

Colin squinted, then gasped. The chain wasn't going around this unfortunate's wrist; it went *through* the wrist, a thick link penetrating the flesh between the radius and ulna.

"Colin! You okay?"

Butts's voice made Colin jump.

"Come on down, Butts! I think I need you!"

"There is no need to be afraid. I will not bite. Even if I desired to do so."

The old man stretched his mouth open, exposing sticky, gray gums. Both the upper and lower teeth were gone.

"I knocked them out quite some time ago. I could not bear to be a threat to anyone. May I ask to whom I am addressing?"

"Eh?"

"What is your name, dear sir?"

Colin started to lie, then realized there was no point. He was going to snuff this poor sod, anyway.

"Colin. Colin Willoughby."

"The pleasure is mine, Mr. Willoughby. Allow me. My name is Dr. Abraham Van Helsing, professor emeritus at Oxford University. Will you allow me one more question?"

Colin nodded. It was eerie, watching this man talk. His body was ravaged to the point of disbelief, but his manner was polite and even affable.

"What year of our Lord is this, Mr. Willoughby?"

"The year? It's nineteen sixty-five."

Van Helsing's lips quivered. His sad, sunken eyes went glassy.

"I have been down here longer than I have imagined. Tell me, pray do, the nosferatu; were they wiped out in the war?"

"What war? And what is a nosfer-whatever you said?"

"The war must have been many years ago. There were horrible, deafening explosions that shook the ground. I believe it went on for many months. I assumed it was a battle with the undead."

Was this crackpot talking about the bombing from World War II? He couldn't have been down here for that long. There was no food, no water . . .

"Mary, Mother of God!"

Butts stepped off the ladder and crouched behind Colin. He held another torch, this one made from the broom they'd used to sweep the kitchen floor.

"Whom am I addressing now, good sir?"

"He's asking your name, Butts."

"Oh. It's Butts."

"Good evening to you, Mr. Butts. Now if I may get an answer to my previous inquiry, Mr. Willoughby?"

"If you mean World War Two, the war was with Germany."

"I take it, because you both are speaking in our mother tongue, that Germany was defeated?"

"We kicked the kraut's arses," Butts said from behind Colin's shoulder.

"Very good, then. You also related that you do not recognize the term nosferatu?*"*

"Never heard of it."

"How about the term vampire?*"*

Butts nodded, nudging Colin in the ribs with his elbow. "Yeah, we know about vampires, don't we, Colin? They been in some great flickers."

"Flickers?"

"You know. Movie shows."

Van Helsing knitted his brow. His skin was so tight, it made the corners of his mouth draw upwards.

"So the nosferatu attend these movie shows?"

"Attend? Blimey, no. They're in the movies. Vampires are fake, old man. Everyone knows that. Dracula don't really exist."

"Dracula!" Van Helsing took a step forward, the chain tugging cruelly against his arm. *"You know the name of the monster!"*

"Everyone knows Dracula. Been in a million books and movies."

Van Helsing seemed lost for a moment, confused. Then a light flashed behind his black eyes.

"My memorandum," he whispered. *"Someone must have published it."*

"Eh?"

"These vampires . . . you say they do not exist?"

"They're imaginary, old man. Like faeries and dragons."

Van Helsing slumped against the wall. His arm jutted out to the side, chain stretched and jangling in protest. He gummed his lower lip, staring into the dirt floor.

"Then I must be the last one."

Colin was getting anxious. He needed some smack, and this old relic was wasting precious time. In Colin's pocket rested a boning knife he kept for protection. Colin'd never killed anybody before, but he figured he could manage. A quick poke-poke, and then they'd be on their way.

"I thought vampires had fangs." Butts approached Van Helsing, his head cocked to the side like a curious dog.

"I threw them in the dirt, about where you are presently standing. Knocked them out by ramming my mouth rather forcefully into this iron weight to which I am chained."

"So you're really a vampire?"

Colin almost told Butts to shut the hell up, but decided it was smarter to keep the old man talking. He fingered the knife handle and took a casual step forward.

"Unfortunately, I am. After Seward and Morris destroyed the Monster, we thought there were no more. Foolish."

Van Helsing's eyes looked beyond Colin and Butts.

"Morris passed on. Jonathan and Mina named their son after him. Quincey. He was destined to be a great man of science; that was the sort of mind the boy had. Logical and quick to question. But on his sixth birthday, they came."

"Who came?" Butts asked.

Keep him talking, Colin thought. He took another step forward, the knife clutched tight.

"The vampiri. Unholy children of the fiend, Dracula. They found us. My wife, Dr. Seward, Jonathan, Mina . . . all slaughtered. But poor, dear Quincey, his fate proved even worse. They turned him."

"You mean, they bit him on the neck and made him a vampire?"

"Indeed they did, Mr. Butts. I should have ended his torment, but he was so small. An innocent lamb. I decided that perhaps, with a combination of religion and science, I might be able to cure him."

Butts squatted on his haunches, less than a yard from the old man. "I'll wager he's the one that got you, isn't he?"

Van Helsing nodded, glumly.

"I kept him down here. Performed my experiments during the day, while he slept. But one afternoon, distracted by a chemistry problem, I stayed too late, and he awoke from his undead slumber and administered the venom into my hand."

"Keep talking, old man," Colin whispered under his breath. He pulled the knife from his pocket and held it at his side, hidden up the sleeve of his coat.

"I developed the sickness. While drifting in and out of consciousness, I realized I was being tended to. Quincey, dear, innocent Quincey, had brought others of his kind back to my house."

"They the ones that chained you to the wall?"

"Indeed they did, Mr. Butts. This is the ultimate punishment for one of their kind. Existing with this terrible, gnawing hunger, with no way to relieve the ache. The pain has been quite excruciating, throughout the years. Starvation combined with a sickening craving. Like narcotic withdrawal."

"We know what that's like," Butts offered.

"I tried drinking my own blood, but it is sour and offers no relief. Occasionally, a small insect or rodent wanders into the cellar, and much as I try to resist it, the hunger forces me to commit horrible acts." Van Helsing shook his head. "Renfield *would have been amused."*

"So you been living on bugs and vermin all this time? You can't survive on that."

"That is my problem, Mr. Butts. I do survive. As I am already dead, I shall exist forever unless extraordinary means are applied."

Butts laughed, giving his knees a smack. "It's a bloody wicked tale, old man. But we both know there ain't no such things as vampires."

"Do either of you have a mirror? Or a crucifix, perhaps? I believe there is one in the jewelry box, on the night stand in the upstairs bedroom. I suggest you bring it here."

Now they were getting somewhere. Jewelry was easy to carry, and easier to pawn. Colin's veins twitched in anticipation.

"Go get it, Butts. Bring the whole box down."

Butts nodded, quickly disappearing up the ladder.

Colin studied Van Helsing, puzzling about the best way to end him. The old man was so frail, one quick jab in the chest and he should be done with it.

"That small knife you clutch in your hand, that may not be enough, Mr. Willoughby."

Colin was surprised that Van Helsing had noticed, but it didn't matter at this point. He held the boning knife out before him.

"I think it'll do just fine."

"I have tried to end my own life many times. On many nights, I would pound my head against this steel block until bones cracked. When I still had teeth, I tried gnawing off my own arm to escape into the sunlight. Yet every time the sun set again, I awoke fully healed."

Colin hesitated. The knife handle was sweaty, uncomfortable. He wondered where Butts was.

"My death must come from a wooden stake through my heart, or, in lieu of that, you must sever my head and separate it from my shoulders." Van Helsing wiped away a long line of drool that leaked down his chin. *"Do not be afraid. I am hungry, yes, but I am still strong enough to fight the urge. I will not resist."*

The old man knelt, lifting his chin. Colin brought the blade to his throat. Van Helsing's neck was thin, dry, like rice paper. One good slice would do it.

"I want to die, Mr. Willoughby. Please."

Hand trembling, Colin set his jaw and sucked in air through his teeth.

But he couldn't do it.

"Sorry, mate. I—"

"Then I shall!"

Van Helsing sprung to his feet, tearing the knife away from Colin. With animal ferocity he began to hack at his own neck, slashing through tissue and artery, blood pumping down his translucent chest in pulsing waterfalls.

Colin took a step back, the gorge rising.

Van Helsing screamed, an inhuman cry that made Colin go rigid with fear.

The old man's head cocked at a funny angle, tilting to the side. His eyes rolled up in their sockets, exposing the whites. But still he continued, slashing away at the neck vertebrae, buried deep within his bleeding flesh like a white peach pit.

Colin vomited, unable to pull his eyes away.

He's going to make it, Colin thought, incredulous. *He's going to cut off his own head.*

But it wasn't to be. Just as the knife plunged into the bone of his spine, Van Helsing went limp, sprawling face first onto the dirt.

Colin stared, amazed. The horror, the violence of what he just witnessed, pressed down upon him like a great weight. After a few minutes, his breathing slowed to normal, and he found his mind again.

Colin reached tentatively for the knife, still clutched in Van Helsing's hand. The gore gave him pause.

"Go ahead and keep it," Colin decided. "I'll buy another one when—"

Alarm jolted through Colin. He realized, all at once, that Butts hadn't returned. Had the bugger run off with the jewelry box?

Colin sped up the ladder, panicked.

"Butts!"

No answer.

Using the torch, he followed Butts's tracks in the dust, into the bedroom, and then back out the front door. Colin swung it open.

"Butts! Butts, you son of a whore!"

No reply.

Colin sprinted into the night. He ran fast as he could, hoping that his direction was true, screaming and cursing Butts between labored breaths.

His foot caught on a protruding root and Colin went sprawling forward, skidding on his chin, his torch flying off into the woods and sizzling out in a bog.

Blackness.

The dark was complete, penetrating. Not even the moon and stars were visible. It felt like being in the grave.

Colin, wracked by claustrophobia, once again called out for Butts.

The forest swallowed up his voice.

Fear set in. Without a torch, Colin would never find his way back to Heysham. Wandering around the woods without fire or shelter, he could easily die of exposure.

Colin got back on his feet, but walking was impossible. On the rough terrain, without being able to see, he had no sense of direction. He tried to head back to the house, but couldn't manage a straight line.

After falling twice more, Colin gave up. Exhausted, frightened, and wracked with the pain of withdrawal, he curled up at the base of large tree and let sleep overtake him.

"This better be it, Butts."

"We're almost there. I swear on it."

Colin opened his crusty eyes, attempted to find his bearings.

He was surrounded by high grass, next to a giant elm. The sun peeked through the canopy at an angle; it was either early morning or late afternoon.

"You've been saying that for three hours, you little wank. You need a little more encouragement to find this place?"

"I'm not holding out on you, Willie. Don't hit me again."

Colin squinted in the direction of the voices. Butts and two others. They weren't street people, either. Both wore clean clothes, good shoes. The smaller one, Willie, had a bowler hat and a matching black vest. The larger sported a beard, along with a chest big as a whiskey barrel.

Butts had taken on some partners.

Colin tried to stand, but felt weak and dizzy. He knelt for a moment, trying to clear his head. When the cobwebs dissipated, he began to trail the trio.

"Tell us again, Butts, how much loot there is in this place."

"It's crammed full, Jake. All that old, antiquey stuff. I'm telling you, that jewelry box was just a taste."

"Better be, Butts, or you'll be wearing your yarbles around your filthy neck."

"I swear, Willie. You'll see. We're almost there."

Colin stayed ten yards back, keeping low, moving quiet. Several times he lost sight of them, but they were a loud bunch and easy to track. His rage grew with each step.

This house was his big break, his shot at a better life. He didn't want to share it with anybody. He may have choked when trying to off Van Helsing, but when they arrived at the house, Colin vowed to kill them all.

"Hey, Willie. Some bloke is following us."

"Eh?"

"In the woods. There."

Colin froze. The man named Jake stared, pointing through the brush.

"Who's there, then? Don't make me run you down."

"That's Colin. He came here with me."

Damned Butts.

"He knows about this place? Jake, go get the little bleeder!"

Colin ran, but Jake was fast. Within moments the bigger man caught Colin's arm and threw him to the ground.

"Trying to run from me, eh?"

A swift kick caught Colin in the ribs, searing pain stealing his breath.

"I hate running. Hate it."

Another kick. Colin groaned. Bright spots swirled in his vision.

"Get up, wanker. Let's go talk to Willie."

Jake grabbed Colin by the ear and tugged him along, dumping him at Willie's feet.

"Why didn't you tell us about your mate, Butts?"

"I thought he'd gone. I swear it."

Jake let loose with another kick. Colin curled up fetal, began to cry.

"Should we kill him, Willie?"

"Not yet. We might need an extra body, help take back some of the loot. You hear me, you drug-addled bastard? We're going to keep you around for awhile, as long as you're helpful."

Butts knelt next to Colin and smiled, brown teeth flashing. "Get up, Colin. They're not going to kill you." He helped Colin gain his footing, keeping a steady arm around his shoulders until they arrived at the house.

In the daylight, the house's aristocratic appearance was overtaken by the many apparent flaws; peeling paint, cracked foundation, sunken roof. Even the stately iron work covering the windows looked drab and shabby.

"This place is a dump." Willie placed a finger on one nostril and blew the contents of his nose onto a patch of clover.

"It's better on the inside," encouraged Butts. "You'll see."

Unfortunately, the inside was even less impressive. The dust-covered furniture Colin had pegged as antique was damaged and rotting.

"You call this treasure?" Willie punched Butts square in the nose.

Butts dropped to the floor, bleeding and hysterical.

"This is good stuff, Willie! It'll clean up nice! Worth a couple thousand quid, I swear!"

Willie and Jake walked away from Butts, and he crawled behind them, babbling.

A moment later, Colin was alone.

The pain in his ribs sharpened with every intake of breath.

If he made a run for it, they'd catch him easily. But if he did nothing, he was a dead man.

He needed a weapon.

Colin crept into the kitchen, mindful of the creaking floorboards. Perhaps the drawers contained a weapon or some kind.

"What you doing in here, eh? Nicking silver?" Jake slapped him across the face.

Colin staggered back, his feet becoming rubber. Then the floor simply ceased to be there. He dropped, straight down, landing on his arse at the bottom of the root cellar.

Everything went fuzzy, and then black.

Colin awoke in darkness.

He felt around, noticed his leg bent at a funny angle.

The touch made him cry out.

Broken. Badly, from the size of the swelling.

Colin peeled his eyes wide, tried to see. There was no light at all. The trap door, leading to the kitchen, was closed. Not that it mattered; he couldn't have climbed up the ladder anyway.

He sat up, tears erupting onto his cheeks. There was a creaking sound above him, and then a sudden burst of light.

"I see you're still alive, eh?"

Colin squinted through the glare, made out the bowler hat.

"No worries, mate. We won't let you starve to death down there. We're not barbarians. Willie will be down shortly to finish you off. Promise it'll be quick. Right, Willie?"

Willie's laugh was an evil thing.

"See you in a bit."

The trap door closed.

Fear rippled through Colin, but it was overwhelmed by something greater. Anger.

Colin had ever been the victim. From his boyhood days, being beaten by his alcoholic father, up to his nagging ex-wife, suing him into the recesses of poverty.

Well, if his miserable life was going to end here, in a foul-smelling dirt cellar, then so be it.

But he wasn't going without a fight.

Colin pulled himself along the cold ground, dragging his wounded leg. He wanted the boning knife, the one he'd left curled in Van Helsing's hand.

When Jake came down to finish him off, the fat bastard was going to get a nice surprise.

Colin's hand touched moisture, blood or some other type of grue, so he knew he was close. He reached into the inky blackness, finding Van Helsing's body, trailing down over his shoulder . . .

"What in the hell?"

Colin brought his other hand over, groped around.

It made no sense.

Van Helsing's head, which had been practically severed from his shoulders, had reattached itself. The neck was completely intact. No gaping wound, no deep cut.

"Can't be him."

Perhaps another body had been dumped down there, possibly Butts. Colin touched the face.

No beard.

Grazing the mouth with his fingers, Colin winced and stuck a digit past the clammy lips.

It was cold and slimy inside the mouth. Revolting. But Colin probed around for almost an entire minute, searching for teeth that weren't there.

This was Van Helsing. And he had completely healed.

Which was impossible. Unless—

"Jesus Christ." Colin recoiled, scooting away from the body.

He was trapped in the dark with a vampire.

When would Van Helsing awake? Damn good thing the bloke was chained down. Who knows what horrors he could commit if he were free?

Colin repeated that thought, and grinned.

Perhaps if he helped the poor sod escape, Van Helsing would be so grateful he'd take care of the goons upstairs.

The idea vanished when Colin remembered Van Helsing's words. All the poor sod wanted was to die. He didn't want to kill anyone.

"Bloody hell. If *I* were a vampire, I'd do things—"

Colin halted mid-sentence. His works were in a sardine can, inside his breast pocket. He reached for them, took out the hypo.

It just might work.

Crawling back to Van Helsing, Colin probed until he found the bony neck. He pushed the needle in, then eased back the plunger, drawing out blood.

Vampire blood.

Tying off his own arm and finding his vein in the dark wasn't a problem; he'd done it many times before.

Teeth clenched, eyes shut, he gave himself the shot.

But there was no rush.

Only pain.

The pain seared up his arm, as if someone was yanking out his veins with pliers.

Colin cried out. When the tainted blood reached his heart, the muscle stopped cold, killing him instantly.

Colin opened his eyes.

He was still in the cellar, but he could see perfectly fine. He wondered where the light could be coming from, but a quick look around found no source.

Colin stood, realizing with a start that the pain in his leg had vanished.

So, in fact, had all of his other pain. He lifted his shirt, expecting to see bruised ribs, but there wasn't a mark on them.

Even the withdrawal symptoms had vanished.

The hypodermic was still in his hand. Colin stared at it, remembering.

"It worked. It bloody well worked."

Van Helsing still lay sprawled out on the floor, face down.

Colin looked at him, and he began to drool. Hunger surged through him, an urge so completely overwhelming it dwarfed his addiction to heroin.

Without resisting the impulse, he fell to the ground and bit into the old man's neck. His new teeth tore through the skin easily, but when his tongue touched blood, Colin jerked away.

Rancid. Like spoiled milk.

A sound, from above. Colin listened, amused at how acute his hearing had become.

"All right, then. Jake, you go downstairs and mercy-kill the junkie, and then we'll be off."

Mercy kill, indeed.

Colin forced himself to be patient, standing stock-still, as the trap door opened and a figure descended.

"Well well well, look who's up and about. Be brave, I'll try to make it painless."

Jake moved forward. Colin almost grinned. Big, sweating, dirty Jake smelled delicious.

"You got some fight left in you, eh?"

Colin lunged.

His speed was unnatural; he was on Jake in an instant. Even more astounding was his strength. Using almost no effort at all, he pulled the larger man to the ground and pinned down his arms.

"What the hell?"

"I'll try to make it painless," Colin said.

But from the sound of Jake's screams, it wasn't painless at all.

This blood wasn't rancid. This blood was ecstasy.

Every cell in Colin's body shuddered with pleasure; an overwhelming rush that dwarfed the feeling of heroin, a full-body orgasm so intense he couldn't control the moan escaping his throat.

He sucked until Jake stopped moving. Until his stomach distended, the warm liquid sloshing around inside him like a full term embryo.

But he remained hungry.

He raced up the ladder, practically floating on his newfound power. Butts stood at the table, piling dishes into a wooden crate.

"Colin?"

Butts proved delicious, too. In a slightly different way. Not as sweet, sort of a Bordeaux to Jake's Cabernet. Colin's tongue was a wild thing. He lapped up the blood like a mad dog at a water dish, ravenous.

"What the hell are you doing?"

Colin let Butts drop, whirling to face Willie.

"Good God!"

Willie reached into his vest, removed a small derringer. He fired twice, both shots tearing into Colin's chest.

There was pain.

But more than pain, there was hunger.

Willie turned to run, but Colin caught him easily.

"I wonder what you'll taste like," he whispered in the screaming man's ear.

Honey mead. The best of the three.

Colin suckled, gulping down the nectar as it pulsed from Willie's carotid. He gorged himself until one more swallow would have caused him to burst.

Then, in an orgiastic stupor, he stumbled from the house and into the glorious night.

No longer dark and silent and scary, the air now hummed with a bright glow, and animal sounds from miles away were clear and lovely.

Bats, chasing insects. A wolf, baying the moon. A tree toad, calling out to its mate.

Such sweet, wonderful music.

The feeling overwhelmed Colin, and he shuddered and wept. This is what he'd been searching for his entire life. This was euphoria. This was power. This was a fresh start.

"I see you have been busy."

Colin spun around.

Van Helsing stood at the entrance to the house. His right hand still gripped Colin's bone knife. His left hand was gone, severed above the wrist where the chain had bound him. The stump dripped gore, jagged white bone poking out.

Colin studied Van Helsing's face. Still sunken, still anguished. But there was something new in the eyes. A spark.

"Happy, old man? You finally have your freedom."

"Freedom is not what I seek. I desire only the redemption that comes with death."

Colin grinned, baring the sharp tips of his new fangs.

"I'll be happy to kill you, if you want."

Van Helsing frowned.

"The lineage of nosferatu ends now, Mr. Willoughby. No more may be allowed to live. I have severed the heads of the ones inside the house. Only you and I remain."

Colin laughed, blood dripping from his lips.

"You mean to kill me? With that tiny knife? Don't you sense my power, old man? Don't you see what I have become?" Colin spread out his arms, reaching up into the night. "I have been reborn!"

Colin opened wide, fangs bared to tear flesh. But something in Van Helsing's face, some awful fusion of hate and determination, made Colin hesitate.

Van Helsing closed the distance between them with supernatural speed, plunging the knife deep into Colin's heart.

Colin fell, gasping. The agony was exquisite. He tried to speak, and blood— his own rancid blood—bubbled up sour in his throat.

"Not . . . not . . . wood."

"No, Mr. Willoughby, this is not a wooden stake. It will not kill you. But the damage should be substantial enough to keep you here for an hour or so."

Van Helsing drove the knife further, puncturing the back of Colin's rib cage, pinning him to the ground.

"I have been waiting sixty years to end this nightmare, and I am tired. So very tired. With our destruction, my wait shall finally be over. May God have mercy on our souls."

Colin tried to rise, but the pain brought tears.

Van Helsing rolled off, and sat, cross-legged, on the old cobblestone road. He closed his eyes, his thin, colorless lips forming a serene smile.

"I have not seen a sunrise in sixty years, Mr. Willoughby. I remember them to be very beautiful. This should be the most magnificent of them all."

Colin began to scream.

When sunrise came, it cleansed like fire.

Zen and the Art of Vampirism
Kelley Armstrong

Kelley Armstrong's best-selling Women of the Otherworld series was launched in 2001 with Bitten, *a novel featuring Elena Michaels—an everyday woman who also happens to be the only known female werewolf. Unlike other contemporary fantasy series with female protagonists that mix in mystery and a bit of romance, the Otherworld books didn't stick with a single lead character (or werewolves or women for that matter). In "Zen and the Art of Vampirism," we meet Zoe Takano, the only vampire in Toronto—until some southern fangsters decide to take over her territory. But don't expect the stereotypical from either the author or her vampire.*

Armstrong has been telling stories since before she could write. Her earliest written efforts were disastrous. If asked for a story about girls and dolls, hers would invariably feature undead girls and evil dolls, much to her teachers' dismay. All efforts to make her produce "normal" stories failed. Today, she continues to spin tales of ghosts and demons and werewolves, while safely locked away in her basement writing dungeon. Other than the Otherworld paranormal suspense series, she's authored the Darkest Powers young adult urban fantasy trilogy, and the Nadia Stafford crime series. She lives in southwestern Ontario with her husband, kids, and far too many pets.

IN MILLER'S bar, the only thing that smelled worse than the bathroom was the clientele. Of the three humans there that night, two were already so pissed I could walk over, sink my teeth into their necks, and they'd never flinch. Tempting, but Rudy likes me sticking to beer.

Cultural assimilation is a lofty goal, but every minority needs a place to kick back with her own kind, a place to trade news and gossip that wouldn't interest anyone outside the group. For supernaturals in Toronto, that place is Miller's.

The clientele wasn't exclusively supernatural. That kind of thing is hard to enforce without calling attention to yourself, which none of us wants to do. But the ambiance itself is usually enough to discourage outsiders.

Tonight the only sober human was a guy in a suit sitting at the bar, drinking in his surroundings and telling himself that, despite his house in the suburbs and corporate parking spot, he was still a badass. And as long as he was misbehaving, that Japanese girl in the short skirt and knee-high boots looked like just the thing to cap off his evening. I'd already rejected the two drinks he'd sent, but he wasn't getting the message, not even when I openly eyed the blond half-demon girl at the other end of the bar.

While I'd settle for an introduction to the half-demon, what I really wanted was a job. My rent was due, my bar tab was overdue and if I didn't get a gig in the next week, I'd be digging through my stash of goodies, looking for something to fence. I suppose I could return my new red leather jacket and matching boots. Or not.

A job, though, might be forthcoming. The bartender Rudy said a guy had come by last night, interested in hiring me. I don't usually take jobs without referrals, but desperate times . . .

I swore I heard the bells of St. James toll midnight when my guy walked in. If that bit of theatrics didn't mark him as a first-timer, the way he entered did—slinking through the door, looking around furtively, hands stuffed in his overcoat pockets like a perv getting ready to flash. The overcoat didn't help. Nor did the rest of the outfit—skin-tight pleather pants, an open-necked shirt and chains. Someone had watched Underworld one too many times.

Rudy said the guy had introduced himself as José. If there was an ounce of Hispanic blood in him, I'd drink cow's blood for a week. Probably christened Joe, but decided it wasn't exotic enough for a supernatural.

He made it halfway to the bar before Rudy pointed me out to him. The guy stopped. He looked at me. He looked some more.

Obviously I wasn't what he expected. Unfortunately, he was exactly what I expected—scruffy, stringy hair, wild eyes. Toronto doesn't get a lot of new supernaturals and those who do emigrate are usually on the run from trouble south of the border. I only hoped José didn't want me to fix that trouble for him. I'm a thief, not an assassin, but I've had more than one client imply that it shouldn't make a difference. Vampires kill; therefore, they should have no compunction about doing it for money.

José walked to my table. "Zoe Takano?"

I motioned to the chair across from me.

"It's uh, about a job," he said.

I motioned at the chair again.

His gaze skittered about the bar. "Shouldn't we, uh, take this outside?"

"Does anyone in here look like an undercover cop?"

He gave a nervous chuckle. "I guess not."

Actually, the hulking half-demon in the corner was one, but we had an understanding.

"Tell me what you have in mind," I said. "Just leave out the details until I've agreed."

It was a theft, something about a ring. I didn't pay much attention because after two lines of his story, I knew there was no job. That's when he turned to call a drink order to Rudy, and his hair swung off his neck, revealing the ghosts of a half-dozen puncture wounds.

Vamp freak.

Just as there are humans who get off on bloodletting, there are supernaturals who do, too. The difference is that supernaturals don't need to find someone to play vampire for them. They can get a real one.

In Toronto, there weren't any vamp freaks. There was no point. I was the only vampire here.

I let José natter on, then set my beer aside. "You're right. Let's take this outside."

He jumped up so fast he set the table wobbling. Rudy stood at the bar, scowling, José's drink in hand.

"Pay the man," I said.

José opened his wallet and stared in confusion at the multicolored bills.

"This one's pretty," I said, plucking out a red fifty. I handed it to Rudy, mouthing for him to apply the extra to my tab. Then I waved José out of the bar.

I led José to an alley two blocks over. He trailed at my heels even when I said he could walk beside me. Someone had him trained well. I shivered and briefly wondered who.

I got far enough down the alley to be hidden from the street, then turned sharply.

"No," I said.

"No?"

"I'm not interested."

"In the job? I thought—"

He stopped as I moved in, getting so close our clothing brushed. Then I lifted onto my tiptoes. I didn't say a word. Just gave him the look. His pupils dilated. His heart raced, the sound of it echoing through the alley, the sight of it pulsing in his neck making my fangs lengthen. He let out a groan and shifted forward, his erection rubbing my leg.

I stepped back. "That's what I meant. And the answer is no."

"Please? Just a bite. Just a taste."

I swallowed my revulsion. My fangs retracted. As I took another step back, a crackle sounded behind me. A foot treading on trash.

He kept babbling. "I'm a clean-living Druid. Totally clean. No booze. No dope. No cigarettes. I haven't even taken aspirin in months."

"And do you know what all that healthy living is going to get you? A comfy berth in the morgue."

He shook his head. "No, I'm always careful. I know what it feels like when you have to stop. I have a safe word—"

"Which works just fine until it's time for your master's annual kill. That's how it ends, José. That's how it always ends. So take my advice and find a human playmate who'll bite your neck for you and—"

I spun, my kick connecting with the kneecap of a hulking figure behind me. Another spin, another kick—this one to the back of her knee—and she went down.

The woman lying on the ground was at least six-foot-two and well-muscled. A flaxen-haired Amazon. Admittedly, I have a weakness for strong blondes, but I knew drag queens who could pass for female more easily than this woman.

"Brigid Drescher, I presume," I said. "Pleased to meet you."

She snarled, spittle speckling my boots. I bent to wipe it off, then spun fast, fists and foot flying up. The dark-ponytailed vampire sneaking up behind me raised his hands.

"Hey, Hans," I said. "It's been a while."

Forty years, give or take a decade. Last time I saw Hans, he was still going by his real name: John. Now I kicked myself for not figuring out who "owned" José. If his rechristening didn't give it away, his costume should have. Last I heard, Hans was on an Anne Rice kick, but apparently he'd progressed to Underworld gear. Either that or he spent his off-hours in a bordello.

As Brigid got to her feet, he turned to her. "I told you there wasn't any use trying to trick Zoe."

Brigid brushed off her leather corset. "I thought you said she didn't fight."

"Only in self-defense. Isn't that right, Zoe?"

I ignored his mocking lilt and managed a perky smile. "You got it. So what brings you two to Toronto?" I had an idea, and hoped I was wrong.

"José," Brigid said before Hans could answer.

She snapped her fingers, and motioned the vamp freak to her side. He pretended not to notice and kept slinking closer to me. I sidestepped. He slunk. Sidestepped. Slunk.

Hans laughed. "I think your boy found something he likes better, Brig. Sorry, José, but you're not Zoe's type. Or gender."

José frowned, taking a moment to get it. Then he smiled and sidled closer.

"Go," I said, flicking my fingers at him. "Shoo."

"José!" Brigid barked.

He slid a look her way, shuddered and wriggled closer to me. Brigid strode over and grabbed him, yelping, by the collar.

"When I tell you to come, you come."

His gaze shunted my way, and Brigid's head shot down to his neck, fangs sinking in. I started to say this wasn't the time for a snack. Then Brigid's head ripped back, a chunk of José's neck in her teeth, arterial blood spurting against the wall. She dropped him and spat out the flesh. José convulsed on the ground, gasping and jerking, hands pressed to his neck, eyes rolling as he tried to stop the flow.

I looked down at him, knowing there was nothing I could do, feeling the old serpent of rage uncoil in my gut. My gaze shot to Brigid but, at the last second, I wrenched it away and turned aside.

"What's the matter, Takano?" Brigid said. "Don't like the sight of blood?"

I counted to five, until the serpent relaxed and slid back into hiding. Then I turned and smiled.

"I have a weak stomach, what can I say?"

José lay on his back now, sightless eyes staring up.

"Well, that was a waste," Hans said, stepping away as the blood seeped toward his boots. "You really need to control your temper, Brig."

"Can we get this conversation over with?" I said. "I'd really rather not be found standing over a dead body." I kept my gaze on Hans, my tone light. "And I do hope you plan to clean this mess up. It's terribly bad form to leave bodies in another vamp's town."

"That's what we're here to talk about," he said. "Your town."

"It's not yours anymore," Brigid said.

That's what I was afraid they were here for. Hans and his little gang had lived in New Orleans. From what I'd heard, they'd been thrilled when Hurricane Katrina hit—a chaos-gripped city makes for easy pickings. But after a year, they'd realized trailer park life really wasn't their style. Since then, they'd been hunting for a new place to settle.

"So you're looking at Toronto?" I laughed. "Seriously? Sure, it's a world-class city, multicultural, blah, blah. But it's Toronto. There's a reason a third-rate vamp like me lives here. No one else wants it. Long cold winters. Hot humid summers.

Smog so thick you can taste it. Taxes are outrageous, and for what? Free health care? Like we need that."

"You aren't going to give us any trouble, are you, Zoe?"

His voice was smooth and soft, but there was an arrogant tilt to his chin and a condescending twist to his words.

For a moment, I reveled in the visions of what I would have done if he'd said those words a hundred years ago. A vampire's invulnerability makes it difficult to inflict any sensation like pain. But there are ways. And I know them all.

"You're welcome to fight for your territory." Brigid strolled over to stand beside Hans. "But I hear you're a bit of a coward."

"Coward is a strong word."

She walked up until she stood so close I could see a shred of José's skin caught between her teeth. Then she took another step and towered over me.

"Is it?" she said.

I sidestepped to face Hans. "I'll be gone by Friday."

I was born Kioko Takano in 1863. My name meant "happy child" and I fulfilled its promise. My life was unremarkable. I was a cheerful girl with loving parents, who grew into a cheerful young woman with a loving fiancé.

A month before my wedding, a group of missionaries came to our village. One of them was Jane Bowman, a blond English girl not much older than myself. When I met her, I realized why, as dearly as I cared for my fiancé, I could feel no more passion for him than for a brother.

I fell in love with Jane. Madly, desperately in love. She was so vibrant and brilliant and worldly, all the things I was not. I soon learned why she had so much experience for her youth—she was a hundred-year-old vampire. I didn't care. It only made her more exotic and wonderful. I loved her. She loved me. Nothing else mattered.

I ran away with Jane. The next few years were glorious. Then came my twentieth birthday and, for it, she offered me the gift of eternal life. Become a vampire. Be young forever. Be with her forever.

I refused. She wheedled, pleaded, begged. I refused. She called me a coward. I laughed and refused.

Being a gracious hostess, I offered to show Hans and Brigid around Toronto before I left. I'd introduce them to the supernatural community and make the transition easy. For a fee, of course.

We had to wait until after dark. Apparently, Hans was sensitive to daylight.

He seemed to think this made him a more authentic vampire. I thought it made him an idiot.

And I wasn't the only one. Rudy got one look at the pair, dressed like they were heading to a BDSM convention, and marched into the back room. He emerged only when I hopped over the bar and helped myself to a beer.

"Not until you pay your tab, Zoe." He plucked the bottle from my hand. "And if you think you're cutting town and not paying? I will hunt you down and rip that pretty little—"

"I'll pay. Just give me a couple weeks to settle into my new place."

Rudy put the beer back and turned to Hans. "You're the new vamps Zoe told me about?"

Hans glanced about us, but it was early and the only patron in Miller's was passed out, probably from the night before.

"Yes," Hans said. "We'll be taking over—"

Rudy slapped a paper onto the bar. "Pay her tab."

Brigid snorted. "We aren't going to—"

"You ever want to set foot in this place again?" Rudy asked.

Hans looked around. "Not particularly."

"You want to take Zoe's place in this city? Be part of the community?"

"We aren't really joiners."

Rudy stuffed the tab into his pocket. "Fine. Just remember, we've got over a hundred sorcerers, witches, half-demons, necromancers and shamans in this city, and the only vampire they've ever known is Zoe. Now, if a real vampire comes to town, it's going to make folks nervous—"

"How much?" Hans said.

"Seven-hundred and eighty-two dollars."

Hans pivoted to me. "How much do you drink?"

"One beer a night. It's the paying part that gives me trouble."

"Make it an even grand and you'll get my personal seal of approval," Rudy said.

Hans sighed, pulled a wad of cash from his pocket and peeled off the bills.

As Rudy counted them, he said, "My first piece of advice? Make sure this one—" He pointed at me. "—shows you the ropes."

"That's what I'm doing."

He met my gaze. "All of them."

"What do you mean?" Brigid asked.

Rudy looked at her. "Toronto has its peculiarities."

"Like the transit system," I said. "Buses, subways, street cars, high-speed trains to the suburbs." I rolled my eyes. "It's so confusing. Let's go check out the subways now."

I hustled them off, leaving Rudy glaring after me.

Back when I'd refused to become a vampire, Jane had invited me to a weekend with her undead friends. To persuade me, she teased. Only there was to be no persuasion. Just a conversion.

Like Jane, most vampires inherit the genes and are reborn on death. There is a second way to become one, but the process is horrific. They say you can't force it on another person. They're wrong.

Months later, when Jane and her friends finished with me, I was half mad. But I was a vampire. She expected me to be grateful. Hadn't she proven how much she loved me, to what lengths she'd go to keep me?

I killed her. As slow and horrible a death as my own conversion. When she was finally gone, I hunted down her friends. Then I slaughtered their human servants and thralls.

Next stop on our Toronto tour: Trinity Church.

As I walked to the front doors, Hans and Brigid stopped short, earning choice words from the stream of shoppers exiting the mall next door.

"What is that?" Brigid said.

"The Church of the Holy Trinity. Pretty, isn't it?"

They stared at me. I reached through the open doors and wiggled my fingers.

"See any smoke yet? I hope not. I really like this jacket."

When they didn't answer, I walked in and waved my arms. A homeless guy circled warily around me.

"We are not going in there," Brigid said.

"Suit yourself."

In the side courtyard, I found a dark-skinned fortyish guy in a gym shirt and sweat pants tending to one of the regulars who refused to set foot in a building. I led Hans and Brigid around to him.

"You need to have that tooth pulled, Frank," Randy was telling the old man, who was dressed in ten layers of clothes despite the warm night. "A dentist should do it, but I will if you want."

"What's he doing?" Hans whispered.

"Running a medical clinic for the homeless," I said.

"Why?"

I lifted myself up to his ear. "For the money."

Hans shot me a look.

"Seriously," I said. "Why do you think they wear all those clothes? They're stuffed with cash."

Hans snorted, but Brigid started eyeing the old man.

"I'm kidding," I said, before I was responsible for a wave of homeless deaths.

As the old man tottered away, Randy packed his medical bag.

"Hey, Doc," I said.

"Don't 'hey' me." Randy straightened. "Are these the vamps taking over?"

"Yep. Randall Tolliver, meet—"

"Are they taking over your work for me, too?"

"Um, no, I don't think—"

"What work?" Brigid asked.

"Medical supplies," Randy said. "The clinic can't run without them and we're too underfunded to buy all we need. So Zoe obtains them."

"Steals them," I said.

"How much does that pay?" Brigid asked.

"If I could afford to pay for the theft, I could afford to pay for supplies."

"So it doesn't pay?"

"Sure it does," I chirped. "Huge dividends in self-satisfaction. You'd love it."

They looked at me as if they'd rather swallow a crucifix.

"Well, that's just great," Randy said. "You piss off and leave me in the lurch with, what, two days notice? Thank you, Zoe."

He turned to leave, then slowly pivoted back. "She has warned you about Tee, hasn't she?"

"Tee?" Hans said.

"Tea," I said, taking Hans's arm and leading him away. "Being part of the British Commonwealth, Canadians like their tea. Hot tea, not iced. It takes some getting used to."

"If you don't warn them, Zoe—" Randy called after us.

I coughed to cut him off. "Now, ahead, you'll see the Eaton Centre, one of Toronto's largest shopping malls."

Hans waited until we were at the mouth of a deserted walkway, then stopped me.

"You really think I'm stupid, don't you?" he said.

I decided it was best not to answer that.

He went on anyway. "I see what you're doing, Zoe, and it's not going to work."

"Doing?"

"First the bartender warns us of some unknown danger in Toronto, then your doctor friend mentions a monster named Tee."

"Monster?" I gave a nervous laugh. "There's no monster."

"Of course there isn't. Really, Zoe, I gave you credit for being a lot more clever than this silly scheme. Do you think Brigid and I are going to be scared off by wild stories? I've been around for two hundred years—too long to be frightened by demons."

"Who said anything about—?" I blurted, then stopped. I stepped back into the shadows and shoved my hands into my pockets. After a moment, I sighed. "I'm sorry. The guys were having some fun with you—playing a prank on the new vamps. I was running interference because I was afraid you'd take it the wrong way."

I adjusted my collar. "I really don't want to cause any trouble."

"Of course you don't," he said smoothly as Brigid rolled her eyes. "That's why we want to make this transition as painless as possible."

"So do I."

"Good. Let's get on with it then."

For my first ten years as a vampire, I never fed and left a living victim. I didn't bother to learn how. And I didn't need to—I found enemies everywhere. If someone so much as shoved me at the market, it would awaken that serpent of rage. I killed and I killed and I killed, and the rage was never sated.

Eventually, I stopped.

There was no dramatic epiphany. No wise vampire showed me a better path. One day I was sitting by a river, caught a glimpse of myself in the water and wished the old myths were true—that vampires cast no reflection. I realized then that the lifetime of a vampire was too long to spend being someone you couldn't bear to see in the mirror.

I moved to the New World and rechristened myself Zoe—a light-hearted, cheerful name. I'd been light-hearted and cheerful once and I vowed I would be again.

And so I reinvented myself. Zoe Takano, cat burglar extraordinaire. The always calm, always cool Zen master of vampirism. Fun, good-natured and easy-going. If you need someone to liven up a party, I'm your girl. To help you in a fight? Not so much.

That's the problem with swearing off the dark stuff. Like an alcoholic, I'm only one good fight away from losing control. It's happened before and it was a long, ugly road to recovery. I can't travel that route again. I might not find my way back.

The next evening, I played realtor, showing Hans and Brigid my apartment.

"It's one of the few units in the building that's still rent-controlled," I said as I led them down the hall. "Being downtown, you get mainly young, single tenants. They come and go so often that I've been here thirty-seven years and no one has noticed I haven't aged a day."

I put my key in the lock.

"And how much would this illegal transfer of tenancy cost us?" Hans asked.

"Three grand, which is an absolute steal. Around here, that wouldn't buy you first and last month's rent for a place like this."

"And that's on top of the thousand I already paid you for playing tour guide?"

"Er, yes, but it's negotiable."

"Seeing as how we've been such good customers," he said dryly.

I faced him. "Whether I leave tomorrow has nothing to do with whether you pay my bar tab or hire my guide services or take over my apartment. I could say you owe me relocation expenses, but we both know I'm not going to challenge you on that. If you don't want to see the apartment, fine. I just thought—"

"Show it to us," he said.

I didn't move.

"Show us the damned apartment," Brigid growled.

When they walked in, I could tell they were impressed. Why wouldn't they be? I'd spent twenty years in Toronto searching for exactly the right place to live, and this apartment was it, with its huge bank of windows taking in a postcard view of the skyline.

They admired the night sky and the panorama of colored lights below, then Hans checked out the apartment itself. Again, it was perfect. Minimalist, but warm and inviting. Every piece had been selected with care, from the leather chairs to the ebony dining set to the priceless artifacts I'd "picked up" over decades of museum heists.

"How much for the whole thing?" Hans asked. "Fully furnished."

Brigid's gaze swept over the apartment, her lip curling. "It's not really my style—"

"It's mine." He met my gaze. "How much?"

"A lot. I don't think you want—"

"I do."

His tone said either I named a price or he'd take it. The serpent uncoiled. I clenched my stomach muscles, sending it back to sleep.

"We'll discuss it," I murmured. "For now, if the location is to your—"

A shuffling rasp came from the bedroom. I went still. But they didn't hear it, only frowned, wondering why I'd stopped.

I put my hands on Hans's back, propelling him toward the door. "Actually, let's discuss this over drinks. My treat. I know this amazing place on Queen's West. Much more your style than Miller's."

He let me push him two feet before locking his knees. "I want this apartment, Zoe."

"Actually, you know, transferring the tenancy might not be that easy . . . "

The shuffling sound reached the bedroom hall. Brigid heard it now, pivoting that way.

"You want more money?" Hans said. "Is that what this is about? It better not be, because I've dealt fairly with you, and if you screw me over—"

"Mein Gott," Brigid whispered. "What is that?"

Lurching from the bedroom hall was a woman. I already knew her gender—otherwise, it would be impossible to tell. Gauzy rags encased her skeletal limbs. A tangled mass of matted white hair hid her face. As she shuffled forward, her bony fingers waved in front of her as if she was conducting an orchestra no one else could see. Her head bobbed, sunken eyes glittering with madness, fleshless lips moving soundlessly.

Seeing me, the woman stopped. She squinted, head weaving like a hawk trying to get a better look at its prey.

"Tee," I said, "Hi. I, uh, was just—"

"Going somewhere, Zoe?"

I bit off a nervous laugh. "Uh, no. Of course not."

"That's not what Tee heard. She heard you're leaving us. Running off because big bad vampires have come to town again." She looked at Brigid and Hans and sniffed. "Are these them? Nasty creatures."

"Hey!" Brigid stepped toward Tee, then thought better of it and stopped, crossing her arms over her chest. "Whatever that monster is—"

"Monster?"

Tee unfurled her limbs, pulling herself up until she was almost as tall as Brigid. She shuffled toward her, rags whispering against the hardwood floor. Brigid tried holding her ground, but when she caught a whiff of Tee, she drew back.

"A monster kills and does not feed," Tee said. "A monster leaves pretty boys to die in ugly alleys."

"José?" Hans said. "That was—"

"There was another, last night. The one this naughty vampire didn't tell you about." She drew herself up again to look Brigid in the eye. "The pretty boy with the pretty red hair and the pretty red shirt and all that pretty red blood."

"How did you—?" Brigid began.

"Tee knows everything. Her friends tell her."

Tee swept a hand around the room. Brigid and Hans followed it, but saw nothing.

I stepped forward. "And that is the great thing about you, isn't it, Tee? You have a regular army of spirit informants."

Tee rocked back on her heels, lips smacking in self-satisfaction. "Tee and her friends help little Zoe."

"Exactly, and now you can help Hans and Brigid."

Her lips pursed and she eyed them. "One vampire is enough for any city." She sidled toward Hans and whispered. "Give Tee the naughty one, and she won't ask for morsels for a very long time."

"Morsels?" Hans's gaze shot to me.

"Er, yes. See . . . "

I motioned him off to the side. When Tee tried to follow, I waved her away. She grumbled, then stumped over to a chair.

"Tee's a demon," I said, voice lowered. "She got trapped in a human body a hundred years ago. Being a demon, she can't die, which is why she . . . looks like that. But over the years, she's misplaced a few of her marbles."

"A few?"

"Most of the bag. Anyway, she's convinced that she's alive because she's found the key to immortality: consuming the flesh of the living."

"What?"

I motioned for him to keep his voice down. "Usually she just takes a few nibbles off dead bodies. Sometimes she does hunt—"

"Tee eats what she hunts," she called. "Not like some people." She glowered at Brigid.

I lowered my voice another notch. "We discourage the hunting. It's messy. Instead, Tee and I have an arrangement. Her spirit friends help me and I feed her."

"Feed her what?"

"If you're looking for immortality, what's better than the flesh of the living?"

Hans stared at me. He blinked. Then he eased back with a harsh laugh. "If you really expect me to believe that you feed her—"

I took a penknife from my pocket, sliced a strip of flesh from the underside of my forearm, then walked over and gave it to Tee. She gobbled it down like a strip of bacon.

Behind me, the room went silent. I flexed my arm. The flesh was already filling in the furrow. In an hour, it would be back to normal.

"So." I smiled brightly. "That's all there is to it. Now, let's get that drink and we can talk terms. There are a few pieces here I couldn't bear to part with, but the rest is negotiable."

I walked to the door. Hans and Brigid didn't move.

"We don't like them," Tee muttered. "We don't like them at all. Nasty things. We like Zoe."

I sighed. "Yes, it'll be an adjustment, Tee, but you'll get used to them." Another bright smile. "I'm sure we all taste the same."

"Okay," Brigid said, hands flying up. "That's it. Zoe might put up with your shit, demon, but I won't. If you ever try to take a bite of me—"

Brigid sailed off her feet, smacked into the wall and collapsed at the bottom.

"She's a demon, remember?" I whispered. "You don't say no to a demon."

"The hell I don't," Brigid snarled.

She leaped up . . . and got hit in the gut with an energy bolt. The smell of burning flesh filled the room. Tee hadn't budged, just sat placidly stroking the leather chair.

"We don't like her." Tee looked at Hans. "We don't like you, either, but we like her less. Give her to Tee. Tee has a good hiding place, dark and cold. She'll save all the naughty vampire's bits and eat them slowly."

Brigid let out a growl, pawing the ground like a bull.

I swung over to Tee and squeezed her shoulder. "Ah, Tee, you're such a joker. You'd never do that, would you? Not to a big, strong vampire like Brigid."

"Even vampires sleep," Tee murmured. "Yes, they do." Her gaze darted around, listening to her spirit counsel. "That's how we'll do it. We'll get her when—"

"Tee," I said sharply.

She pouted and grumbled under her breath.

"I'm not staying in the same city as that thing," Brigid said. "Either she goes or I do."

Tee launched herself at Brigid. The vampire stumbled back, arms sailing up to ward her off. Then she stiffened and fell over.

"Shit!" I said. "Her binding powers. Hans, grab her before—"

Too late. Tee was on Brigid, biting chunks of flesh from her shoulder. Hans and I managed to get her off. I restrained her, thrashing and howling, as the binding spell broke and Brigid scrambled to her feet. As they ran for the door, I dropped Tee and tore after them.

"Wait! We had a deal! I'll give you a discount on the apartment—"

I caught up with them in the stairwell. We had a brief discussion, the upshot being that I could keep my damned city and they were never setting foot in this godforsaken town again. I begged. I pleaded. I cajoled. All to no avail.

I walked back into my apartment. Rudy and Randy were helping themselves to my bar.

"That went well," I said. "Thanks for the spells, guys."

Rudy and Randy were half-brothers. With different mothers and twenty years between them, they didn't look much alike. The only thing they shared was their father's sorcerer blood.

Tee was back in her chair, now stroking a Maori mask she'd plucked from the shelf. She whispered under her breath. Talking to her spirits. Tee wasn't a demon—just a very old, very powerful, very crazy necromancer terrified of death, certain it would condemn her to an eternity of serving ghosts.

I cut another strip from my arm and handed it to her. She gobbled it down. Randy turned away; Rudy glowered at me.

"It grows back," I said. "And it's better than having her hunt humans."

"Well, don't do it while I'm here, okay?" Rudy helped himself to my daiginjō-shu.

"That'll be twenty bucks," I said. "You can add it to my credit."

"Credit?"

"You got a grand for a fifty-dollar tab, most of which José already paid off. I expect at least five-hundred in credit."

"Sure, we could do that." He headed for the couch, circling wide around Tee. "Or I could introduce you to the blond half-demon. She asked about you last night. Of course, not having any experience with vampires, she's a little nervous about introducing herself . . . "

"Keep the money."

He sat. "I'm sure you had fun with this scheme, but you could have saved yourself a lot of trouble and just killed them."

"Me?"

He gave me a look that said I didn't fool him. I never had.

Randy handed Tee a glass of my cheaper sake. She whispered under her breath and petted his hand before he continued on to the sofa.

"Normally, I'd be all for the humane solution," Randy said. "But in this case, killing them might have been the humane solution. At least for everyone else."

True. I did the world no favors by sparing Brigid's life. I could argue that in killing her, I could unleash a worse predator inside me. But that's bullshit rationalization. I let her live because I wouldn't risk the personal hell that could come with killing her.

I have a good life here. A damned near perfect one. Would I kill to keep it? I'd rather not find out. Someday, I'll be tested. Just not today.

I pulled out the watch I'd swiped from Hans when we were struggling with Tee.

"Anyone want a Rolex?"

La Vampiresse
Tanith Lee

British author Tanith Lee has written around ninety books and close to three hundred short stories in a variety of genres including both adult and young adult fantasy, science fiction, Gothic romance, historical novels, and horror. Her prose is always intelligent, often darkly twisted, exotic, and lush. Vampiric themes appear frequently in her fiction, most notably in short novel Sabella: or the Bloodstone *and the novels of the* Blood Opera *series—*Dark Dance, Personal Darkness, *and* Darkness, I—*which reveal the life of the Scarabae: elegant, mysterious, seductive creatures of few words and many secrets. Additional vampire novels include* The Blood of Roses, *and* Vivia. *Some of her shorter works are considered vampire classics. These include "The Beautiful Biting Machine," "Red As Blood," (which twists Snow White's tale into something darker), "Bite-Me-Not, Or Fleur de Fur," and "Nunc Dimittis" (adapted for the cable TV series* The Hunger *in 1999). The title character of "La Vampiresse" embodies the charisma, power, and presence of the vampire in an unusual way. This story is another with the makings of a classic.*

Tanith Lee has won the British Fantasy Society's August Derleth Award, two World Fantasy Awards, and two Spanish Gilgames Awards. She was named a Grand Master at the World Horror Convention in 2009. She is married to the writer-artist-photographer John Kaiine. They live on the Sussex Weald, near the sea, in a house full of books and plants. Norilana Books is currently reissuing some of Lee's early novels: including The Birthgrave Trilogy *and the five books of the* Tales of the Flat Earth *opus.*

GOING UP in the elevator, he felt a wave of depression so intense at what he was about to do, that he almost rushed out at another floor. But then what would he see? The eerie elongate building was frosted with a dry desert cold. On the ground floor he had already encountered strange sliding, creeping or slipping shades. He had glimpsed creatures—things—he didn't want to be at large among. And anyway, there was the man with him in the lift, "helping" him to reach the proper place.

How is she today?" he had asked, when they first got in.

"As always."

"Ah."

And that was all.

Ornamental, the elevator had fretted screens of delicately wrought white metal. Its internal light was soft, but not warm. When the cage finally rattled to a halt, and the screens parted, a cold blast hit him from an open window.

"Is that safe?"

"What?" asked the man.

"That window—surely—"

"That's fine. See the grill?"

He looked and saw the grill. And in any case, now they were in the heart of a desert night. The sunset had been sucked under, sucked up like red blood, in the minute or so of the elevator's ascent. Stars glittered out in the black sky, undimmed even by the lights of this immense, automated mansion. Soon a moon would rise.

"Thanks," he said humbly to the attendant. Should he tip him? Perhaps not. The man was already undoing a door, and it seemed *he* should go through—go through alone. And now after the depression, for a moment he was afraid.

"Am I okay in there?" He tried to sound flippant.

The attendant smiled suddenly, contemptuous as a wolf. "Sure. It's all right, you know. She's sated."

"She is?"

"Yes. Quite."

"Sated."

"Yes."

"How?" he heard himself ask. The ghoulish word hung there in the slightly-warmed cold air.

The attendant said. "Best not to ask, mister."

"No . . ."

"Best not to ask," the man repeated, as fools or the nervous or the indomitable often did.

But this time he resisted, himself, doing so.

And then he was through the door, which—as it seemed with its own laughter—shut fast and closed him in.

❦

The first thing he saw in the great wide room was the Christmas tree. It was that blue-green variety, about two meters tall and growing in a stone pot. He knew of the tree, had indeed seen pictures of it, both stills and film. Probably not the *same* tree. but the same type of tree and decorated in the same way, for it was hung with long pearl necklaces.

The room was luxurious. Thickly carpeted with deep chairs upholstered in what looked like velvet, or leather. The drapes were looped back from two tall windows, in one of which the moon was now coming up from the desert.

In fact, this whole room was very like the other room, the room he had seen photographs of. Not absolutely, he supposed, but enough.

He looked around carefully. On a gallery up a stair were book-stacks lined with volumes of calf and silk, gilded. A globe stood up there on a table, and down here, one long decanter filled with dark fluid and two crystal goblets.

"It isn't blood."

He snapped around so fast a muscle twanged at the top of his neck.

Christ. She had risen up silent as the moon rose, out of that chair in the corner, in he half light beyond the lamps, a shadow.

"No, truly, not blood. Alcohol. I keep it for my guests."

He knew what to do. And if he hadn't known, he had had it droned into him by everyone he had had to deal with, lawyers, his own office, and inevitably, the people here. So he bowed to her, the short military bow of a culture and a world long over. But not, of course, for her.

"Madame Chaikassia."

"Ah," she said. "At last. One who knows how to say my name."

Naturally he knew. He had known from the day he saw her in the interview on TV. Rather as he had seen the actress Bette Davis in an interview years before and she had been asked how her first name was pronounced. So that he therefore knew it was not pronounced, as most persons now did, in the French way, Bett, but—for he had heard the actress herself reply—as Betty. And in the same way he knew the female being before him now did not pronounce her name as so many did: not Che´-kasee-ah, but Ch´-high-kazya.

She did not ask who *he* was. They would have told her when they said he would be coming. After all, without her permission, he would never have been allowed into this room. And all the way here, if the truth were known, he had been sweating, thinking she would, after his journey of two thousand miles and more, suddenly change her mind.

"Help yourself," she said idly, "to a drink."

So he thanked her, and went and poured himself one. To his surprise, when he sipped it, it was a decent malt whisky. Despite her words he expected anything but alcohol. Yet obviously, they knew *she* would never drink *this*.

When she beckoned to him, he sat down facing her where she had once more sat down. The side lamps cast the mildest glow, but behind her the harsh white neon of the moon was coming up with incredible rapidity. It would shine into his face, not hers.

In the soft flattering light, he studied her.

Even under these lamps she looked old. He had been prepared for that. No one knew her exact age, or those who did kept quiet. But twenty, twenty-five years ago, when he had seen her in that interview, or more recently in little remaining clips of film, she had looked only a glamorous thirty, forty. Now he would have said she was well into her sixties. She looked like that. Except, of course, she still was glamorous, and she still had her wonderful mask of bones on which the flesh stayed pinned, not by surgery, but by that random good luck which chance sometimes handed out, just now and then, to the chosen few.

In fact, she was still beautiful, and he had a feeling even when she looked seventy, eighty, one hundred, she would still keep those two things, the glamour and the beauty.

Although, again, probably she wouldn't live that long, not now. Now she was in captivity and ruined.

She lost a little more each day, they had told him that. A little more.

But you'd never know.

Her hair was long as in the old pictures and just as lustrous and thick, though fine silver wires of the best kind of gray silked through it. She wore a minimum of makeup, eye shadow, and false lashes. No powder he could detect. And though her lips were a startling scarlet, it was a softer scarlet to suit the aging of her face.

Her body, like her throat, was long and slender. She wore one of those long black gowns, just close enough in fit he had seen, in her rising and sitting, her figure looked, at least when clothed, like that of a woman half her apparent age. And she had on high heels—black velvet pumps on slender tapering pins. She had surrendered very little. that way.

As for her hands, always the big giveaway, she wore mittens of thin black lace, and her nails were long and painted dull gold.

"Well," she said. "What do you wish to know?"

"Whatever you are kind enough to tell me."

"There is so much."

"Yes."

"Time," she said. She shrugged.

"We have some time."

"I mean, my time. Such a great amount. Like the snows and the forests. Like the mountains I saw from the beginning of my life. And always in moonlight or the light of the stars. So many nights. Centuries, and all in the dark."

She had hypnotized him. He felt it. He didn't struggle. But she said, "Don't be nervous," as if he had stuttered or flinched or drawn back. "You know, don't you, you are perfectly safe with me tonight?"

"Yes, Madame Chaikassia."

"That's good. Not everyone is able to relax."

"I know," he said, "that you've given your word. You never break your word."

She smiled then. She had beautiful teeth, but they were all caps. Thank God, he thought, with a rare compassion, she had not needed new teeth until such excellent dentistry had become available.

He could remember the little headline in the scurrilous magazine: *False Fangs for a Vampire.*

"Do you know my story?" she asked, not coyly, but with dignity.

Surely it would be impossible not to respond to this pride and self-control? At least, for him.

"Something of it. But only from the movies and the book."

"Oh, my book." She was dismissive. Any authorial arrogance had left her, or else she had never had any. "I did not write everything I should have done. Or they would not let me. Always there are restraints."

"Yes," he said.

She said, "It must surprise you to find me here."

He waited, careful.

She sighed. She said, "As the world shrinks, I have been taken like an exotic animal and put into this zoo—this menagerie. And I have allowed it for there was nothing else I could do. I am the last of my kind. A unique exhibit. And of course, they feed me."

At the vulgar flick of her last words, he found, to his slight dismay, the hair crawled on his scalp. Then curiosity, his stock-in-trade, made him say, "Can I ask you, Madame, in the realm of food, on what do they—?"

"On what do you *think*?"

She leaned forward. Her black eyes that had no aging mark on them beyond a faint reddening at their corners, burned into his. And he felt, and was glad to feel, an electric weakening in his spine.

If only I could give you what you need.

He heard the line in his head, as he had heard and read it on several occasions. But he kept the sense not to say it.

She had given him her word, La Vampiresse, that she would not harm him. But there was one story, if real or false he hadn't been able to find out. One journalistic interviewer had teasingly gone too far with her, and left this place in an ambulance.

So he only waited, letting the recorder tick unheard in his pocket—they had said she didn't object to such machines, providing she didn't have to see or hear them.

And she leaned back after moment and said, "They bring me what I must have. It is taken quite legally. And only from the willing and the healthy."

He risked it. "Blood, Madame."

"*Blood*, monsieur. But I will tell you something. They must, by law, disguise what it is."

"How is that possible?"

"They add a little juice, some little meat extract or other. This is required by the government. Astonishing, their hypocrisy, would you not say?"

"I'd say so, yes."

"For everyone knows what I am and what I must have to live. But in order to protect the sensibility of a few, they perpetrate a travesty. However," she folded her hands, her rings dark as her eyes, "I can taste what it really is, under its camouflage. And it does what it must. As you see. I am still alive."

He had been an adolescent when he saw her first, and that was on film. He was not the only one whose earliest sexual fantasies had been lit up all through by La Vampiresse.

But also, romantically, he had fallen in love with her world, recreated so earnestly on the screen. A country and landscape of forests, mountains, spired cities on frozen rivers, or winter palaces and sleighs and wolves, and of darkness, always that, where the full moon was the only sun. Russia, or some component of Russia, but a Russia vanished far away, where the aristocrats spoke French and the slavery of serfdom persisted.

As he grew up, found fleshly women that, for all their faults, were actually embraceable, actually penetrable, he lost the dreams of blood and moonlight. And with them, perhaps strangely, or not, lost too the romance of *place*. So that when, all these years after, he had been looking again at the film, or at those bits of it which had been—aptly—dug up, he was amused. At himself, for ever liking these scenarios at all. At the scenarios themselves, their naivety and censored charms. Oh yes, the imagination, in those days, sexual and otherwise, had had to work overtime. And from doing it, the imagination had grown muscular and strong. So that in memory after, you saw what you had not been shown, the fondling behind the smoky drape, that closed boudoir door, or even the rending among the hustle of far-off feeding wolves . . .

Altogether, he was sorry the romance had died for him with his youth. What was more—though they had only been, to begin with, such images, a recreation—coming here he grew rather afraid she too, La Vampiresse herself, would also disappoint. Worse, that she would horrify him with scorn or pity or disgust.

But now, sitting facing her, he had to admit he was nearly aroused. Oh, not in any erotic way. Better than that—*imaginatively*. Those strong imagination-muscles hadn't after all wasted completely away. For here and now he was filling in once more the hidden or obscured vision. So that under her age, still, he could make out what she had been and was, in her own manner.

And when she spoke of her food, the blood, he didn't want to smile behind his hand or gag at the thing she told him. He felt a kind of wild rejoicing. Despite the fact she was here in this building in the desert, despite her growing old and—nearly—tame, she had remained *Chaikassia*.

Because of this, he was finding it easy to talk to her, and would find it easy to perform the interview. And he wondered if others had found this too. He even wondered if that had been the problem for the one who left under the care of paramedics—it had been, for him, *too* easy.

At the nineteenth hour, when the moon was at the top of the first window and crossing to the top of the second, someone came in to check on them.

They had been talking about two and a half hours.

Verbally, they had crossed vast tracts of land, lingered in crypts and on high towers, seem armies gleam and sink, and sunrise slit the edge of air like a knife. And she had been, through memory, a child, a girl, a woman.

She had spoken of much of her life, even of her childhood, of which, until now, he had known little. A vampire's childhood, unrevealed in her book, or in any other medium. He had even been able to glimpse her own adolescence, where she stood for him, frosted like the finest glass with candle-shine and ghostly falling snow.

As the door was knocked on, this contemporary and unforgivable door, in such an old fashioned and fake way, Chaikassia threw back her head and laughed.

"They must come in. To see whether I have attacked you."

He knew quite well that there were three concealed cameras in the room, perhaps for her protection as much as his. He suspected she knew about these cameras too.

But he said, "They see, surely, you would never do that."

She glanced playfully at him. "But I might after all be tempted."

He said, "You're flattering me."

"Yes," she said. "But also I am telling you a fact. But again, I have given my word, and you are safe."

Then a uniformed man and woman were in the room. Both gave a brief bow to La Vampiresse. Then the man came over and handed her a beaker like a little silver thimble on a silver tray.

"Oh," she said, "is it time for this, now?"

"Yes, Madame."

She glanced at him again. "Did you know they make me also swallow such drugs?"

"I knew something about it."

"Here is the proof. For my health, they say. Do you not?" she addressed the man. He smiled and stood waiting. Chaikassia tipped the contents of the silver thimble into her mouth. Her throat moved smoothly, used to this. "But really, it is to subdue me," she murmured softly. And then, more softly, almost lovingly, "As if it ever could."

The uniformed woman had come over and stood by his chair.

She said to him politely, "Do you wish for coffee, sir, hot tea, or a soft drink?"

"No, thank you."

"I must remind you, sir, your three hours are nearly through."

"Yes, I'm keeping count."

When they had gone out again, Chaikassia stood up.

"Three hours," she murmured. "Have we talked so long?"

"We have twenty-four minutes left."

"Twenty-four. So exact. Ah, monsieur, what a captain you would have made."

He too had got up, courteous, in the old style, He saw now, taken aback for a moment, that even in her high heels she was shorter than he. He had gained the impression, entertaining, approaching, she was about a tenth of a meter taller, for he wasn't tall.

She had always seemed tall to him, as well. Perhaps she had shrunk a little. Despite their best efforts—the diet she now lived on . . . like the loss of her own teeth.

"What else shall I tell you?" she asked.

"Anything, Madam. Everything you wish to."

So she began one of her vivid rambling anecdotes. Only now and then was he required to lead her with a question or comment. Of all the things she had already told him, many he recognized from other material. Yet others had proved changeable, or quite fresh, like the childhood scenes, different and new. He was aware they alone might make a book. The tape chugged on over his heart, a full four hours of it, to be on the safe side, its clever receptor catching every nuance. Even when, for a moment, she might turn her head. And he marveled at her coherence. So much and all so perfectly rendered. If she repeated herself, he barely noticed. It didn't matter. This was really more real than anything else, surely? More impactful and apposite than any tragedy which was human.

"Look at the moon," she suddenly said. "How arid and cold and old she is tonight." Her voice altered. "Have they told you? I'm always better when the moon is up. When it's full. I wonder why the hell that is? Crazy, isn't it?"

And something in him stumbled, as it seemed something had done in her. For not only the pattern of her speech had changed, the faint accent wiped away, but as she looked back at him her face was fallen and stricken. And from her eyes ran two thin shining tears. Lost tears, all alone.

Made dumb, he stood there, seeing her oldness and her shrunkenness. Then he heard his voice come from him and, for a second, was afraid of what it would say.

"Madame Chaikassia, how you must miss your freedom, it must be so intense, the lonely sorrow of all these hundreds of years you have lived—and you are the last of your kind. You must feel the moon is your only friend at last, the only thing that can comprehend you."

And then her face was smoothing over, the strength of imagination working its power upon her. The trite banality of his words, like some splash of bad dialogue from the worst of the scripts, but able to change her, give her back her courage and her center. So that again she rose, towering over him, her eyes wiser than a thousand nights, older than a million moons.

"You are a poet, monsieur, And you are perceptive. Come to the window. Do you see? The bars are of the finest steel, otherwise they think, my captors, I will escape them. But they have forgotten—oh, shall I tell you my secret?"

They leaned together by the cold glass, observing the slender bars.

She said, "Unlike most of my kind, I am able to make myself visible, monsieur, in mirrors—have they ever told you? Oh yes, it is an old trick. How else was I able for so long to deceive your race and live among you? But there is, through this, a reverse ability. I can pass through glass. Through *this* glass, through *these* bars. I do go out, therefore, into the vastness of the night. But I am then invisible. I see you believe me."

"Yes, Madame Chakassia. Many of us have long thought this was what you must be doing."

She leaned back from him, triumphant, and laughed sharply again. He caught the faint tang of the drug on her breath, the drug they gave her to "subdue" her.

"I fly by night. And though I return then to this prison-cage—one night, one night when I am ready—believe me, *I shall be gone forever.*"

Her eyes glittered back the stars.

He knew what to do. He took her hand and brushed the air above it with his lips.

"I'm so glad, so very glad, Madame, you are no longer shut in. I salute your intrepid spirit and your freedom."

"You will tell no one." Not a plea, an order. (Yes, she had now forgotten the cameras.)

"I *swear* I will tell no one."

"Not when you print your story-piece about me?"

"Not even then. Of *course* not then."

Flirtatiously she said, "You are afraid I will kill you otherwise?"

"Madame," he said, "you could kill me, I'm well aware, at any instant. But you've given your word and will not. Now I have given *my* word, and your secret is secure with me, to my grave."

He found his eyes had filled, as hers had, with tears. This would embarrass him later, but at the time it had been, maybe, necessary.

She saw his emotion. Still smiling, she turned from him and walked away across the room, and up the steps to her gallery of books. She did this with the sublime indifference of her superior state, dismissing him, now and utterly, for all her unfathomable length of time, in which he had only been one tiny dot.

So he went to the door and pressed the button, but it opened at once, because the cameras had shown the interview was over.

A copy of the piece he wrote—less story or interview than article—would be sent to her, apparently. She had stipulated this as part of the deal.

And so had he. He made sure, too, the copy she received which would be only one of three, one for her, one for himself, and one for the archive, was exactly and precisely right. Which meant it stayed faithful to the flawless lie she was now living.

He didn't want her or intend her ever to see the real article, the commissioned one. Nobody wanted her to see that. But that was the one the public would see. Christ, he would cut his throat if she ever saw *that* one—well, perhaps not go so far as cutting his throat . . . But he had made absolutely certain. The truth was the truth, but he'd never grasped why truth always had to be used to hurt someone. To her, life had done enough. And death would do the rest.

So in his version of the article which Chaikassia would later receive and glance over in her great room, in the tall building in the cold, moon-bled desert, an article complete with a most beautiful photograph of her, taken some twenty years before, she would see, if she looked, only what she might expect from one devoted, loyal, and bound by her magical spell. But that was not what the rest of them would read, marveling and sneering, or simply turned to stone by fear at the tricks destiny or God could play.

But the real article would anyway make little stir. It wasn't even going to be very lucrative for him, since the travel expenses had been so high. And it was only of interest to certain cliques and cults and elderly admirers, and to himself, of course, which was why he had agreed to write it, providing he could interview her, by which he had meant meet her, look at her, be with her those three hours.

The photograph used in the real article was chosen by his editor. It was very cruel. It showed her as she had become—not even, he thought, as she had appeared to him. But perhaps some of them, with imaginative muscles, would still see something in it of who she was, had been. Was, *was*. This phantom of his adolescence, who would now be the haunting of his dying middle-age.

Who remembers Pella Blai?

She was once said to be one of the most beautiful women in the world, or at least on TV. She had the eponymous rôle in that fantasy series of the previous century, *La Vampiresse*.

The storylines of the series were gorgeous if slender. It was all about a (seemingly, somewhat) Russian vampire, located (somewhere) between the Caucasus and Siberia, though God knows where. A winter country around eighteen-something of moonlit gardens and gravestones, and wolf-scrambled forest. And here she flew by night under the moon, gliding at first light down into her coffin, as any vampire must.

Though never at the top of the tree (not even her famous pearl-hung Christmas tree at Bel Delores), Pella enjoyed much success, and most of us forty years and up know the name. But then the whole ethos of this kind of romantic celluloid vampirism slunk from prominence.

What she did with her between-years remains something of a mystery. And even the lady herself never now talks of them. But there is one very good reason for that.

Diagnosed in her fifties with Alzheimer's disease, Pella lives out her final years in a luxurious private clinic somewhere south of the northern U.S.A. It is a clinic for the rich and the damned, a salutary lesson for any visitor of what fate may bring. But in the case of Pella Blai, there is one extraordinary factor.

For the strangest thing has happened. Another blow of fate—but whether savage or benign, who dare say? For Pella Blai's disintegrating brain has by now wholly convinced her that she is not herself at all, but the heroine she played all those years back on TV, on screen, and about whom she wrote her own novel: the one true vampire left alive on Earth.

Her only memories, then, and perhaps continually reinvented, concern the rôle she acted and has now come to live, Chaikassia, the eternal vampire. (And please note, that is pronounced Ch´-high-kazya.)

Bizarrely, inside this framework, she is pretty damn near perfectly coherent. It is only, they tell you, when she comes out of it, and just now and then she does, that she grows confused, distressed, forgetful, and enraged. When she is Chaikassia—and that takes up around ninety per cent of her time—she is word perfect. No one seems to know why that is. But having spoken some while to her, I can confirm the fact.

Chaikassia's wants and wishes too, are all those of a vampire—let me add, a graceful and well-bred vampire. And to this end, the amenable if expensive clinic permits her to sleep in some sort of box through the day. While at mealtimes she is served "blood"—which is actually a concoction of fruit juice, bouillon, and vitamins—the only nourishment she will knowingly take. They can even leave a decanter of malt whisky in her room. She never touches it—what decent vampire would? "For guests" she tells you, with her Russian aristocrat's grace, learnt in her earliest youth in a winter palace of the mind—*her* mind. Which is all so unlike the real Pella Blai, the hard-drinking daughter of an immigrant family dragged up somewhere in lower London, England.

Frankly, having met her only last month, I venture to say there is nothing left of that real Pella at all. Instead, I talked with a being who can make herself *appear* in mirrors to deceive us all, and who passes at will out through the bars of her nocturnal windows. A being too who never takes your blood if she has promised not to, but who once, with one of the fake books from her gallery, broke the nose of a reporter who offended her.

And this being lives in a high white tower in the middle of a moon-leached desert, as far away from the rest of us as it is possible to get. And, until the last of her mind sets in oblivion and night, and finally lets her free forever, I swear to you she is—without any doubt—La Vampiresse.

Dead Man Stalking
A Morganville Vampires Story
Rachel Caine

Rachel Caine is the author of more than thirty novels, including the internationally best-selling Morganville Vampires series, the Weather Warden series, and the Outcast Season series. She's been fascinated by the undead since she first got a glimpse of Barnabas Collins on Dark Shadows, *and has never lost her interest in the subject. She was writing vampire fiction when vampire fiction was cool, when it wasn't, and when it was cool again, and probably will keep on writing it as long as they'll let her. She lives in Fort Worth, Texas. Outcast Season's* Unseen *was recently released in February 2011, and Morganville Vampire's* Bite Club (*the tenth in the series*) *will be released in May 2011. She starts a new series, The Revivalist, with the release of* Working Stiff *in August 2011.*

Caine's Weather Warden series (beginning with Ill Wind *in 2003) brought her a considerable following, but The Morganville Vampires, a young adult series (initial book:* Glass Houses, 2006) *brought even greater fame and* New York Times *best-selling status. Claire Danvers is the central character of the series. The precocious sixteen-year-old attends Texas Prairie University in Morganville, Texas. Although most of its human inhabitants are unaware, Morganville was founded and is secretly controlled by vampires. Claire lives off campus in an unusual house with three other young adults: gothy Eve, the not entirely human Michael, and Shane, who becomes her boyfriend early in the series. Shane takes the lead role in "Dead Man Stalking," a story that shows Caine's flair for creating a convincing setting, exciting adventure, and indelible characters who young people—and anyone who was ever young—can identify with.*

Living in West Texas is sort of like living in Hell, but without the favorable climate and charming people. Living in Morganville, Texas, is all that and a takeout bag of worse. I should know. My name is Shane Collins, and I was born here, left here, came back here—none of which I had much choice about.

So, for you fortunate ones who've never set foot in this place, here's the walking tour of Morganville: It's home to a couple of thousand folks who breathe, and some crazy-ass number of people who don't. Vampires. Can't live with 'em, and in Morganville, you definitely can't live without 'em, because they run the town. Other than that, Morganville's a normal, dusty collection of buildings—the kind the oil boom of the '60s and '70s rolled by without dropping a dime in the banks. The university in the center of town acts like its own little city, complete with walls and gates.

Oh, and there's a secluded, tightly guarded vampire section of town too. I've been there, in chains. It's nice, if you're not looking forward to a horrible public execution.

I used to want to see this town burned to the ground, and then I had one of those things, what are they called, epiphanies? My epiphany was that one day I woke up and realized that if I lost Morganville and everybody in it I'd have nothing at all. Everything I still cared about was here. Love it or hate it.

Epiphanies suck.

I was having another one of them on this particular day. I was sitting at a table inside Marjo's Diner, watching a dead man walk by the windows outside. Seeing dead men wasn't exactly unusual in Morganville; hell, one of my best friends is dead now, and he still gripes at me about doing the dishes. But there's vampire-dead, which Michael is, and then there's dead-dead, which was Jerome Fielder.

Except Jerome, dead or not, was walking by the window outside Marjo's.

"Order up," Marjo snapped, and slung my plate at me like a ground ball to third base; I stopped it from slamming into the wall by putting up my hand as a backstop. The bun of my hamburger slid over and onto the table-mustard side up, for a change.

"There goes your tip," I said. Marjo, already heading off to the next victim, flipped me off.

"Like you'd ever leave one, you cheap-ass punk."

I returned the gesture. "Don't you need to get to your second job?"

That made her pause, just for a second. "What second job?"

"I don't know, grief counselor? You being so sensitive and all."

That earned me another bird, ruder than the first one. Marjo had known me since I was a baby puking up formula. She didn't like me any better now than she had then, but that wasn't personal. Marjo didn't like anybody. Yeah, go figure on her entering the service industry.

"Hey," I said, and leaned over to look at her retreating bubble butt. "Did you just see who walked by outside?"

She turned to glare at me, round tray clutched in sharp red talons. "Screw you, Collins, I'm running a business here, I don't have time to stare out windows. You want something else or not?"

"Yeah. Ketchup."

"Go squeeze a tomato." She hustled off to wait another table—or not, as the mood took her.

I put veggies on my burger, still watching the parking lot outside the window. There were exactly six cars out there; one of them was my housemate Eve's, which I'd borrowed. The gigantic thing was really less a car than an ocean liner, and some days I called it the Queen Mary, and some days I called it Titanic, depending on how it was running. It stood out. Most of the other vehicles in the lot were crappy, sun-faded pickups and decrepit, half-wrecked sedans.

There was no sign of Jerome, or any other definitely dead guy, walking around out there now. I had one of those moments, *those did I really see that?* moments, but I'm not the delusional type. I had zero reason to imagine the guy. I didn't even *like* him, and he'd been dead for at least a year, maybe longer. Killed in a car wreck at the edge of town, which was code for *shot while trying to escape*, or the nearest Morganville equivalent. Maybe he'd pissed off his vampire Protector. Who knew?

Also, who cared? Zombies, vampires, whatever. When you live in Morganville, you learn to roll with the supernatural punches.

I bit into the burger and chewed. This was why I came to Marjo's . . . not the spectacular service, but the best hamburgers I'd ever eaten. Tender, juicy, spicy. Fresh, crisp lettuce and tomato, a little red onion. The only thing missing was.

"Here's your damn ketchup," Marjo said, and slid the bottle at me like a bartender in an old western saloon. I fielded it and saluted with it, but she was already moving on.

As I drizzled red on my burger, I continued to stare out the window. Jerome. That was a puzzle. Not enough to make me stop eating lunch, though.

Which shows you just how weird life in Morganville is, generally.

I was prepared to forget all about Jerome, post-lunch, because not even Marjo's sour attitude could undo the endorphin high of her burger and besides, I had to get home. It was five o'clock. The bottling plant was letting out, and pretty soon the diner would be crowded with adults tired from a hard day's labor, and not many of them liked me any better than Marjo did. Most of them were older than me; at eighteen, I was starting to get the get-a-job-you-punk stares.

I like a good ass-kicking, but the Good Book is right: It's better to give than to receive.

I was unlocking the door to Eve's car when I saw somebody behind me on the window glass, blocking the blazing westerly sun. The reflection was smeared and indistinct, but in the ripples I made out some of the features.

Jerome Fielder. What do you know, I really *had* seen him.

I had exactly enough time to think, *Dude, say some thing witty*, before Jerome grabbed a handful of my hair and rammed me forehead-first into hot metal and glass. My knees went rubbery, and there was a weird high-pitched whine in my ears. The world went white, then pulsed red, then faded into darkness when he slammed me down again.

Why me? I had time to wonder, as it all went away.

I woke up some time later, riding in the backseat of Eve's car and dripping blood all over the upholstery. *Oh, crap, she's gonna kill me for that*, I thought, which was maybe not the biggest problem I had. My wrists were tied behind my back, and Jerome had done some work on my ankles too. The bonds were so tight I'd lost feeling in both hands and feet, except for a slow, cold throb. I had a gash in my forehead, somewhere near the hairline I thought, and probably some kind of concussion thing, because I felt sick and dizzy.

Jerome was driving Eve's car, and I saw him watching me in the rearview mirror as we rattled along. Wherever we were, it was a rough road, and I bounced like a rag doll as the big tank of a car charged over bumps.

"Hey," I said. "So. Dead much, Jerome?"

He didn't say anything. That might have been because he liked me about as much as Marjo, but I didn't think so; he didn't look exactly *right*. Jerome had been a big guy, back in high school-big in the broad-shouldered sense. He'd been a gym worshipper, a football player, and winner of the biggest neck contest hands down.

Even though he still had all the muscles, it was like the air had been let out of them and now they were ropy and strangely stringy. His face had hollows, and his skin looked old and grainy.

Yep: dead guy. Zombified, which would have been a real mindfreak anywhere but Morganville; even in Morganville, though, it was weird. Vampires? Sure. Zombies? Not so you'd notice.

Jerome decided it was time to prove he still had a working voice box. "Not dead," he said. Just two words, and it didn't exactly prove his case because it sounded hollow and rusty. If I'd had to imagine a dead guy's voice, that would have been it.

"Great," I said. "Good for you. So, this car theft thing is new as a career move, right? And the kidnapping? How's that going for you?"

"Shut up."

He was absolutely right, I needed to do that. I was talking because hey, dead guy driving. It made me just a bit uncomfortable. "Eve's going to hunt you down and dismember you if you ding the car. Remember Eve?"

"Bitch," Jerome said, which meant he did remember. Of course he did. Jerome had been the president of the Jock Club and Eve had been the founder and nearly the only member of the Order of the Goth, Morganville Edition. Those two groups never got along, especially in the hothouse world of high school.

"Remind me to wash your mouth with soap later," I said, and shut my eyes as a particularly brutal bump bounced my head around. Red flashed through my brain, and I thought about things like aneurysms, and death. "Not nice to talk about people behind their backs."

"Go screw yourself."

"Hey, *three* words! You go, boy. Next thing you know, you'll be up to real sentences. . . . Where are we going?"

Jerome's eyes glared at me in the mirror some more. The car smelled like dirt, and something else. Something rotten. Skanky homeless unwashed clothes brewed in a vat of old meat.

I tried not to think about it, because between the smell and the lurching of the car and my aching head, well, you know. Luckily, I didn't have to not-think-about-it for long, because Jerome made a few turns and then hit the brakes with a little too much force.

I rolled off the bench seat and into the spacious legroom, and *ow.* "Ow," I made it official. "You learn that in Dead Guy Driver's Ed?"

"Shut up."

"You know, I think being dead might have actually given you a bigger vocabulary. You ought to think of suggesting that to the U. Put in an extension course or something."

The car shifted as Jerome got out of the front seat, and then the back door opened as he reached in to grab me under the arms and haul. Dead he might be; skanky, definitely. But still: strong.

Jerome dumped me on the caliche-white road, which was graded and graveled, but not recently, and walked off around the hood of the car. I squirmed and looked around. There was an old house about twenty feet away-the end of the pale road-and it looked weathered and defeated and sagging. Could have been a hundred years old, or five without maintenance. Hard to tell. Two stories, old-fashioned and square. Had one of those runaround porches people used to build to catch the cool breezes, although cool out here was relative.

I didn't recognize the place, which was a weird feeling. I'd grown up in Morganville, and I knew every nook and hiding place-survival skills necessary to making it to adulthood. That meant I wasn't in Morganville proper anymore. I knew there were some farmhouses outside of the town limits, but those who lived in them didn't come to town much, and nobody left the city without express vampire permission, unless they were desperate or looking for an easy suicide. So I had no idea who lived here. If anyone but Jerome did, these days.

Maybe he'd eaten all the former residents' brains, and I was his version of takeout. Yeah, that was comforting.

I worked on the ropes, but Jerome tied a damn good knot and my numbed fingers weren't exactly up to the task.

It had been quitting time at the plants when I'd gone out to the parking lot and ended up road kill, but now the big western sun was brushing the edge of the dusty horizon. Sunset was coming, in bands of color layered on top of each other, from red straight up to indigo.

I squirmed and tried to dislocate an elbow in order to get to my front pocket, where my cell phone waited patiently for me to text 911. No luck, and I ran out of time anyway.

Jerome came back around the car, grabbed me by the collar of my T-shirt, and pulled. I grunted and kicked and struggled like a fish on the line, but all that accomplished was to leave a wider drag-path in the dirt. I couldn't see where we were going. The backs of Jerome's fingers felt chilly and dry against my sweaty neck.

Bumpily-bump-bump up a set of steps that felt splintersharp even through my clothes, and the sunset got sliced off by a slanting dark roof. The porch was flatter, but no less uncomfortably splintered. I tried struggling again, this time really putting everything into it, but Jerome dropped me and smacked the back of my head into the wood floor. More red and white flashes, like my own personal emergency signal.

When I blinked them away, I was being dragged across a threshold, into the dark.

Shit.

I wasn't up for bravado anymore. I was seriously scared, and I wanted out. My heart was pounding, and I was thinking of a thousand horrible ways I could die here in this stinking, hot, closed-up room. The carpet underneath my back felt stiff and moldy. What furniture there was looked abandoned and dusty, at least the stuff that wasn't in pieces.

Weirdly, there was the sound of a television coming from upstairs. Local news. The vampires' official mouthpieces were reporting safe little stories, world events, nothing too controversial. Talk about morphine for the masses.

The sound clicked off, and Jerome let go of me. I flopped over onto my side, then my face, and inchwormed my way up to my knees while trying not to get a mouthful of dusty carpet. I heard a dry rattle from behind me.

Jerome was laughing.

"Laugh while you can, monkey boy," I muttered, and spat dust. Not likely he'd ever seen *Buckaroo Banzai*, but it was worth a shot.

Footsteps creaked on the stairs from the second floor. I reoriented myself, because I wanted to be looking at whatever evil bastard was coming to the afternoon matinee of my probably gruesome death. . . .

Oh. Oh, *dammit*.

"Hello, son," my dad Frank Collins said. "Sorry about this, but I knew you wouldn't just come on your own."

The ropes came off, once I promised to be a good boy and not rabbit for the car the second I had the chance. My father looked about the same as I'd expected, which meant not good but strong. He'd started out a random pathetic alcoholic; after my sister had died-accident or murder, you take your pick-he'd gone off the deep end. So had my mom. So had I, for that matter.

Sometime in there, my dad had changed from random pathetic drunk to mean, badass vampire-hunting drunk. The vampire-hating component of that had been building up for years, and it had exploded like an ancient batch of TNT when my mother died—by suicide, maybe. I didn't believe it, and neither did my dad. The vampires had been behind it, like they were behind every terrible thing that had ever happened in our lives.

That's what I used to believe, anyway. And what Dad still did.

I could smell the whiskey rising up off of him like the bad-meat smell off of Jerome, who was kicked back in a chair in the corner, reading a book. Funny. Jerome hadn't been much of a reader when he'd been alive.

I sat obligingly on the ancient, dusty couch, mainly because my feet were too numb to stand, and I was trying to work circulation back into my fingers. Dad and I didn't hug. Instead, he paced, raising dust motes that glimmered in the few shafts of light that fought their way through smudged windows.

"You look like crap," Dad said, pausing to stare at me. I resisted the urge, like Marjo, to give him a one-fingered salute, because he'd only beat the crap out of me for it. Seeing him gave me a black, sick feeling in the pit of my stomach. I wanted to love him. I wanted to hit him. I didn't know what I wanted, except that I wanted this whole thing to just go away.

"Gee, thanks, Dad," I said, and deliberately slumped back on the couch, giving him all the teen attitude I could. "I missed you too. I see you brought all your friends with you. Oh, wait."

The last time my dad had rolled into Morganville, he'd done it in a literal kind of way—on a motorcycle, with a bunch of badass motorcycle biker buddies. No sign of them this time. I wondered when they'd finally told him to shove it, and how hard.

Dad didn't answer. He kept staring at me. He was wearing a leather jacket with lots of zippers, faded blue jeans, sturdy boots. Not too different from what I was wearing, minus the jacket, because only a stupid jerk would be in leather in this heat. Looking at you, Dad.

"Shane," he said. "You knew I'd come back for you."

"Yeah, that's really sweet. The last time I saw you, you were trying to blow my ass up along with a whole building full of vampires, remember? What's my middle name, Collateral Damage?" He'd have done it too. I knew my dad too well to think anything else. "You also left me to burn alive in a cage, Dad. So excuse me if I'm not getting all misty-eyed while the music swells."

His expression—worn into a hard leather mask by wind and sun—didn't change. "It's a war, Shane. We talked about this."

"Funny thing, I don't remember you saying, *If you get caught by the vampires, I'll leave you to burn*, dumbass. But maybe I'm just not remembering all the details of your clever plan." Feeling was coming back into my fingers and toes. Not fun. It felt like I'd dipped them in battery acid and then rolled them in lye. "I can get over that. But you had to go and drag my friends into it."

That was what I hated the most. Sure, he'd screwed me over—more than once, actually. But he was right, we'd kind of agreed that one or the other of us might have to bite it for the cause, back when I believed in his cause.

We hadn't agreed about innocent people, especially my friends, getting thrown on the pile of bodies.

"Your *friends*, right," Dad said, with about a bottle's worth of cheap whiskey emphasis. "A half-vampire, a wannabe morbid freak, and—oh, you mean that girl, don't you? The little skinny one. She melted the brains right out of your head, didn't she? I warned you about that."

Claire. He didn't even remember her name. I closed my eyes for a second, and there she was, smiling up at me with those clear, trusting eyes. She might be small, but she had a kind of strength my dad wouldn't ever understand. She was the first really pure thing that I'd ever known, and I wasn't about to let him take her away. She was waiting for me right now, back at the Glass House, probably studying and chewing a pencil. Or arguing with Eve. Or . . . wondering where the hell I was.

I had to get out of this. I had to get back to Claire.

Painful or not, my feet were functional again. I tested them by standing up. In the corner, Dead Jerome put aside his book. It was a battered, water-stained copy of *The Wizard of Oz*. Who did he think he was? The Cowardly Lion? The Scarecrow? Hell, maybe he thought he was Dorothy.

"Just like I thought, this is all about the girl. You probably think you're some knight in shining armor come to save her." Dad's smile was sharp enough to cut diamonds. "You know how she sees you? A big, dumb idiot she can put on a leash. Her own pet pit bull. Your innocent little schoolgirl, she's wearing the Founder's symbol now. She's working for the vampires. I sure as hell hope she's like a porn star in the sack for you to be betraying your own like this."

This time, I didn't need a knock on the head to see red. I felt my chin going down, my lungs filling, but I held on to my temper. Somehow.

He was trying to make me charge him.

"I love her, Dad," I said. "Don't."

"Love, yeah, right. You don't know the meaning of the word, Shane. She's working for the leeches. She's helping them regain control of Morganville. She has to go, and you know it."

"Over my dead body."

In the corner, Jerome laughed that scratchy, raspy laugh that made me want to tear out his voice box once and for all. "Could be arranged," he croaked.

"Shut up," my dad snapped without taking his eyes off of me. "Shane, listen to me. I've found the answer."

"Wait—let me guess—forty-two?" No use. Dad wasn't anywhere near cool enough to be a Douglas Adams fan. "I don't care what you've found, Dad, and I'm not listening to you anymore. I'm going home. You want to have your pet dead guy stop me?"

His eyes fixed on my wrist, where I was wearing a bracelet. Not one of those things that would have identified me as vamp property—a hospital bracelet, white plastic with a big red cross on it.

"You wounded?" Not, of course, was I sick. I was just another foot soldier, to Dad. You were either wounded, or malingering.

"Whatever. I'm better," I said.

It seemed, for just a second, that he softened. Maybe nobody but me would have noticed. Maybe I imagined it too. "Where were you hurt, boy?"

I shrugged and pointed to my abs, slightly off to one side. The scar still ached and felt hot. "Knife."

He frowned. "How long ago?"

"Long enough." The bracelet would be coming off in the next week. My grace period was nearly over.

He looked into my eyes, and for a second, just a second, I let myself believe he was genuinely concerned.

Sucker.

He always had been able to catch me off guard, no matter how carefully I watched him, and I didn't even see the punch coming until it was too late. It was hard, delivered with surgical precision, and it doubled me over and sent me stumbling back to flop onto the couch again. Breathe,

I told my muscles. My solar plexus told me to stuff it, and my insides throbbed, screaming in pain and terror. I heard myself making hard, gasping noises, and hated myself for it. *Next time. Next time I hit the bastard first.*

I knew better, though.

Dad grabbed me by the hair and yanked my head back. He pointed my face in Jerome's direction. "I'm sorry, boy, but I need you to listen right now. You see him? I brought him back, right out of the grave. I can bring them all back, as many as I need. They'll fight for me, Shane, and they won't quit. It's time. We can take this town back, and we can finally end this nightmare."

My frozen muscles finally unclenched, and I pulled in a whooping, hoarse gasp of air. Dad let go of my hair and stepped away.

He'd always known when to back off too.

"Your definition of—the end of the nightmare—is a little different—from mine," I wheezed. "Mine doesn't include zombies." I swallowed and tried to slow my heart rate. "How'd you do it, Dad? How the hell is he standing here?"

He brushed that aside. Of course. "I'm trying to explain to you that it's time to quit talking about the war, and time to start fighting it. We can win. We can destroy all of them." He paused, and the glow in his eyes was the next best thing to a fanatic with a bomb strapped to his chest. "I need you, son. We can do it together."

That part, he really meant. It was sick and twisted, but he did need me.

And I needed to use that. "First, tell me how you do it," I said. "I need to know what I'm signing up for."

"Later." Dad clapped me on the shoulder. "When you're convinced this is necessary, maybe. For now, all you need to know is that it's possible, I've done it. Jerome's proof."

"No, Dad. Tell me how. Either I'm in it or I'm not. No more secrets."

Nothing I was saying was going to register with him as a lie, because they weren't lies. I was saying what he wanted to hear. First rule of growing up with an abusive father: you cope, you bargain, you learn how to avoid getting hit.

And my father wasn't bright enough to know I'd figured it out.

Still, some instinct warned him; he looked at me with narrowed eyes, a frown wrinkling his forehead. "I'll tell you," he said. "But you need to show me you can be trusted first."

"Fine. Tell me what you need." That translated into, *Tell me who you need me to beat up*. As long as I was willing to do that, he'd believe me.

I was hoping it would be Jerome.

"Of everybody who died in the last couple of years, who was the strongest?"

I blinked, not sure it was a trick question. "Jerome?"

"Besides Jerome."

"I guess—probably Tommy Barnes." Tommy was no teenager; he'd been in his thirties when he'd kicked it, and he'd been a big, mean, tough dude even the other big, mean, tough dudes had given a wide berth. He'd died in a bar fight, I'd heard. Knifed from behind. He'd have snapped the neck off of anybody who'd tried it to his face.

"Big Tom? Yeah, he'd do." Dad nodded thoughtfully. "All right, then. We're bringing him back."

The last person on Earth I'd want to bring back from the grave would be Big Tommy Barnes. He'd been crazy-badass alive. I could only imagine death wouldn't have improved his temper.

But I nodded. "Show me."

Dad took off his leather jacket, and then stripped off his shirt. In contrast to the sun-weathered skin of his arms, face, and neck, his chest was fish-belly white, and it was covered with tattoos. I remembered some of them, but not all the ink was old.

He'd recently had our family portrait tattooed over his heart.

I forgot to breathe for a second, staring at it. Yeah, it was crude, but those were the lines of Mom's face, and Alyssa's. I didn't realize, until I saw them, that I'd nearly forgotten how they looked.

Dad looked down at the tat. "I needed to remind myself," he said.

My throat was so dry that it clicked when I swallowed. "Yeah." My own face was there, frozen in indigo blue at the age of maybe sixteen. I looked thinner, and even in tattoo form I looked more hopeful. More sure.

Dad held out his right arm, and I realized that there was more new ink.

And this stuff was *moving*.

I took a step back. There were dense, strange symbols on his arm, all in standard tattoo ink, but there was nothing standard about what the tats were doing—namely, they were revolving slowly like a DNA helix up and down the axis of his arm, under the skin. "*Christ*, Dad—"

"Had it done in Mexico," he said. "There was an old priest there, he knew things from the Aztecs. They had a way to bring back the dead, so long as they hadn't been gone for more than two years, and were in decent condition otherwise. They used them as ceremonial warriors." Dad flexed his arm, and the tattoos flexed with him. "This is part of what does it."

I felt sick and cold now. This had moved way past what I knew. I wished wildly that I could show this to Claire; she'd probably be fascinated, full of theories and research.

She'd know what to do about it.

I swallowed hard and said, "And the other part?"

"That's where you come in," Dad said. He pulled his T-shirt on again, hiding the portrait of our family. "I need you to prove you're up for this, Shane. Can you do that?"

I gulped air and finally, convulsively nodded. *Play for time.* I was telling myself. *Play for time, think of something you can do.* Short of chopping off my own father's arm, though. . . .

"This way," Dad said. He went to the back of the room. There was a door there, and he'd added a new, sturdy lock to it that he opened with a key from his jacket.

Jerome gave me that creepy laugh again, and I felt my skin shiver into gooseflesh.

"Right. This might be a shock," Dad said. "But trust me, it's for a good cause."

He swung open the door and flipped on a harsh overhead light.

It was a windowless cell, and inside, chained to the floor with thick silver-plated links, was a vampire.

Not just any vampire. Oh no, that would have been too easy for my father.

It was Michael Glass, my best friend.

Michael looked—white. Paler than pale. I'd never seen him look like that. There were burns on his arms, big raised welts where the silver was touching, and there were cuts. He was leaking slow trickles of blood on the floor.

His eyes were usually blue, but now they were red, bright red. Scary monster red, like nothing human.

But it was still my best friend's voice whispering, "Help."

I couldn't answer him. I backed up and slammed the door.

Jerome was laughing again, so I turned around, picked up a chair, and smashed him in the face with it. I could have hit him with a powder puff, for all the good it did. He grabbed the chair, broke the thick wood with a snap of his hands, and threw it back at me. I stumbled, and would have gone down except for the handy placement of a wall.

"Stop. Don't touch my son," my father said. Jerome froze like he'd run into a brick wall, hands working like he still wanted to rip out my throat.

I turned on my dad and snarled, "That's my friend!"

"No, that's a vampire," he said. "The youngest one. The weakest one. The one most of them won't come running to rescue."

I wanted to scream. I wanted to punch somebody. I felt pressure building up inside, and my hands were shaking. "What the hell are you doing to him?"

I didn't know who he was, this guy in the leather jacket looking at me. He looked like a tired, middle-aged biker, with his straggly graying hair, his sallow, seamed face, his scars and tats. Only his eyes seemed like they belonged to my dad, and even then, only for a second.

"It's a vampire," he said. "It's not your friend, Shane. You need to be real clear about that—your friend is dead, just like Jerome here, and you can't let that get in the way of what needs to be done. When we go to war, we get them all. *All*. No exceptions."

Michael had played at our house. My dad had tossed a ball around with him and pushed his swing and served him cake at birthday parties.

And my dad didn't care about any of that anymore.

"How?" My jaw felt tight. I was grinding my teeth, and my hands were shaking. "How did you do this? What are you doing to him?"

"I'm bleeding it and storing the blood, just like they do us humans," Dad said. "It's a two-part spell—the tattoo, and the blood of a vampire. It's just a creature, Shane. Remember that."

Michael wasn't a creature. Not *just* a creature, anyway; neither was what Dad had pulled out of Jerome's grave, for that matter. Jerome wasn't just a mindless killing machine. Mindless killing machines didn't fill their spare time with the adventures of Dorothy and Toto. They didn't even know they *had* spare time. I could see it in Jerome's wide, yellowed eyes now. The pain. The terror. The anger.

"Do you want to be here?" I asked him, straight out.

For just that second, Jerome looked like a boy. A scared, angry, hurt little boy. "No," he said. "Hurts."

I wasn't going to let this happen. Not to Michael, oh hell no. And not even to Jerome.

"Don't you go all soft on me, Shane. I've done what needed doing," Dad said. "Same as always. You used to be weak. I thought you'd manned up."

Once, that would have made me try to prove it by fighting something. Jerome, maybe. Or him.

I turned and looked at him and said, "I really would be weak, if I fell for that tired bullshit, Dad." I raised my hands, closed them into fists, and then opened them again and let them fall. "I don't need to prove anything to you. Not anymore."

I walked out the front door, out to the dust-filmed black car. I popped the trunk and took out a crowbar.

Dad watched me from the door, blocking my way back into the house. "What the hell are you doing?"

"Stopping you."

He threw a punch as I walked up the steps toward him. This time, I saw it coming, saw it telegraphed clearly in his face before the impulse ever reached his fist.

I stepped out of the way, grabbed his arm, and shoved him face-first into the wall. "Don't." I held him there, pinned like a bug on a board, until I felt his muscles stop fighting me. The rest of him never would. "We're done, Dad. Over. This is over. Don't make me hurt you, because God, I really want to."

I should have known he wouldn't just give up.

The second I let him go, he twisted, jammed an elbow into my abused stomach, and forced me backward. I knew his moves by now, and sidestepped an attempt to hook my feet out from under me.

"Jerome!" Dad yelled. "Stop my—"

The end of that sentence was going to be son, and I couldn't let him put Jerome back in the game or this was over before it started.

So I punched my father full in the face. Hard. With all the rage and resentment that I'd stored up over the years, and all the anguish, and all the fear. The shock rattled every bone in my body, and my whole hand sent up a red flare of distress. My knuckles split open.

Dad hit the floor, eyes rolling back in his head. I stood there for a second, feeling oddly cold and empty, and saw his eyelids flutter.

He wouldn't be out for long.

I moved quickly across the room, past Jerome, who was still frozen in place, and opened the door to the cell. "Michael?" I crouched down across from him, and my friend shook gold hair back from his white face and stared at me with eerie, hungry eyes.

I held up my wrist, showing him the bracelet. "Promise me, man. I get you out of here, no biting. I love you, but no."

Michael laughed hoarsely. "Love you too, bro. Get me the hell out of here."

I set to work with the crowbar, pulling up floorboards and gouging the eyebolts out for each set of chains. I'd been right; my dad was too smart to make chains out of solid silver. Too soft, too easy to break. These were silver-plated— good enough to do the job on Michael, if not one of the older vamps.

I only had to pull up the first two; Michael's vampire strength took care of yanking the others from the floor.

Michael's eyes flared red when I leaned closer, trying to help him up, and before I knew what was happening, he'd wrapped a hand around my throat and slammed me down, on my back, on the floor. I felt the sting of sharp nails in my skin, and saw his eyes fixed on the cut on my head.

"No biting," I said again, faintly. "Right?"

"Right," Michael said, from somewhere out beyond Mars. His eyes were glowing like storm lanterns, and I could feel every muscle in his body trembling. "Better get that cut looked at. Looks bad."

He let me up, and moved with about half his usual vampire speed to the door. Dad might not let Jerome have at me, but he wasn't going to hold back with Michael, and Michael was—at best—half his normal strength right now. Not exactly a fair fight.

"Michael," I said, and put my back against the wall next to him. "We go together, straight to the window. You get out, don't wait for me. The sun should be down far enough that you can make it to the car." I gathered up a handful of silver chain and wrapped it around my hand. "Don't even think about arguing right now."

He sent me an are-you-kidding look, and nodded.

We moved fast, and together. I got in Jerome's way and delivered a punch straight from the shoulder right between his teeth, reinforced with silver-plated metal.

I only intended to knock him back, but Jerome howled and stumbled, hands up to ward me off. It was like years fell away, and all of a sudden we were back in junior high again-him the most popular bully in school, me finally getting enough size and muscle to stand up to him. Jerome had made that same girly gesture the first time I'd hit back.

It threw me off.

A crossbow bolt fired from the far corner of the living room hissed right over my head and slammed to a vibrating stop in the wooden wall. "Stop!" Dad ordered hoarsely. He was on his knees, but he was up and very, very angry. He was also reloading, and the next shot wouldn't be a warning.

"Get out!" I screamed at Michael, and if he was thinking about staging a reenactment of the gunfight at the OK Corral, he finally saw sense. He jumped through the nearest window in a hail of glass and hit the ground running. I'd been right. (The sun was down, or close enough that it wouldn't hurt him too badly.

He made it to the car, opened the driver's side door, and slid inside. I heard the roar as the engine started. "Shane!" he yelled. "Come on!"

"In a second," I yelled back. I stared at my father, and the moving tattoo. He had the crossbow aimed right at my chest. I twirled the crowbar in one hand, the silver chain in the other. "So," I said, watching my father. "Your move, Dad. What now? You want me to do a cage match with Dead Jerome? Would that make you happy?"

My dad was staring not at me, but at Dead Jerome, who was cowering in the corner. I'd hurt him, or the silver had; half his face was burned and rotting, and he was weeping in slow, retching sobs.

I knew the look Dad was giving him. I'd seen it on my father's face more times than I could count. Disappointment.

"My son," Dad said in disgust. "You ruin everything."

"I guess Jerome's more your son than I am," I said. I walked toward the front door. I wasn't going to give my father the satisfaction of making me run. I knew he had the crossbow in his hands, and I knew it was loaded.

I knew he was sighting on my back.

I heard the trigger release, and the ripped-silk hiss of wood traveling through air. I didn't have time to be afraid, only—like my dad—bitterly disappointed.

The crossbow bolt didn't hit me. Didn't even miss me.

When I turned, at the door, I saw that he'd put the crossbow bolt, tipped with silver, through Jerome's skull. Jerome slid silently down to the floor. Dead. Finally, mercifully dead.

The Wizard of Oz fell face down next to his hand.

"Son," my dad said, and put the crossbow aside. "Please, don't go. I need you. I really do."

I shook my head.

"This thing—it'll only last another few days," he said. "The tattoo. It's already fading. I don't have time for this, Shane. It has to be now."

"Then I guess you're out of luck."

He snapped the crossbow up again.

I ducked to the right, into the parlor, jumped the wreckage of a couch, and landed on the cracked, curling floor of the old kitchen. It smelled foul and chemical in here, and I spotted a fish tank on the counter, filled with cloudy liquid. Next to it was a car battery.

DIY silver plating equipment, for the chains.

There was also a 1950s-era round-shouldered fridge, rattling and humming.

I opened it.

Dad had stored Michael's blood in bottles, old dirty milk bottles likely scavenged from the trash heap in the corner. I grabbed all five bottles and threw them one at a time out the window, aiming for a big upthrusting rock next to a tree.

Smash. Smash. Smash. Smash. . . .

"Stop," Dad spat. In my peripheral vision I saw him standing there, aiming his reloaded crossbow at me. "I'll kill you, Shane. I swear I will."

"Yeah? Lucky you've already got me tattooed on your chest, then, with the rest of the dead family." I pulled back for the throw.

"I could bring back your mother," Dad blurted. "Maybe even your sister. Don't."

Oh, God. Sick black swam across my vision for a second.

"You throw that bottle," he whispered, "and you're killing their last chance to live."

I remembered Jerome—his sagging muscles, his grainy skin, the panic and fear in his eyes.

Do you want to be here?

No. Hurts.

I threw the last bottle of Michael's blood and watched it sail straight and true, to shatter in a red spray against the rock.

I thought he'd kill me. Maybe he thought he'd kill me too. I waited, but he didn't pull the trigger.

"I'm fighting for humanity," he said. His last, best argument. It had always won me over before.

I turned and looked him full in the face. "I think you already lost yours."

I walked out past him, and he didn't stop me.

Michael drove like a maniac, raising contrails of caliche dust about a mile high as we sped back to the main highway. He kept asking me how I was doing. I didn't answer him, just looked out at the gorgeous sunset, and the lonely, broken house fading in the distance.

We blasted past the Morganville city limits sign, and one of the ever-lurking police cars cut us off. Michael slowed, stopped, and turned off the engine. A rattle of desert wind shook the car.

"Shane."

"Yeah."

"He's dangerous."

"I know that."

"I can't just let this go. Did you see—"

"I saw," I said. "I know." But he's still my father, some small, frightened kid inside me wailed. He's all I have.

"Then what do you want me to say?" Michael's eyes had faded back to blue, now, but he was still white as a ghost, blue-white, scary-white. I'd spilled all his blood out there on the ground. The burns on his hands and wrists made my stomach clench.

"Tell them the truth," I said. If the Morganville vampires got to my dad before he could get the hell out, he'd die horribly, and God knew, he probably deserved it. "But give him five minutes, Michael. Just five."

Michael stared at me, and I couldn't tell what was in his mind at all. I'd known him most of my life, but in that long moment, he was just as much of a stranger as my father had been.

A uniformed Morganville cop tapped on the driver's side window. Michael rolled it down. The cop hadn't been prepared to find a vampire driving, and I could see him amending the harsh words he'd been about to deliver.

"Going a little fast, sir," he finally said. "Something wrong?"

Michael looked at the burns on his wrists, the bloodless slices on his arms. "Yeah," he said. "I need an ambulance."

And then he slumped forward, over the steering wheel. The cop let out a squawk of alarm and got on his radio. I reached out to ease Michael back. His eyes were shut, but as I stared at him, he murmured, "You wanted five minutes."

"I wasn't looking for a Best Supporting Actor award!" I muttered back.

Michael did his best impression of Vampire in a Coma for about five minutes, and then came to and assured the cop and arriving ambulance attendants he was okay.

Then he told them about my dad.

They found Jerome, still and evermore dead, with a silver-tipped arrow through his head. They found a copy of *The Wizard of Oz* next to him.

There was no sign of Frank Collins.

Later that night—around midnight—Michael and I sat outside on the steps of our house. I had a bottle of most illegal beer; he was guzzling his sixth bottle of blood, which I pretended not to notice. He had his arm around Eve, who had been pelting us both with questions all night in a nonstop machine gun patter; she'd finally run down, and leaned against Michael with sleepy contentment.

Well, she hadn't quite run down. "Hey," she said, and looked up at Michael with big, dark-rimmed eyes. "Seriously. You can bring back dead guys with vampire juice? That is so wrong."

Michael almost spit out the blood he was swallowing. "Vampire juice? Damn, Eve. Thanks for your concern."

She lost her smile. "If I didn't laugh, I'd scream."

He hugged her. "I know. But it's over."

Next to me, Claire had been quiet all night. She wasn't drinking—not that we'd have let her, at sixteen—and she wasn't saying much, either. She also wasn't looking at me. She was staring out at the Morganville night.

"He's coming back," she finally said. "Your dad's not going to give it up, is he?"

I exchanged a look with Michael. "No," I said. "Probably not. But it'll be a while before he gets his act together again. He expected to have me to help him kick off his war, and like he said, his time was running out. He'll need a brand-new plan."

Claire sighed and linked her arm through mine. "He'll find one."

"He'll have to do it without me." I kissed the soft, warm top of her hair.

"I'm glad," she said. "You deserve better."

"News flash," I said. "I've got better. Right here."

Michael and I clinked glasses, and toasted our survival.

However long it lasted.

The Ghost of Leadville
Jeanne C. Stein

Jeanne Stein is the best-selling author of the urban fantasy series, The Anna Strong Chronicles, but "The Ghost of Leadville" is a different sort of fantasy. Set primarily in the past it features a historical character—Doc Holliday—who was a legend in his own lifetime and later became part of a larger mythology. You don't have to be a vampire to achieve a form of immortality.

Stein lives in Denver (which isn't far from Leadville) where she is active in the writing community, belonging to Sisters in Crime, Romance Writers of America, and Rocky Mountain Fiction Writers. In 2008 she was named RMFW's Writer of the Year and last year, her character, Anna Strong, received a Romantic Times Reviewers Choice Award for Best Urban Fantasy Protagonist. The sixth in the Anna Strong series, Chosen, *was released in August 2010. She has numerous short story credits, as well. She is also one of the editors of RMFW's award-winning anthology,* Broken Links, Mended Lives.

My name is Rose Sullivan. Although I've been on the earth for two hundred years, I was turned on my twenty-fifty birthday. I am eternally frozen in the physical form of a twenty-five year old. Blond hair, blue eyes, five feet two inches tall, one hundred pounds. I am small in stature which means men sometimes make the mistake of thinking a childish mind resides in this rather childish body. They only make the mistake once. I am preternaturally strong, as are all vampires, and have no tolerance toward those who try to intimidate me—or others. If I see an injustice, it is in my nature to correct it.

It isn't always easy being vampire. There are rules to be followed. Most humans are unaware of our existence. Just as they are unaware of other supernatural beings living amongst them. It has to be. The great secret must be preserved. Humanity has shown how it reacts to that which it does not understand. Destroy first. Ask questions later.

And so I have survived as a vampire for two hundred years. Living in big cities, mostly. Able to last as long as forty years in one guise—the latest a museum curator in New York. My specialty was early Americana. Convenient since I was born to missionary parents in the American west in 1809.

But one can only do so much to disguise a face and body that do not age. It becomes apparent when all those around you take note of your "youthful" appearance that is time to move on. A hasty resignation because of "family problems," a quick transfer of funds to whatever new identity I've adopted and a brief goodbye to the human hosts who have provided me sustenance during my stay. They, the few who are guardians of the secret, do not question. They are used to the plight of the vampire. They know to take the money and pleasure offered in return for blood and form no attachment. It has always been so.

And so I shed the skin of the old persona and adapt a new one in Leadville, Colorado in the year 2009.

I've decided this time around to eschew bright lights and settle into a quiet existence in a quiet little town. I've also decided to write a book. Why not? Look at a current bestseller list. The one hot topic on all the charts is vampire romance. Who is in a better position to write about vampire romance than a female vampire who has certainly experienced her share of romance? And besides, it's a chance to set the record straight, albeit under the ruse of *fiction,* about many things having to do with living a modern vampire life. It's not all bad. Not by a long shot.

There is another reason I chose to make this incarnation that of a writer. It's a solitary existence. I've had my fill of city life and being forced to live among people. The smells, the noises, the *desperation* of a population trying to cram all of life into a few decades burdens the spirit of a vampire. I'm ready for a change.

I bought a nicely restored Victorian on the edge of Leadville. I stumbled on the place last year while on a research trip, visiting early mining sites in preparation for a museum exhibit. Leadville nestles in a fold of the Rocky Mountains, hidden, protected. At the height of the gold rush, fifty thousand called this place home. Now there are barely two thousand people living here. The climate is harsh, the most often heard comment is that Leadville has two seasons—this winter and last winter. But temperature is irrelevant to a vampire. And Leadville's one lasting claim to fame is an opera house, built to entertain the miners during the long winter. It has been restored and opens its door to the public in the summer when a flock of faithful opera fans make the trek up from Denver to enjoy the old building's perfect acoustics. It is a gentle reminder of a gentler time. I fell in love with it at first sight.

And so I find myself comfortably ensconced on my living room couch, laptop computer open, finger poised over the keys to begin this novelist's journey. My eyes, however, keep drifting upwards, through the window at the other side of the room, drawn to the mountains rising like stark, grey monoliths against a cloudless November sky.

A familiar landscape.

Truth be told, this is not the first time I've lived in Leadville.

Memories flood back.

No, I lived here once before.

Leadville, 1884

Hyman's Saloon

"Rose. Come on over here, gal. I have someone for you to meet."

I look up. Sunny Tom's face is wreathed in a grin, his dozen gold teeth flashing in the bar light like fireflies on a summer night.

Are you sure? I ask him. I've been keeping an eye on the poker table. Miners flush with gold dollars and full to the brim with whiskey are normally good for business. But when the cards turn against them, the whiskey takes over. Bullets are never good for business and at this moment, both the whiskey and the cards are turning against one youngster new to both. I raise an eyebrow at Tom. *This could turn ugly.*

He shrugs. *He pay for his drinks?*

A nod.

Then fuck him. This is more important.

My gaze sweeps over the slight figure of a man standing beside him. Sunny Tom is six feet tall, two hundred pounds. The stranger with him is maybe five foot ten, one hundred forty pounds. He's dressed like a dandy, striped pants, white shirt, cravat with a diamond stickpin that winks at me as I approach. He has a hat in his hand and a big Colt revolver on his hip.

He watches me with a predator's eye. He's even-featured with a square chin, light brown hair, full mustache. Not bad looking. Must be a big spender if Tom is sending him to me.

I tilt my head, taste the air around him. He's sick. Consumption. It hovers about him in a bilious cloud.

I hold out my hand. "Rose."

He takes it, brings it to his lips. "John Holliday, ma'am. Pleased to meet you."

Sunny Tom probes my head, waiting for the connection to be made. I lift a shoulder in a half-shrug which prompts an exasperated, *John Holliday? You don't know the name? How about Doc Holliday? That ring any bells?*

Tom turns his smile back on Doc Holliday. "I will leave you in Rose's most capable hands. Have a very good evening."

He saunters away to take my place near the poker table, winking as he passes. *Have fun.*

With a consumptive? Tom is past before I can skewer him with a properly caustic reply.

He runs the saloon, I run the girls who work it. There are only two people who know the truth of our relationship. Sunny Tom and me. We are both vampires. Running a bar that specializes in whores and whiskey keeps us both in what we need. Human blood.

He's set me up tonight with a consumptive. It's not the illness I resent. Vampires are impervious to human disease. It's the *taste* of the blood.

My shoulders bunch a little at the prospect but I put on a sweet smile and take my place beside Doc at the bar. He half turns toward me and the diamond at his neck catches and reflects the light in a rainbow burst. I reach up and touch it with the tip of a finger. "Nice bauble, Mr. Holliday."

His smile is tinged with bitterness and regret. "A gift from my mother before she died. Unfortunately not the only thing she left me." He is looking down the bar and with a flick of a finger, summons the barkeep.

Holliday orders whiskey for himself, turns to me. "What will you have?"

"Gin." I tap a finger on the bar. Sam has worked for us for twenty years and he interprets my order with a nod and a grin.

He turns his back on us and pours.

I touch Holliday's hand. "What brings such a famous person to Leadville?"

"I guess you could say my mother." This time there's no mistaking the irony heavy in his tone.

He reads the question in my eyes. He shakes his head, but the hard lines of his mouth soften. "The climate. I've been told it is better for one who suffers with consumption to live in a dry climate."

An honest answer. My eyebrows lift in surprise. It is only in the last few years that consumption has been found to be infectious. Yet he says it openly. Maybe because I am only a whore, bought and paid for, and the answer is of no consequence. The health of his wallet is all I should be interested in.

The bartender places our drinks in front of us. Holliday takes a long pull, draining the glass, orders another. I sip at my drink. It's only water. I learned long ago to keep a clear head when working. Alcohol goes directly into a vampire's system and we are as susceptible to its effects as humans. It took an unexpected and unprovoked attack from a drunken miner to teach me that lesson. Vampires are not easily killed, but we feel pain. I bore the marks of that attack for two days. The miner suffered the consequences for a much briefer period. He was dead in two minutes.

I watch Holliday surreptitiously, over the rim of my glass. Standing this close to him, his reputation as a cold-blooded killer seems exaggerated. His speech is soft, his inflection subtle. He is neither loud nor imposing.

Not an indication that he doesn't like his sex rough, I remind myself. The mildest mannered men are often the ones who find it satisfying to take their frustrations out on a female.

"So, Rose." Holliday dabs at his mouth with a finger. "What do you do for excitement in Leadville?"

"The gaming tables here, of course," I reply with a smile. "And Horace Tabor opened his opera house just last week. Emma Abbott is performing. Her voice is wonderful. If you're planning to stay for awhile, you really should catch a performance."

He nods and signals for another drink. "Perhaps I will." He looks toward the tables. "Business appears to be good."

"It is. Silver was discovered two years ago and those lodes are as rich as the gold. There's money to be made for sure."

Holliday is watching me now, over the rim of *his* glass. "You don't talk like a whore. You don't look like one either. Your skin is milky white. Your hair shiny. Good teeth. Why hasn't some rich city boy plucked you up?"

I wave a hand and laugh. "You see any rich city boys around here? I'm doing what I want to do. I like men. They seem to like me. Men are allowed to indulge their passions. What's wrong with a woman doing the same thing?"

His eyebrows raise a bit. "Plain talk. I like that. I say let's you and me follow that passion right up to a room." He signals the bartender. "A bottle, if you please, and two glasses."

He tucks the bottle under an arm, scoops the glasses into one hand, places his other hand at the small of my back. "Time to properly make your acquaintance, Miss Rose," he says with a little bow. "Lead the way."

Tom's eyes follow us to the staircase at the back of the saloon. I feel his thoughts reaching out. *You need anything, you call, he says.*

I smile at him over my shoulder. *You watch out for the other girls. Trixie should be back down in fifteen minutes. Annabelle just went up. Those two miners in the corner have monopolized Jane and Kate for too long. If they aren't ready to pony up for a fuck in ten minutes, kick 'em out.*

He grins and throws me a salute. *Yes, sir. How long should I give you and Doc?*

I put my arm through Holliday's. *As long as it takes.*

My room is at the back of the hallway, facing Main Street. It has big windows that are left open nearly year around. The cold doesn't bother me and the bracing smell of air heavy with snow flushes out the human smell of sweat and semen that often permeates these walls.

Holliday crosses right over to the windows and pulls them shut. "Damn, woman. It's cold in here. Don't you feel it?"

No, the vampire answers. The human answers, "I forget sometimes, to close the windows. Here. I'll stoke the fire. It will be warm as a spring day in a minute."

He holds up the bottle. "Good thing I brought a little something to help heat us up."

He pours two glasses and hands one to me. I pretend to take a sip, then place the glass on the table next to the bed. "I know better ways to heat our blood." I slip the straps of my gown down over my shoulders.

His eyes follow my movements. He still has his own glass in his hand. By the time I've stripped down to my undergarments, that hand is trembling a little.

"You have a beautiful body," he says. "Tiny. You're no bigger than a minute."

"How about you, cowboy? You no bigger than a minute?"

He puts his glass down beside mine, crosses the room, eyes blazing with the challenge. He shrugs out of his jacket, lets it fall to the floor. He pulls the tie off, strips off his shirt. Only then does he take his gun belt off. He lets the holster fall to the floor. The gun he places on one of the pillows.

"You afraid you need protection from me?" I ask with a playful smile. I don't like guns, especially one within arm's reach of a man I'm fucking. Bullets can't kill me, but they sure as hell can hurt.

I reach out to move the gun. He's faster. He stops my hand, gives it a little shake. "Uh-huh. The gun stays where it is."

I twist free. "You paid for my time. This is my bedroom. I will fuck you anyway you want, but not with a gun on my pillow. It either gets moved, or you both do. Out the door."

His face darkens with quick anger. Then it's over. The cloud clears from his eyes first. Then the corners of his mouth turn up in a grin. "Do you fuck as good as you give orders?"

My hand drifts down his stomach, rubs at the bulge pushing against the fabric of his pants. "Take these off and we'll find out."

He fumbles a little with the buttons, impatience and desire making him clumsy. I push his hands away and free him myself. His member thrusts out at me, hard and ready. I throw him back on the bed, pull off his boots and slide his trousers down over his ankles. He reaches for me, but I've got the gun in my hand and have stepped out of reach to place it across the room on the bureau.

When I turn around, he's watching me with that predator's glare again, wary, suspicious, until I pull my chemise up over my head and stand in front of him as naked as he is.

Suspicion and doubt are swept from his mind. The only thing he feels now is a powerful lust, a hunger. My blood responds to the fire in his eyes. I let him pull me down on top of him, our bodies press together. My breasts are crushed against his chest, his erection between my legs, probing, insistent. He grabs my shoulders and rolls me over. He thrusts himself deep inside me, pounding into me until he comes with a gasp and a moan.

It's over for him. The weight of his body on mine grows heavier as his breathing becomes deep and regular. I let him drift off, used to the ways of men. I am a whore whose value is limited to one thing—the vessel into which men pour their seed. But I am also vampire. I have needs of my own.

I have learned how best to fulfill those needs. When Holliday has slept for some minutes, I begin. I roll him gently off me and start first by calling up my own desire. My fingers probe my sex, finding the spot that brings the release denied me with our first coupling. Then, breathless, eager, I turn my attention to him. I take his sex in my hands, gently, using strokes as light as a butterfly's kiss to call back the hunger. Holliday awakens, startled, to find this woman, this whore fondling him. But his body is already responding. He moans and lets me continue until he is fully aroused. He reaches for me. This time, I have my way.

I straddle him, pinning him beneath me with my thighs. I guide him into me and begin moving, slowly, his sex filling me, pressing against the pleasure point, tension rising until my blood sings with it. He tries once to grab my shoulders, thrust me back under him, but I am vampire. This is my game now.

He gives in, surrendering to my control. His hands grasp my buttocks, his hips grind against mine. He's moaning again, a low, keening sound. His eyes are closed and I bend forward, kiss each eyelid, brush my lips against his. I trace a path with my tongue from the corner of his mouth to his jaw line, find the pulse point just beneath the surface, wait until I feel the first spasms of his release, and bite.

Need consumes us both. He comes with a groan as his body pushes up against mine. I come with a shudder as I taste his blood, roll it around in my mouth, savor the life essence of this man. His blood is not as bitter as I expect. I drink, great breathless droughts of blood that warm and revive me. But I know when to stop. When to relegate the vampire back to the shadow. When to call the human back.

Holliday lies spent once more beneath me. I use my lips to close and heal the puncture marks. This is when I secrete the enzymes that make my host forget. The sex. The feeding.

But I don't want this one to forget. He won't remember my opening his neck. He won't remember my taking his blood. But he will remember the coupling, the pleasure we've given each other. I lay still and quiet beside him.

While I'm cradled against his shoulder, his right hand comes up and caresses the back of my neck. He doesn't fall asleep this time. He gathers me into his arms.

Imagine that.

Holding a whore after sex.

It makes me smile.

I'm sitting at the vanity, still naked, brushing my hair. Holliday watches, leaning against the headboard, a blanket thrown over his hips.

"You are no ordinary whore."

I shrug. "What kind of whore am I?"

He tilts his head, studying me. "I don't know."

He throws off the blanket, comes to stand behind me, takes the brush from my hand. He draws it gently through my hair. When he leans toward me, I feel his sex press into the small of my back.

"Are you ready to go again so soon?"

He lays the brush down, puts his hands on my shoulders, pulls me up. "If you do what you did before, I may never want to leave this room."

He is smiling and for a moment, I see the younger, healthier man he must have been before illness and the fortunes of life claimed him.

A startling thought flashes into my head. He could be that man again. I could make it happen. I could make him forever young and healthy. I could make him vampire.

I feel him watching me. I've never done it before—made another like me. Would he want it?

His hands cup my face. "What are you thinking?"

A rap on the door brings me back to the present with a little jump. I stand back and away from Holliday and snatch up a robe. "Yes?"

"There's someone here says he's looking for Doc Holliday."

Sunny Tom's voice carries through the thick door. His thoughts project even better. *This could be trouble.*

Holliday reaches for his trousers. "Got a name?"

I've crossed to the door, pulled it open. Sunny Tom steps inside. "Says his name is Billy Allen. Says he's gunning for you. Name mean anything?"

A frown pulls at the corners of his mouth. "Yeah. The name means something." He shrugs into his shirt, tucks it into his trousers, straps on the holster. He grabs the gun from the top of the bureau, spins the chamber, slips it into the holster in a single, fluid motion.

"You don't have to go down there. There's a back entrance. Tom could show you and you could be out of town before Allen knows you're gone."

Holliday shakes his head. "No."

The answer sends a spark of irritation burning through me. "Why not? Why risk dying?"

His expression this time is one of amused indulgence. He chucks my chin. "I am dying, lady. Consumption, remember?"

"But what if you didn't have to die?"

What are you doing, Rose? Tom's voice in my head is sharp-edged and heavy with disapproval.

Holliday is at my vanity, smoothing his hair back from his face, straightening the diamond tiepin at the neck of his shirt. "We all have to die, Rose. I'd prefer to do it with my boots on."

He turns toward me and smiles. "How do I look?"

"Good. You look good."

He takes another step closer, close enough to lean down and brush his lips against mine. "Keep that bed warm. I reckon to be back."

And then he's gone, Tom on his heels.

Tom doesn't leave without a parting shot. He pauses at the door, grins back at me. *He must be one hell of a fuck.*

I push the door closed at his back and scramble for my clothes. There are too many of them with too many hooks and too many buttons. I give up, wrap the robe around me again and cinch it with the sash. Barefoot, I run into the hall.

The retort of the gunshot reaches me at the top of the stairs. I race down in time to see Holliday leaning over the end of the bar. In two seconds, I'm at his side.

Billy Allen is on the floor, his right arm bloody. He's yelling and clutching at the arm, his face twisted in pain and fear.

Holliday stands over him, pistol cocked, and takes aim.

"No." I put my hand on his arm, tug. "If you kill him like this, it's cold blooded murder. If you stop now, it's self-defense. You'll have a fighting chance with a jury."

I recognize in Holliday's face a feeling I'm well acquainted with—the blood lust—when adrenaline is hot in your veins and the need for satisfaction swallows up your humanity. But I'm not sure he heard or understood what I said. His heart is pounding with such force, I feel it deep in my own chest.

The crowd in the saloon has grown quiet. The only noise is the sound of sobbing from Billy Allen. Holliday remains poised over him. He glances down at me.

I shake my head. "Don't. Please."

He smiles.

Then he fires.

I jump, gasping.

There's a strangled cry from Billy Allen that continues to grow in volume until as one, all of us take a step forward to look.

The floor is splintered just above Allen's head. He's curled himself into a fetal position, rocking and crying. The air is foul with the smell of his body's waste. He's pissed and shit himself and all around, laughter erupts.

Holliday holsters his gun. "Sorry for the mess," he says.

He looks around at the crowd. "I reckon someone should get Marshal Kelly. And call whoever you have in town who serves as a medical man to tend to Allen here. I'll be at the bar."

He holds out his arm and I take it. "You know you're going to pay for the damage to the floor."

Holliday grins. "You are no ordinary whore. That's a fact."

Sunny Tom is directing the music man back to his playing and the girls back to their hustling. He herds players toward the gaming tables to resume their interrupted poker game. I signal the bartender to give everyone a drink on the house. Soon Billy Allen is nothing more than a mewling distraction to be stepped around until the town's doctor arrives to cart him off.

Holliday and I sip whiskey at the bar.

"What's going to happen?" I ask. It's a stupid question. I know the answer.

Holliday's smile acknowledges that we both do. "I'll be arrested. If I'm lucky, they'll let me out on bail. If not, I'll be in jail until the trial."

"It's self-defense, though, pure and simple. Sunny Tom said Allen was gunning for you. You have a right to protect yourself."

Holliday laughs. "I'll be sure you're called as a defense witness."

"It will be my pleasure."

We lapse into silence. I can't quantify what it is about this man, this stranger, that has touched me. I only know that I want him to stay with me, if not forever, than at least as long as human life allows.

"You better come right back here the minute you're released, y'hear?"

Another rumbling laugh. "You sure like to give orders."

"I do. And I'm used to those orders being followed. Don't make me come after you."

He puts his hand over mine on the bar and squeezes. "I'll do my best."

I lean toward him, resting my head on his shoulder, wondering again if I told him what I was and offered him eternal life what he might say. Would he believe me?

No. Worse, he might think me mad. Better to wait until he comes back. Until I have time to explain the gift I have to offer. What it means to me. What it can mean to him.

My heart is pounding so hard, I'm sure he must hear it. Maybe if I remind him of what we shared upstairs. Give him a hint of what could be. What *will* be when he returns.

I move closer, my lips at his ear.

He bends his head. "Yes, Rose?"

I don't get the chance. Marshal Kelly and two deputies appear at the door to the saloon and Holliday pushes himself away from the bar to meet him. He lets them take his gun and cuff his hands behind his back. He doesn't look my way. Not once. He carries himself straight and tall and with quiet dignity as they lead him away.

Sunny Tom comes to stand beside me at the bar. "Damn girl. Are you crying?"

I swipe at tears and snot with the back of my hand. "Of course not." I look around. "The excitement doesn't seem to have hurt business."

"Nope." He leans his elbows back on the bar and rests a foot on the copper rail. "Think we'll see Holliday again?"

"Of course. I told him he'd better come back the minute he's out of jail."

"And nobody disobeys one of your orders, do they?"

"Not if they're smart. I figure between all the legal wrangling and the trial, he should be walking through that door in six months at the outside."

Sunny Tom shakes his head. "Hope you're right. I'd hate to see you get your heart broke."

"What heart?"

One of the girls calls for Tom and he leaves me with a pat on the arm.

But I know.

Holliday will be acquitted and he'll come back.

He has to.

Turns out I am right and I am wrong.

Doc Holliday is acquitted. A jury agrees that Billy Allen spent the morning he was shot walking up and down Main Street telling everyone that he was out for Holliday's blood. They reasoned it would have been foolish on Holliday's part not to be prepared to counter force with force.

But I am wrong about something else. I am wrong about the most important part. I am wrong that Holliday will come back to me.

He never does.

For some weeks, I follow his story in the newspaper. How during the trial, Holliday's health deteriorated. How when it was over, he headed south for Glenwood Springs, to partake of medicinal waters found there that are said to relieve the suffering of consumptives. How somewhere along the way, he picked up a traveling companion.

At that point, I stop reading the stories. Stop waiting for him to appear. Stop making plans for when he does. It is finally clear that whatever we shared those brief hours six months before meant far more to me than it did to him.

Sunny Tom and I continue to run our saloon. We know it won't be long before we have to move on. The silver veins are petering out and prices are falling. In preparation we begin hoarding more and more of our take.

On November 14, 1887, I come downstairs to find Sunny Tom having breakfast at his usual table, the *Leadville Carbonate Chronicle* spread out in front of him. His hand stills and his eyes grow round as he reads.

I pour myself a cup of coffee and came round to join him. *What's wrong?*

He looks up at me, pity reflected in his expression. It's an emotion quite alien to his usually gruff nature. I raise an eyebrow in surprise.

He turns the paper around so that I see what sparked the reaction.

It is Doc Holliday's obituary.

I thrust it away. *I don't want to know.*

Sunny Tom takes the paper back. "You should at least hear this, " he says aloud. He settles the paper on the table and begins to read:

"There is scarcely one in the country who had acquired a greater notoriety than Doc Holliday, who enjoyed the reputation of being one of the most fearless men on the frontier, and whose devotion to his friends in the climax of the fiercest ordeal was inextinguishable. It was this, more than any other faculty, that secured for him the reverence of a large circle who were prepared on the shortest notice to rally to his relief."

He meets my gaze across the table. "He was a good man. It's all right to grieve."

No. I won't grieve any human. It's pointless. They die. We do not.

I push myself away from the table, turning to flee back upstairs when a man from the stage office appears at the saloon doors.

"Can I help you?" I ask.

He has a small package in his hand. "I'm looking for Rose Sullivan."

"I am she."

He holds the package out to me. "This came for you on the morning stage."

I fish a coin from my pocket and press it into his palm as I accept the package.

Sunny Tom asks from his table, "Sir, would you like a drink?"

I don't wait for the answer, but seat myself at a table in the far corner to examine the package. It's wrapped in plain brown paper, my name and Hyman's Saloon, Leadville, printed in block letters on the top. There is no indication of who it's from.

But something inside me knows. My hands tremble as I tear at the paper, fumble the top off the tiny box inside.

A diamond winks up at me.

Under it, a note. "For Rose. To remember me by. John Holliday."

Leadville

Present Day

A chiming tone from my computer brings me back with a start. I have an instant message coming in from my friends at the museum in New York. They tell me they miss me and ask how I'm doing and when I'm coming back.

We know you won't last in bumfuckville six months, one of them writes. *Rose Sullivan living in a ghost town? Never gonna work.*

My fingers play with the small diamond pendant I've worn around my neck for over a hundred years. Holliday was the first and only man I ever considered offering immortality. If he'd come back after his trial, maybe he'd be seated beside me right now, adding his own words to mine.

My face is wet with tears I haven't shed in as long. I am surprised how the memory of a man I knew only a few hours has power still to touch me. Or is it this place? Was coming back here a mistake?

Deep inside, I know it's not.

My fingers begin to move over the keyboard. Doc Holliday is here with me. I hear his voice, see his face and the words flow.

This will be more than a novel.

This will be the way it could have been. This will be our story.

Author's Note: I've telescoped time and circumstances to fit this story. Doc Holliday spent most of the last years of his life in Leadville, Colorado before dying in Glenwood Springs in 1887. The shooting of Billy Allen, the opening of Tabor Opera House, Hyman's Saloon are all part of the Leadville Holliday would have known during his stay. I've taken the liberty to reorder time so that what actually took place over years, takes place in one.

Holliday always wore a diamond stickpin given him by his mother. When he died, the pin was found in his effects. The diamond was not.

WASTE LAND
Stephen Dedman

As we know, those who hunt vampires do not always meet with success and Stephen Dedman provides a frightening first-person narrative that puts the reader uncomfortably into a very tight place indeed. At least one has the "comfort" of poetry.

Dedman is the author of four novels, a nonfiction book, and more than one hundred and twenty published short stories (some of which are gathered on his two collections). He teaches creative writing at the University of Western Australia and is co-owner of the Fantastic Planet bookshop in Perth. His website is www.stephendedman.com.

THE TRUNK is small, but so am I, and small places have never scared me all that badly. And dark, of course, but darkness is bearable. At least it isn't airtight. I hope. Maybe it only feels as though I can't breathe. Rats, rats I'm scared of, but there's no way a rat could squeeze in. My nerves are bad, but if the darkness gets too bad, there's a light in my watch—not a bright light, but at least it lets me know what time it is. I've set the alarm for seven; the sun should be well and truly up by then, and I'll be safe.

I wish I knew what sort of vampires they all are. You can't trust the movies to get these things right. Russian vampires have purple faces. Mexican vampires have fleshless skulls. Albanian vampires are supposed to wear high-heeled shoes. Bulgarian vampires have one nostril, and they've been eaten inside by some sort of fungus, so they're solid but squishy the whole way through, and they don't cast shadows. German vampires, nosferatu, control rats and so bring the Black Death, as though I don't have enough to worry about already. But they all drink blood, and most of them sleep through the day. Bavarian vampires are supposed to sleep with their thumbs crossed and one eye open, though I've never found any like that.

Hammering a stake through the heart isn't always enough to kill one, and different books have different ideas about what sort of wood you're supposed to use, or whether iron works. Romanians recommend driving iron forks through the heart and eyes, then re-burying the body face downwards—and there's always a body, none of the ones we've killed ever disintegrated into a handful of dust. Decapitation always seems to work, and burning them is good, if you can get a fire hot enough to cremate them. The Bulgarian vampires burn beautifully, like marshmallows, though they smell more like car tires.

The Poles say that if you impale or decapitate a vampire, they scream horribly and blood gushes out until it fills the grave, all of which is true; even the Bulgarians bleed. The Poles also say that if you mix flour with this blood and bake it into bread and eat it, vampires will never persecute you again. We drew lots and three of us tried it, two didn't, as a control, but the myth seems to have been garbled, as myths often are. Vampires weren't able to touch those of us who'd eaten the bread, but Clark was ripped apart by dogs, and someone with a crossbow killed Marie. Of course, that might not have been a vampire, the sun was up and there may be other humans left alive, hunters like us who mistook her for a vampire, or Quislings, Renfields . . . but if there are, they're doing a good job of hiding from us, even during the day. That's really why I'm staying here in Amsterdam, even after a Bulgarian got Jack, the faint hope of finding other humans. Going on alone is . . .

I hear sounds of movement from outside the trunk, and keep my breathing as quiet as possible. I don't know how well vampires hear.

We were in Moscow, eight of us, when it began. Or ended. Four of us made it across Germany; we'd hoped that the NATO bases might have been well enough fortified to hold out, that maybe there'd be an airlift to somewhere safe. It was probably only bloody-mindedness that kept us walking into the sunset (they've blocked most of the roads) after that. With Marie dead and Jack probably turned, maybe I'll stay here. When there were three of us, or even two, one could sleep while the other kept watch, and we kept each other sane by talking about our dissertations, poetry, folklore, things that had mattered to us once. Jack was doing his thesis on Eliot's poems, "The Love Song of J. Alfred Prufrock," "The Waste Land," "Portrait of a Lady," he was fanatical about them and quoted them as though they were a prayer to keep the vampires away, keeping himself sane and driving the rest of us crazy. Now he's out there somewhere, probably looking for me, like the rest of them, it's as though they can smell me, the only fresh blood for miles . . . unless that's how the bread works, making me smell like a vampire, I've never seen any sign of them harming each other, they may be even more civilised than we were in that way, but I don't even know whether they've kept any of their memories, as some of the legends say, or whether they're just smart animals, I've never heard one

Speak to me. Why do you never speak? Speak.

"The Waste Land." Jesus, he's got me doing it now. But it's true, I've never heard them speak. Maybe they don't need to speak to each other, maybe they use telepathy or something to communicate with each other, sounds that living humans can't hear, heat vision, or pheromones, they must have a strong sense of smell. I press the button on my watch. Only nine twenty-one. I should sleep, but I can't. Not since the Bulgarian took Jack; if I'd managed to wake him, we might have both gotten away . . .

Even if they can't feed on me, they can still kill me, which is fair in its way, because we've killed as many of them as we could.

What is that noise? Movement. Something in the room, almost heavy enough to be human. A Bulgarian, maybe; they're light, not having any bones, they don't make much noise when they walk, *oh Jesus, it just bumped against the trunk* . . .

Silence. Maybe it was just a dog—maybe not even one of their dogs. Or another sort of animal. At least it didn't sound like rats. Maybe it was the wind. Maybe there was nothing there at all, nothing; maybe I was falling asleep and beginning to dream but I'm not going to open the lid and look out just in case it is one of them and oh Jesus the trunk just moved, it was lifted off the floor—

I stay quiet. If it opens the trunk, I'll try to get away. I have a cross, but they're not all scared of crosses, either, or garlic, or mirrors, or roses, or anything else we've been able to find. We tried staying in a church once, in Krakow, and they came in. We stayed in a brothel in Hamburg, mirrors everywhere, and they came in. Maybe I could have found a safer place than this junk shop, but I needed food—canned food, stuff that the rats and roaches haven't gotten to yet, and I saw this place opposite a supermarket, saw the trunk in the window, and opened it in case there was a vampire inside.

The trunk lurches; I'm being carried . . . somewhere. I didn't see any canals within walking distance, and the vampires have wrecked anything that could be used as a crematorium. Oh Jesus, what if they bury me alive—I draw a deep breath, slowly, quietly, and try to stay calm, wondering if they can smell fear, like dogs. I try to distract myself by reciting poetry, but all I can think of is bloody Eliot—

I hear laughter, and the trunk is dropped. We haven't gone far, just around a few corners, halfway around the block maybe, or out behind the shop . . . Something says, in Jack's voice but not Jack's voice, if he's become a Bulgarian then his jaw and his teeth and his larynx must be turning to mush:

"Stay with me.

"Speak to me. Why do you never speak? Speak.

"What are you thinking of? What thinking? What?

"I never know what you are thinking. Think."

I'm about to open the lid, but I hear scurrying, tiny claws, a faint sound of chewing . . .

I think we are in rat's alley, where the dead men lost their bones.

A Gentleman of the Old School
Chelsea Quinn Yarbro

Chelsea Quinn Yarbro's Count Saint-Germain was the first truly "good guy" romantic vampire. The books and stories of the Saint-Germain Cycle combine historical fiction, romance, and horror and feature the heroic vampire first introduced in Hôtel Transylvania (1978) *as Le Comte de Saint-Germain. In that first novel, the character—cultured, well-traveled, articulate, elegant, and mysterious—appears in the court of France's King Louis XV. Since then, Yarbro has presented—in a non-chronological manner and with name variations suitable to language, era, locale, and circumstance—the Count's life and undeath from 2119 BC and (as the story included here shows) into the twenty-first century. (Roger, the houseman in "A Gentleman of the Old School," became the vampire's right-hand ghoul in Rome in AD 71.) An Embarrassment of Riches has just been published;* Commedia della Morte *will be the twenty-third novel in the series. (With two short story collections, that makes them numbers twenty-four and twenty-five, respectively, in the Chronicles as a whole.)*

Chelsea Quinn Yarbro is the first woman to be named a Living Legend by the International Horror Guild (2006). She was honored in 2009 with a Bram Stoker Lifetime Achievement Award by the Horror Writers Association. Yarbro was named as Grand Master of the World Horror Convention in 2003. She is the recipient of the Fine Foundation Award for Literary Achievement (1993) and (along with Fred Saberhagen) was awarded the Knightly Order of the Brasov Citadel by the Transylvanian Society of Dracula in 1997. She has been nominated for the Edgar, World Fantasy, and Bram Stoker Awards and was the first female president of the Horror Writers Association. The author of scores of novels in many genres, her manuscripts are being archived at Bowling Green University.

"BUT SURELY the Count is willing to talk to the press? He's been very generous, and I would have thought he'd want to make sure people know about it." The reporter was a crisply attractive woman in her mid-twenties, bristling with high fashion and ambition; she was hot on the scent of a story. She lingered in the door of the somewhat secluded house in an elegant section of Vancouver, a tape recorder in one hand, a small digital camera in the other. "And there is the problem of the murder, isn't there? The VPMNC audience wants to know."

The houseman—a lean, middle-aged man with sandy hair and faded-blue eyes, roughly the same height as the reporter: about five-foot seven—remained unfailingly polite. "I am sorry, but my employer has a pronounced dislike of all public attention, even if the intention is benign." He nodded to the young woman once. "I am sure there are many on the hospital board who will be delighted to give you all the information you seek. As to the murder, you should speak to the police—they will know about it."

"Everyone's talked to them, and there's nothing new to get out of them," the reporter complained. "Everyone's looking for a new angle on the case, and the Center was a good place to start. That led me to the Count, and I only found out about the Count through the Donations Administrator's secretary, and that was over a very expensive lunch." She frowned. "I was told that the Count only visited the facilities twice: shortly after construction began and just before it was opened: The Vancouver Center for the Diagnosis and Treatment of Blood Disorders. Ms. Saunders said the Count's donation covered more than seventy percent of the cost of building and equipping the facility, and that he provides an annual grant for on-going research. That's got to be a lot of money. I was wondering if the Count would care to confirm the amount? Or discuss the body found on the roof of the Center two days ago?"

"Neither is the sort of matter my employer likes to talk about. He is not inclined to have his fortune bruited about, and the investigation of crime is not his area of expertise. He leaves such things to the police and their investigators." The houseman stepped back, preparing to close the door.

"Then he's talked to them?" the reporter pursued.

"A crime scene technician named Fisk has asked for various samples from the Count, and he has provided them." The houseman started to swing the door shut.

"Fisk—the new tech?"

"That was his name. I have no idea if he is new or old to his position. If you will excuse me—" There was less than three inches of opening left.

"I'll just return, tonight or tomorrow, and I may have some of my colleagues with me: I am not the only one with questions." This last was a bluff: she was relishing the chance for an exclusive and was not about to give up her advantage to any competition.

"You will receive the same answer whenever you call, Ms. . . . Is it Barradis? If you want useful information, I would consult the police, Ms. Barradis." The houseman lost none of his civility, but he made it clear that he would not change his mind.

"Barendis," she corrected. "Solange Barendis."

"Barendis," the houseman repeated, and firmly closed the door, setting the door-crossing bolt into its locked position before withdrawing from the large entry-hall, bound for the parlor on the west side of the house that gave out on a deck that was added to the house some fifty years before. It had recently been enlarged to make the most of the glorious view afforded down the hill, colored now with the approaching fires of sunset.

The house had been built in 1924 in the Arts and Crafts style, with cedar wainscoting in most of the rooms, and stained glass in the upper panes of many of the windows, all in all, a glorious example of the style, for although it did not appear to be large from the outside, it had three stories, and thirteen rooms, all of generous proportions. The parlor, with its extensive bow windowand the deck beyond provided the appearance of an extension of the room through two wide French doors into the outside, making it one of Roger's favorite places in all the house. Here he lingered until a beautiful Victorian clock chimed five; then he started toward the stairs that led to the upper floors, to the room on the south side of the second floor, a good-sized chamber that once held a pool table but was now devoted to books. He went along to the library and tapped on the door, opening it as soon as the occupant of the room called out, "Do come in, Roger."

Roger opened the door and paused on the threshold, watching his employer, who was dressed in black woolen slacks and black cashmere turtleneck, up a rolling ladder where he busied himself shelving books at the tops of the cases. "The reporter was back." The French he spoke was a in a dialect that had not been heard for more than two centuries.

"Ms. Barendis?" the Count asked. "I'm not surprised to hear it. I'm a little puzzled that she hasn't brought more press with her, considering."

"She has threatened to do so. She said she was asking about the Center, but it—"

The Count sighed. "She had another topic in mind, I suspect."

"You mean the body they found?" Roger knew what the response would be.

"That, and her reporter's inclination to uncover information that appears to be hidden."

"Such as the size of your donation to the Blood Center; a legitimate story as well as a workable excuse to talk to you to find out about the murder victim," said Roger, a bit disgusted. "She asked about the money as well as about the body."

"I doubt she will pursue the money: it isn't scandalous enough. The murder is more intriguing than money, since it appears to be one of a series," said the Count dryly. "Even the Canadians are fascinated by human predators, it would seem."

"And this young woman is stoking the furnace," said Roger.

"All the more reason for her to find more combustible fuel to consume— money hasn't the engrossing power of serial murders, especially such messy ones as this man commits—he is seeking as much gore as he can create," said the Count. "The murder is scary and exciting—large donations only spur a moment of greed, which is insufficient to hold the audience's attention."

"Whatever the public may find interesting, this reporter is proving as persistent as a burr." Roger came a few steps into the room and flipped on the light-switch, banishing the thickening shadows with the gentle glow of wall-sconces. "She says she'll be back tomorrow."

"I would not doubt it," said the Count, coming down the ladder. "So long as she confines her pursuit to the daytime, she will be nothing more than inconvenient. We have dealt with far worse than she." As he said the last, he put his foot on the floor.

"She may expand her inquiries," said Roger, sitting on an upholstered rosewood bench and giving his attention to the end table beside it; he picked up a small ivory carving of Ganesh riding his Rat and moved it to a less vulnerable place on the end table. "I recommended she speak to the police."

"If they lead her away from me, so much the better," said the Count, sitting down in a leather recliner. "You know, when we first came here in—was it '38?— well, after we left California, near the start of the war—I didn't appreciate what a handy place this would be, or how pleasant. Who could have foreseen the expansion of the Pacific Rim, especially then, as the war was getting under way? This has been a much better investment than the house in Winnipeg." He reached over and turned on a floor lamp with a frosted tulip motif, banishing the last of the gloom; the shining paneling, along with the array of spines, gave the place a cozy elegance.

"Winter is easier here than in Winnipeg," Roger observed.

"You have the right of it," said the Count.

Roger brushed his hand over the embossed leather cover of a book printed in Amsterdam almost five hundred years before. "Do you think you will want to remain here much longer?"

"Perhaps year or two, until the Center Is fully established. It will depend somewhat on the state of the world then; I am not in any particular hurry to return to my homeland, not as things are going now. The government has already seized half the money I left for the university I endowed on the pretext of using it for cultural projects: I would just as soon not provide them more occasions for another raid." He shoved the recliner back, sighing luxuriously as he did so. "These are wonderful inventions."

"So they are," Roger agreed, knowing it was prudent not to press the Count about his plans "And it is not difficult to conceal your native earth inside them."

"Another advantage," said the Count, and closed his eyes.

"A fifth body," Solange exclaimed as she stared at her computer screen some twelve days after her second fruitless visit to the Count's house. "Near the university, this time." She shoved back from her workstation and stood so she could see over the top of her cubical. "Hey, Baxter! You seen this?"

The night city editor came over to her, his silk regimental tie loosened and his well-cut hair slightly mussed. "Seen what?"

She pointed to the computer screen. "Another one with a cut throat, blood everywhere, and mutilations. Fair-haired, cut short, above average height, on the plumpish side, between twenty-five and thirty-five years of age—a cookie-cutter victim for this guy." She stamped her foot. "And Hudderston isn't doing anything! Crime desk—yeah, right!"

"How do you mean?" Baxter asked. "I have his column on the daily report from the police—they say they've doubled patrols, and the crimes are getting top priority, the crime scene tech is preparing a new report."

"Fisk also says the forensics are inconclusive, even though there are pools of blood around the victims, the same thing you can get off the Internet, or on the hourly news spots," said Solange. "You saw the report on the confusing DNA results—animal blood mixed with human and both contaminated with chemical additives. Any identification they may make from the analysis of the blood, even though it's accurate, won't hold up under rigorous cross examination."

"But five women with cut throats, multiple stab wounds in the upper bodies, and perforated uteruses! The public won't stand for much more of this, and arrest—let alone a trial—is a long way off." Baxter sighed. "McKenna has the story on days; if you want to take it on for nights, I won't stop you. I'll clear it with Sung." Louie Sung worked the night crime desk, and was known to be territorial about his fiefdom.

Solange tried to contain her excitement. "Sung could say no."

"Not to me," Baxter told her.

"Okay, then. You clear it." Eyes glistening with excitement, Solange picked up her recorder, her camera, and her tote, then reached for her coat. "I'm on it, boss," she vowed, and tapped in her code to block access to her terminal. "I'll call in before one, and I'll report before six."

"Sounds good," said Baxter, and stood aside as Solange swept out of the city room of the Vancouver Print and Media News Corporation, bound for the parking lot and her hybrid hatchback.

At police headquarters, Solange avoided the press office and the front desk where the usual assortment of denizens of the night were gathered with arresting officers; she made straight for the squad room and the desk of Neal Conroy, who shook his head as soon as he caught sight of her. "Barendis, get out of here," he said cordially. "You know I can't talk to you." He was slightly stooped, slightly scruffy: pushing forty, and forty was pushing back.

"Sure you can: here or at your house, Uncle-in-law—you know Aunt Melanie won't keep me out. If you don't tell me what I want to know, she will. And don't tell me you don't talk to her about your cases, because you do," she said, sitting down in the old, straight-backed chair that was intended for visitors and victims of crimes. "The murders. What's happening? And why is the DNA inconclusive? It is identifiable or it isn't."

"You're too nosy for your own good, Barendis," said Conroy.

"That's how I earn my living," she countered, undeterred by the frown he offered.

"Well, use a little good sense for once in your life and keep clear of this one. For your own protection. Melanie would agree with me, if you bother to ask her," Conroy advised her seriously. "This murderer targets women alone, in their late-twenties to early-thirties, cuts their throats and then chops at the bodies, and adds cows' blood to mess up the crime scene. You know the basics already."

"Chops—with a knife?" Solange asked, pulling out her pen and notebook, saying nothing about her recorder in her tote's outer pocket, already in the *on* position.

"Stop it, Barendis," said Conroy, sounding tired. "I hate it when you fish."

She shook her head, undeterred. "Not a knife, but it cuts throats? For all five women?"

"What can I say—the guy likes blood, lots and lots of it," Conroy told her, deliberately harsh. "Don't put that in your story."

Eyes sparkling, Solange shrugged. "I can't promise anything, but I'll try not to get you into trouble."

"It's not getting *you* into trouble that concerns me," Conroy riposted. "I mean it, Solange. Don't try to make your mark on this one—it won't do you any good, and you could become a target."

"Not a knife, but something that slices, that's for sure," said Solange, paying no attention to Conroy's last statement. "A dagger—I do know the difference between a knife and a dagger—or a poignard . . . no."

Conroy took a long, slow breath. "If you will give me your word you won't go after Melanie about any of this, I'll tell you what the medical examiner thinks made the wounds, but you have to keep this out of your story, or you compromise the whole investigation."

Solange sat upright in the chair, and managed to say, "I promise," all the while staring at Conroy.

"It's some kind of curved sword—a saber, a scimitar, a katana—or something like a Medieval battle-hammer, with a long, pointed claw at the back of the head—we can't say for sure. There's too much damage." He had lowered his voice and now was more pale than he had been.

"That's really . . . " She stopped before she said something she would regret.

"Appalling," said Conroy.

"God, what grisly stuff," said Solange. "I wish I could use it."

"You try and I'll have your press-badge pulled until the perpetrator is caught."

"You know you won't do that. Aunt Melanie would never permit it." She showed him a smug smile.

Conroy sat back. "You're probably right, but that doesn't change anything. Let Fisk and the M.E. do their jobs, and keep your two cents out of it. You can screw this investigation royally if you don't play by the rules, and that would mean more people getting killed."

"You mean more *women* getting killed," Solange corrected as she got out of the uncomfortable chair. "I'll go along for now, but you had better give me a first call on the story when it breaks."

"Certainly," said Conroy. "You know I'll do that."

"Yes. Or Aunt Melanie won't—"

"—let me hear the end of it," he finished for her.

The restaurant was elegant, the lights low and golden instead of brilliant and white, the upholstery heavy tapestry to match the draperies, the silverware was sterling, the napery linen, the china Spode, the glassware Reidel. Solange, in her second-best cocktail dress—a designer-label, bias-cut, cobalt-blue, bat-sleeved sheath—was trying to conceal how impressed she was while reading from the six-page menu. Finally she looked up at her host and asked, "Why did you change your mind, Count?"

"About the interview?" he countered, his demeanor urbane and genial; he was in a tailor-made black silk suit, a very white silk shirt, a burgundy-red damask tie, tie-tack and cufflinks in white-gold with discreet black sapphires for ornamentation.

"Yes," she said, glancing at the approaching waiter. "What are you having?"

"The pleasure of your company, but do not let that deter you in ordering anything you want." He waited for her to ask something more, and when she did not, he went on, "I fear I have a number of . . . allergies, I suppose you could call them. I must constrain my dining, and so, to avoid any unpleasantness, I take my nourishment in private. I am used to having others eat when I do not." He signaled the waiter to take down her order. "And if you have a wine list I would like to see it."

Solange's eyes lit up. "Then you *drink*—" she began.

"The wine will be for you," he said, adding, "I do not drink wine."

She laughed aloud. "You know who says that, don't you?"

With a swift, ironic smile, he answered, "Vampires."

Her laughter increased, and she had to choke back her amusement in order to tell the waiter, "I'd like the cream of wild mushroom soup to start, then the broiled scallops in terrine; for an entrée, the duck with cherries and pearl onions in port, next the endive salad, and I'll think about dessert when I've finished dinner."

"Very good, ma'am," said the waiter. "I will bring the wine list, Count."

"Thank you, Franco."

"So they know you here," said Solange, her curiosity engaged again.

"I have a minor investment in this restaurant, and the hotel across the court-yard." He held out his hand for the wine list as the waiter approached, bringing it and a basket of small fresh-baked loaves of bread and a ramekin of sweet butter.

"You are a man of surprises, Count," said Solange, idly wondering if his investments might be a story worth pursuing at another time.

"Am I," he said, and opened the wine-list, settling on a Cotes Sauvage. "It may not go well with the scallops, but it will compliment the soup and the duck."

"For a man who doesn't drink wine, you have a discriminating palette."

He turned his dark eyes on her. "I hope so, Ms. Barendis."

To her astonishment, she felt herself blushing, and she tried to stop the color rising in her face. "I . . . Well, thank you for ordering such an unusual wine."

This sounded lame, even to her own ears, so she made another attempt. "I'm very flattered that you're willing to talk to me." That was a little better.

"You're a very persistent young woman, Ms. Barendis; I decided we might as well arrange a discussion, and if we are to discuss difficult questions, we may also be comfortable."

"I wish all my subjects were so reasonable," said Solange archly. She broke one of the small loaves of bread in half and set it down on the bread plate. "It smells wonderful, doesn't it?"

"Yes, it does," he said, rather distantly.

She paused in the act of cutting butter. "Will my eating bother you, considering we will be talking about murder during the meal?"

"No; it is not my appetite that could be compromised," he said wryly, and went on, "I realize you are on assignment tonight."

"Yes," she said, as if she had forgotten it. "This is an assignment, and an important one."

"That is why I agreed to the meeting," he said.

"Then I'll thank you for the very civilized way you have of conducting it, even to this public setting, so my reputation wouldn't be damaged. As if gossip can damage a reporter." She took a bite of the bread, feeling somewhat embarrassed for being hungry.

"It may be an unnecessary precaution," he said, "but you are not the only one who could be endangered by the appearance of collusive arrangements."

Her smile was at once worldly-wise and relieved. "You mean that you don't want it said that you are influencing or being influenced by me—it's not worry about people speculating what our relationship might be."

Before he could speak, the waiter brought her soup, promising to return at once with the wine; for the moment all aspects of her story were set aside in favor of the meal.

Mid-way through the duck, Solange was able to return to the matter that had brought them there; she began to ask the Count questions about the bodies and their ties—if any—to the Blood Center. "Some so-called experts have speculated that the man is close to the investigation, and that is making the police nervous. My aunt's husband is a cop, and he said he feels as if he's under suspicion."

"Do you find your aunt's husband reliable?" the Count inquired. "Some policemen are more so than others."

"Conroy is a model of rectitude," said Solange, and decided the wine was going to her head—she would rarely use the word *rectitude*, especially to describe

Neal Conroy; she did her best to soften her meaning. "Dependable, honorable, hard-working, responsible."

"Commendable qualities in any man," the Count approved.

"Yes. He let me know he has questions about the state of the investigation, including similar ones to the reservations expressed by the expert. He's a bit worried about the kind of questions being raised in the press, as well. He wants everything in the case to be above doubt." She was delighted with the meal, in part because it allowed her to spar with the Count while she had this excellent repast.

"Do you recall which expert said the things that bother your aunt's husband— about the killer being close to the investigation?" the Count asked, unperturbed. He studied her face. "Did your aunt's husband have any opinions on the current uncertainty?"

She pondered for several seconds. "Not about the investigation, not directly, no. The expert isn't a cop: I think it was Fisk; the crime scene tech: he's been talking to the media recently."

"No doubt he has," said the Count, a suggestion of a frown forming between his brows.

Now Solange was alert. "What do you mean?" She had the uneasy suspicion that the Count, not she, was guiding their conversation, and so she prepared a number of lines of inquiry to pursue.

The Count shrugged. "Unlike Fisk, I am no expert, but I find it strange that a man who is so responsible for the quality and preservation of the evidence in this case should call so much of it into question. He has an obligation to keep an open mind, but from what I have read, Fisk is doing more than that." He took the bottle of wine and poured her a third glass.

Much struck, Solange gave this her consideration. "He is only living up to his function, and gathering evidence impartially—evidence is just that: evidence. It has no opinions, only existence."

"That may be, but Doctor Fisk certainly has opinions," said the Count. "He impugns his own work at almost every turn. Had an arrest been made, I would have thought Fisk was a member of the defense,"

To give herself a little time to think, Solange took a long sip of the wine, then remarked, "When you put it that way, I see what you mean."

"Is there anything in his past to account for his behavior? Did he give testimony in a trial that was found to be—"

"That could be it!" Solange exclaimed. "He used to work in Moose Jaw, or so he says. I'll check with the cops there."

The Count held up his hand. "I can understand wanting not to appear too much a part of the prosecution instead of an investigator, but this man Fisk has—"

"I know," she interrupted. "Thanks for the observation. You have a point. I'll look into it." Drinking more wine, she had to resist the urge to call Baxter at once; instead she asked one of her mental lists of queries, "Do you think the murder has taken away any of the community benefits the Blood Center promises?"

"For some, no doubt it has," said the Count. "But once the murders are solved and the guilty party brought to book, then the Center will quickly show its value."

"Aren't you being a bit too optimistic?" She cut a little more duck. "This is very good. I'm sorry you can't enjoy it."

"That's kind of you," said the Count. "No, I don't think my optimism is unrealistic. But time will tell, and time is often the test in these cases."

"Then you're thinking in the long run?" Solange asked.

"For a man in my position, it is the only perspective that makes sense," he told her as she went on with her dinner.

Applause burst out in the city room as Solange sauntered in, twenty-six days after her first dinner with the Count. She went to her cubicle, but stood outside it to curtsy three times, smiling proudly. "Thank you, thank you. You're all too kind."

Baxter, who had hung back, now came up to her. "Don't be modest, Barendis," he advised. "Conroy says you were the linchpin in their investigation."

"I'm not being modest," she said. "I know how much luck had to do with catching the guy."

"You put them on the scent, and you kept at the story," Sung said from his office doorway. "You could have followed the rest, hassling the cops for not getting the guy, but you went after Fisk, asking about his reluctance to do anything to break the case. The thing about saying animal blood and human blood could not be separated enough for a valid DNA profile. Very good."

"Thanks," she repeated. "It seemed a good place to begin."

"Did you think it was Fisk?' Hill, who covered building and expansion, made his question sharp.

"I didn't know who it was," said Solange, delighted she had accomplished so much. "I just thought it was odd that Fisk kept running down the evidence he himself was collecting. A crime scene tech needs to be skeptical, but what Fisk was doing was well beyond skepticism and leaning toward subversion."

"Well, you helped bring him to justice, and you're a credit to the paper,"

Baxter approved, then went on, "Everyone back to work. You don't want to have to chase the paper tonight."

The celebratory mood vanished at once, and the night staff of the Vancouver Print and Media News Corporation returned to their tasks.

"Management is preparing a bonus for you, Solange," said Baxter, lingering in the opening of her cubicle.

"Thanks," she said.

After a short silence, Baxter said, "So what are you looking at now?"

"I got a lead on a smuggling operation. Not drugs, but high-quality antiques," she told him, unfamiliar hesitation in her response.

"What about the Count—the exile?" Baxter prompted. "The one with so much money in the Blood Center."

Her smile was slow and had a sensuality to it that Baxter had never seen before. "He's a gentleman of the old school—no real story there, except that he still exists."

Baxter pounced on her remark. "Something going on there that I should know about?"

She shook her head. "Only dreams."

"*Those* kind of dreams?" Baxter asked her.

"None of your business, boss," said Solange.

Baxter chuckled. "So long as it doesn't get in the way of your work, dream away."

She contemplated his profile. "It was something the Count said that got me thinking about the smuggling scheme."

"He fed you information?" Baxter seemed surprised.

"No; not even enough to qualify as an unnamed source—he mentioned something a week ago, about trouble his shipping business was having. I decided to ask around, to see if his problems were isolated."

"And I gather they're not," said Baxter and slapped the side of her cubicle. "Well, keep me up-to-date on your project." He started away from her cubicle.

"You can depend on me, boss," she responded, and began to work on her new story, all the while anticipating the late-night supper she would have with the Count, three hours from now. Grinning inwardly, she promised herself she would have particularly delicious dreams tonight, as a reward for her tenacity, and the result of her rendezvous with the Count.

No Matter Where You Go
Tanya Huff

Tanya Huff lives in rural Ontario, Canada with her partner Fiona Patton and, as of last count, nine cats. Her twenty-six novels and sixty-eight short stories include horror, heroic fantasy, urban fantasy, comedy, and space opera. She's written four essays for Ben Bella's pop culture collections. Her Blood series was turned into the twenty-two-episode Blood Ties *(which premiered on Lifetime in March 2007) and writing episode nine allowed her to finally use her degree in Radio & Television Arts. Her latest novel is* The Truth Of Valor. *A sequel to* The Enchantment Emporium *is also planned. When not writing, she practices her guitar and spends too much time online.*

Huff's Blood books (five novels and a collection of short stories) mixed vampires, mystery, suspense, and romance. Blood Price *(1991) introduced Vicki Nelson, a homicide detective forced to retire when her eyesight fails due to Retinitis Pigmentosa. Vicki teams up with Henry Fitzroy—a 450-year-old vampire and bastard son of Henry VIII who now writes historical romances—and becomes a private investigator. The other man in her life is Detective-Sergeant Mike Cellucci. The series is set in Toronto. The three books of her Smoke and Shadows were a follow-up to the Blood books. Tony Foster, one of Fitzroy's ex-loves, is the series protagonist.*

We catch up with Vicky, Mike, and Tony here in "No Matter Where You Go," which was published just last year.

"I OVERHEARD a couple of uniforms talking today."

Her head pillowed on Mike's shoulder, palm of her right hand resting over his heart, Vicki made a non-committal *hmm*.

"There's been some vandalism in Mount Pleasant Cemetery the last couple of nights."

She tapped her fingers on sweat-damp skin to the rhythm of the rain against the window, wrapping it around the steady bass of his heartbeat. "You don't say."

Mike closed his hand around hers, stopping the movement. "Someone dug a small firepit on a grave and cremated a mouse. The officers responding found wax residue on the gravestone, chalk marks on the grass, and evidence of at least four people."

"Uh huh." Vicki rose up on her left elbow so that she could see Mike's expression. He seemed to be completely serious. Although the pale spill of streetlight around the edges of the blind provided insufficient illumination for him to see her in turn, his eyes were locked on her face, waiting for her to draw her own conclusions.

"You think some idiot's trying to call up a demon."

"I think it's possible."

"And you think I should . . . ?"

He shrugged, a minimum movement of one shoulder. "I think *we* should check it out."

"We?"

His fingers tightened, thumb moving down to stroke the scar on her wrist. "I don't want you there alone."

She had a matching scar on the other wrist, a pair of thin white lines against pale skin, a reminder written in flesh of a demon nearly unleashed on the city by her blood. But that had been years ago, when Vicki Nelson, ex-police detective, not particularly successful private investigator, had only just discovered that creatures out of nightmare were real.

"Things have changed." Turning her hand in his, she stroked in turn the puncture wound on his wrist, already healing even though it had been less than an hour since she'd fed. "I'm pretty sure vampire trumps wannabe sorcerer." When he didn't answer, merely continued to look up at her, brown eyes serious, she sighed. "Fine. A vampire and an exceedingly macho police detective *definitely* trumps wannabe sorcerer. Worst case scenario, it won't be much of a demon if all they're sacrificing is a mouse. We'll check it out tomorrow night."

Dark brows rose. "Why tomorrow? It's barely midnight."

"And it's pouring rain. They won't be able to keep their fire lit."

"So tonight . . . "

Vicki grinned, tugged her hand free, and moved it lower on his body. "Well, if you're so set on not sleeping, I'm sure we'll think of something to do."

Mike Celluci had spent most of his career in Violent Crimes. One night, back before the change, when alcohol had still been able to breach the barriers Vicki kept around her more philosophical side, she'd called the men and women who worked homicide the last advocates of the dead—bringing justice if not peace.

Over the last few years Mike had learned that, on occasion, the dead were quite capable of advocating for themselves. That knowledge had added a whole new dimension to walking in graveyards at night.

By day, Mount Pleasant Cemetery was a green oasis in the center of Toronto, the dead sharing their real estate with a steady stream of people looking for a respite from the press of the city. At night, when shadows pooled in the hollows and under the trees and clustered around the hundreds of headstones, the dead seemed less willing to share.

"Isn't this romantic." Vicki tucked her hand in the crock of Mike's elbow and leaned toward him with exaggerated enthusiasm. "You, me, midnight, a grave-yard. Too bad we don't have a picnic." She grinned up at him, fingers tightening over his pulse. "Oh, wait . . . "

Mike snorted and shook his head but he understood her mood. It had been too long since they'd worked a case together. And okay, a cremated mouse and some wax residue wasn't exactly a case but it was more than they'd had for a while.

He tugged her off the path, following the landmarks from the original police report. "It was this way."

As they moved further from the lines of asphalt and the circles of light that barely touched the grass, Vicki took the lead.

"Do you know where you're going?" he asked. With no moonlight, no star-light, and, more importantly, his flashlight off so as not to give away their posi-tion, he stayed close.

"I can smell the wet ash from their fire. The candle wax." She frowned. "Smells like gardenia."

And then she froze.

Mike froze with her. "Vicki?"

"Burning blood. This way."

He knew she was holding back so he could match her pace, his hand wrapped around her elbow as he ran full out, trusting her to steer him around any obstacle. They headed into the older part of the cemetery where ornate mausoleums housed the elite of the early 1900's. Clutching at her outstretched arm as she suddenly stopped, he nearly fell but found his balance at the last minute. They were close enough together, he could see her turning in place, head cocked.

"There." A mausoleum set off a little from the rest. "I hear four heartbeats."

Not for the first time, he wished she could return to the force. They had a canine unit, they had mounted unit, they had a mountain bike unit for Christ's sake—why not a bloodsucking undead unit? Her abilities were wasted within the narrow focus of her PI's license.

He could see a flicker of light through the grill in the mausoleum's door as they moved closer.

Teenagers. Peering carefully through the ornate ironwork, Mike could see four—three watching the fourth as she chanted over the smoking contents of a stainless steel mixing bowl set between the four white candles burning on the marble crypt in the center of the mausoleum. A triple circle about six feet in diameter had been drawn in what looked like sidewalk chalk on the back wall—a blue ring, then a red ring, then a white ring. In the center of the innermost circle was a complex scrawl of loops and angles.

Mike knew better than to equate youth with an absence of threat but nothing about the kids looked dangerous. Two of them—a thin white female and a tall East Indian male—were all but bouncing out of their black hightops. One of them—white male, shortest of the four—stood with his shoulders hunched and hands shoved into his hoodie's pockets, looking a little scared. The body language of the girl doing the chanting suggested she wasn't going to accept failure as an option.

He glanced down at Vicki and mouthed, "Demon?"

She shrugged and lifted her head to murmur, "I have no idea," against his ear.

Whatever it was they were doing, they hadn't done it yet. Teenagers, he could handle. Demons . . .

He could, but he'd rather not.

Pushing his coat back to expose the badge on his belt, he pushed open the door. "Tell me," he snapped in his best voice-of-authority, "that you're not raising the dead because that never turns out well."

The scared boy made a sound Mike was pretty sure he'd deny later. The other two froze in place, mouths open. The chanting girl stopped chanting and turned—white female, pierced eyebrow, pierced lower lip. She had what looked like a silver fish knife in one hand an impressive scowl for someone her age. This close, he doubted any of them were over fifteen.

"Ren!" Scared boy took a step toward her. "It's the cops."

"I can see that." She shoved a fall of black and white striped hair back off her face. "It doesn't matter. It's done!"

"What's done?" Vicki asked.

Mike hadn't seen Vicki move so he was damned sure Ren hadn't. In all fairness, he had to admire her nerve—if he hadn't been watching her, he wouldn't have seen the flinch as she turned to find Vicki smiling at her from about ten centimeters away.

"The ritual."

"I don't see a demon." Vicki peered into the bowl. "Unless it's a very small demon. Another mouse," she added, glancing over at Mike.

"Demons." The bouncing boy rolled his eyes. "As if."

"That's so last millennium," the girl beside him snorted.

Ren's gaze skittered off Vicki's face but, with the Hunter so close to the surface, Mike gave her points for the attempt. "If you must know," she said as pride won out over a preference to keep the adults in the dark, "I've opened a portal."

"A portal?" Mike repeated, glancing around the mausoleum.

"Might be a very small portal," Vicki offered.

All four teenagers looked over at the circles chalked on the rear wall.

"It takes time!" Ren said defensively. She set the knife down forcefully enough that the metal rang against the stone then moved around the crypt so that nothing stood between her and the wall.

Given that Vicki made no move to stop her, Mike figured the odds of the portal opening were small.

"Come on." Ren beckoned to the others. "We need to be ready."

"But Ren, they're cops!" the scared boy protested, hanging back as the other two joined her.

"Their laws have no relevance here."

Mike sighed. The last things he wanted to do was spend the night arguing with teenagers. "Okay, guys, I get that you're bored and looking for some excitement but at the very least this is trespassing so let's just pack things up, promise to take up hobbies that don't involve graveyards, and we'll see you get home."

Ren ignored him. Spearing the scared boy with an imperious gaze, she snapped, "Cameron!"

The scared boy ran to join the others just as the center of the chalked circle flared white then black then cleared to show a dark sky filled with stars too orange to be familiar. Mike thought he saw the dark silhouettes of buildings and was certain he could smell rotting meat.

"We are so out of here," Ren sneered as she stepped back through the circle pulling Cameron with her. An instant later, Vicki stood holding the black and silver hoodie of the unnamed girl as the other two followed.

Almost immediately, someone began to scream.

Cameron.

The circle started to close. The first fifteen centimeters in from the white chalk line already returned to grubby stone and flaking mortar.

Mike knew what Vicki was going to do before she did it. As he charged around the crypt—to stop her, to join her, he had no idea—she shot him a look that said half a dozen things he didn't want to consider too closely and dove through a hole no more than a meter across. Then half a meter. He couldn't follow.

All four kids were screaming now.

Vicki was stronger, faster, and damned hard to kill but in another world she might be no more of a threat than Cameron was.

Barely a handspan of portal remained. Mike snapped his extra clip off his belt, threw it and his weapon as hard as he could into the dark, then stood staring at a blank stone wall.

The silence was so complete he could hear the candles flickering on the crypt behind him.

Vicki had no idea what the hell she was facing. It looked a bit like The Swamp Thing, only a phosphorescing gray with three large yellowing fangs about ten centimeters long—two on the top, one on the bottom across a wobbling lip from a jagged stub. It was big—three, three and a half meters high although it was hard to tell for certain given that it rested its weight on the knuckles of one clawed hand as it stuffed bits of Cameron into its mouth. The other three teenagers crouched among the rubble at the base of a crumbling wall and screamed.

Moonlight and starlight reflected off the pale stone of the ruins, denying them the merciful buffer of full darkness. It was light enough, they'd seen their friend die.

The scent of Cameron's blood pulled the Hunger up and, although Vicki drew her lips back off her teeth and shifted her weight onto the balls of her feet, she held her position. She could do nothing for Cameron.

If the creature was willing to move on, she'd let it.

It wasn't.

The kids realized that the same time she did.

On the bright side, as it lurched toward them, ramped up terror stopped the screaming.

It roared and swatted at her as she raced up the closest pile of rubble, too slow to connect. When the rubble ended, she launched herself onto its shoulders, wrapping both hands around its head.

Her fingers sank deep into rubbery flesh but got a grip on the bone beneath as she twisted. Back home, bipedal meant a spine and a spinal column but she wasn't in Kansas anymore. Nothing cracked.

It wrapped a hand around her leg.

Snarling, she wrapped her hand in turn around one of the upper fangs, snapping it off at the base and jabbing it deep into the creature's neck as it yanked her off its shoulders. The flesh parted like tofu wrapped in rubber and it essentially cut its own throat.

Just before she hit the ground, Vicki realized that the orange fluid spilling from the gash was not what she knew as blood.

One problem at a time! She rolled with the impact and bounced up onto her feet ready for round two.

Rising up to its full height, throat gaping, it staggered back a step. Cameron's leg fell from lax fingers. It wobbled in place for a moment, then it collapsed with an entirely unsatisfactory squelch.

Under normal circumstances, Vicki'd make sure it was dead but nothing about this even approached normal so she turned instead to check on the kids. Heads down, huddled close and weeping, all three still cowered at the base of the wall. Stepping toward them, she kicked something that skittered across the uneven pavement.

The 19 round magazine for a Glock 17.

Mike's scent clung to it.

A heartbeat later she had the Glock in her hand. He hadn't been able to follow her through the contracting portal so he'd . . .

Which was when it hit her.

Even through the nearly overpowering scent of Cameron's blood, Vicki knew exactly where she'd first touched the ground in this new world. There was no sign of the portal.

No way to get . . .

The air currents against her cheek changed. She threw herself down and to the side as an enormous flock of black, featherless birds dropped out of the sky—those that could landing on the fallen creature, the rest, circling, waiting for their chance to feed.

Scavengers. With curved raptor beaks, they ripped off chunks of flesh, fighting challengers for their place on the corpse with the bone spurs on the tips of their pterodactyl-like wings. About a dozen fought over the pieces of Cameron.

They weren't particularly large, but there was one hell of a lot of them.

A shriek of pain brought her back up onto her feet and racing toward the kids. Denied their place at the feast, a few of the birds were making a try for fresher meat, wheeling and diving and easily avoiding Ren's flailing arms. Vicki could smell fresh blood. One of the kids had taken a hit.

Twisting her head just far enough to avoid a bone spur ghosting past her cheek, she grabbed the attacking bird out of the air, crushed it, tossed it aside. And then another. And then she was standing over the kids, with blood that wasn't blood dripping from her hands, teeth bared, killing anything that came close enough.

After a few moments, nothing did.

Recognizing a predator, those scavengers not feeding pulled back to circle over the corpse.

Ren screamed when Vicki turned toward her.

"Be quiet!" Vicki snapped, giving thanks for the whole *Prince of Darkness* thing when Ren gave one last terrified hiccup and fell silent. Considering the welcome they'd already had, the odds were very good screaming would not attract bunnies and unicorns. "Now do whatever it is you have to do to get us the hell out of here."

The girl's eyes widened. "What?"

"Open the portal that'll take us home." Vicki gave her points for looking in the right direction but, given Ren's rising panic, didn't wait for a response. "You can't, can you?" She kept her tone matter-of-fact, used it to smack the panic back down, didn't let her own need to scream out denial show. "Not from this side."

"We weren't going to go back." Ren waved a trembling hand at the corpse and the scavengers and the sky of red stars. "It wasn't supposed to be like this!"

"Yeah, well, surprise." A scavenger with more appetite than survival instinct tried to take a piece out of the top of her head and Vicki crushed it almost absently, wiping her hand on her jeans as she watched the circling birds. Some of them were flying fairly high. They'd be visible as silhouettes against the night to anyone—or anything—with halfway decent vision. It reminded her of lying on the sofa with Mike, soaking up his warmth, and watching television . . .

"They're going to draw other scavengers. The way vultures do. Maybe other predators. We have to find cover."

"How do you know that?"

"Animal Planet."

"But you're a . . . " Even though she was clearly fine with poking holes into other realities, Ren couldn't seem to say it.

This was neither the time nor the place for denial.

"Vampire. Nightwalker. Member of the bloodsucking undead." Vicki frowned, trying to remember the rest and coming up blank. Three would have to do. "I have cable. And I'm your best bet if you want to survive this little adventure." Hand on the girl's shoulder, Vicki could feel her trembling but whether it was from Cameron's grizzly death or the proximately to one of Humanity's ancient terrors there was no way to be sure. Unfortunately, Vicki had no time for kindness that didn't involve keeping these three kids alive.

No time to give into fear of her own.

She studied the area, for the first time able to look beyond the immediate need to kill. This wasn't the night she knew. The portal had opened on a broad street that looked a bit like University Avenue by way of a hell dimension, the paving cracked and buckled. The closest stone buildings were ruins but some offered more shelter than others. The solidest of the lot was on the other side of the corpse—not worth the risk—but about two hundred meters away, where the road began a long sweeping arc to the left, was a structure that still had a second and third floor even though the actual roof was long gone. Better still, it looked as the though the colonnaded entrance had partially collapsed leaving an opening too small to admit Cameron's killer—or more specifically, under the circumstances, its friends and family.

"There." She pointed with her free hand, giving Ren a little shake to focus her. "We need to get those two up and moving and into that building. What are their names?"

"I don't . . . "

"What? You don't know?"

"Of course I know!" A hint of the girl who'd faced them in the tomb emerged in response to Vicki's mocking tone. Vicki gave herself a mental high five; anger wouldn't hobble the way fear would. "Their names are Gavin and Star."

"Star? Seriously?"

"What's wrong with Star?" Ren demanded, jerking her shoulder out from under Vicki's hand. "It's her name and it's better than the dumbass name her mother gave her!"

Vicki didn't care who gave her the name, as long as she answered to it.

Gavin had a long, oozing cut along the top of his forehead and she let the scent of fresh blood block the stink coming from the creature's corpse as unfamiliar internal organs were exposed. The kid's eyes were squeezed shut and he had both arms wrapped around Star. Star's eyes were open, her pupils so dilated the blue was no more than a pale halo around the black. Calling their names had little effect.

Vicki could feel terror rising off them like smoke.

Given what a joy this place had been so far, if she could feel it, so could other things.

She could work with terror if she had to. When she snarled, Star blinked and focused on her face. Gavin opened his eyes. As she pulled her lips back off her teeth, she could hear their hearts begin to pound faster and faster as adrenaline flooded their system. *She* was a terror they understood. Hauling them onto their feet, she pointed them the right way and growled, "Run."

Hindbrains took over.

Stumbling and crying, they ran.

Ren shot her a look that promised retribution, and raced to catch up.

"So a teenage girl opened a portal to another reality on the wall of a mausoleum, went through with her friends and Vicki followed them then the portal closed—is that it?"

"That's it."

"Are you bullshitting me?"

"Why the fuck would I joke about something like that," Mike growled into his phone.

Thousands of kilometers away in Vancouver, Tony Foster sighed. "Yeah. Good point. Okay, it's eleven now, if I can get on the first plane out in the morning, I won't be there until around three in the afternoon, given the time difference, so . . ."

"Too long." Over the years, Mike had heard more screaming than he was happy admitting to. The kid on the other side of the portal had been screaming in pain, not fear. Not under threat; under attack. And Vicki had landed right into the middle of it. "You need to reopen that thing, now."

"Over the phone?"

"Now," Mike repeated. Years ago, Tony Foster had been Vicki's best set of eyes and ears on the street then Henry fucking Fitzroy had gotten his bloodsucking undead self wrapped up in the kid's life and Tony'd headed out west with them while Henry taught Vicki how to handle the *change*. After Vicki'd come home, Tony'd stayed with Henry. Next thing Mike knew, Tony'd actually had the balls to walk away and make a life for himself—a life that included a job, a relationship, and magic. Real magic. Not rabbits out of a hat magic, that much Mike knew but not much more. In all honesty, he hadn't asked too many questions. Vicki was about all the *it's a weird new wonderful world* he could cope with.

Tonight, his ability to cope with the fact Tony had gone all Harry Potter was moot. He needed to get Vicki and the kids back. Tony was the only one he knew who might be able to do it.

Who *could* do it.

"All right." On the other end of the phone, Tony took a deep breath. "Was one of them a sixty year old Asian dude?"

"No, I told you . . ."

"I know what you told me but I had to check. That means the girl who opened the portal wasn't actually a wizard; she just found a spell and had enough will power and need to make it work. So all you have to do is repeat exactly what she did."

Mike glanced around the mausoleum at the bowl and the candles and the chalked circles. "*All* I have to do?"

"Send me pictures of everything she used. As much detail as you can. Doesn't matter how small or insignificant. I'll run it through my database and see if I can identify the verbal portion."

"You have a database for this sort of shit?"

"Yeah, well, I like my shit organized."

"She burned a dead mouse."

"She probably killed it first. Send me the pictures then go looking for a mouse of your own."

A mouse of his own? "Tony, where the fuck am I going to find a live mouse in Toronto at one in the morning?"

"No idea. You may have to use your badge and go all fake official business on a pet store owner."

"I can't . . . " He rubbed at his temples and sighed. "Yeah. Maybe. Pictures are on their way . . . "

The ruins were dry and didn't smell too bad and if something skittered *away* while Vicki checked the first floor, well, it was skittering *away*. Good enough. She let Ren maneuver her friends through the partially blocked entrance while she kept watch then slipped in behind them.

The gaping windows threw patches of grey against the marble floor. Ren tucked the other two at the angle where the grey met a pile of fallen masonry. Hands clasped, knees drawn up to their chests, they stared out into the darkness and shuddered at every sound.

As Vicki moved past her, Ren grabbed her arm and snarled, "Leave them alone!"

The scent of blood was still too strong for Vicki to push the Hunger completely back but she damped it down as far as she could before she turned. Not quite far enough if Ren's reaction was any indication but, in spite of a surge of fear so intense Vicki could all but taste it, the girl maintained her grip and repeated, "Leave them alone!"

"I'm not going to hurt them."

Ren snorted. "Yeah, right." She tipped her head to one side, exposing her throat. "Come on then. If you're going to do it, do me."

Tempting.

"Let's table that offer until I have to feed," Vicki sighed. If she hadn't fed before meeting Mike at the cemetery, she doubted she'd have been able to tear her gaze away from the pulse-throbbing humming bird fast under the pale—and slightly grubby—skin. As it was, she glanced down at the fingers still clutching her arm and said, "Let go; I'm only going to put them to sleep. Give them a bit of a break from this place."

"Why should I trust you?"

"Because I'm asking you to, when I could be telling you to."

"Oh. Right."

When Ren released her, Vicki ignored the way the girl's fingers trembled, nodded once, and moved to deal with the other two. A command to *Sleep. Dream of pleasant things* wasn't the way she'd been trained to deal with shock but hey, whatever worked. Star's hoodie was back in the mausoleum so she shrugged out of her jacket and spread it over them before straightening and returning to Ren's side.

"So how was it supposed to be?" she asked from just behind the girl's left shoulder.

Ren flinched but kept her gaze locked on the road outside the entrance to their shelter. "How was what supposed to be?"

"This. You told me that this wasn't how it was supposed to be. So . . . ?"

"It was supposed to be . . . " She swiped at her cheek with the palm of her left hand. "I thought it said, it was the home we always wanted."

Vicki waited.

"My grandma died," Ren continued after a moment. "I hadn't seen her since we moved to Toronto, like four years ago but she wanted me to have her bible. My mom, she checked to make sure there wasn't any money in it but totally missed this piece of stuff like leather that had writing on it. Probably because it was in Greek and my mom never learned to read Greek. My grandma taught me when I was little." She paused to swallow a sob and rub her nose against her sleeve before repeating, "I thought it said this was the home we always wanted."

"What was wrong with the homes you had?" The look Ren shot her suggested she not be an idiot as clearly as if the girl had said the words out loud. "So no one cared that you were sneaking out at night?" None of the kids looked like they'd been starved or beaten but Vicki knew that didn't have to mean anything as far as indicators of abuse went. "And no one's going to care if you never make it back?"

Ren snorted. "You really don't get it do you?"

"Actually . . . " Vicki didn't bother finishing and Ren clearly didn't need her to.

"This my fault. I told them about this. I convinced them to come."

"You didn't force them to come here."

"I didn't tell them we were coming *here*."

"True."

"You're not very comforting."

"Not my . . . "

The skittering returned.

Pulling Mike's Glock from where she'd tucked it up against the small of her back, Vicki whirled and blew the head off something that looked like a cross between a rat and a rotweiller seconds before it took a bite out of Star's leg.

" . . . job," she finished, ignoring Ren's scream in favor of grabbing the rat thing by the tail, carrying it outside, and whipping it about forty meters back toward the flock of scavengers. On her way back inside, she scooped up a double handful of grey sand from where the building met the road.

She could feel Ren watching her as she scattered the sand over the blood and brain spatter on the floor.

"You have a gun. What kind of vampire carries a gun?"

"One that'd like to keep us all alive until morning." Vicki told her, rejoining her at the door. With any luck the bang had scared off the rat things and hadn't attracted anything else. "The gun's Detective Celluci's. He must've tossed it through as the portal was closing."

They turned together to face back down the road where the arc of ribs stripped clean of flesh gleamed in the spaces between the black birds.

Vicki could hear Ren's heartbeat and breathing speed up. "We're never going back, are we?"

"Please." Given the light levels, Vicki made sure the eye-roll could be heard in her tone as she stretched the truth a bit. "This isn't our first portal; Mike'll work it out."

"The cop?"

"He's got resources." He'd probably been on the phone to Tony before Vicki'd hit the ground on the other side and Tony'd know how to fix this. Tony had to know how to fix this.

"But he's a real cop?"

"He is."

"And you're a real vampire?"

"I am."

"Oh man, that's totally like a bad romance novel!" And this time, Vicki could hear the eye-roll in Ren's voice.

She grinned, thinking of Henry. "Kid, you don't know the half of it."

Something skittered in the background but didn't come close enough to shoot. Ren's shoulder pressed up against hers although Vicki doubted the girl had consciously sought out the contact. "You're a vampire, right? And given the whole non-sparkling, lack of emo thing, I'm guessing you're like a traditional vampire?"

Vicki frowned, decided not to bother translating the teen speak, and shrugged. "Traditional enough, I guess. Why?"

"If there's like even a sun here, what happens to you when it rises?"

"All right, I've got the mouse." It was in a little, green plastic carrying cage and Mike felt like shit every time he looked in at it. He'd had to drive out to the Super Walmart at Eglinton and Warden to get it and that went on the growing list of experiences he never wanted to repeat.

"What color is it?"

"What fucking difference does the color make?"

"It's probably safest if we keep as close to the original ritual as possible."

Setting the cage on the crypt, Mike took a deep breath and reminded himself that he—and more importantly, Vicki—needed Tony. "Probably?"

"Well, magic is mostly a matter of will so you should be able to bull through any minor variations but . . . "

There was a whole wealth of things Tony clearly didn't want to say in that *but*. And that was fine because Mike didn't want to hear them. He shone his flashlight down into the bowl and scowled. "I can't tell what color it was—too burned. She must have used an accelerant."

"That was the spell working. Is there dirt in the bowl? Toss it out and get fresh," Tony instructed when Mike grunted an affirmative. "I've sent you the symbol you have to draw in the middle of the circles."

"That's not what was there before." Mike squinted down at his screen. "It's, I don't know, backwards."

"It's supposed to be. This thing's a cut-rate gate; one way only. This is the inbound symbol."

He found a broken piece of sidewalk chalk, no doubt tossed aside by the idiot teenager who'd gotten them all into this mess. "I'll call you back when I'm done."

"Don't take too long, remember . . . "

"You don't have to fucking remind me about the time," Mike snapped and hung up. Sunrise hadn't been his friend for some years now.

Returning from disposing of another rat thing's body, Vicki glanced up at the sky where the stars were definitely a little dimmer. Clearly it had been too much to hope that this shithole would be a shithole without a dawn. Sitting down next to Ren, she sighed. "Okay, I didn't want to do this but, can you shoot?"

"A gun? Eww, no. Guns are stupid."

"Guns are dangerous. People are stupid. And we don't have time for that lecture right now." Vicki pulled out Mike's weapon and held it resting across her palms. "If I shut off at dawn, you're going to have to keep us all alive until sunset."

Ren shook her head. "I can't."

"Kid, you opened a portal between worlds. In my book, that says there's not a lot you can't do if it comes down to it. Hopefully, it won't come down to it, but, if it does . . ."

"I don't even like first person shooter games!"

Vicki ignored the protest and held up the Glock. "How much *can* you see?"

"What?"

"I can see in the dark. How much can you see?"

Frowning, Ren leaned away from the gun. "It's not as dark as it was."

Not an answer but it would have to do. "Okay, these are the sights—ramped front sight and a notched rear sight with white contrast. You aim with them but I'll use some wreckage to build a shelter with a limited access so all you'll have to do is point and shoot. Now the Glock has a triple safety system to prevent accidental discharge but once you've released the external safety, here, the two internal safeties automatically disengage when the trigger is pulled."

"Forget it!" Ren shoved at Vicki's arm. "I'm not going to shoot anything!"

"Would you rather be eaten by a giant rat?"

"No, but . . ."

"Then pay attention."

"It's arunda-*ay*!"

"It's nonsense!" Mike protested. "It doesn't mean shit!"

On the other end of the phone, Tony sighed. "It means we get Vicki back," he said quietly. "Try it again from the top."

One hand gripping the edge of crypt, Mike, glanced over at the square of sky he could see through the grill, took a deep breath, and started again.

And then again.

One more time before Tony muttered, "Close enough."

"Close enough?"

"Look, like I said before, it's mostly a matter of will. The rest is just a way to focus power."

"I don't have that kind of power."

"How badly do you want Vicki back?" The phone casing cracked in Mike's grip and although he couldn't have heard it, Tony snorted. "That's plenty of power, trust me. Light the candles and get the mouse."

The mouse seemed oblivious to its fate. Mike thanked heaven for small mercies. He couldn't have coped with a terrified animal. "Why . . . ?"

"Its death symbolizes the journey from one world to another. I don't like this either but I don't think you can skip it. Put it in the bowl and cut its throat then set it on fire and start the chant. When you finish, the gate should open."

"And if it doesn't?"

"I'll be on the first plane to Toronto. Don't hang up, just set the phone down. I'll chant with you."

"Will that help?"

"It can't hurt."

The silver knife was surprisingly sharp. The mouse's head came right off. It helped, a little, that it didn't have time to suffer. Its fur had just started to smolder when Mike began the chant.

The rat things were getting bolder. She'd killed two more and had just given thanks that they didn't hunt in packs when she saw a large shadow moving through the building across the road. Back home, a lot of predators hunted at dusk and dawn. It figured, Vicki noted silently, that would hold true here as well.

No, not *moving* through the building. *Slithering.*

All things considered, she supposed she shouldn't be surprised by giant snakes. "And no fucking sign of Samuel Jackson when I could really use him," she muttered rubbing the back of her neck. She could feel the dawn approaching. The shelter she'd built would give Ren and the kids a chance against the rat things but giant snakes were a whole different ball game.

"What are you looking at?"

Vicki glanced down the road to where the portal wasn't, and shook her head. "Nothing."

The portal wasn't opening.

The stone under the symbol remained solid.

He should have known this magic shit wouldn't have a hope in hell of working. Charging around the crypt, Mike smacked the wall with both palms. "God damn it! Open up!" And again. And then with his fists. "Open the fuck up!"

There was a whoosh behind him.

He turned to see the mixing bowl melting in the heat of the flames.

Turned again to see the center of the circle flare white, then grey under a smear of blood.

"All right, you're going to have to . . . " The flash of light she caught in the corner of her eye had probably been nothing more than an indicator that dawn was closer than she thought, but Vicki turned toward it anyway.

"Is that?" Ren's fingers closed around her arm hard enough to hurt.

"It is."

"But what if it doesn't lead home!"

Vicki took another look across the road. She couldn't see the snake. Probably not a good thing. "Trust me, we'll still be trading up." It was hard to find the Hunter this close to sunrise but, somehow. she managed it. "Gavin! Star! Wake up and come here. Quickly!"

Still wrapped in her imperative, they did as they were told.

Vicki shoved Ren out into the road and the other two out behind her. "Get them through the portal," she growled. "Get them home."

"What will you be doing?"

"I'll be right behind you." She could *hear* the slithering now. "Run!"

To her credit, Ren grabbed her friend's hands before she started to move.

They'd made maybe twenty meters when the rush of wind at her back had Vicki spin around and squeeze off five quick shots.

Giant snake.

With arms, of a sort.

And no visible eyes.

The bullets dug gouges in the charcoal grey scales. It paused, head and arms weaving about three meters off the ground, but seemed more puzzled than injured.

"Vicki!"

"Keep running!" Next time she ended up on another world with teenagers, she'd add *don't look behind you*.

On the bright side, the giant snake thing had to be keeping the rat things under cover.

Fifty meters further and hunger apparently won over annoyance. Vicki felt air currents shift as the snake lunged. She dropped, rolled, came up, and grabbed the nearest limb above the . . . well, fingers given their position, snapping it at the elbow.

Leaping clear of the flailing, she raced down the street and hauled Gavin back up onto his feet. He'd torn his jeans and his palm was bleeding and desperate times . . .

She dragged her tongue across the torn flesh and shoved him toward Ren adding what should have been a redundant, "RUN!"

Pain did not seem to make the creatures of this world cautious. If forced to guess, Vicki'd say the snake thing was pissed.

Diving under its charge to the far side of the road, she got a grip on its other arm, braced herself against a piece of broken pavement, and hauled it sideways. There was a wet crack at the point where the arm met the body.

And more flailing.

Ren had shoved Star through the portal and was working on Gavin by the time the snake got moving forward again.

Another time, Vicki might have admired that kind of single-minded determination. But not right now. She grabbed the polished leg bone of the creature she'd killed when they arrived, made it between the snake and the portal just in time, and slammed it as hard as she could on the nose.

"Vicki, come on!"

A glance over her shoulder. The kids were through.

And the portal was about twice as big around as the snake.

The snake didn't seem to know the meaning of the word *quit*.

She hit it again.

"Vicki! It's closing!"

Mike.

The portal was still bigger than the snake.

And the sun was rising.

She threw the bone. It skittered off the scales. When the snake lunged, she stood her ground and emptied the Glock into its open mouth. Changed magazines, kept firing. Ignored the pain as a fang sliced into her upper arm.

Stumbling back, she could smell burning blood.

A hand grabbed her shirt then she was on her back, on the floor of the mausoleum, still firing into the snake's open mouth.

The portal closed.

The snake head dropped onto her legs.

"Vicki!"

She felt Mike pull the weapon from her hand. Grabbed his hand in turn and sank her teeth into his wrist. Mike swore, she hadn't been particularly careful, but he didn't pull away. One swallow, two, and she had strength enough to tie up a couple of loose ends. "Star, Gavin, forget this night ever happened!"

"I don't . . . " Ren began.

Vicki cut her off. "Your choice."

"I want to remember. Well, I don't really want to remember but . . . "

A raised hand cut her off and Vicki managed to growl, "Sunrise."

"Got it covered."

She was heavier than she had been but Mike lifted her and dropped her into the open crypt. The open occupied crypt.

And then the day claimed her.

"Okay, I'm impressed with your quick thinking . . . " Vicki shimmied into the clean jeans Mike had brought her. " . . . but waking up next to a decomposed body was quite possibly the grossest thing that's ever happened to me."

"At least the body didn't wake up," Mike pointed out handing her a shirt. "Given our lives of late, that's not something you can rule out."

"True." She shrugged into the shirt and moved into his arms, head dropping to rest on his shoulder.

"You need to feed."

The wound in her arm had healed over but was still an ugly red.

"Later." She needed more than he could give and right now, she needed him. "The kids?"

"They're all home. The two you told to forget are . . . " She felt him shrug. "I don't know . . . teenagers. The other girl, Ren, she's something. You're going to have to talk to her."

"I know. Cameron?"

The arms around her tightened. "Teenagers run away all the time."

She could tell he hated saying it. "I was too late to save him."

"Yeah, Ren told me." He sighed, breath parting her hair, warm against her scalp. "There isn't enough crap in this world, they had to go looking for another."

Vicki shifted just far enough to press the palm of her right hand over his heart. "There isn't enough love in this world, they had to go looking for another."

Outfangthief
Conrad Williams

The title of this chilling story is an archaic word meaning "the right of a lord to pursue a thief outside the lord's own jurisdiction and bring him back within his jurisdiction to be punished." But there's nothing medieval about it. The bloodsuckers involved are the antithesis of benign. If you want "lite bite" fiction—this one is not for you. Of course if you are acquainted with the work of Conrad Williams, you'll not be expecting "lite." The author of six novels, four novellas, and around one hundred short stories, some of which are collected in Use Once Then Destroy, *Williams has won the British Fantasy Award three times, most recently for Best Novel (One). He is also a past recipient of the International Horror Guild Award and the Littlewood Arc Prize. His latest novel is* Loss of Separation. *He has a new collection,* Penetralia, *forthcoming from PS Publishing, who are also releasing his first foray into editing, with* Gutshot, *an anthology of weird west stories. Conrad lives in Manchester, UK, with his wife, three sons, and a monster Maine Coon cat. You can find out more at www.conradwilliams.net*

AT THE moment the car slid out of control, Sarah Running had been trying to find a radio station that might carry some news of her crime. She had been driving for hours, risking the M6 all the way from Preston. Though she had seen a number of police vehicles, the traffic had been sufficiently busy to allow her to blend in and anyway, Manser would hardly have guessed she would take her ex-husband's car. Michael was away on business in Stockholm and would not know of the theft for at least another week.

But Manser was not stupid. It would not be long before he latched on to her deceit.

As the traffic thinned, and night closed in on the motorway, Sarah's panic grew. She was convinced that her disappearance had been reported and she would be brought to book. When a police Range Rover tailed her from Walsall to the M42 turn off, she almost sent her own car into the crash barriers at the center of the road.

Desperate for cover, she followed the signs for the A14. Perhaps she could make the one hundred and thirty miles to Felixstowe tonight and sell the car, try to find passage on a boat, lose herself and her daughter on the continent. In a day they could be in Dresden, where her grandmother had lived; a battered city that would recognize some of its own and allow them some anonymity.

"Are you all right back there, Laura?"

In the rear view mirror, her daughter might well have been a mannequin. Her features were glacial; her sunglasses formed tiny screens of animation as the sodium lights fizzed off them. A slight flattening of the lips was the only indication that all was well. Sarah bore down on her frustration. Did she understand what she had been rescued from? Sarah tried to remember what things had been like for herself as a child, but reasoned that her own relationship with her mother had not been fraught with the same problems.

"It's all okay, Laura. We'll not have any more worries in this family. I promise you."

All that before she spotted the flashing blue and red lights of three police vehicles blocking her progress east. She turned left on to another A road bound for Leicester. There must have been an accident; they wouldn't go to the lengths of forming a roadblock for her, would they? The road sucked her deep into darkness, on either side wild hedgerows and vast oily swells of countryside muscled into them. Head lamps on full beam, she could pick nothing out beyond the winding road apart from the ghostly dusting of insects attracted by the light. Sarah, though, felt anything but alone. She could see, in the corner of her eye, something blurred by speed, keeping pace with the car as it fled the police cordon. She took occasional glances to her right, but could not define their fellow traveller for the dense tangle of vegetation that bordered the road.

"Can you see that, Laura?" she asked. "What is it?"

It could have been a trick of the light, or something silver reflecting the shape of their car. Maybe it was the police. The needle on the speedometer edged up to eighty. They would have to dump the car somewhere soon, if the police were closing in on them.

"Keep a look out for a B&B, okay?" She checked in the mirror; Laura's hand was splayed against the window, spreading mist from the star her fingers made. She was watching the obliteration of her view intently.

Sarah fumbled with the radio button. Static filled the car at an excruciating volume. Peering into the dashboard of the unfamiliar car, trying to locate the volume control, she perceived a darkening in the cone of light ahead. When she looked up, the car was drifting off the road, aiming for a tree. Righting the swerve only took the car more violently in the other direction. They were still on the road, but only just, as the wheels began to rise on the passenger side.

but i wasn't drifting off the road, was i?

Sarah caught sight of Laura, expressionless, as she was jerked from one side of the car to the other and hoped the crack she heard was not caused by her head slamming against the window.

i thought it was a tree big and black it looked just like a tree but but but

And then she couldn't see much because the car went into a roll and everything became part of a violent, circular blur and at the centre of it were the misted, friendly eyes of a woman dipping into her field of view.

but but but how can a tree have a face?

She was conscious of the cold and the darkness. There was the hiss of traffic from the motorway, soughing over the fields. Her face was sticky and at first she thought it was blood, but now she smelled a lime tree and knew it was its sap being sweated on to her. Forty meters away, the road she had just left glistened with dew. She tried to move and blacked out.

Fingers sought her face. She tried to bat them away but there were many fingers, many hands. She feared they might try to pluck her eyes out and opened her mouth to scream and that was when a rat was pushed deep into her throat.

Sarah came out of the dream, smothering on the sodden jumper of her daughter, who had tipped over the driver's seat and was pressed against her mother. The flavor of blood filled her mouth. The dead weight of the child carried an inflexibility about it that shocked her. She tried to move away from the crushing bulk and the pain drew gray veils across her eyes. She gritted her teeth, knowing that to succumb now was to die, and worked at unbuckling the seat belt that had saved her life. Once free, she slumped to her left and her daughter filled the space she had occupied. Able to breathe again, she was pondering the position in which the car had come to rest, and trying to reach Laura's hand, when she heard footsteps.

When she saw Manser lean over, his big, toothy grin seeming to fill the shattered window frame, she wished she had not dodged the police; they were preferable to this monster. But then she saw how this wasn't Manser after all. She couldn't understand how she had made the mistake. Manser was a stunted, dark man with a face like chewed tobacco. This face was smooth as soapstone and framed by thick, red tresses; a woman's face.

Other faces, less defined, swept across her vision. Everyone seemed to be moving very fast.

She said, falteringly: "Ambulance?" But they ignored her.

They lifted Laura out of the window to a cacophony of whistles and cheers. There must have been a hundred people. At least they had been rescued. Sarah would take her chances with the police. Anything was better than going home.

The faces retreated. Only the night stared in on her now, through the various rents in the car. It was cold, lonely and painful. Her face in the rear view mirror: all smiles.

He closed the door and locked it. Cocked his head against the jamb, listened for a few seconds. Still breathing.

Downstairs, he read the newspaper, ringing a few horses for the afternoon races. He placed thousand pound bets with his bookies. In the ground floor wash room, he took a scalding shower followed by an ice cold one, just like James Bond. Rolex Oyster, Turnbull & Asser shirt, Armani. He made four more phone calls: Jez Knowlden, his driver, to drop by in the Jag in twenty minutes; Pamela, his wife, to say that he would be away for the weekend; Jade, his mistress, to ask her if she'd meet him in London. And then Chandos, his police mole, to see if that cunt Sarah Running had been found yet.

Sarah dragged herself out of the car just as dawn was turning the skyline milky. She had drifted in and out of consciousness all night, but the sleet that had arrived within the last half hour was the spur she needed to try to escape. She sat a few feet away from the car, taking care not to make any extreme movements, and began to assess the damage to herself. A deep wound in her shoulder had caused most of the bleeding. Other than that, which would need stitches, she had got away with pretty superficial injuries. Her head was pounding, and dried blood formed a crust above her left eyebrow, but nothing seemed to be broken.

After quelling a moment of nausea when she tried to stand, Sarah breathed deeply of the chill morning air and looked around her. A farmhouse nestled within a crowd of trees seemed the best bet; it was too early for road users. Cautiously at first, but with gathering confidence, she trudged across the muddy, furrowed field towards the house, staring all the while at its black, arched windows, for all the world like a series of open mouths, shocked by the coming of the sun.

She had met Andrew in 1985, in the Preston library they both shared. A relationship had started, more or less, on their hands bumping each other while reaching for the same book. They had married a year later and Sarah gave birth to Laura then, too. Both of them had steady, if unspectacular work. Andrew was a security guard and she cleaned at the local school and for a few favoured neighbors. They eventually took out a mortgage on their council house on the right-to-buy scheme and bought a car, a washing machine, and a television on the never-never. Then they both lost their jobs within weeks of each other. They owed £17,000. When the law center they depended on heavily for advice lost its funding and closed down, Sarah had to go to hospital when she began laughing so hysterically, she could not catch her breath. It was as Andrew drove her back from the hospital that they met Malcolm Manser for the first time.

His back to them, he stepped out in front of their car at a set of traffic lights and did not move when they changed in Andrew's favor. When Andrew sounded the horn, Manser turned around. He was wearing a long, Nubuck trench coat, black Levi's, black boots and a black T-shirt without an inch of give in it. His hair was black save for wild slashes of gray above his temples. His sunglasses appeared to be sculpted from his face, so seamlessly did they sit on his nose. From the trench coat he pulled a car jack and proceeded to smash every piece of glass and dent every panel on the car. It took about twenty seconds.

"Mind if I talk to you for a sec ?" he asked, genially, leaning against the crumbled remains of the driver's side window. Andrew was too shocked to say anything. His mouth was very wet. Tiny cubes of glass glittered in his hair. Sarah was whimpering, trying to open her door, which was sealed shut by the warp of metal.

Manser went on: "You have two-hundred-six pieces of bone in your body, fine sir. If my client, Mr. Anders, does not receive seventeen grand, plus interest at ten per cent a day—which is pretty bloody generous if you ask me—by the end of the week, I will guarantee that after half an hour with me, your bone tally will be double that. And that yummy piece of bitch you've got ripening back home—Laura? I'll have her. You test me. I dare you."

He walked away, magicking the car jack in to the jacket and giving them an insouciant wave.

A week later, Andrew set himself on fire in the car which he had locked inside the garage. By the time the fire services got to him, he was a black shape, thrashing in the back seat. *Set himself on fire.* Sarah refused to believe that. She was sure that Manser had murdered him. Despite their onerous circumstances, Andrew was not the suicidal type. Laura was everything to him; he'd not leave this world without securing a little piece of it for her.

What then? A nightmare time. A series of safe houses that were anything but. Early morning flits from dingy addresses in Bradford, Cardiff, Bristol, and

Walsall. He was stickier than anything Bostik might produce. "Bug out," they'd tell her, these kind old men and women, having settled on a code once used by soldiers in some war or another. "Bug out." Manser had contacts everywhere. Arriving in a town that seemed too sleepy to even acknowledge her presence, she'd notice someone out of whack with the place, someone who patently did not fit in but had been planted to watch out for her. Was she so transparent? Her migrations had been random; there was no pattern to unpick. And yet she had stayed no longer than two days in any of these towns. Sarah had hoped that returning to Preston might work for her in a number of ways. Manser wouldn't be expecting it for one thing; for another, Michael, her ex-husband, might be of some help. When she went to visit him though, he paid her short shrift.

"You still owe me fifteen hundred quid," he barked at her. "Pay that off before you come groveling at my door." She asked if he could use his toilet and passed any number of photographs of Gabrielle, his new squeeze. On the way, she stole from a hook on the wall the spare set of keys to his Alfa Romeo.

It took twenty minutes to negotiate the treacherous field. A light frost had hardened some of the furrows while other grooves were boggy. Sarah scuffed and skidded as best she could, clambering over the token fence that bordered an overgrown garden someone had used as an unauthorized tipping area. She picked her way through sofa skeletons, shattered TV sets, collapsed flat-pack wardrobes, and decaying, pungent black bin bags.

It was obvious that nobody was living here.

Nevertheless, she stabbed the doorbell with a bloody finger. Nothing appeared to ring from within the building. She rapped on the door with her knuckles, but half-heartedly. Already she was scrutinizing the windows, looking for another way in. A narrow path strangled by brambles led around the edge of the house to a woefully neglected rear garden. Scorched colors bled into each other, thorns, and convulvulus savaged her ankles as she pushed her way through the tangle. All of the windows at the back of the house had been broken, probably by thrown stones. A yellow spray of paint on a set of storm doors that presumably led directly into the cellar picked out a word she didn't understand: *scheintod*. What was that? German? She cursed herself for not knowing the language of her elders, not that it mattered. Someone had tried to obscure the word, scratching it out of the wood with a knife, but the paint was reluctant. She tried the door but it was locked.

Sarah finally gained access via a tiny window that she had to squeeze through. The bruises and gashes on her body cried out as she toppled into a gloomy larder.

Mingled into the dust was an acrid, spicy smell; racks of ancient jars and pots were labeled in an extravagant hand: *cumin, coriander, harissa, chili powder.* There were packs of flour and malt that had been ravaged by vermin. Dried herbs dusted her with a strange, slow rain as she brushed past them. Pickling jars held back their pale secrets within dull, lusterless glass.

She moved through the larder, arms outstretched, her eyes becoming accustomed to the gloom. Something arrested the door as she swung it outwards. A dead dog, its fur shaved from its body, lay stiffly in the hallway. At first she thought it was covered in insects, but the black beads were unmoving. They were nicks and slashes in the flesh. The poor thing had been drained. Sarah recoiled from the corpse and staggered further along the corridor. Evidence of squatters lay around her in the shape of fast food packets, cigarette ends, beer cans, and names signed in the ceiling by the sooty flames of candles. A rising stairwell vanished into darkness. Her shoes crunched and squealed on plaster fallen from the bare walls.

"Hello?" she said, querulously. Her voice made as much impact on the house as a candy-floss mallet. It died on the walls, absorbed so swiftly it was as if the house was sucking her in, having been starved of human company for so long. She ascended to the first floor. The carpet that hugged the risers near the bottom gave way to bare wood. Her heels sent dull echoes ringing through the house. If anyone lived here, they would know they were not alone now. The doors opened on to still bedrooms shrouded by dust. There was nothing up here.

"Laura?" And then more stridently, as if volume alone could lend her more spine: *"Laura!"*

Downstairs she found a cozy living room with a hearth filled with ashes. She peeled back a dust cover from one of the sofas and lay down. Her head pounded with delayed shock from the crash and the mustiness of her surroundings. She thought of her baby.

It didn't help that Laura seemed to be going off the rails at the time of their crisis. Also, her inability, or reluctance, to talk of her father's death worried Sarah almost as much as the evidence of booze and drug use. At each of the safe houses, it seemed there was a Laura trap in the shape of a young misfit, eager to drag someone down with him or her. Laura gave herself to them all, as if glad of a mate to hasten her downward spiral. There had been one boy in particular, Edgar—a difficult name to forget—whose influence had been particularly invidious. They had been holed up in a Toxteth bedsit. Sarah had been listening to City FM. A talkshow full of languid, catarrhal Liverpool accents that was making her drowsy. The sound of a window smashing had dragged her from slumber. She caught the boy trying to drag her daughter through the glass. She had shrieked at him and hauled him into the room. He could have been no older than ten or eleven. His eyes were rifle green and would not stay still. They darted around like steel bearings in a bagatelle game. Sarah had drilled him, asking him if he had been sent from Manser. Panicked, she had also been firing off instructions to Laura, that they must pack immediately and be ready to go within the hour. It was no longer safe. And then:

Laura, crawling across the floor, holding on to Edgar's leg, pulling herself up, her eyes fogged with what could only be ecstasy. Burying her face in Edgar's crotch. Sarah had shrank from her daughter, horrified. She watched as Laura's free hand traveled beneath her skirt and began to massage at the gusset of her knickers while animal sounds came from her throat. Edgar had grinned at her, showing off a range of tiny, brilliant white teeth. Then he had bent low, whispering something in Laura's ear before charging out of the window with a speed that Sarah thought could only end in tragedy. But when she rushed to the opening, she couldn't see him anywhere.

It had been the Devil's own job trying to get her ready to flee Liverpool. She had grown wan and weak and couldn't keep her eyes off the window. Dragging her on to a dawn coach from Mount Pleasant, Laura had been unable to stop crying and as the day wore on, complained of terrible thirst and unbearable pain behind her eyes. She vomited twice and the driver threatened to throw them off the coach unless Laura calmed down. Somehow, Sarah was able to pacify her. She found that shading her from the sunlight helped. A little later, slumped under the seat, Laura fell asleep.

Sarah had begun to question ever leaving Preston in the first place. At least there she had the strength that comes with knowing your environment. Manser had been a problem in Preston but the trouble was that he remained a problem. At least back there, it was just him that she needed to be wary of. Now it seemed Laura's adolescence was going to cause her more of a problem than she believed could be possible. But at the back of her mind, Sarah knew she could never have stayed in her home town. What Manser had proposed, sidling up to her at Andrew's funeral, was that she allow Laura to work for him, whoring. He guaranteed an excellent price for such a perfectly toned, *tight* bit of girl.

"Men go for that," he'd whispered, as she tossed a fistful of soil on to her husband's coffin. "She's got cracking tits for a thirteen-year-old. High. Firm. Nipples up top. Quids in, I promise you. You could have your debt sorted out in a couple of years. And I'll break her in for you. Just so's you know it won't be some stranger nicking her cherry."

That night, they were out of their house, a suitcase full of clothes between them.

"You fucking *beauty*."

Manser depressed the call end button on his Motorola and slipped the phone into his jacket. Leaning forward, he tapped his driver on the shoulder. "Jez. Get this. Cops found the bitch's car in a fucking field outside Leicester. She'd totaled it."

He slumped back in his seat. The radio masts at Rugby swung by on his left, lights glinting through a thin fog. "Fuck London. You want the A5199. Warp Factor two. And when we catch the minging little tart, we'll show her how to have a road accident. Do the job properly for her. Laura though, Laura comes with us. Nothing happens to Laura. Got it?"

At Knowlden's assent, Manser closed his eyes. This year's number three had died just before he left home. It had been a pity. He liked that one. The sutures on her legs had healed in such a way as to chafe his thigh as he thrust into her. But there had been an infection that he couldn't treat. Pouring antibiotics down her hadn't done an awful lot of good. Gangrene set in. Maybe Laura could be his number four. Once Dr Losh had done his bit, he would ask him the best way to prevent infection. He knew what Losh's response would be: *let it heal*. But he liked his meat so very rare when he was fucking it. He liked to see a little blood.

Sarah woke up to find that her right eye had puffed closed. She caught sight of herself in a shard of broken mirror on the wall. Blood caked half her face and the other half was black with bruises. Her hair was matted. Not for the first time, she wondered if her conviction that Laura had died was misplaced. Yet in the same breath, she couldn't bear to think that she might now be suffering with similar, or worse, injuries. Her thoughts turned to her saviours—if that was what they were. And if so, then why hadn't she been rescued?

She relived the warmth and protection that had enveloped her when those willowy figures had reached inside the car and plucked out her child. Her panic at the thought of Laura either dead or as good as had been ironed flat. She felt safe and, inexplicably, had not raged at this outrageous kidnap; indeed, she had virtually sanctioned it. Perhaps it had been the craziness inspired by the accident, or endorphins stifling her pain that had brought about her indifference. Still, what should have been anger and guilt was neutralized by the compulsion that Laura was in safe hands. What she didn't want to examine too minutely was the feeling that she missed the rescue party more than she did her own daughter.

Refreshed a little by her sleep, but appalled at the catalogue of new aches and pains that jarred each movement, Sarah made her way back to the larder where she found some crackers in an airtight tin. Chewing on these, she revisited the hallway and dragged open the heavy curtains, allowing some of the late afternoon light to invade. Almost immediately she saw the door under the stairs. She saw how she had missed it earlier; it was hewn from the same dark wood and there was no door handle as such, just a little recess to hook your fingers into. She tried it but it wouldn't budge. Which meant it was locked from the inside. Which meant that somebody must be down there.

"Laura?" she called, tapping on the wood with her fingernails. "Laura, it's Mum. Are you in there?"

She listened hard, her ear flush against the crack of the jamb. All she could hear was the gust of subterranean breezes moving through what ought to be the cellar. She must check it out; Laura could be down there, bleeding her last.

Sarah hunted down the kitchen. A large pine table sat at one end of the room, a dried orange with a heart of mould at its center. She found a stack of old newspapers bound up with twine from the early 1970s by a back door that was forbiddingly black and excessively padlocked. Ransacking the drawers and cupboards brought scant reward. She was about to give in when the suck of air from the last yanked cupboard door brought a small screwdriver rolling into view. She grabbed the tool and scurried back to the cellar door.

Manser stayed Knowlden with a finger curled around his lapel. "Are you carrying?"

Knowlden had parked the car off the road on the opposite side to the crash site. Now the two men were standing by the wreck of the Alfa. Knowlden had spotted the house and suggested they check it out. If Sarah and her daughter had survived the crash—and the empty car suggested that they had—then they might have found some neighborly help.

"I hope you fucking are," Manser warned.

"I'm carrying okay. Don't sweat it."

Manser's eyebrows went north. "Don't tell me to not sweat it, pup. Or you'll find yourself doing seventy back up the motorway without a fucking car underneath you."

The sun sinking fast, they hurried across the field, constantly checking the road behind them as they did so. Happy that nobody had seen them, Manser nodded his head in the direction of the front door. "Kick the mud off your boots on that bastard," he said.

It was 5:14 p.m.

Sarah was halfway down the cellar stairs and wishing she had a torch with her when she heard the first blows raining down on the door. She was about to return to the hallway when she heard movement from below. A *lot* of movement. Creaks and whispers and hisses. There was a sound as of soot trickling down a flue. A chatter: teeth in the cold? A sigh.

"Laura?"

A chuckle.

The door gave in just before Knowlden was about to. His face was greasy with sweat and hoops of dampness spoiled his otherwise pristine shirt.

"Gun," Manser said, holding his hand out. Knowlden passed him the weapon, barely disguising his disdain for his boss. "You want to get some muesli down you, mate," Manser said. "Get yourself fit." He checked the piece was loaded and entered the house, muzzle pointing ahead of him, cocked horizontally. Something he'd done since seeing Brad Pitt do the same thing in *Se7en*.

"Knock, knock," he called out. "Daddy's home."

Sarah heard, just before all hell broke loose, Laura's voice firm and even, say: "Do not touch her." Then she was knocked back on the stairs by a flurry of black leather and she was aware only of bloody-eyed, pale-skinned figures flocking past her. And teeth. She saw each leering mouth as if in slow motion, dark lips peeled back to reveal teeth so white they might have been sculpted from ice.

She thought she saw Laura among them and tried to grab hold of her jumper but she was left clutching air as the scrum piled into the hallway, whooping and screaming like a gang of kids let out early from school. When the shooting started she couldn't tell if the screaming had changed in pitch at all, whether it had become more panicked. But at the top of the stairs she realized she was responsible for most of it. There appeared to be some kind of stand-off. Manser, the fetid little sniffer dog of a man, was waving a gun around while his henchman clenched and unclenched his hands, eyeing up the opposition, which was substantial. Sarah studied them properly for the first time, these women who had rescued her baby and left her to die in the car. And yet proper examination was beyond her. There were four of them, she thought. Maybe five. They moved around and against each other so swiftly, so lissomely that she couldn't be sure. They were like a flesh knot. Eyes fast on their enemy, they guarded each other with this mesmerizing display. It was so seamless it could have been choreographed.

But now she saw that they were not just protecting each other. There was someone at the heart of the knot, appearing and disappearing in little ribbons and teasers of color. Sarah need see only a portion of face to know they were wrapped around her daughter.

"Laura," she said again.

Manser said, "Who the fuck are these clowns? Have we just walked into Goth night down the local student bar, or what?"

"Laura," Sarah said again, ignoring her pursuer. "Come here."

"Everyone just stand back. I'm having the girl. And to show you I'm not just pissing in my paddling pool . . . " Manser took aim and shot one of the women through the forehead.

Sarah covered her mouth as the woman dropped. The three others seemed to fade somewhat, as if their strength had been affected.

"Jez," said Manser. "Get the girl."

Sarah leapt at Knowlden as he strode into the pack but a stiff arm across her chest knocked her back against the wall, winding her. He extricated Laura from her guardians and dragged her kicking back to his boss.

Manser was nodding his head. "Nice work, Jez. You can have jelly for afters tonight. Get her outside."

To Sarah he said: "Give her up." And then he was gone.

Slumped on the floor, Sarah tried to blink a fresh trickle of blood from her eyes. Through the fluid, she thought she could see the women crowding around their companion. She thought she could see them lifting her head as they positioned themselves around her. But no. No. She couldn't accept that she was seeing what they began to do to her then.

Knowlden fell off the pace as they ran towards the car. Manser was half-dragging, half-carrying Laura who was thrashing around in his arms.

"I'm nearly ready," she said. "I'll bite you! I'll bite you, I swear to God."

"And I'll scratch your eyes out," Manser retorted. "Now shut the fuck up. Jesus, can't you do what girls your age do in the movies? Faint, or something?"

At the car, he bundled her into the boot and locked it shut. Then he fell against the side of the car and tried to control his breathing. He could just see Knowlden plodding towards him in the dark. Manser could hear his squealing lungs even though he had another forty meters or so to cover.

"Come on Jez, for fuck's sake! I've seen mascara run faster than that."

At thirty meters, Manser had a clearer view of his driver as he died.

One of the women they had left behind in the house was moving across the field at a speed that defied logic. Her hands were outstretched and her nails glinted like polished arrowheads. Manser moved quickly himself when he saw how she slammed into his chauffeur. He was in third gear before he realized he hadn't taken the handbrake off and he was laughing harder than he had ever laughed in his life. Knowlden's heart had been skewered on the end of her claws like a piece of meat on a kebab. He didn't stop laughing until he hit the M1, southbound.

Knowlden was forgotten. All he had on his mind now was Laura, naked on the slab, her body marked out like the charts on a butcher's wall.

Dazed, Sarah was helped to her feet. Their hands held her everywhere and nowhere, moving along her body as soft as silk. She tried to talk but whenever she opened her mouth, someone's hand, cold and rank, slipped over it. She saw the pattern in the curtains travel by in a blur though she could not feel her feet on the floor. Then the night was upon them, and the frost in the air sang around her ears as she was swept into the sky, embedded at the center of their slippery mesh of bodies, smelling their clothes and the scent of something ageless and black, lifting off the skin like forbidden perfume. *Is she all right now?* she wanted to ask, but her words wouldn't form in the ceaseless blast of cold air. Sarah couldn't count the women that cavorted around her. She drifted into unconsciousness thinking of how they had opened the veins in their chests for her, how the charge of fluid had engulfed her face, bubbling on her tongue and nostrils like dark wine. How her eyes had flicked open and rolled back into their sockets with the unspeakable rapture of it all.

Having phoned ahead, Manser parked the car at midnight on South Wharf Road, just by the junction with Praed Street. He was early, so instead of going directly to the dilapidated pub on the corner he sauntered to the bridge over Paddington Basin and stared up at the Westway, hoping for calm. The sounds emanating from that elevated sweep were anything but soothing. The mechanical sigh of speeding vehicles reminded him only of the way those witches' mouths had breathed, snake-like jaws unhinged as though in readiness to swallow him whole. The hiss of tires on rain-soaked tarmac put him in mind of nothing but the wet air that had sped from Knowlden's chest when he was torn open.

By the time he returned, he saw in the pub a low-wattage bulb turning the glass of an upstairs window milky. He went to the door and tapped on it with a coin in a pre-arranged code. Then he went back to the car and opened the boot. He wrestled with Laura and managed to clamp a hand over her mouth, which she bit, hard. Swearing, he dragged a handkerchief from his pocket and stuffed it in her mouth, punching her twice to get her still. The pain in his hand was mammoth. She had teeth like razors. Flaps of skin hung off his palm; he was bleeding badly. Woozy at the sight of the wound, he staggered with Laura to the door, which was now open. He went through it and kicked it shut, checking the street to make sure he hadn't been seen. Upstairs, Losh was sitting in a chair containing more holes than stuffing.

"This was a good boozer before it was closed down," Manser said, his excitement unfolding deep within him.

"Was," Losh said, keeping his eyes on him. He wore a butcher's apron that was slathered with blood. He smoked a cigarette, the end of which was patterned with bloody prints from his fingers. A comma of blood could be mistaken for a kiss-curl on his forehead. "Everything changes."

"You don't," Manser said. "Christ. Don't you ever wash?"

"What's the point? I'm a busy man."

"How many years you been struck off?"

Losh smiled. "Didn't anybody ever warn you not to piss off the people you need help from?"

Manser swallowed his distaste of the smaller man. "Nobody warns me nothing," he spat. "Can't we get on?"

Losh stood up and stretched. "Cash," he said, luxuriously.

Manser pulled a wad from his jacket. "There's six grand there. As always."

"I believe you. I'd count it but the bank gets a bit miffed if they get blood on their bills."

"Why don't you wear gloves?"

"The magic. It's all in the fingers." Losh gestured towards Laura. "This the one?"

"Of course."

"Pretty thing. Nice legs." Losh laughed. Manser closed his eyes. Losh said, "What you after?"

Manser said, "The works."

Wide eyes from Losh. "Then let's call it eight thou."

A pause. Manser said, "I don't have it with me. I can get it tomorrow. Keep the car tonight. As collateral."

Losh said, "Done."

The first incision. Blood squirted up the apron, much brighter than the stains already painted upon it. A coppery smell filled the room. The pockets of the pool table upon which Laura was spread were filled with beer towels.

"Soft tissue?"

Manser's voice was dry. He needed a drink. His cock was as hard as a house brick. "As much off as possible."

"She won't last long," Losh said.

Manser stared at him. "She'll last long enough."

Losh said, "Got a number five in mind already?"

Manser didn't say a word. Losh reached behind him and picked up a Samsonite suitcase. He opened it and pulled out a hacksaw. Its teeth entertained the light and flung it in every direction. At least Losh kept his tools clean.

The operation took four hours. Manser fell asleep at one point and dreamed of his hand overpowering the rest of his body, dragging him around the city while the mouth that slavered and snarled at the center of his palm cupped itself around the stomachs of passers-by and devoured them.

He wakened, rimed with perspiration, to see Losh chewing an errant hangnail and tossing his instruments back into the suitcase. Laura was wrapped in white bath towels. They were crimson now.

"Is she okay?" Manser asked. Losh's laughter in reply was infectious and soon he was at it too.

"Do you want the off cuts?" Losh asked, wiping his eyes and jerking a thumb at a bucket tastefully covered with a dishcloth.

"You keep them,' Manser said. "I've got to be off."

Losh said, "Who opened the window?"

Nobody had opened the window; the lace curtains fluttering inward were being pushed by the bulge of glass. Losh tore them back just as the glass shattered in his face. He screamed and fell backwards, tripping on the bucket and sprawling on to the floor.

To Manser it seemed that strips of the night were pouring in through the broken window. They fastened themselves to Losh's face and neck and munched through the flesh like a caterpillar at a leaf. His screams were low and already being disguised by blood as his throat filled. He began to choke but managed one last, hearty shriek as a major blood vessel parted, spraying color all around the room with the abandon of an unmanned hosepipe.

How can they breathe with their heads so deep inside him? Manser thought, hypnotized by the violence. He felt something dripping on his brow. Touching his face with his fingers, he brought them away to find them awash with blood. He had time to register, as he looked up at the ceiling, the mouth as it yawned, dribbling with lymph, the head as it vibrated with unfettered anticipation. And then the woman dropped on him, ploughing her jaws through the meat of his throat and ripping clear. He saw his flesh disappear down her gullet with a spasm that was almost beautiful. But then his sight filled with red and he could understand no more.

She had been back home for a day. She couldn't understand how she had got here. She remembered being born from the warmth of her companions and standing up to find both men little more than pink froth filling their suits. One of the men had blood on his hands and a cigarette smouldered between his fingers. The hand was on the other side of the room, though.

She saw the bloody, tiny mound of towels on the pool table. She saw the bucket; the dishcloth had shifted, revealing enough to tell her the game. Two toes was enough. She didn't need to be drawn a picture.

And then somehow she found herself outside. And then on Edgware Road where a pretty young woman with dark hair and a woven shoulder bag gave her a couple of pounds so that she could get the tube to Euston. And then a man smelling of milk and boot polish she fucked in a shop doorway for her fare north. And then Preston, freezing around her in the early morning as if it were formed from winter itself. She had half expected Andrew to poke his head around the corner of their living room to say hello, the tea's on, go and sit by the fire and I'll bring some to you.

But the living room was cold and bare. She found sleep at the time she needed it most, just as her thoughts were about to coalesce around the broken image of her baby. She was crying because she couldn't remember what her face looked like.

When she revived, it was dark again. It was as if daylight had forsaken her. She heard movement towards the back of the house. Outside, in the tiny, scruffy garden, a cardboard box, no bigger than the type used to store shoes, made a stark shape amid the surrounding frost. The women were hunched on the back fence, regarding her with owlish eyes. They didn't speak. Maybe they couldn't.

One of them swooped down and landed by the box. She nudged it forward with her hand, as a deer might coax a newborn to its feet. Sarah felt another burst of unconditional love and security fill the gap between them all. Then they were gone, whipping and twisting far into the sky, the consistency, the trickiness of smoke.

Sarah took the box into the living room with her and waited. Hours passed; she felt herself become more and more peaceful. She loved her daughter and she hoped Laura knew that. As dawn began to brush away the soot from the sky, Sarah leaned over and touched the lid. She wanted so much to open it and say a few words, but she couldn't bring herself to do it.

In the end, she didn't need to. Whatever remained inside the box managed to do it for her.

Dancing with the Star
Susan Sizemore

New York Times *best-selling author Susan Sizemore's debut novel was a time-travel romance,* Wings of the Storm *(1992). She continued writing romance, but after penning a media tie-in novel based on the television series* Forever Knight, *she was inspired her to create an original vampire world. The result was the five-book* The Laws of the Blood *dark fantasy series. She later created an entirely different vampire world for the Vampire Prime paranormal romance series. The eleventh in this series,* Primal Instincts, *was published in 2010. The vampires in both series deal with the challenges of undeath much as humans deal with life, but otherwise are quite distinct: the Laws vamps are still monsters, the Primes are romantic fun. "Dancing With the Star" is definitely an example of the author in her lighter romantic vein. Sizemore lives in the Midwest and knits when she's not writing. She's the author of over thirty novels and more than a dozen short stories—a great many of them are about vampires.*

THERE ARE plenty of people who come into the Alhambra Club for the things we regulars can offer. It's a nice place, not flashy on the inside, hard to spot from the outside. You have to want to find the place and search for it through friends of friends of friends. If you're a mortal, that is. The rest of us have used it as a hangout for the better part of a century.

There's a television set over the bar, a big, flat-panel model, always playing with the sound off. I wasn't paying attention to it because I was engaged in seducing a handsome young man with far too many body piercings for my usual taste. I mean, if you want piercings I'm perfectly capable of providing them for you. But, he had nice eyes and a lovely voice, and the place wasn't all that full of human patrons this evening. A girl goes with what she can sometimes. I wasn't all that hungry, so I wasn't trying too hard.

I wasn't paying attention to the TV but my friend Tiana was. I was surprised when she came up and put her cold hand on my shoulder, cause she isn't normally rude enough to interrupt me when I'm working a fresh feed.

"Did you hear? There's been a twelve car pile up on Mulholland."

This isn't the sort of thing that would normally interest me, but her excitement got my attention. I shifted my gaze to the television. It showed a scene of fire and carnage spotlighted in beams of white light shooting down from circling helicopters. A crawl on the bottom of the screen was showing statistics about dead and injured and the amount of emergency rescue equipment called to the scene. A windblown blond girl reporter was excitedly talking about the same things.

Beside me, Tiana was starting to breath heavily. I wasn't sure who was getting off on the disaster more, my friend or the reporter.

I looked back at Tiana. "So?"

Her eyes were glowing, not quite the death-eating electric blue she gets when she's feeding, but her pupils held pinprick sparks of anticipation. "You want to go have a look, Serephena?" she asked.

Normally I wouldn't have been interested, but the pleading in her voice got to me. Tiana's been my best friend for a very long time. If you know what we are you wouldn't think she and I would have that much in common. I'm a vampire, and she's—well, all right—she's my ghoul friend. I feed on the living, she feeds on the energy of the dying. But we both like to shop.

"Maybe there's a dying movie star out there I can latch onto," she said. She rubbed her hands together. "A producer would be even better."

I know what that sounds like, but it really had more to do with psychic power levels than celebrity stalking. There are a lot of high energy types in show business, a lot of people who are psychic and don't even know it.

I got up and telepathically told the pierced boy that we'd never met. "Sure," I said to Tiana. "It's been a slow night. Let's go have a look."

It was gruesome up on Mulholland Drive. Tiana ate it up—literally soaking the energy of fear and pain in through her pores. It was the scent of blood that got to me, but not in a good way. There's no fun in spilled blood. I need to take blood from the living, breathing source, to taste it fresh and hot, with the heartbeat still pulsing through it. And preferably from a volunteer because we live in modern, humane times. Unlike some of my notorious forebears I do not get off on pain. The blood on the crash victims gave off a sick scent that roiled my stomach, but I did find hiding in the shadows and watching the emergency crews work exciting. Hey, I'm as interested in all that forensics and rescue stuff as anyone else who watches the geek TV channels, but this was *live and direct* like Max Headroom used to say on the television show nobody but me probably remembers.

It was interesting, but after a while I glanced at the sky and sighed. The night was getting on. "Had enough yet?" I asked Tiana. "You'll outgrow your size 2 clothes if you feed much longer. Besides, it's an hour to sunrise."

Tiana came out of her happy trance and turned glowing blue eyes on me. "Oh, Sorry, I lost track of the time."

"No problem," I said, and took her arm to help her walk away, knowing from experience that she was drunk and dizzy from feeding.

Help me! Where are you?

Here! I shouted to the voice in my head. *Where—*

"Serephena!"

I looked up into pinpoints of blue light. Tiana. I was on my knees, and she was standing over me. The fierce pain in my head block out most thought, but I knew that our positions were all wrong. I was supposed to be helping her.

I wanted to run into the wreckage behind us. But when I stood my legs were too shaky. I glanced back. "I—"

Tiana shook my shoulders. "We have to go. Sunrise," she added.

That was one word I understood in all of its myriad implications of pain, suffering, death. I had to go. Now. Whatever had just happened I had to get home.

I took Tiana's hand, and we ran together.

I have a nice studio apartment, where I sleep on a daybed in the huge windowless bathroom. The bathroom door is reinforced and has a strong lock, panic-room style and the building, which I own and rent mostly to my sort of people, has state of the art security. So, normally I have no reason not to sleep very well. Normally I don't dream, either. I go to sleep. I wake up. It all happens so quickly . . . normally . . .

The path was made of brick, laid out in a chevron pattern. It was lined with rose bushes and night blooming jasmine. The air was so fragrant I could taste it. The stars overhead formed a thick blanket of light brighter than I'd seen them for a very long time.

"I need to get out of the city more," I said, and continued walking toward the music in the distance.

I was wearing a dress, the skirt long and floaty and pale blue sprinkled with a pattern of glittering crystals that mirrored the sky. This was not the slinky black sort of garment I favored, but it felt right, feminine, beautiful.

I was wearing honest to god glass slippers. Cinderella? Me? Well, it was a dream.

And my feet—my whole body—wanted nothing more than to dance.

When the gazebo came into sight, as pretty as a white confection on top of a wedding cake, I ran toward it. Something more than wonderful waited for me there.

"You!" I said, skidding to a halt at the entrance as I spied the man leaning with his arms crossed against a pillar.

"Me," he replied, a stranger with a familiar voice.

"But—you're a movie star!"

It was an accusation. I didn't expect my very rare dreams to go off on such grandiose tangents.

"And I worked very hard to become a genuine movie star," he answered, totally unashamed for showing up in my fantasy. "Would you prefer meeting a celebrity?" His gesture took in the small building. "Here? In our space?"

Our space? Yeah, it was, wasn't it?

I turned around, my skirts belling out around my legs. I could see my reflection in the highly polished white marble floor. And his reflection as he came to join me. He moved with the grace of Fred Astaire—I've been around long enough to see Fred and his sister Estelle dance on the stage, I know what I'm talking about.

His hands touched me, one at my waist, one gently gripping my fingers. His warmth against my coolness. The next thing I knew we were circling the room, caught up in the music.

"We're waltzing," I said. "I don't know how to waltz."

"I learned it when I auditioned for Mr. Darcy. Didn't get the role, though."

"But you learned how to dance."

"Silver linings," he said.

I studied his face. There was a sweep of dark hair across his brow, high arching eyebrows over penetrating green eyes, severe high cheekbones softened by a lush, full mouth. "You would have made a great Darcy," I told him.

Of course he had the body of a god—or at least of a man who spent a fortune working long hours with a personal trainer—and now that body was pressed to mine. I liked it. A lot. The longer we danced the more I liked it.

My skin wasn't cool anymore.

"This is—nice," he said.

"In a strange way," I answered.

"You've noticed that, have you?"

I nodded. His green eyes twinkled at me. We danced around in circles for a long, long time, caught up in the music and the flow of energy between us. That's what it was all about for me—flow and energy, give and take. For once I knew that I was giving as much as I was taking, and it felt—nice.

"What are you—we—doing here?" I asked.

"Dreaming about dancing," he answered. His smile devastated me. "I'm as surprised by this as you are. One moment I was floating in gray clouds. I think I was screaming, but there was no one to hear me, not even me. Then I was here with you."

"I was in blackness," I said. "That's normal for me."

"The gray was terrifying," he said. He whirled me around faster, until we both laughed. "This is much better," he said. He pulled me closer. We weren't dancing anymore, but the music played on and the world continued to spin.

"No one should be in darkness," he said. "Gray or black or any other kind, especially not alone."

I started to say that I didn't mind being alone, but being with him made me realize that I did mind. "I've been lonely and didn't know it." Though I was looking into his eyes, I was talking more to myself.

Neither of us spoke for an unknowable time after that but we continued to look into each others' eyes and shared. What? Our emotions, our souls, the essences of our beings? All of the above, I guess.

"This is such bullshit," I finally said.

"But you like it."

My gaze flicked away from his, but I couldn't stand the loss of contact for long. "If I could blush, I'd be blushing," I told him when our gazes locked again.

"We live in a time and place that's cynical about love."

"Darlin', I come from New York. People in L.A. are amateurs about cynicism."

He shook his head. "I used to live in New York," he said. "Where I tended bar while I went to drama school. I saw plenty of broken hearts there."

"Broke a few, too, I bet."

"Too bad I didn't meet you there."

I laughed. "I left long before you were born."

"Really? When were you there? How did you get to be—?" He looked puzzled for a moment, then said it. "A vampire?"

Those in the know generally don't ask. Maybe they think it's rude, or mystery is part of the mystique, or are afraid of getting their throats ripped out. I hadn't told this story for a long time. "I worked at the Plaza back in the 1930s."

"The hotel?"

I nodded. "I was a telephone operator. There was a mob boss that lived there."

"Lucky Luciano?"

"You've heard of him?"

"I've been doing research to play him in a film."

"Too bad. I hate seeing that bastard glamorized."

"He did bad things to you," he guessed.

"He had me killed. He wrongfully thought I'd overheard some conversations and might testify about them in court. A hitman was sent after me. It turned out that the killer was a hungry vampire. He drained me and left me for dead."

"But—"

"But the vampire didn't realize I was one of his bloodline."

"You were already a vampire?"

"No, no! My family came from Walachia. There's some sort of genetic mutation that kicks in when a vampire bites us. Old Vlad the Impaler really is Dracula, and the king of us all."

"That's amazing. I'm part Hungarian, could I be a vampire?"

"Depends on if your grandmas got raped by the right sort of invaders, I guess. Do you want to be a vampire?"

He shrugged. "I want to hear more about you."

"Nice answer. The gist of it is I woke up dead and had to start over from there."

"Did you go after the one who turned you?"

"You've been watching vampire movies."

"Been in one."

"I saw it, had nothing to do with my world. But you were good," I added.

"You're lovely when you're bullshitting. What happened to the evil one who turned you?"

"I don't know if he was evil."

"He was a mob hitman."

His indignation was adorable. "I'll concede his profession was evil."

"You've never done anything like that."

His certainty of my goodness was even more adorable. "No, I haven't," I assured him. "But after a while of wrestling with all the implications of immortality you get some perspective on good, evil, expediency, stuff like that. And no, I haven't seen him again, at least, not that I know of. I didn't get a good look at him while he was sucking the lifeblood out of me."

"But—how did you survive? Didn't you have to have a teacher, a mentor? Didn't another vampire bring you into the dark world?"

I laughed and stroked his cheek. "I suppose there's melodrama somewhere, but I've never been involved in any—other than being rubbed out by a mobster, which I did find pretty melodramatic at the time."

He traced his hand up and down my back, sending tingling shivers all through me. His sympathy warmed me even more than his touch. "I'm sorry you went through such trauma. How did you survive?"

"I found the right bar and ordered a beer. Getting all the blood drained out of you makes you thirsty."

"It was a vampire bar?"

I nodded.

"Did some instinct kick in that drew you to your own kind and they taught you how to survive?"

I nodded again. He was smart and quick on the uptake. The man had many great qualities. And he could dance in a way that made me feel like I was having sex standing up, fully clothed and not ruffling a hair or breaking a sweat. Not that vampires sweat.

"I've explained me," I said. "How about you? How did you get here? Wherever here is."

"That is the problem isn't it? We seem to be dancing in limbo. Though I like being here with you."

From anyone else, any other time, I would have considered that a line. But his eyes held genuine pleasure, genuine sincerity.

"I'm falling like a rock, you know," I told him.

"Me, too. Is that a bad thing?"

We both shrugged, and that became part of the dance. We laughed together, and that was part of the music.

"As for me," he went on. "I remember being with friends at their house. We played Scrabble."

I love word games. "Scrabble? Is that any way for a movie star to spend an evening?"

"Now you know why the paparazzi hate me. I lead a quiet life."

"Me too. But how did you get here?"

We danced in silence for a while. I watched as every possible emotion crossed his face. He finally said, "It has something to do with ice cream." He looked deep into my eyes. "Is that crazy?"

"Probably," I told him. "But much of life makes no sense."

"Life and death? Am I dead?"

I pulled him close and we stood still in the center of the gazebo for a long time, holding each other tight, giving comfort for the frightening questions that had no answers.

"You're so good for me," he said at last. "I don't even know your name."

"Everyone knows yours." I gave a faint, sad laugh. "No one really knows mine anymore. I became Serephena back in my hippie phase."

It was his turn to laugh, at me, but not mocking. "Oh, no, that won't do. That name isn't you. It's a flighty name. You're solid and strong and grounded."

It was like he was giving me back myself. "Stella," I admitted. "My name is Stella."

His smile was a blessing. It was sunshine. It was—

I awoke as I always did, at the moment the sun went down. It was normally the most pleasant moment of the night. This time I woke with an anguished shout. I lay on my back with my eyes squeezed shut and tried to will myself back to sleep. That didn't work, of course. All I ended up doing was crying and the tears that rolled down onto the pillowcase made a disgusting mess—vampire tears having blood mixed in with the salt water.

I stripped the bed and threw the sheets in the laundry and paced around restlessly for a while wondering what the hell was going on in my head. Was I going senile? Worst of all loneliness well up in me and grief shook me and the heartache—

The heartache was a very real sensation. Physical pain radiated out of the core of my being where my shattered soul ached for the loss of half my being.

Or something like that.

I hurt. I really emotionally and physically hurt from what I knew had only been a dream. It took a couple of hours before I could get myself together enough to head off to the Alhambra in hopes of staving off the painful loneliness.

There wasn't a huge crowd at the club, but the place was jumping when I showed up. Everybody was gathered around the bar, abuzz with conversation.

I spotted Tiana and went up to her. "What happened."

"Anton went up in flames this morning," she answered.

"Why'd he do a thing like that without having a goodbye party first?" I asked. Anton was the bartender. He lived on the second floor. Used to.

"He didn't want to make a fuss."

"How'd it happen?"

"Usual way. He walked outside to see the dawn."

It happens. Every few decades the urge to end eternity gets hold of a vampire. I hadn't succumbed to the depression yet, but the way I was feeling tonight I sympathized with Anton's choice. I wasn't sure my usual panacea of buying lots of shoes was going to be enough.

"Did anybody sweep up his ashes?"

"Oh, yes," Tiana answered. "He's already in a nice urn over the bar with a sticky note reminder attached to sprinkle some blood on him in a year or two. The problem is what are we going to do for a bartender now?"

Blood brings us back and we usually are ready to carry on after an ash vacation. I wasn't in the mood to join in the "what are we going to do to replace Anton" discussion occupying everyone else's attention, but I did manage to elbow my way to a seat at the bar. I found myself looking up at the television overhead.

The local news was still dwelling on last night's multi-car crash. Slow news night, I supposed. "Isn't there a gang war or a car chase you could cover?" I complained to the television. "I'm bored."

"You don't feel bored," Tiana said, coming up beside me. "You're unhappy. I don't mean to snack on your emotions," she added when I glared at her. "You know I can't help it. Why are you unhappy? Anton?"

I snorted. "May he rest in peace, but I don't give a damn about Anton." I turned my glare back on the TV screen. "What's so important about last night's car crash?"

"Four people died on scene," she said, "Everybody else is hospitalized, most of them in critical condition. But the real reason the networks are still covering it is—"

Her timing was perfect, because at that moment *his* picture appeared on the screen.

"Oh, good God!" My heart felt like a knife had been plunged into it.

Tiana's hand touched my shoulder. "I know you're a fan, but—"

"He's not dead! Tell me he isn't dead?"

I only realized I was shaking her when she shouted, "Stop it! Let go of me!"

I did. I pointed at the television. "That's the man in my dream."

"The man of your dreams? He's an actor you've got a crush on."

"I do not get crushes. And I mean he's the man that was in my dream last day. We were dancing."

"Vampires don't dream. And he was in intensive care while you were sleeping."

The relief might have killed me if that was possible. As it was, it felt like I was having a heart attack. "Intensive care? So he isn't dead?"

"Not yet, but it's only a matter of time." She glanced at the face of the reporter now on the screen. "His deathwatch is what all the media fuss is about. They're worse ghouls than I am."

I automatically patted her shoulder, knowing that this admission hurt her pride, but my mind was racing on another matter. It hadn't been a dream. Somehow, it hadn't been a dream. He'd been there and I'd been there, only, where the hell was there?

"How did it happen?"

"He and some friends were going out for ice cream when they ended up in the pile up and the car went off the side of the mountain. He was the only survivor, but he's on life support and he's been declared brain dead."

"His brain isn't dead," I said. "It's been out dancing."

I was sure this was true. We'd been in telepathic contact. But how?

I heard the voice that speared into my brain back at the crash site in my head again—*Help me! Where are you?*

"Of course! He's psychic. He called out for help when we were up at the crash—and I answered him! That's how we met!"

I grabbed Tiana's cold, gray hand. "Come on, ghoulfriend!"

"Where are we going?" she asked as I pulled her toward the door.

I laughed, all my depression blown away by exaltation. "To the rescue, of course!"

"We're here. Now what?" Tiana asked as we moved across the ER waiting room.

"Go up to the ICU," I answered. "And take him home."

"He's on life support. There's probably cops and private security in the halls."

"I'll take care of them. All you have to do is create a diversion."

She licked her lips and nodded. Her skin was flushed to an almost normal human color. This was one of her feeding grounds and she'd showed me where to sneak in. It had been easy, even with the circus in the streets.

Outside the media and fan frenzy was as thick and chaotic as I'd ever seen it in all my decades of dwelling in this town. There were news vans sprouting satellite and lighting equipment and chuffing power generators. Reporters looked solemnly into cameras as they spoke. Paparazzi were thick as roaches in a tenement. Helicopters circled. Cops held a crowd back beyond a cordon surrounding the hospital. People held signs and candles and flowers. Some were singing the theme song from one of his movies.

I wondered if what I was doing was any less ridiculous than the behavior of his grieving fans.

In the ER people were bleeding and screaming and crying through their own problems. It was quiet and peaceful compared to what was going on outside. No one paid any attention as we made our way through a wide doorway, down a hallway and to a door past a row of elevators. You learn to take the stairs when you want to live an under the radar life.

"There are three people ready to die here," Tiana said after we reached the critical care floor and slipped into an empty room. She looked sad.

Hey, she's a ghoul, but that doesn't mean she isn't a kind person.

"Can you work with that?" I asked. Hey, I'm a vampire, remember?

She nodded. She prefers living off residual death energy instead of any direct involvement. "I hate doing the soul sucking thing, but, yeah, there's nothing that can be done for any of them."

"Is my guy one of the three?" I asked worriedly.

She looked thoughtful, shook her head. "Low energy, but stable. Now let me get to work."

I backed out of the room as she opened her mouth for one of those screams that only the dying could hear. The dying would give up their energy to the ghoul when they heard that sound. Pretty soon there was almost as much activity on this floor of the hospital at there was outside. Alarms went off at the nursing station, crash carts were hurried into rooms. There was running and shouting and I moved unnoticed to the room with the guard outside the door.

The guard wasn't a problem. I made him look into my eyes and he was instantly stunned. "Is there a security camera in there?" I asked.

"No. There's a nurse," he volunteered.

"Tell the nurse to respond to the code blues. Follow the nurse and volunteer to help." I hoped that was enough of an excuse to keep the guard from getting into too much trouble when I kidnapped his charge. I rushed into his room once he was alone.

Inside the door I stopped with my mouth hanging open. The man on the bed was hooked up to so many tubes and gadgets I didn't know how to start freeing him. I didn't have much time, so I whispered an apology for any pain I caused him and started ripping and pulling the life support equipment off him. Trails of his blood stained my clothes when I picked him up. The scent and warmth of it was intoxicating, but I fought off the sudden blood lust. My fangs ached like a virgin's on her first hunt as I carried him away with me.

His weight was no problem, but I'm a small woman and he's a very tall man. Carrying him was awkward, but you manage what you have to.

I took him downstairs, through the closed cafeteria and to a courtyard garden beyond it where I set him down gently beneath a squat palm tree. I sat beside him and settled his head in my lap. My fingers touched his temples.

Are you there? I thought.

You came for me! His voice called from so far away I barely sensed it.

Do you want to live? I asked. *You know I'm a vampire. I will try to change you if you want me to. Think carefully before you choose.*

In the long silence that followed I had to fight very hard to keep my fangs from sinking into his flesh. I'd never been so aroused by the scent of blood before, but I wasn't going to taste a drop without his permission. He had to make the choice.

I thought I'd have to be Wallachian, his thought came at last.

You're part Hungarian. There's a chance you'll change.

It depends on if my grandmas got raped by the right sort of invaders?

Pretty much.

I'll die otherwise, won't I?

Yes. But that shouldn't be why you choose to become a blood drinker, a night-walker, an exile from every part of the daylight world.

It really isn't all that bad being a vampire, but there are difficulties and the lifestyle should not be glamorized for potential newbies. No matter how much you want to share a coffin with them.

Can I stay with you if I change?

My heart sang at his question. And, oh, how my fangs ached!

Yes, I told him. For as long as you want. Forever if you want.

Forever sounds good to me. Do it.

Remember that it might not take. That—

Shut up and bite me.

I couldn't argue with that. So I did.

And I'd never had a rush like it in all my years of sucking the good stuff! I couldn't count the orgasms that shook me before every drop of him was flowing inside me.

I didn't have to share my blood with him. Some sort of enzyme in my saliva was transferred to him from the bite and the enzyme would trigger the change if it was going to happen. But, just in case, I bit my wrist and poured a few drops of my blood into his mouth. Not that he was capable of swallowing. At this point he was essentially dead. He'd either get better or I'd have to dispose of his body in a way that the marks on his throat would never be seen.

I didn't want to think about disposal. I didn't want to think of him ever being dead. I held his limp body and felt it grow heavier and colder and worried and cried those disgusting blood-drenched vampire tears. I don't know for how long. Long enough for my mood to turn bleak and heartbroken.

Long enough for me to be aware that the sun would be up in an hour or so.

There's an almost physical pressure on the skin the closer daylight comes. Normally I'd be starting to think about getting to cover. Instead, I vowed I'd stay here and let the sun take me if he didn't come around before the end of the night. I didn't care if my ashes blew away so far there wouldn't be anything left of me. Perhaps the fire that took me would burn him as well, and our ashes would blend together.

Sentimental, aren't you?

I heard the thought but it took a long time before I came out of my grief enough to realize that the voice wasn't my imagination.

"You're alive!"

Don't shout. I have a hangover. That's not right. My throat hurts. I'm thirsty. My mouth tastes like sweet copper.

"That's my blood. You're alive," I repeated, the words whispered in his ear as I helped him sit up. "You're a vampire."

"I guess the right Cossacks raped my grandmas."

His voice was a rough croak, but the most delicious sound I'd ever heard. He struggled to his feet, and insisted on giving me his hand to help me up. Living or dead, he was always a gentleman. When I was on my feet his arms came around me. He was weak enough that I ended up holding him up as we embraced.

"We could dance like this forever," he said.

I sighed romantically. "We could." I looked around. "We could if the sun wasn't coming up soon. We need to get out of here."

He cupped my cheek and looked at me with his new night vision. "You're as beautiful as I dreamed you were, my Stella. Thank you—for saving me, thank you for being with me now and forever."

There's no way a girl can't respond to that. I kissed him, and he kissed back and it was real and deep and better than any dream.

After a while he lifted his head and gave a dry, hacking cough. "S-sorry. Thirsty."

I put my arm around his waist and helped him toward the garden door. "I know just the place where we can get a beer. Now that you've changed you can find it on your own."

"I'd rather go with you."

You have no idea how much this meant to me.

Tiana met us outside the cafeteria and guided us along her secret route out of the hospital and away from the crowd. He noticed all the fuss as we drove away, he and I squeezed into the trunk of Tiana's car.

"You have no idea how happy I am to leave the celebrity era of my life behind," he told me.

"You'll miss acting."

"I'll think of a way to get back to it. Do vampires work? Do I need a job?"

"I'm a real estate mogul. You can live off me. Wait—" I'd remembered Anton. "The place we're heading, the Alhambra Club, needs a bartender. I know the owner." That would be me. "If you're interested."

We were squeezed in pretty tightly, but he managed to pull me closer. "Does this place have a dance floor?"

I laughed, happier than I'd ever imagine I could be. "It will when we're done with it if that's what you want," I promised.

"I think dancing—being—with you is all I ever wanted."

"Me too." I couldn't stop the girlish giggle from escaping. "I guess this is a real—"

"Hollywood ending," he finished, not having to be psychic to know what I was thinking.

A TRICK OF THE DARK
Tina Rath

This haunting tale takes us back to the period between two World Wars when chrome was shockingly modern, a young man might be thought to be an anarchist if he went about with long curly hair and wore no hat, and the best a young woman in poor health could hope for was to stay home in bed and await her demise . . . or perhaps not.

Tina Rath gained her doctorate from London University with a thesis on The Vampire in Popular Fiction *and her MA with a dissertation on* The Vampire in the Theatre. *She has made radio and television appearances and lectured on vampires and other aspects of Gothic literature for various groups and societies. Her fiction has been published in periodicals such as* All Hallows, Ghosts and Scholars, The Magazine of Fantasy & Science Fiction, Supernatural Tales 16, Visionary Tongue, *and* Weird Tales. *Anthology appearances include* Strange Tales, Exotic Gothic 3, *and* The Mammoth Book of Vampires. *She edited the anthology* Conventional Vampires *for the Dracula Society in 2003.*

"What job finishes just at sunset?"

Margaret jumped slightly. "What a weird question, darling. Park keeper, I suppose." Something made her turn to look at her daughter. She was propped up against her pillows, looking, Margaret thought guiltily, about ten years old. She must keep remembering, she told herself fiercely, that Maddie was nineteen. This silly heart-thing, as she called it, was keeping her in bed for much longer than they ever thought it would, but it couldn't stop her growing up . . . she must listen to her, and talk to her like a grown-up.

Intending to do just that she went to sit on the edge of the bed. It was covered with a glossy pink eiderdown, embroidered with fat pink and mauve peonies. The lamp on Maddie's bed-side table had a rosy shade, Maddie was wearing a pink bed jacket, lovingly crocheted by her grandmother, and Maddie's pale

blond hair was tied back with a pink ribbon . . . but in the midst of this plethora
of pink Maddie's face looked pale and peaky. The words of a story she had read
to Maddie once—how many years ago?—came back to her: "Peak and pine,
peak and pine." It was about a changeling child who never thrived, but lay in
the cradle, crying and fretting, peaking and pining . . . in the end the creature
had gone back to its own people, and, she supposed that the healthy child had
somehow got back to his mother, but she couldn't remember. Margaret shivered,
wondering why people thought such horrid stories were suitable for children.

"What made you wonder who finishes work at sunset?" she asked.

"Oh—nothing," Maddie looked oddly shy, as she might have done if her mother
had asked her about a boy who had partnered her at tennis, or asked her to a dance.
If such a thing could ever have happened. She played with the pink ribbons at her
neck and a little, a very little colour crept into that pale face. "It's just—well—I can't
read all day, or—" She hesitated and Margaret mentally filled in the gap. She had
her embroidery, her knitting, those huge complicated jigsaws that her friends were
so good about finding for her, a notebook for jotting down those funny little verses
that someone was going to ask someone's uncle about publishing . . . but all that
couldn't keep her occupied all day.

"Sometimes I just look out of the window," she said.

"Oh, darling . . . " She couldn't bear to think of her daughter just lying
there—just looking out of the window. "Why don't you call me when you get
bored? We could have some lovely talks. Or I could telephone Bunty or Cissie
or—" it's getting quite autumnal after all, she thought, and Maddie's friends
won't be out so much, playing tennis, or swimming or . . . You couldn't expect
them to sit for hours in a sick-room. They dashed in, tanned and breathless from
their games and bicycle rides, or windblown and glowing from a winter walk,
and dropped off a jigsaw or a new novel . . . and went away.

"I don't mind, Mummy," Maddie was saying. "It's amazing what you can see,
even in a quiet street like this. I mean, that's why I like this room. Because you
can see out."

Margaret looked out of the window. Yes. You could see a stretch of pavement,
a bit of Mrs. Creswell's hedge, a lamppost, the post box and Mrs. Monkton's
gate. It was not precisely an enticing view, and she exclaimed, "Oh, darling!"
again.

"You'd be amazed who visits Mrs. Monkton in the afternoons," Maddie said
demurely.

"Good heavens, who—" Margaret exclaimed, but Maddie gave a reassuringly
naughty giggle.

"That would be telling! You'll have to sit up here one afternoon and watch for yourself."

"I might," Margaret said. But how could she? There was always so much to do downstairs, letters to write, shopping to do, and cook to deal with. (Life to get on with?) She too, she realized, dropped in on Maddie, left her with things to sustain or amuse her. And went away.

"Perhaps we could move you downstairs, darling," she said. But that would be so difficult. The doctor had absolutely forbidden Maddie to use the stairs, so how on earth could they manage what Margaret could only, even in the privacy of her thoughts, call *the bathroom problem*? Too shame-making for Maddie to have to ask to be carried up the stairs every time she needed—and who was there to do it during the day? Maddie was very light—much too light—but her mother knew that she could not lift her let alone carry her by herself.

"But you can't see anything from the sitting room," Maddie said.

"Oh darling—" Margaret realized she was going to have to leave Maddie alone again. Her husband would be home soon and she was beginning to have serious doubts about the advisability of re-heating the fish-pie . . . She must have a quick word with Cook about cheese omelettes. If only Cook wasn't so bad with eggs . . . "What's this about sunset anyway?" she said briskly.

"Sunset comes a bit earlier every day," Maddie said. "And just at sunset a man walks down the street."

"The same man, every night?" Margaret asked.

"The same man, always just after sunset," Maddie confirmed.

"Perhaps he's a postman?" Margaret suggested.

"Then he'd wear a uniform," Maddie said patiently. "And the same if he was a park-keeper I suppose—they wear uniform too, don't they. Besides he doesn't look like a postman."

"So—what does he look like?"

"It's hard to explain," Maddie struggled for the right words, "but—can you imagine a beautiful skull?"

"What! What a horrible idea!" Margaret stood up, clutching the gray foulard at her bosom. "Maddie, if you began talking like this I shall call Dr. Whiston. I don't care if he doesn't like coming out after dinner. Skull-headed men walking past the house every night indeed!"

Maddie pouted. "I didn't say that. It's just that his face is very—sculptured. You can see the bones under the skin, especially the cheekbones. It just made me think—he must even have a beautiful skull."

"And how is he dressed?" Margaret asked faintly.

"A white shirt and a sort of loose black coat," Maddie said. "And he has quite long curly black hair. I think he might be a student."

"No hat?" her mother asked, scandalized. "He sounds more like an anarchist! Really, Maddie, I wonder if I should go and have a word with the policeman on the corner and tell him a suspicious character has been hanging about outside the house."

"No, Mother!" Maddie sounded so anguished that her mother hastily laid a calming hand on her forehead.

"Now, darling, don't upset yourself. You must remember what the doctor said. Of course I won't call him if you don't want me to, or the policeman. That was a joke, darling! But you mustn't get yourself upset like this . . . Oh dear, your forehead feels quite clammy. Here, take one of your tablets. I'll get you a glass of water."

And in her very real anxiety for her daughter, worries about the fish pie and well-founded doubts about the substitute omelettes, Margaret almost forgot about the stranger. Almost but not quite. A meeting with Mrs. Monkton one evening when they had both hurried out to catch the last post and met in front of the post-box, reminded her and she found herself asking if Mrs. Monkton had noticed anyone "hanging about."

"A young man," that lady exclaimed with a flash of what Margaret decided was rather indecent excitement, "but darling, there are no young men left." Margaret raised a hand in mute protest only to have brushed aside by Mrs. Monkton. "Well, not nearly enough to go round anyway. I expect this one was waiting for Elsie."

Elsie worked for both Mrs. Monkton and Margaret, coming in several times a week to do "the rough," the cleaning that was beneath Margaret's cook and Mrs. Monkton's extremely superior maid. She was a handsome girl, with, it was rumored, an obliging disposition, who would never have been allowed across the threshold of a respectable household when Margaret was young. But nowadays . . . Mrs. Monkton's suggestion did set Margaret's mind at rest. A hatless young man—yes, he must be waiting for Elsie. She might "have a word" with the girl about the propriety of encouraging young men to hang about the street for her, but, on the other hand, she might not . . . She hurried back home.

Bunty's mother came to tea, full of news. Bunty's elder sister was getting engaged to someone her mother described as "a bit nquos, but what can you do . . . " *Nquos* was a rather transparent code for "not quite our sort." The young man's father was, it appeared, very, very rich, though no one was quite sure where he had made his money. He was going to give—to give—outright, Bunty's mother had gasped, a big house in Surrey to the young couple. And he was going to furnish it too, unfortunately, according to his own somewhat . . . individual taste . . .

"Chrome, my dear, chrome from floor to ceiling. The dining room looks like a milk bar. And as for the bedroom—Jack says—" she lowered her voice, "he says it looks like an avant garde brothel in Berlin. Although how he knows anything about them I'm sure I'm not going to ask. But he's having nothing to do with the wedding," she added, sipping her tea as if it were hemlock. "I wonder my dear—would dear little Maddie be well enough to be a bridesmaid? It won't be until next June. I want to keep Pammy to myself for as long as I can . . . " she dabbed at her eyes.

"Of course," Margaret murmured doubtfully. And then, with more determination, "I'll ask the doctor."

And, rather surprising herself, she did. On his next visit to Maddie she lured him into the sitting room with the offer of a glass of sherry and let him boom on for a while on how well Maddie was responding to his treatment. Then she asked the Question, the one she had, until that moment, had not dared to ask.

"But when will Maddie be—quite well? Could she be a bridesmaid, say, in June next year?"

The doctor paused, sherry halfway to his lips. He was not used to being questioned. Margaret realized that he thought she had been intolerably frivolous. "Bridesmaid?" the doctor boomed. And then thawed, visibly. Women, he knew, cared about such things. "Bridesmaid! Well, why not? Provided she goes on as well as she has been. And you don't let her get too excited. Not too many dress fittings, you know, and see you get her home early after the wedding. No dancing and only a tiny glass of champagne . . . "

"And will she ever we well enough . . . to . . . to . . . marry herself and to . . . " But Margaret could not bring herself to finish that sentence to a man, not even a medical man.

"Marry—well, I wouldn't advise it. And babies? No. No. Still, that's the modern girl, isn't it? No use for husbands and children these days—" and he boomed himself out of the house.

Margaret remembered that the doctor had married a much younger woman. Presumably the marriage was not a success . . . then she let herself think of Maddie. She wondered if Bunty's mother would like to exchange places with her. Margaret would never have to lose her daughter to the son of a nouveau riche war profiteer. Never . . . and she sat down in her pretty chintz covered armchair and cried as quietly as she could, in case Maddie heard her. For some reason she never asked herself how far the doctor's confident boom might carry. Later she went up to her daughter, smiling gallantly.

"The doctor's so pleased with you, Maddie," she said. "He thinks you'll be well enough to be Pammy's bridesmaid! You'll have to be sure you finish her present in nice time."

Margaret had bought a tray cloth and six place mats stamped with the design of a figure in a poke bonnet and a crinoline, surrounded by flowers. Maddie was supposed to be embroidering them in tasteful naturalistic shades of pink, mauve, and green, as a wedding gift for Pammy, but she seemed to have little enthusiasm for the task. Her mother stared at her, lying back in her next of pillows. "Peak and pine! Peak and pine!" said the voice in her head.

"Do you ever see your young man any more?" she asked, more to distract herself than because she was really concerned.

"Oh, no," Maddie said, raising her shadowed eyes to her mother. "I don't think he was ever there at all. It was a trick of the dark."

"Trick of the light, surely," Margaret said. And then, almost against her will, "Do you remember that story I used to read you? About the changeling child?"

"What, the one that lay in the cradle saying 'I'm old, I'm old, I'm ever so old?' " Maddie said. "Whatever made you think of that?"

"I don't know," Margaret gasped. "But you know how you sometimes get silly words going round and round your head. It's as if I can't stop repeating those words from the story—'Peak and pine!'—to myself over and over again." There, she had said it aloud. That must exorcise them, surely.

"But that's not from the changeling story," Maddie said. "It's from 'Christabel,' you know, Coleridge's poem about the weird Lady Geraldine. She says it to the mother's ghost 'Off wandering mother! Peak and pine!' We read it at school, but Miss Brownrigg made us miss out all that bit about Geraldine's breasts."

"I should think so, too," Margaret said weakly.

Autumn became winter, although few people noticed by what tiny degrees the days grew shorter and shorter until sunset came at around four o'clock. Except perhaps Maddie, sitting propped up on her pillows, and watching every day for the young man who still walked down the street every evening, in spite of what she had told her mother. And even she could not have said just when he stopped walking directly passed the window, and took to standing in that dark spot just between the lamp post and the post box, look up at her . . .

"Where's your little silver cross, darling?" Margaret said, suddenly, wondering vaguely when she had last seen Maddie wearing it.

"Oh, I don't know," Maddie said, too casually. "I think the clasp must have broken and it slipped off."

"Oh, but—" Margaret looked helplessly at her daughter. "I do hope Elsie hasn't picked it up. I sometimes think . . . "

"I expect it'll turn up," Maddie said. Her eyes slid away from her mother's face and returned to the window.

"How's Pammy's present coming along?" Margaret asked, speaking to that white reflection in the dark glass, trying to make her daughter turn back to her. She picked up Maddie's work bag. And stared. One of the place mats had been completed. But the figure of the lady had been embroidered in shades of black and it was standing in the midst of scarlet roses and tall purple lilies. It was cleverly done: every fold and flounce was picked out . . . but Margaret found it rather disturbing. She was glad that the poke bonnet hit the figure's face . . . She looked up to realize that Maddie was looking at her almost slyly.

"Don't you like it?" she said.

"It's—it's quite modern, isn't it?"

"What, lazy daisies and crinoline ladies, modern?" How long had Maddie's voice had that lazy mocking tone? She sounded like a world-weary adult talking to a very young and silly child.

Margaret put the work down.

"You will be all right, darling, won't you?" Margaret said, rushing into her daughter's room one cold December afternoon. "Only I must do some Christmas shopping, I really must . . . "

"Of course you must, Mummy," Maddie said. "You've got my list, haven't you? Do try to find something really nice for Bunty, she's been so kind . . . "

And what I would really like to give her, Maddie thought is a whole parcel of jigsaws . . . and all the time in the world to see how she likes them . . . She leaned against her pillows, watching her mother scurry down the street. She would catch a bus at the corner by the church, and then an underground train, and then face the crowded streets and shops of a near-Christmas West End London. Maddie would have plenty of time to herself. She knew (although her mother did not) that Cook would be going out to have tea with her friend at Mrs. Cresswell's at half-past three, and for at least one blessed hour she would be entirely alone in the house.

She pulled herself further up in the bed, and fumbled in the drawer of her bedside table to find the contraband she had managed to persuade Elsie to bring in for her. Elsie had proved much more useful than Bunty, or Cissie or any of her kind friends. She sorted through the scarlet lipstick, the eye-black, the face-powder, and began to draw the kind of face she knew she had always wanted on the blank canvas of her pale skin. After twenty minutes of careful work she felt she had succeeded rather well.

"I'm old, I'm old, I'm ever so old," she crooned to herself. She freed her hair from its inevitable pink ribbon, and brushed it sleekly over her shoulders, then she took off her lacy bed-jacket and the white winceyette nightie beneath it. Finally she slid into the garment the invaluable Elsie had found for her (Heaven knows where—although Maddie had a shrewd suspicion it might have been stolen from another of Elsie's clients—perhaps the naughty Mrs. Monkton). It was a nightdress made of layers of black and red chiffon, just a little too large for Maddie, but the way it tended to slide from her shoulders could have, she felt, its own attraction.

All these preparations had taken quite a long time, especially as Maddie had had to stop every so often to catch her breath and once to take one of her tablets . . . but she was ready just before sunset. She slipped out of bed, crossed the room, and sat in a chair beside the window. So. The trap was almost set (but was she the trap or only the bait . . . ?) Only one thing remained to be done.

Maddie took out her embroidery scissors, and, clenching her teeth, ran the tiny sharp points into her wrist . . .

The bus was late and crowded. Margaret struggled off, trying to balance her load of packages and parcels and hurried down the road, past the churchyard wall, past Mrs. Monkton's red-brick villa, past the post box—and hesitated. For a moment she thought she had seen something—Maddie's strange man with the beautiful skull-like face? But no, there were two white faces there in the shadows—no . . . there was nothing. A trick of the dark . . . She dropped her parcels in the hall and hurried up the stairs.

"Here I am, darling, I'm so sorry I'm late . . . Oh, Maddie—Maddie darling . . . whatever are you doing in the dark?"

She switched on the light.

"Maddie. Maddie, where are you?" she whispered. "What have you done?"

When Gretchen Was Human
Mary A. Turzillo

"When Gretchen Was Human" is a story about love, but that doesn't mean—as you will see—it is romantic.

Mary Turzillo's Nebula-winning story, "Mars Is No Place for Children," and her novel An Old-Fashioned Martian Girl, *have been selected as recreational reading on the International Space Station. Her poetry and fiction appears in* Asimov's, The Magazine of Fantasy & Science Fiction, Interzone, Weird Tales, Crafty Cat Crimes, Electric Velocipede, Lady Churchill's Rosebud Wristlet, The Ultimate Witch, Dark Terrors, Oceans of the Mind, *and anthologies and magazines in the U.S., Great Britain, Japan, Italy, Germany, and the Czech Republic. Her poetry collection,* Your Cat & Other Space Aliens, *was a Pushcart nominee. Her most recent book is* The Dragon Dictionary, *with Marge Simon (Sam's Dot, 2010), and she has a vampirish tale coming out in* Ladies of Trade Town *from Harp Haven. She lives in Ohio with her mad scientist-writer husband, Geoff Landis and four cats with surprisingly long canines.*

"You're only human," said Nick Scuroforno, fanning the pages of a tattered first edition of *Image of the Beast*. The conversation had degenerated from half-hearted sales pitch, Gretchen trying to sell Nick Scuroforno an early Pangborn imprint. Now they sat cross-legged on the scarred wooden floor of Miss Trilby's Tomes, watching dust motes dance in August four o'clock sun. Gretchen was wallowing in self disclosure and voluptuous self-pity.

"Sometimes I don't even feel human," Gretchen settled her back against the soft, dusty-smelling spines of a leather-bound 1910 imprint *Book of Knowledge*.

"I can identify."

"And given the choice, who'd really want to be?" asked Gretchen, tracing the grain of the wooden floor with chapped fingers.

"You have a choice?" asked Scuroforno.

"See, after Ashley was diagnosed, my ex got custody of her. Just as well." She rummaged her smock for a tissue. "I didn't have hospitalization after we split. And his would cover her, but only if she goes to a hospital way off in Seattle." Unbidden, a memory rose: Ashley's warm little body, wriggly as a puppy's, settling in her lap, opening *Where the Wild Things Are*, striking the page with her tiny pink index finger. *Mommy, read!*

Scuroforno nodded. "But can't they cure leukemia now?"

"Sometimes. She's in remission at the moment. But how long will that last?" Gretchen kept sneaking looks at Scuroforno. Amazingly, she found him attractive. She thought depression had killed the sexual impulse in her. He was a big man, chunky but not actually fat, with evasive amber eyes and shaggy hair. Not bad looking, but not handsome either, in gray sweat pants, a brown T-shirt, and beach sandals. He had a habit of twisting the band of his watch, revealing a strip of pale skin from which the fine hairs of his wrist had been worn.

"And yet cancer itself is immortal," he mused. "Why can't it make its host immortal too?"

"Cancer is immortal?" But of course cancer would be immortal. It was the ultimate predator. Why shouldn't it hold all the high cards?

"The cells are. There's some pancreatic cancer cells that have been growing in a lab fifty years since the man with the cancer died. And yet, cancer cells are not even as intelligent as a virus. A virus knows not to kill its host."

"But viruses do kill!"

He smiled. "That's true, lots do kill. Bacteria, too. But there are bacteria that millennia ago decided to infect every cell in our bodies. Turned into—let me think of the word. Organelles? Like the mitochondrion."

"What's a mitochondrion?"

He shrugged, slyly basking in his superior knowledge. "It's an energy-converting organ in animal cells. Different DNA from the host. You'd think you could design a mitochondrion that would make the host live forever."

She stared at him. "No. I certainly wouldn't think that. "

"Why not?"

"It would be horrible. A zombie. A vampire."

He was silent, a smile playing around his eyes.

She shuddered. "You get these ideas from Miss Trilby's Tomes?"

"The wisdom of the ages." He gestured at the high shelves, then stood. "And of course the World Wide Web. Here comes Madame Trilby herself. Does she like you lounging on the floor with customers?"

Gretchen flushed. "Oh, she never minds anything. My grandpa was friends with her father, and I've worked here off and on since I was little." She took Scuroforno's proffered hand and pulled herself to her feet.

Miss Trilby, frail and spry, wafting a fragrance of face powder and moldy paper, lugged in a milk crate of pamphlets. She frowned at Gretchen. Strange, thought Gretchen. Yesterday she said I should find a new man, but now she's glaring at me. For sitting on the floor? I sit on the floor to do paperwork all the time. There's no room for chairs. It has to be for schmoozing with a male customer.

Miss Trilby dumped the mail on the counter and swept into the back room.

"Cheerful today, hmm?" said Scuroforno.

"Really, she's so good to me. She lends me money to go to Seattle and see my daughter. She's just nervous today."

"Ah. By the way, before I leave, do you have a cold, or were you crying?"

Gretchen reddened. "I have a chronic sinus infection." She suddenly saw herself objectively: stringy hair, bad posture, skinny. How could she be flirting with this man?

He touched her wrist. "Take care." And strode through the door into the street.

"Him you don't need," said Miss Trilby, bustling back in and firing up the shop's ancient Kaypro computer.

"Did I say I did?"

"Your face says you think you do. Did he buy anything?"

"I'm sorry. I can never predict what he'll be interested in."

"I'll die in the poorhouse. Sell him antique medical texts. Or detective novels. He stands reading historical novels right off the shelf and laughs. Pretends to be an expert, finds all the mistakes."

"What have you got against him, besides reading and not buying?"

"Oh, he buys. But Gretchen, lambkin, a man like that you don't need. Loner. Crazy."

"But he listens. He's so understanding."

"Like the butcher with the calf. What's this immortal cancer stuff he's feeding you?"

"Nothing. We were talking about Ashley."

"Sorry, lambkin. Life hasn't been kind to you. But be a little wise. This man has delusions he's a vampire."

Gretchen smoothed the dust jacket of *Euryanthe and Oberon at Covent Garden*. "Maybe he is."

Miss Trilby rounded her lips in mock horror. "Perhaps! Doesn't look much like Frank Langella, though, does he?"

No, he didn't, thought Gretchen, as she sorted orders for reprints of Kadensho's *Book of the Flowery Tradition* and de Honnecourt's *Fervor of Buenos Aires.*

But there was something appealing about Nick Scuroforno, something besides his empathy for a homely divorcee with a terminally ill child. His spare, dark humor, maybe that was it. Miss Trilby did not understand everything.

Why not make a play for him?

Even to herself, her efforts seemed pathetic. She got Keesha, the single mother across the hall in her apartment, to help her frost her hair. She bought a cheap cardigan trimmed with Angora and dug out an old padded bra.

"Lambkin," said Miss Trilby dryly one afternoon when Gretchen came in dolled up in her desperate finery, "The man is not exactly a fashion plate himself."

But Scuroforno seemed flattered, if not impressed, by Gretchen's efforts, and took her out for coffee, then a late dinner. Mostly, however, he came into the bookstore an hour before closing and let her pretend to sell him some white elephant like the Reverend Wood's *Trespassers: How Inhabitants of Earth, Air, and Water Are Enabled to Trespass on Domains Not Their Own.* She would fiddle with the silver chain on her neck, and they would slide to the floor where she would pour out her troubles to him. Other customers seldom came in so late.

"You trust him with private details of your life," said Miss Trilby, "but what do you know of his?"

He did talk. He did. Philosophy, history, details of Gretchen's daughter's illness. One day, she asked, "What do you do?"

"I steal souls. Photographer."

Oh.

"Can't make much money on that artsy stuff," Miss Trilby commented when she heard this. "Rumor says he's got a private source of income."

"Illegal, you mean?"

"What a romantic you are, Gretchen. Ask him."

Gambling luck and investments, he told her.

One day, leaving for the shop, Gretchen opened her mail and found a letter— not even a phone call—that Ashley's remission was over. Her little girl was in the hospital again.

The grief was surreal, physical. She was afraid to go back into her apartment. She had bought a copy of Jan Pieńkowski's *Haunted House,* full of diabolically funny pop-ups, for Ashley's birthday. She couldn't bear to look at it now, waiting like a poisoned bait on the counter.

⌒—✦—⌒

She went straight to the shop, began alphabetizing the new stock. Nothing made sense, she couldn't remember if O came after N. Miss Trilby had to drag her away, make her stop.

"What's wrong? Is it Ashley?"

Gretchen handed her the letter.

Miss Trilby read it through her thick lorgnette. Then, "Look at yourself. Your cheeks are flushed. Eyes bright. Disaster becomes you. Or is it the nearness of death bids us breed, like romance in a concentration camp?"

Gretchen shuddered. "Maybe my body is tricking me into reproducing again."

"To replace Ashley. Not funny, lambkin. But possibly true. I ask again, why this man? Doesn't madness frighten you?"

Next day, Gretchen followed him to his car. It seemed natural to get in, uninvited, ride home with him, follow him up two flights of stairs covered with cracked treads.

He let her perch on a stool in his kitchen darkroom while he printed peculiar old architectural photographs. The room smelled of chemicals, vinegary. An old Commodore 64 propped the pantry door open. She had seen a new computer in his living room, running a screen saver of Giger babies holding grenades, and wraiths dancing an agony-dance.

"I never eat here," he said. "As a kitchen, it's useless."

He emptied trays, washed solutions down the drain, rinsed. Her heart beat hard under the sleazy Angora. His body, sleek as a lion's, gave off a male scent, faintly predatory.

While his back was turned, she undid her cardigan. The buttons too easily slipped out of the cheap fuzzy fabric, conspiring with lust.

She slipped it off as he turned around. And felt the draft of the cold kitchen and the surprise of his gaze on her inadequate chest.

He turned away, dried his hands on the kitchen towel. "Don't fall in love with me."

"Not at all arrogant, are you?" She wouldn't, wouldn't fall in love. No. That wasn't quite it.

"Not arrogance. A warning. I'm territorial; predators have to be. For a while, yes, I'd keep you around. But sooner or later, you'd interfere with my hunting. I'd kill you or drive you away to prevent myself from killing you."

"I won't fall in love with you." Level. Convincing.

"All right." He threw the towel into the sink, came to her. Covered her mouth with his.

She responded clumsily, overreacting after the long dry spell, clawing his back.

The kiss ended. He stroked her hair. "Don't worry. I won't draw blood. I can control the impulse."

She half-pretended to play along with him. Half of her did believe. "It doesn't matter. I want to be like you." A joke?

He sat on the kitchen chair, pulled her to him and put his cheek against her breasts. "It doesn't work that way. You have to have the right genes to be susceptible."

"It really is an infection?" Still half-pretending to believe, still almost joking.

"A virus that gives you cancer. All I know is that of all the thousands I've preyed upon, only a few have gotten the fever and lived to become—like me."

"Vampire?"

"As good a word as any. One who I infected and who lived on was my son. He got the fever and turned. That's why I think it's genetic." He pulled her nearer, as if for warmth.

"What happens if the prey doesn't have the genes?"

"Nothing. Nothing happens. I never take enough to kill. I haven't killed a human in over a hundred years. You're safe."

She slid to her knees, wrapping her arms around his waist. He held her head to him, stroking her bare arms and shoulders. "Silk," he said finally, pulling her up, touching her breast. She had nursed Ashley, but it hadn't stopped her from getting leukemia. Fire and ice sizzled across her breasts, as if her milk were letting down.

"Are you lonely?"

"God, yes. That's the only reason I was even tempted to let you do this. You know, I have the instincts of a predator, it does that. But I was born human."

"How did you infect your son?"

"Accident. I was infected soon after I was married. Pietra, my wife, is long dead."

"Pietra. Strange name."

"Not so strange in thirteenth century Florence. I turned shortly after I was married. I was very ill. I knew I needed blood, but no knowledge of why or how to control my thirst. I took blood from a priest who came to give me last rites. My thirst was so voracious, I killed him. Not murder, Gretchen. I was no more guilty that a baby suckling at breast. The first thirst is overpowering. I took too much, and when I saw that he was dead, I put on my clothes and ran away."

"Leaving your wife—"

"Never saw her again. But years later, I encountered this young man at a gambling table. Pretended to befriend him. Overpowered him in a narrow dark street. Drank to slake my thirst. Later I encountered him, changed. As a rival for the blood of the neighborhood. I had infected him, he had gotten the fever, developed into—what I am. Later I put the pieces together; I had left Pietra pregnant, this was our son, you see. He had the right genes. If he hadn't, he would have never even noticed that modest blood loss." His hand stroked her naked shoulder.

"Where is he now?"

"I often wonder. I drove him off soon after he finished the change. Vampires can't stand one another. They interfere with each other's hunting."

"Why have you chosen to tell me this?" She tried to control her voice, but heard it thicken.

"I tell people all the time what I am. Nobody ever believes it." He stood, pulling her to her feet, kissed her again, pressing his hips to her body. She ran her hands over his shoulders and loosened his shirt. "You don't believe me, either."

And then she smiled. "I want to believe you. I told you once, I don't want to be human."

He raised his eyebrows and smiled down at her. "I doubt you have the right genes to be anything else."

His bedroom was neat, sparsely furnished. She recognized books from Miss Trilby's Tomes, *Red Dragon, Confessions of an English Opium Eater* on a low shelf near the bed. Unexpectedly, he lifted her off her feet and laid her on the quilt. They kissed again, a long, complicated kiss. He took her slowly. He didn't close the door, and from the bed she could see his computer screen in the living room. The Giger wraiths in his screen saver danced slowly to their passion. And then she closed her eyes, and the wraiths danced behind her lids.

When they were finished, she knew that she had lied; if she did not *feel* love, then it was something as strong and as dangerous.

She traced a vein on the back of his hand. "You were born in Italy?"

He kissed the hand with which she had been tracing his veins. "Hundreds of years ago, yes. Before my flesh became numb."

"Then why don't you speak with an accent?"

He rolled onto his back, hands behind his head, and grinned. "I've been an American longer than you have. I made it a point to get rid of my accent. Aren't you going to ask me about the sun and garlic and silver bullets?"

"All just superstition?"

"It would seem." He smiled wryly. "But there is the gradual loss of feeling."

"You say you can't love."

He groped in the bedside table for a pen. He drove the tip into his arm. "You see?" Blood welled up slowly.

"Stop! My god, must you hurt yourself?"

"Just demonstrating. The flesh has been consumed by the—by the cancer, if that's what it is. It starts in the coldest parts of the body. No nerves. I don't feel. It has nothing to do with emotion."

"And because you are territorial—"

"Yes. But the emotions don't die, exactly. There's this horrible conflict. And physically, the metastasis continues, very slowly. I heard of a very old vampire whose brain had turned. He was worse than a shark, a feeding machine—"

She pulled the sheets around her. The room seemed cold now that they were no longer entwined. "You seemed human enough, when you—"

"You didn't feel it when I kissed you?"

"Feel—"

He guided her index finger into his mouth, under the tongue. A bony little organ there, tiny spikes, retracted under the root of the tongue.

She jerked her hand away, suddenly afraid. He caught it and kissed it again, almost mockingly.

She shuddered, tenderness confounded with terror, and buried her face in the pillow. But wasn't this what she had secretly imagined, hoped for?

"Next time," she said, turning her face up to him, like a daisy to the sun, "draw blood, do."

The wraiths in his screen saver danced.

The idea of a bus trip to Seattle filled her with dread, and she put it off, as if somehow by staying in Warren she could stop the progress of reality. But a second letter, this from her ex-sister-in-law Miriam, forced her to face facts. The chemotherapy, Miriam wrote, was not working this time. Ashley was "fading".

"Fading"!

The same mail brought a postcard from Scuroforno. *Out of town on business, seeing to investments. Be well, human*, he wrote.

She told Miss Trilby she needed time off to see Ashley.

"Lambkin, you look awful. Don't go on the bus. I'll lend you money for the plane, and you can pay me back when you marry some rich lawyer."

"No, Miss Trilby. I have a cold, that's all." Her skin itched, her throat and mouth were sore, her head throbbed.

They dusted books that afternoon. When Gretchen came down from the stepladder, she was so exhausted she curled up on the settee in the back room with a copy of *As You Desire*. The words swam before her eyes, but they might stop her from thinking, thinking about Ashley, about cancer, immortal cells killing their mortal host. Thinking, *immortal*. It might have worked. A different cancer. And then she stopped thinking.

And awoke in All Soul's Hospital, in pain and confusion.

"Drink. You're dehydrated," the nurse said. The room smelled of bleach and dead flowers.

Who had brought her in?

"I don't know. Your employer? An elderly woman. Doctor will be in to talk to you. Try to drink at least a glass every hour."

In lucid moments, Gretchen rejoiced. It was the change, surely it was the change. If she lived, she would be released from all the degrading baggage that being human hung upon her.

The tests showed nothing. Of course, the virus would not culture in agar, Gretchen thought. If it was a virus.

She awoke nights thinking of human blood. She whimpered when they took away her roommate, an anorexic widow, nearly dry, but an alluring source of a few delicious drops, if only she could get to her while the nurses were away.

Miss Trilby visited, and only by iron will did Gretchen avoid leaping upon her. Gretchen screamed, "Get away from me! I'll kill you!" The doctors, unable to identify her illness, must have worried about her outburst; she didn't get another roommate. And they didn't release her, though she had no insurance.

Miss Trilby did not come back.

They never thought of cancer. Cancer does not bring a fever and thirst, and bright, bright eyes, and a numbness in the fingers.

Finally, she realized she had waited too long. The few moments of each day that delirium left her, she was too weak to overpower anybody.

Scuroforno came in when she was almost gone. She was awake, floating, relishing death's sweet breath, the smell of disinfectants.

"I'm under quarantine," she whispered. This was not true, but nobody had come to see her since she had turned on Miss Trilby.

He waved that aside and unwrapped a large syringe. "What you need is blood. They wouldn't think of that, though."

"Where did you get that?" Blood was so beautiful. She wanted to press Scuroforno's wrists against the delicate itching structure under her tongue, to faint in the heat from his veins.

"You're too weak to drink. Ideally, you should have several quarts of human blood. But mine will do."

She watched, sick with hunger, as he tourniqueted his arm, slipped the needle into the vein inside his elbow and drew blood.

She reached for the syringe. He held it away from her. She lunged with death-strength. He put the syringe on the table behind him, caught her wrists, held them together.

"You're stronger than I expected." He squeezed until the distant pain quelled her. She pretended to relax, still fixated on the sip of blood, so near. She darted at his throat, but he held her easily.

"Stop it! There isn't enough blood in the syringe to help you if you drink it! If I inject it, you'll get some relief. But my blood is forbidden."

Yes, she would have killed him, anybody, for blood. She sank back, shaking with desire. The needle entered her vein and she never felt the prick. She shuddered with pleasure as the blood trickled in. She could taste it. Old blood, sour with a hunger of its own, but the echo of satiety radiated from her arm.

"Here are some clothes. You should be just strong enough to walk to the car. I'll carry you from there."

She fumbled for his wrists. "No. Any more vampire blood would kill you. Or," he laughed grimly, "you might be strong enough to kill me. On your feet." He lifted her like a child.

In his apartment, he carried her to the bedroom and laid her on the bed. She smelled blood. Next to her was an unconscious girl, perhaps twenty, very blond, dressed in white suede jeans, boots, a black lace bra.

Ineptly, she went for the girl's jugular. The girl was wearing strong jasmine perfume, a cheap knockoff scent insistent and sexy.

"Wait. Don't slash her and waste it all. Be neat." He leaned over, pressed his mouth to the girl's neck.

Gretchen lunged.

She thrilled to sink her new bloodsucking organ into the girl's neck, but discovered it was at the wrong place. Hissing with anger, she broke away and tried a third time. Salty, thick comfort seeped into her body like hot whisky.

In an instant, Gretchen felt Scuroforno slip his finger into her mouth, breaking the suction. She came away giddy with frustration. Scuroforno held her arms, hurting her. The pain was in another universe. She tried to twist away.

"You're going to kill her," he warned.

"Who is she?" She shook herself into self control, gazed longingly at the girl, who seemed comatose.

"Nobody. A girl. I take her out now and then. I never take enough blood to harm her. I don't actually enjoy hurting people."

"She's drugged?"

"No, no. I—we have immunity to bacteria and so on, but drugs are bad. I hypnotized her."

"You hypnotized—she sleeps through all this?"

"She thinks she's dead drunk. Here, help me get her sweater back on."

"She thinks you made love to her?"

Scuroforno smiled.

"You did make love to her?"

He busied himself with adjusting the girl's clothes.

Gretchen lay back against the headboard. "I need more, God, I need more."

"I know. But you'll have to find your own from now on."

"How do I get them to submit?"

Scuroforno yawned. "That's your problem. Rescuing you was hard work. Now you'll have to find your own way. You're cleverer and stronger than humans now. Did you notice your sinus infection is gone?"

"Nick, help."

He did not look at her. "It would be better if you left town now."

"But you saved me."

"You're my competitor now. Leave before the rage for blood takes you, before we go after the same prey."

She held the hunger down inside her, remembering human emotions. "It makes no difference that I love you?" And suddenly, she did love him.

"Tomorrow you'll know what hate is, too."

On the way out, she noticed he had a new screen saver: red blood cells floating on black, swelling, bursting apart.

On the bus to Seattle, she wept. Yes, she had loved him, and she had learned what hate was, too. She played with a sewing needle, stabbed her fingers. Numb. But her feelings were not numb, not yet. Would that happen? Was Nick emotionally dead?

Would the physical numbness spread? If her body was immortal, why would she need nerves, pain, to warn of danger?

Maybe she would regret the bargain she had made.

The numbness did spread. Her fingers and hands were immune to pain. but she still felt thirst. The cancer metastasized into her tongue and nerves, wanted to be fed.

Her seat-mate was a Mormon missionary, separated from his partner because the bus was crowded. In Chicago, he asked her to change seats, so he could sit with his partner. But she refused. It didn't fit her plan.

She stroked his cheek, held the back of his neck in a vice grip, all the while smiling, catlike. Scarcely feeling her own skin, but vividly feeling the nourishment under his. He tried to repel her, laughing uneasily, taking it for an erotic game. A forward, sluttish gentile woman. Then he was fighting, uselessly. He twisted her thumb back, childish self-defense. She felt no pain. Then he was weeping, softening, falling into a trance. She kissed his throat with her open mouth. Drank from him. Drank again and again. Had he fought, she could have broken his neck. She was completely changed.

In Seattle, the floor nurse in Pediatrics challenged her. Sniffing phenol and the sweet, sick urine that could never quite be cleaned up, Gretchen glanced at her reflection in a dead computer screen behind the nurse. She did look predatory now. Like a wax mannequin, but also like a cougar. Powerful. Not like anybody's mother. Two other nurses drifted up, as if sensing trouble

She showed the nurse her driver's license. They almost believed her, then. Let her go down the hall, to room 409. But still the nurses' eyes followed her. She had changed.

She opened the door. The floor nurse drifted in behind her.

This balding, emaciated tyke, tangled in tubing, could not be her Ashley.

Ashley had changed, too. From a less benign cancer.

The nurse sniffed. "I'm sorry. She's gone downhill a lot in the last few weeks." The nurse clearly did not approve of noncustodial mothers. Maybe still did not believe this quiet, strong woman *was* the mother.

When Gretchen had been human, she would have been humiliated, would have tried to explain that Ashley had been taken from her by legal tricks. Now, she considered the nurse simply as a convenient beverage container from which, under suitable conditions, she might sip. She smiled, a cat smile, and the nurse could not hold her gaze.

"Ashley," said Gretchen, when they were alone. She had brought the Jan Pieńkowski book, wrapped in red velvet paper with black cats on it. Ashley liked cats. She would love the scary haunted house pop-ups. They would read them together. Gretchen put the gift on the chair, because first she must tend to more important things. "Ashley, it's Mommy. Wake up, darling."

But the little girl only opened her eyes, huge and bruised in the pinched face, and sobbed feebly.

Gretchen lowered the rail on the bed and slid her arm under Ashley. The child was frighteningly light.

Gretchen felt the warmth of her feverish child, smelled the antiseptic of the room, the sweet girl-smell of her daughter's skin. But those were all at a distance. Gretchen was being subsumed by something immortal.

We are very territorial. Isn't that what Nick had said? It's not an emotional numbness; it's physical. And the memory of him jabbing the pen into his arm, the needle into his vein, her own numb fingers, how everything, even her daughter's warmth and the smell of the child and the room were all receding, distant. Immortal. Numb. Strong beyond human strength. Alone.

She touched her new, predatory mouth to her child's throat. Would Ashley thank her for this?

Now she must decide.

Conquistador de la Noche
Carrie Vaughn

Carrie Vaughn is the best-selling author of the Kitty series, about a werewolf who hosts a talk radio advice show for the supernaturally disadvantaged. "Conquistador de la Noche" tells the story of how a friend of Kitty's—Rick, the vampire master of Denver in "our" day and age—became a vampire. Set in sixteenth century New Spain, "Conquistador" demonstrates how vampiric immortality can allow an imaginative writer to take the reader into a different era and culture.

*Vaughn's also written for young adults (*Voices of Dragons, Steel*), has two stand-alone novels (*Discord's Apple, After the Golden Age*), and many short stories. She lives in Colorado. Find out more at www.carrievaughn.com.*

His LIFE was becoming a trail of blood.

Ricardo de Avila fired his crossbow at the crowd of natives. The bolt struck the chest of a Zuni warrior, a man no older than his own nineteen years. The native fell back, the dark of his blood splashing, along with dozens of others. The army's few arquebuses fired, the sulfur stink clouding the air. The horses danced, tearing up the grass and raising walls of dust. Between keeping control of his horse and trying to breathe, Ricardo could not winch back his crossbow for another shot.

Not that he needed to fire again. The general was already calling for a cease fire, and the few remaining Zuni, running hard and shouting in their own language, were fleeing back to their city.

City. Rather, a few baked buildings clustered on the hillside. The expedition had become a farce. Cíbola did not exist—at least, not as it did in the stories the first hapless explorers had brought back. So many leagues of travel, wasted. Dead men and horses, wasted. The land itself was not even worth much. It had little water and was cut through with unforgiving mountains and canyons. The Spanish should turn around and leave it to the natives.

But the friars who traveled with Coronado were adamant. Even if they found no sign of treasure, it was their duty as Christians to save the souls of these poor heathens.

They had believed that Coronado would be a new Cortés, opening new lands and treasures for the glory of Spain. The New World was more vast than any in Europe had comprehended. Naturally they assumed the entire continent held the same great riches Spain had found in Mexico. As quickly as Spain was eating through that treasure, it would need to find more.

Coronado tried to keep up a good face for his men. His armor remained brightly polished, gleaming in the harsh sun, and he sat a tall figure in his horse. But with the lack of good food, his face had become sunken, and when he looked across the despoblado, the bleak lands they would have to cross to reach the rumored Cities of Gold, the shine in his eyes revealed despair.

This expedition should have made the fortune of a third son of a minor nobleman like Ricardo. Now, though, he was thirsty, near to starving, and had just killed a boy who had come at him with nothing but a stone club. His dark beard had grown unkempt, his hair long and ratted. Sand had marred the finish of his helmet and cuirass. No amount of wealth seemed worth the price of this journey. Rather, the price he was paying had become so steep, it would have taken streets paved with gold in truth to restore the balance. What was left, then? When you had already paid too much in return for nothing?

Ricardo had sold himself for a mouthful of dust.

Ten years passed.

It was dark when Ricardo rode into the main plaza at Zacatecas. Lamps hung outside the church and Governor's buildings, and the last of the market vendors had departed. A small caravan of a dozen horses and mules from the mine was picketed, awaiting stabling. The place was hot and dusty, though a cool wind from the mountains brought some refreshment. Ricardo stopped to water his horse and stretch his legs before making his way to the fort.

At the corner of the garrison road, a man stepped from the shadows to block his path. His horse snorted and planted its feet. Ricardo's night vision was good, but he had trouble making out the figure.

"Don Ricardo? I was told you were due to return today," the man said.

Ricardo recognized the voice, though it had been a long time since he'd heard it. "Diego?"

"Ah, you do remember!"

He'd met Diego in Mexico City, where they'd both listened to the stories of Cíbola and joined Coronado's expedition. Side by side they'd ridden those thousands of miles. They'd both grown skinny and shaggy, and, on their return, Diego had broken away from the party early to seek his own fortune. Ricardo hadn't seen him since.

"Where have you been? Come into the light, let me look at you!"

A lamp shone over the doorway on the brick building on the corner. Ricardo touched Diego's shoulder and urged him over. His old compatriot turned, but didn't move from the spot. Ricardo squinted to see him better. Diego had not changed much in the last decade. If anything, he seemed more robust. He had a brightness to him, a sly smile, as if he had come into some fortune, discovering what the rest of them had failed to attain. His clothing, a leather doublet, breeches, and sturdy boots, were worn but well made. His hair and beard were well kept. He wore a gold ring in one ear and must have seemed dashing.

"You look very well, Diego," Ricardo said finally.

"And you look tired, my friend."

"Only because I have ridden fifteen miles today over hard country."

Diego grimaced. "Yes, playing courier for the garrisons along the road to Mexico City. How do you come to do such hard labor? It's not fit for one of your station."

Typical hidalgo attitude. Ricardo was used to the reaction. Smiling, he ducked his gaze. "The work suits me, and it won't be forever."

"Hoping to earn your way to a land grant? A silver mine of your very own, with a fine estancia and a well-bred girl from Spain to marry and give you many sons? So you can return to Spain a made man?" Diego spoke with a mocking edge.

"Isn't that the dream of us all?" Ricardo said, spreading his arms and making a joke of it. He really was that transparent, he supposed. Not dignified enough to lead the life of dissolute nobility like so many others of his class. Too proud and restless to wait for his fortune to find him. But the secret that he told no one was that he didn't want to leave and take his fortune back to Spain. He had come to love this land, the wide desert spaces, hot sun and cold nights, green valleys ringed by brown mountains. He wanted to be at home here.

Diego stepped close and put a hand on Ricardo's arm. "I have a better idea. A great opportunity. I was hoping to find you, because I know no one as honest and deserving as you."

The schemes to easy wealth were as common in this country as cactus and mountains. Ricardo sounded skeptical. "You have found some secret silver lode, is that it? You need someone in the government to push through the claim, and you'll give me a percentage."

Diego's smile thinned. "There is a village a day's ride away, deep in the western hills. The land is rich, and the natives are agreeable. A Franciscan has started a church there, but he needs men to lead. To make their mark upon the land." He pressed a folded square of paper into Ricardo's hand. A map, directions. "You are a good, honest man, Ricardo. Come and help us make a respectable town out of this place. And reap the rewards for doing so."

Such a village should have fallen under the Governor of Zacatecas' jurisdiction. Ricardo would have heard of a priest in that region. Something wasn't right.

"I still dream of gold, Ricardo," Diego said. "Do you?"

"The Cities of Gold never existed."

"Not as a place. But as a symbol—this whole continent is a Cíbola, waiting for us to claim it."

"Just as we did the last time?" Ricardo said, scowling.

"But you'll come to this village. I'll wait for you."

Diego patted Ricardo on the shoulder, then slipped back into shadows. Ricardo didn't even hear him go. Thoughtful, worried, Ricardo made his way to the fort for the evening.

Ricardo followed Diego's map into the hills, not because he was lured by the promise of easy wealth, but because he wanted to discover what was wrong with the story.

The day was hot, and he traveled slowly, keeping to shade when he could and resting his horse by dismounting and climbing up steep hills alongside it. He followed the ridge of mountains and hoped he had not lost the way.

Then he climbed a rise that opened into a valley, as Diego had described. A large pond, probably filled by a spring, provided water, and fruit trees grew thickly. A meadow covered the valley floor, and Ricardo could imagine sheep or goats grazing here, or crops growing. Much could be done with land like this.

A small village sat a hundred yards or so from the pond. The Franciscan's church was little more than a square cottage made of adobe brick, with a narrow tower. Wood and grass-thatched huts gathered around a dusty square.

No people were visible, no hearth fires burned. Not so much as a chicken scratched in the dirt. Four horses grazed in the meadow beyond the village. They glanced at Ricardo, then continued grazing. Riding into the village, he shouted a hail, which fell flat, as if the empty settlement absorbed sound. Dismounting, he left his horse by a trough that was dry.

A smarter man might have traveled with a troop of guards, or at least servants to ease his way. He had thought it easier to travel alone, learn what he could, and return as quickly as possible to report this to the Governor. Now, the skin of his neck crawled, and he wondered if he might need a squad of soldiers before the day was through. He kept his hand on the hilt of his sword, slung on his belt.

He went into the chapel.

The place might have been new. A few benches lined up before a simple altar. The wood was freshly cut, but they seemed to have been poorly built: rickety legs slotted into flat boards. Those seated would have to be careful if they didn't want to tumble to the dirt floor.

In front, the wood altar was bare, without even a cloth to cover it. No cross hung on the wall. The place had the sickly beeswax candle smell that imbued churches everywhere. At least that much was familiar. Nothing else was. He almost hoped to find signs of violence, because then he'd have some idea of what had happened here. But this . . . nothing . . . was inexplicable.

"Hola!" he called, cringing at his own raised voice. He had the urge to speak in a whisper, if at all.

A door in the back of the chapel opened. A small body in a gray robe looked out. "Who is it?"

A shiver crawled up Ricardo's spine, as if a ghost had stepped through the wall. He peered at the door, squinting, but the man was hidden in shadow.

"I am Captain Ricardo de Avila. Diego Ruiz asked me to come."

"Ah, yes! He told me of you." He straightened, shedding the air of suspicion. "Come inside, let us speak," the friar said, opening the door a little wider. Ricardo went to the back room as the friar indicated.

Like the chapel, this room had no windows. There was a table with a lit candle on it, several chairs, and a small, dirty portrait of the Blessed Virgin. There was a trapdoor in the floor, with a big iron ring to lift it. Ricardo wondered what was in the cellar.

"Take a seat. I have some wine," the friar said, going to a cabinet in the corner. "Would you like some?"

"Yes, please." Ricardo sat in the chair closest to the door.

The friar put one pewter cup on the table, poured from an earthenware jug, and indicated that Ricardo should take it. He took a sip; it was weak, sour. But his mouth was dry, and the liquid helped.

The friar didn't pour a drink for himself. Sitting on the opposite side of the table, he regarded Ricardo as if they were two men in a plaza tavern, not two dusty, weary colonials in a dark room lit by a candle. The man was pale, as if he spent all his time indoors. His hands, resting on the table, were thin, bony. Under his robes, his entire body might have been skeletal. He had dark hair trimmed in a tonsure and a thin beard. He was a stereotype of a friar who had been relegated to the outer edges of the colony for too long.

"I am Fray Juan," the man said, spreading his hands. "And this is my village."

Ricardo couldn't hide confusion. "Forgive me, Fray Juan, but Señor Ruiz told me this was a rich village. I expected to see farmers and shepherds at work. Women in the courtyard, weaving and grinding corn."

"Oh, but this is a prosperous village. You must take my word that appearances here aren't everything." His lips turned in a smile.

"Then what is going on here?" He had started to make guesses: Fray Juan was smuggling something through the village, he'd failed utterly at converting the natives and putting them to useful work and refused to admit it, or everyone had died of disease. But even then there ought to be some evidence. Bodies, graves, something.

Juan studied him with cold eyes, blue and hard as stones. Ricardo wanted to hold the stare, but something made him glance away. His heart was pounding. He wanted to flee.

The friar said, "You rode with Coronado, didn't you? The expedition to find Cíbola?"

Surviving that trip at all gave one a certain reputation. "Yes, I did. Along with Ruiz."

"Even if he hadn't told me I would have guessed. You have that look. A weariness, like nothing will ever surprise you again."

Ricardo chuckled. "Is that what it is? Something different than the usual cynicism?"

"I see that you are not a youth, but you are also not an old man. Not old enough to have the usual cynicism. Therefore, you've lived through something difficult. You're the right age for it."

A restless caballero wandering the northern provinces? He supposed there were a few of that kind. "You've changed the subject. Where is Ruiz?"

"He will be here," Frey Juan said, soothing. "Captain, look at me for a moment." Ricardo did. Those eyes gleamed in the candlelight until they seemed fill the room. The man was all eyes, shining organs in a face of shadows. "Stay here tonight. It's almost dusk, far too late to start back for Zacatecas. There are no other settlements within an hour's ride of here. Take the clean bed in the house next door, sleep tonight, and in the morning you'll see that all here is well."

They regarded one another, and Ricardo could never recall what passed through his mind during those moments. The Franciscan wouldn't lie to him, surely. So all must be well, despite his misgivings.

And Frey Juan was right; Ricardo must stay the night in any case. "When will Ruiz return?"

"Rest, Captain. He'll be at your side when you wake."

Ricardo found himself lulled by the friar's voice. The look in his eyes was very calming.

A moment later, he was sitting at the edge of a rope cot in a house so poorly made he could see through the cracks in the walls. He didn't remember coming here. Had he been sleepwalking? Was he so weary that a trance had taken him? For all his miles of travel, that had never happened before. He hadn't eaten supper. He wondered how much of the night had passed.

His horse—He didn't remember caring for his horse; he'd left the animal tacked up near the trough. That jolted him to awareness. It was the first lesson of this vast country, take care of your horse before yourself, because you'd need the animal if you hoped to survive the great distances between settlements.

Rushing outside, he found his bay mare grazing peacefully, chewing grass around its bit while dragging the reins. He caught the reins, removed the saddle and bridle, rubbed the animal down, and picketed it to a sturdy tree that had access to good grazing, since no cut hay or grain seemed available.

Fully awake now, studying the valley under the light of a three quarters moon, Ricardo's suspicions renewed. This village was dead. He should have questioned the friar more forcefully about what had happened here. Nothing about this place felt right, and Fray Juan's calm assurances meant nothing.

Ricardo had reason to doubt the word of a man of God. It was a friar, another man of God, who brought back the story of Cíbola, of a land covered in lush pastures and rich fields, of cities with wealth that made the Aztec Empire seem as dust. Coronado had believed those stories. They all had, until they reached the edge of that vast and rocky wasteland to the north. They had whispered to each other, is this it?

Ricardo de Avila would find Diego Ruiz and learn what had happened here.

The wind spoke strangely here, crackling through cottonwoods, skittering sand across the mud-patched walls of the buildings. In the first hut, where he'd been directed to stay, he found a lantern and lit it using his own flint. With the light, he examined the abandoned village.

If disease had struck, he'd have expected to see graves. If there had been an attack, a raid by some of the untamed native tribes in the mountain, he would have seen signs of violence—shattered pottery, interrupted chores. He'd have found bodies and carrion animals. But there was not so much as a drop of blood shed.

The huts were tidy, dirt floors swept and spread with straw, clay pots empty, water skins dry. The hearths were cold, the coals scattered. He found old bread, wrapped and moldy, and signs that mice had gnawed at sacks of musty grain.

In one of the huts, the blankets of a bed—little more than a straw mat in the corner—had been shoved away, the bed torn apart. It was the first sign of violence rather than abandonment. He picked up the blanket, thinking perhaps to find blood, some sure sign that ill had happened.

A cross dropped away from the folds of the cloth. It had been wrapped and hidden away, unable to protect its owner. The thought saddened him.

Perhaps the villagers had fled. He went out a little ways to try to find tracks, to determine what direction the villagers might have gone. Behind the church, he found a narrow path in the grass, like a shepherd might use leading sheep or goats into the hills. Ricardo followed it. He shuttered the lantern and allowed his vision to adjust to moonlight, to better see into the distance.

He was part way across the valley, the village and its church a hundred paces behind him, when he saw a figure sitting at the foot of a juniper. A piece of clothing, the tail of a shirt perhaps, fluttered in the slight breeze that hushed through the valley.

"Hola," Ricardo called quietly. He got no answer and approached cautiously, hand on his sword.

The body of a child, a boy, lay against the tree. Telling his age was impossible because it had desiccated. The skin was blackened and stretched over the bones. His face was gaunt, a leathery mask drawn over a skull, and chipped teeth grinned. Dark pits marked the eye sockets. It might have been part of the roots and branches. Ricardo might have walked right by it and not noticed, if not for the piece of rotted cloth that had moved.

The child had dried out, baked in the desert like pottery. It looked like something ancient. Moreover, he could not tell what had killed it. Perhaps only hunger.

But his instincts told him something terrible had happened here. Fray Juan had to know something of what had killed this boy, and the entire village. Ricardo must find out what, then report this to the Governor, then get word to the Bishop in Mexico City. This land and its people must be brought under proper jurisdiction, if for no other reason than to protect them from people like Fray Juan.

He rushed back to the village, went to the church and marched inside, shouting, "Fray Juan! Talk to me! Tell me what's happened here! Explain yourself!"

But no one answered. The chapel echoed, and no doors cracked open even a little to greet him. Softly now, he went through the strange decrepit chapel with no cross. The door to the friar's chamber was unlocked, but the room was empty. Not even a lamp lit. The whole place seemed abandoned. He tried the trapdoor, lifting the iron ring—the door didn't move. Locked from the other side. He pounded on the door with his boot heel, a useless gesture. So, Fray Juan was hiding. No matter. He'd report to the Governor, and Ricardo would return with a squad to burn the place to the ground to flush the man out. He wouldn't even wait until daylight to set out. He didn't want to sleep out the night in this haunted valley.

When he went to retrieve his horse, a man stood in his way.

In the moonlight, he was a shadow, but Ricardo could see the smile on his face: Diego Ruiz.

"Amigo," he called, his voice light, amused. "You came. I wasn't sure you would."

"Diego, what's happened here? What's this about?"

"I told you, Ricardo. This land is rich. We are looking for men to help us reap those riches."

"I see nothing here but a wasted village," Ricardo said.

A new voice spoke, "You need to see with different eyes."

Ricardo turned, for the voice had come from behind him. He had not heard the man approach—he must have been hiding in one of the huts. Two more came with him, so that together the four circled Ricardo. He could not flee without confronting them. He turned, looking back and forth, trying to keep them all in view, unwilling to turn his back on any of them.

The four were very much like Ricardo—young men with pure Spanish features, wearing the clothing of gentlemen. Others who had swarmed to New Spain seeking fortunes, failing, and turning dissolute.

Ricardo drew his sword. One of them he could fight. But not four. Not when they had every advantage. How had they taken him by surprise? He should have heard them coming. "You've turned bandit. You think to recruit more to run wild with you? No, Diego. I have no reason to join you."

"You do not have a choice, amigo. I brought you here because we can use a man like you. Someone with connections."

Ricardo smiled wryly. "No one will pay my ransom."

They laughed, four caballeros in high spirits. "He thinks we'll ask for ransom," another said.

Ricardo swallowed back panic and remained calm. Whatever they planned for him, he would not make it easy. He'd fight.

"Señor, be at ease," spoke a third. "We won't hold you for ransom. We have a gift for you."

Ricardo chuckled. "I don't think so."

"Oh, yes. We'll bring you to serve our Master. It's a great honor."

"I will not. You all are evil."

The men did not argue.

They began to circle him, jackals moving close for a kill. They watched him, and their eyes were fire. He had to run, grab his horse and fly from here, warn to the Governor of this madness.

It was madness, for Diego lunged at him, weaponless, with nothing but outstretched arms and a wild leer. Ricardo held out his sword, blade level and unwavering, and Diego skewered himself on the point, through the gut. Ricardo expected him to cry out and fall. He expected to have to fight off the others for killing one of their own. But the other three laughed, and Diego kept smiling.

Ricardo held fast to the grip out of habit. Diego stood, arms spread, displaying what he'd done. No blood ran from the wound.

Ricardo pulled the sword back just as Diego wrenched himself off the blade. Still, the man didn't make a sound of pain. Didn't fall. Wasn't bothered at all. Ricardo resisted an urge to make the sign of the cross. Holy God, what was this?

"This is why we follow Fray Juan," Diego breathed. "Now, will you join us?"

Ricardo cried out a denial and charged again. These were demons, and he must flee. He crouched, grabbed a handful of dirt with his left hand. If he could not cut them, perhaps he could blind them. He flung it at the man behind him, who must be moving to attack. In the same motion he whirled, slashing with his blade, keeping some distance around him, enough to clear a space so he might reach his horse. He did not wait to see what happened, did not even think. Only acted. Like those old days of battle, fighting the natives with Coronado's company. That had been a strange, alien world. Like this.

He'd have sworn that his sword met flesh several times, but the men stood firm, unflinching. Ricardo might as well have been a child throwing a tantrum. They closed on him without effort.

Two grabbed his arms, bracing them straight out, holding him still. A third wrenched his sword from him. His captors bent back his arms until his back strained, and presented him to Diego.

Ricardo struggled on principle, with no hope. His boots kicked at the dirt.

Diego regarded him with a look of amusement. He ran a gloved hand along Ricardo's chin, scraping his rough beard. Ricardo flinched back, but his captors held him steady. "You should know that you never had a chance against us. Perhaps you might take comfort in that fact."

"I take no comfort," Ricardo said, his words spitting.

"Good. You will have none." He opened his mouth. They all opened their mouths and came at him. They had the teeth of wild dogs. Of lions. Sharp teeth meant to rend flesh.

And they began to rend his.

He couldn't move. He'd been on a very long journey, and his limbs had turned to iron, chilled iron, that had been left out on a winter's night and was now rimed with frost. That image of himself—stiff flesh mounted on a skeleton of frosted iron, a red body fringed with white—struck him as oddly beautiful. It was an image of death, sunk into his bones. Memory recalled the ambush, arms clinging to him, breath leaving him, and the teeth. Demonic teeth, puncturing his flesh, draining his blood, his life. So he had died.

His next thought: what had he done to find himself relegated to hell? What else could this be? Like Dante's ninth circle, where the damned lay frozen solid in a lake, he was left to feel his body turning to frost, piece by piece. He tried to cry out, but he had no breath.

A hand rested on his forehead. If possible, it felt even colder, burning against Ricardo's skin like ice.

"Ricardo de Avila," the Devil said. "You hear me, yes?"

Nothing would melt his body; he could not even nod. Struggling to speak, he felt his lips move, but nothing else.

"I will tell you what your life is now. You will never again see the daylight. To touch the sun is to burn. You are no longer a son of the Church. The holy cross and baptismal water are poison to you. From now on you are a creature of darkness. But these small sacrifices are nothing to the reward: from now on might be a very long time. You belong to me. You are my son. With your brothers you will rule the night."

Ricardo choked on a breath that tasted stale, as if he had not drawn breath in a very long time. His mouth tasted sour. He said, "Is this hell?"

The Devil sounded wry. "Not necessarily. In this life, you make or escape your own hell."

"Who are you?"

"You know me, Ricardo. I am Fray Juan, and I am your Master."

He shook his head. It wasn't that the numbness was fading. Rather, he was getting used to the cold. This body made of iron could move. "The Governor . . . the King . . . I am loyal . . . "

"You are beyond them now. Open your eyes."

His lids creaked and cracked, like the skin was breaking, but he opened them.

He lay on a bed in a dark room. A few lanterns hung from hooks on the walls, casting circles of light and flickering shadows. Fray Juan sat at the edge of the bed. Arrayed elsewhere stood four men, fierce-looking. The demons.

He felt trapped by the shadows that had invaded his dreams. They would destroy him. In a panic, he waited for the jolt of blood, the racing heartbeat that would drive him from the bed, allow him some chance of fighting and escaping. But he felt nothing. He put his hand around his neck and felt . . . nothing. No pulse. He wanted to sigh—but he had not drawn breath. He had only taken in enough air to speak. Now, the panic rose. This could not be, this was impossible, dead and yet not—

This was hell, and the demon with Frey Juan's shape was lying to him.

"Diego, bring the chalice," Juan said, not with the voice of a sympathetic confessor, but with the edge of a commander.

A figure moved at the far end of the room. Even as Ricardo prayed, his ears strained to learn what was happening, his muscles tensed to defend himself.

"Hold him," Juan said, and hands took him, hauled him into a sitting position, and wrenched back his arms so he could not struggle. Another set of hands pinned his legs.

His eyes opened wide. Three of the caballeros braced him in a sitting position. The fourth—Diego, his old comrade Diego—brought forward a Eucharistic chalice made of pewter. He balanced it in a way that suggested it was full of liquid.

Ricardo drew back, pressing against his captors. "You wear Fray Juan's face, but you are not a priest. You can't do this, this is no time for communion."

Juan smiled, but that did not comfort. "This isn't what you think. What is wine, after the holy sacrament of communion?"

"The blood of Christ," Ricardo said.

"This is better," he said, taking the chalice from Diego.

Ricardo cried out. Tried to deny it. Turned his head, clamped shut his mouth. But Juan was ready for him, putting a hand over his face, digging his thumb between Ricardo's lips and prying open his jaw, as if trying to slide a bit in the mouth of a stubborn horse.

Juan was stronger than he looked. Ricardo screamed, a noise that came out breathless and wheezy. The chalice tipped against his lips.

The liquid smelled metallic. When it struck his tongue—a thick stream sliding down his throat, leaving a sticky trail—it tasted of wine and copper.

With the taste of it came knowledge and instinct. Human blood, it could be no other. Even as his mind rebelled with the obscenity of it, his tongue reached for more, and his throat swallowed, greedy for the sustenance. Its thickness flowed like fire through his own veins, and something in him rose up and sang in delight at its flavor.

The battle was no longer with the demons holding him fast; it was with the demon rising up inside of him. The creature that drank the blood and wanted more. A strange joy accompanied the feeling, a strength in his body he'd never felt before. Weariness, the aches of travel, fell away. He was reborn. He was invincible.

And it was false and wrong.

Roaring, he shoved at his captors, throwing himself out of their grasp. He batted away the chalice of blood. They lunged for him again, and Fray Juan cried, "No, let him go."

Ricardo pushed away from them. He pressed his back to the wall and couldn't go further. He could smell the blood soaking into the blanket at his feet. He covered his face with his hands; he could smell the blood on his breath. He wiped his mouth, but could still taste blood on his lips, as if it had soaked into his skin.

He had an urge to lick the drops of blood that had spilled onto his hand. He pressed his face harder and moaned, an expression of despair welling from him.

"You see what you are now?" Juan said, without sympathy. "You are the blood, and it will feed you through the centuries. You are deathless."

Ricardo stared at him. The blood flowing through his veins now was not his own. He could feel it warming his body, like sunlight on skin. Sunlight, which he would never see again, if Juan spoke true.

He drew a breath and said, "You are a devil."

"We all are."

"No! I don't know what you've done to me, but I am not one of you. I would rather die!"

Juan, a pale face in lamp-lit shadows, nodded to his four henchmen, who backed toward the ladder, which lead to the trap door in the ceiling. One by one, they slipped out, watching Ricardo with glittering, knowing eyes. In a moment, Juan and Ricardo were alone.

"This is a new life," Juan said. "I know it is hard to accept. But remember: you have received a gift."

Then he, too, left the room. The door closed, and a bolt slid home.

Ricardo rushed to the door, and tried to open it, rattling the handle. They had locked him in this hole. A damp chill from the walls pressed against him.

Ricardo lay back on the bed, hands resting on his chest. Eventually, the lamp's wick burned down. The light grew dim, until it was coin-sized, burnished gold, then vanished. Even in the dark, he could see the ceiling. He should not have been able to see anything in the pitch dark of this underground cell. But it was like he could feel the walls closing in. He waited for panic to take him. He waited for his heart to start racing. But he touched his ribs and could not feel his heart at all.

Hours had passed, though the time moved strangely. Even in the darkness, he could see shadows move across the ceiling, like stars arcing overhead. It was nighttime outside, he knew this in his bones. The night passed, the moon rose—past full now, waning. The way the air moved over his face told him this. Eventually, near dawn, he fell asleep.

He started awake when the trapdoor opened. His senses lurched and rolled, like a galleon in deep swells. He knew—again, without looking, without seeing—that Juan and his four caballeros had returned. They had a warmth coursing through them, tinged with metal and rot, the scent of spilled blood. The thing inside him stirred, a hunger that cramped his heart instead of his belly. His mouth watered. He licked his lips, hoping for the taste of it.

Shutting his eyes, he turned his face away.

Another, a sixth being, entered the room with them. This one was different—warm, burning with heat, a flame in the dark, rich and beautiful. Alive. A heartbeat thudded, the footfalls of an army marching double-time. A living person who was afraid.

"Ricardo. Look." Juan stood at the foot of the bed and raised a lantern.

Ricardo sat up, pressed against the wall. Two of the caballeros dragged between them a child, a boy seven or eight years old, very thin. The boy met his gaze with dark eyes, shining with fear. He whimpered, pulling back from the caballeros' grasp, but they held fast, their fingers digging into his skin.

Juan said, "This is one of the things you must learn, to take your place among my knights."

"No." But the new sensations, the new way of looking at the world, wanted this child. Wanted the warm blood that gave this child life. The caballeros hauled the boy forward, and Ricardo shook his head even as he reached for the child. "No, no—"

"You cannot stop it," Juan said.

The child screamed before Ricardo even touched him.

It was not him. It did not feel like his body. Something else moved his limbs and filled his mind with lust. His mouth closed over the artery in the child's neck as if he kissed his flesh. His teeth—he had sharp teeth now—tore the skin, and the blood flowed. The sensation of wet blood on tongue burned through him, wind and fire. His vision was gone, his mind was gone.

This was not him.

The blood, life-giving and terrible, filled him until he seemed likely to break out of his own skin. With enough blood, he could expand to fill the world. When they pulled the dead child away, he was drunk, insensible, his hands too weak to clutch at the body. He sat at the edge of the bed, his arms fallen to his sides, limp, his face turned up, ecstatic. He licked his lips with a blood-coated tongue. But it was not him. His eyes stung with tears. He could not open them to look at the horror he'd wrought.

He was not so cold anymore. Either he was used to it, or he could no longer feel at all. That was a possibility. That was most likely best. Even if this were not hell, what they had forced him to do would surely send him to hell when he did die.

If he did.

"It is incentive to live forever, is it not? Knowing what awaits you for these terrible crimes," Diego said with the smile of a wolf.

The friar had shown him what horrors this life held for him: he brought Ricardo a cross made of pressed gold. He kept it wrapped in silk, did not touch it himself. When Ricardo touched it, his skin burned. He could never touch a holy cross again. Holy water burned him the same. He could never go into a church. His baptism had been burned away from him. The Mother Church was poison to him now. God had rejected him.

But I do not reject God, Ricardo thought helplessly.

There were rewards. Juan kept calling them rewards. Mortal weapons could not kill him. Stabs and slashes with a sword, arquebus shot, falls, cracked bones, nothing would kill him. Only beheading, only a shaft of wood driven through the heart. He was immortal.

You call this reward? Ricardo had shouted. To be forever shut out of God's heavenly kingdom? Then he realized the truth: this was no tragedy for Juan, because the friar did not believe in God or heaven.

"Did you ever believe?" Ricardo whispered at him. "Before you became this thing, did you believe?"

Juan smiled. "Perhaps it is not that I don't believe, but that I chose to join the other side of this war between heaven and hell."

Which was somehow even more awful.

Ricardo stood at the church wall one night. The moon waxed again, past new. Half a month, he'd been here. He didn't know what to do next—what he could do. They held him captive. He belonged with them now, because where else could he go?

They told him that the blood should taste sweet on his tongue, and it did. He still hated it.

Perhaps he looked for rescue. When he did not report to the Governor, wouldn't a party come for him? A troop of soldiers would come to learn what had happened, and Ricardo would intercept them, tell them the truth, and he would help them raze the church to the ground, destroy Juan and his caballeros.

And then they would destroy him, stake his heart, drag him into the sunlight, for being one of them. So perhaps Ricardo wouldn't help them, but would hide.

Did he love existence more than life, then? More than heaven?

A jingling of bridles sounded behind him. Ricardo did not have to look; he sensed the four men approaching with the horses.

"Brother Ricardo, it's good you've finally come into the air. It's not good to be cooped up all the time."

"I'm not your brother," he said. His voice scratched, weak and out of practice. He had taken breathing for granted, and had to relearn how to speak.

Diego laughed. "We're all you have, now. You'll understand soon enough."

"He has lots of time to learn," said Octavio, one of the four demons who had once been men, who followed Juan. Rafael and Esteban were the others.

Diego said, "Ride with us. We hunt tonight, and you'll learn at our side." It was a command, not a request.

He followed, because what else could he do? Except perhaps stand in the open when the sun rose and let it burn him. But suicide was a sin. Even now, he believed it. He would show that he did not forsake God. He would ask for forgiveness every moment of his existence.

Diego seemed to be Fray Juan's lieutenant; he had been the first of them turned to this demon life, years ago now. That was why he looked no older than he had when they returned from Coronado's expedition.

He explained what they did here. "Each of us is as strong as a dozen men. But there are still those who know how to kill us. Those who would recognize certain signs and hunt us down."

"Who?" Ricardo asked. "What signs?"

"Secret members of the Inquisition for one. And what signs? Why, bodies. Too many bodies, all drained of blood!" They all laughed.

"New Spain is the perfect place for us. There are thousands of peasants dying by the score in mines, on campaigns, of disease. Out here on the borders, no one is even looking much. If a whole village dies, we say a plague struck. We take all the blood we need and no one notices."

At the mention of blood, Ricardo's mouth watered. A hunger woke in him, like a creature writhing in his belly. Each time Diego said the word, his vision clouded. He shook himself to remain focused on the hills before them.

"I know how it is with you," Diego said. "We all went through this."

"Though the rest of us were perhaps not so holy to start with." Again they laughed, like young men riding to a night of revelry. That was what they looked like, what anyone who saw them would think. Not that anyone would see them out here. That was the point, to feed on as much blood as they wished without notice. A land of riches. Diego had not lied.

"It's eating away inside of me," Ricardo said under his breath.

"The blood will still that," said Rafael. "The blood will keep you sane."

"Ironic," Ricardo said. "That you must become a monster to keep from going mad."

"Ha. I never thought of it like that," Diego said.

He is already mad, Ricardo thought.

They rode for hours. They could not go far—half the night, he thought. Then they must go back, to take shelter before dawn. He could feel the night slipping away in his bones. It was the same part of him that now called out for blood.

Rafael said, "The villages nearby know of us. They go to the hills to hide, but we find them. Look toward the hills, take the air into your lungs. You can sense them, can't you?"

The air smelled of dust, heat, sunlight that had baked into the land during the day and now rose into the chill of night, lost in the darkness. The breeze spoke of emptiness, of a vast plain where nothing larger than coyotes lived. When he turned toward the hills, though, he smelled something else. The warmth had a different flavor to it: life.

When they brought him the child, he had known what was there before he saw it. He could feel its life in the currents of the air, sense its heartbeat sending out ripples, like a stone tossed into a body of still water. A live person made a different mark on the world than one of these demons.

"Our kind are drawn to them, like iron to a lodestone," Diego said. "We cannot live without taking in the human blood we have lost. We are the wolves to their sheep."

"And now you hunt. Like wolves," said Ricardo.

"Yes. It's good sport."

"It's a thousand childhood nightmares come to life."

"More than that, even. Come on!"

He spurred his horse. Kicking dirt behind them, the other four followed.

It was just as Diego said: a hunt. The leader sent two of the caballeros to ascend the hill from a different direction. They flushed the villagers from their hiding places, where they lived in caves and lean-tos. Like animals, Ricardo could not help but think. Easier to hunt them, then, when one did not think of them as human. It was like facing the native tribes with Coronado all over again. The imbalance in strength between the two parties was laughable.

On horseback, Rafael and Octavio galloped across the hill, chasing a dozen people, many of them old, before them. Diego and Esteban had dismounted and tied their horses some distance away, waiting on foot for the prey to come to them.

Ricardo watched, and time slowed.

It was as if he played the scene out in his mind while someone told him the story. Diego moved too fast to see when he stepped in front of the path of a young man, grabbed his arm with one hand and took hold of his hair with the other. The boy didn't have time to scream. Diego held the body like a lover might, hand splayed across his chest, holding him in place, while pulling back his head, exposing his neck. He bit, then sank with the boy to the ground while he drank. The boy didn't even thrash. He was like a stunned rabbit.

Each of the others chose prey and struck, plucking their chosen victims from the scattered, fleeing peasants. The creature lurking where Ricardo's heart used to be sang and longed to reach out and grab a rabbit for itself. As he watched, the scene changed, and it was not the caballeros who moved quickly, but the villagers who moved slowly. Ricardo had felt like this once in a swordfight. His own skills had advanced to a point where he had some proficiency, his mind was focused, and he knew with what seemed like supernatural prescience what his opponent was going to do. He parried every attack with ease, as if he watched from outside himself.

This was the same.

It was not himself but the unholy monster within who stepped aside as a woman ran past him, then slipped into place behind her and took hold of her shoulders, moving like the shadow of a bird in flight across the land.

Jerked off her feet by his hold on her, she screamed and fell against him, thrashing, panicked, like an animal in a snare. He held her, embraced her against his body to still her, and touched her face. The coiled hunger within him gave him power. As he ran his finger down her cheek and closed his hand against her face, she quieted, stilled, went limp in his grasp. Her heartbeat slowed. He could take her, drink her easily, without struggle. This was better, wasn't it? Would he have this power if this wasn't what he was meant to do? She was young, almost a girl, her skin firm and unlined, lips full, her eyes bright. He could have her in all ways, strip her, lie with her, and he could make her want it, make her open to him in a way their Catholic religion would never allow, even in marriage. In the ghostly moonlight, she was beautiful, and she belonged to him. He lay her on the ground. She clutched his hand, and confusion showed in her eyes.

He couldn't do it. He sat with her as though she were his ill sister, holding her hand, brushing damp hair from her young face. The creature inside him thrashed and begged to devour her. Ricardo felt the needle-sharp teeth inside his mouth. And he turned his gaze inward, shutting it all away.

I am not this creature. I am a child of God. Still, a child of God, like her. And the night is dangerous.

Quickly, he made her sit up. He lay his hand on her forehead and whispered, "Wake up. You must run." She stared at him blankly, groggily. He slapped her cheek. She didn't even flinch. "Wake up, please. You must wake up!"

Her gaze focused. At last she heard him. Perhaps she didn't understand Spanish. But then, which of a dozen native dialects would she understand?

Fine, he thought. He didn't need language to tell her to run. He bared his teeth—the sharp fangs ripe for feeding, wet with the saliva of hunger—and hissed at her. "Run!"

She gasped, scrambled to her feet, and ran across the hillside and into shadow.

Just in time. The world shifted, the action around him sped up and slowed as it needed to, and all appeared normal again. A still night lit by a waxing moon, quiet unto death.

The caballeros surrounded him. Ricardo could sense the blood on their breaths, and his belly rumbled with hunger. He bowed his head, content with the hunger, with the choice he had made.

They could probably smell on him the scent of resignation.

"Brother Ricardo," Diego said. "Aren't you hungry? Were the pickings not easy enough for you?"

"I'm not your brother," Ricardo said.

Diego laughed, but nervously. "Don't starve yourself to spite us," he said.

"Don't flatter yourself," Ricardo said. "I don't starve myself for you."

The four demons looked down on him, where he sat in the dust, content. They would kill him, and that was all right. The demon they had given him screeched and complained. Ricardo sat rigid, keeping it trapped, refusing to give it voice.

"You're not strong enough to survive this," Diego said. "You don't have the will to refuse the call of our kind."

At this, Ricardo looked at him with a hard gaze. Unbelievably, Diego took a step back.

"I was one of the hundred who returned to Mexico City with Coronado. Don't tell me about my will."

To his left, a branch snapped as Octavio broke a twisting limb off a nearby shrub. "Diego, I will finish him. Turning him was a mistake."

"Yes," Diego said. "But we didn't know that."

"We'll leave him. Leave him here and let the sunlight take him," said Rafael.

Diego watched him with the air of a man trying to solve a riddle. "The Master wants to keep him. The Governor will listen to him, and he will keep us safe. He must live. Captain Ricardo de Avila, you must accept what you are, let the creature have its will."

Ricardo smiled. "I am a loyal subject of Spain and a child of God who has been saddled with a particularly troublesome burden."

Diego looked at Octavio. Ricardo was ready for them.

Together, the thing coiled inside him and his honor as a man of Spain rose up to defend, if not his life, then his existence. Octavio made an inhuman leap that crossed the distance between them, faster than eye could see. The perception that made time and the world around Ricardo seem strange and move thickly, like melting wax, served him now. For all Octavio's speed, Ricardo saw him and wasn't there when his enemy struck.

He could learn to revel in this newfound power.

Ricardo longed for a sword in his hand, no matter that steel would do no good against these opponents. He would have to beat them with wood through the heart. Octavio held the torn branch, one end jagged like a dagger. The other three ranged around him, ready to cut off his escape, and a wave of dizziness blurred his vision for a moment. Despair and hunger. If he'd taken blood, he would have more power—maybe enough to fight them all. As it was, he could not fight all four of them. Not if they meant to kill him.

He ran. They reached for him, but with flight his only concern, he drew on that devilish power. *Make me like shadow*, he thought.

The world became a blur, and he was smoke traveling across it. Nothing but air, moving faster than wind. He felt their hands brush his doublet as he passed. But they did not catch hold of him.

He found a cave. Villagers might have hidden here once. Ricardo found the burned remains of a campfire, some scraps of food, and an old blanket that had been abandoned. The back of the cave was narrow and ran deep within the hillside. It would always be dark, and he could stay there, safe from sunlight.

But would they come after him?

They could not tolerate rivals. Animal, demon, or men fallen beyond the point of redemption, they had claimed this territory as their own. He had rebuffed their brotherhood, so now he was an invader. They would come for him.

Ricardo put the blanket over a narrow crag in the rock, deep in the cave. The light of dawn approached. As he lay down in the darkness, he congratulated himself on surviving the night.

He fell asleep wondering how he would survive the next.

At dusk, he hurried over the hill side, gathering fallen sticks, stripping trees of the sturdiest branches he could find, and using chipped stones he had found in the cave to sharpen the ends into points. It was slow going, and he was weak. Lack of blood had sapped his strength. His skin was clammy, pale, more and more resembling a dead man's. *I am a walking corpse*, he thought, and laughed. He had thought that once before, while crossing the northern despoblado with Coronado.

Ricardo had to believe he was not dead, that he would not die. He was fighting for a much nobler cause than the one that had driven him north ten years ago. He'd made that journey for riches and glory. Now, he was fighting to return to God. He was fighting for his soul. But without blood, he couldn't fight at all.

"Señor?" a woman's voice called, hesitating.

Ricardo turned, startled. It was a sign of his weakness that he had not heard her approach. Now that he saw her, the scent of her blood and the nearness of her pounding heart washed over him, filling him like a glass of strong wine. His mind swam in it, and the demon screeched for her blood. Ricardo gripped the branch in his hand, willing the monster to be silent.

The mestiza woman wore a poor dress and a ragged shawl over her head. Her hair wasn't tossed and tangled in flight tonight, but he recognized her. She was the one he'd let go.

"You," he breathed, and discovered that he loved her, wildly and passionately, with the instant devotion of a drunk man. He had saved her life, and so he loved her.

She kept her gaze lowered. "I hoped to find you. To thank you." She spoke Spanish with a thick accent.

"You shouldn't have come back," he said. "My will isn't strong tonight."

She nodded at his roughly carved stake. "You fight the others? The wolves of the night?"

He chuckled, not liking the tone of despair in the sound. "I'll try."

"But you are one of them."

"No. Like them, but not one of them."

She knelt on the ground and drew a clay mug from her pouch. She also produced a knife. She moved quickly, as if she feared she might change her mind, and before Ricardo could stop her, she drew the knife across her forearm. She hissed a breath.

He reached for her. "No!"

Massaging her forearm, encouraging the flow of blood, she held the wound over the mug. The blood ran in a thin stream for several long minutes. Then, just as quickly, she took a clean piece of linen and wrapped her arm tightly. The knife disappeared back in the pouch. She glanced at him. He could only stare back, dumbfounded.

She moved the cup of blood toward him. "A gift," she said. "Stop them, then leave us alone. Please?"

"Yes. I will."

"Thank you."

She turned and ran.

The blood was still warm when it slipped down his throat. His mind expanded with the taste of it. He no longer felt drunk; on the contrary, he felt clear, powerful. He could count the stars wheeling above him. The heat of young life filled him, no matter if it was borrowed. And he could survive without killing. That gave him hope.

He scraped the inside of the cup with his finger and sucked the film of blood off his skin, unwilling to waste a drop. After tucking the mug in a safe place, he climbed to his hiding place over the cave and waited. He had finished his preparations in time.

They came like the Four Horsemen of Revelations, riders bringing death, armed with spears. They weren't going to toy with him. They were here to correct a mistake. Let them come, he thought. Let them see his will to fight.

They pulled to a stop at the base of the hill, within sight of the cave's mouth. The horses steamed with sweat. They must have galloped most of the way from the village.

Diego and the others dismounted. "Ricardo! We have come for you! Fray Juan wants you to return to him, where you belong!"

Ricardo could smell the lie on him. He could see it in the spears they carried, wooden shafts with sharpened ends. The other three dismounted and moved to flank the cave, so nothing could escape from it.

Octavio stepped, then paused, looking at the ground. Ricardo clenched fistfuls of grass in anticipation. Another step, just one more. But how much could Octavio sense of what lay before him?

"Diego? There's something wrong—" Octavio said, and leaned forward. With the extra weight, the ground under him collapsed. A thin mat of grass had hidden the pit underneath.

Almost, Octavio escaped. He twisted, making an inhuman grab at earth behind him. He seemed to hover, suspended in his moment of desperation. But he was not light enough, not fast enough, to overcome his surprise at falling, and he landed, impaled on the half-dozen stakes driven into the bottom of the pit. He didn't even scream.

"Damn!" Diego looked into the pit, an expression of fury marring his features.

Ricardo stood and hurled one of his makeshift spears at the remaining riders. He put all the strength and speed of his newfound power, of the gift of the woman's blood, into it, and the spear sang through the air like an arrow. He never should have been able to throw a weapon so strong, so true.

This curse had to be good for something, or why would people like Juan and Diego revel in it? He would not revel. But he would use it. The bloodthirsty demon in him reveled in this hunt and lent him strength. They would come to an understanding. Ricardo would use the strength—but for his own purpose.

The spear landed in Rafael's chest, knocking him flat to the ground. He clutched at the shaft, writhing, teeth bared and hissing in what might have been anger or agony. Then, he went limp. His skin tightened, wrinkling, drying out, until the sunken cavities of his skull were visible under his face. His clothes drooped over a desiccated body. He looked like a corpse years in the grave. That was how long ago he died, Ricardo thought. He had been living as a beast for years. But now, perhaps he was at peace.

Diego and Esteban were both flying up the hill toward him. Almost literally, with the speed of deer, barely touching earth. Ricardo took up another spear. This would be like fighting with a sword, a battle he understood a little better. They had their own spears ready.

He thrust at the first to reach him, Esteban, who parried easily and came at him, ferocious, teeth bared, fangs showing. Ricardo stumbled back, losing ground, but braced the spear as his defense. Esteban couldn't get through to him. But then there was Diego, who came at Ricardo from behind. Ricardo sensed him there but could do nothing.

Diego braced his spear across Ricardo's neck and dragged him back. Reflexively, Ricardo dropped his weapon and choked against the pressure on his throat, a memory of the old reaction he should have had. But now, he had no breath to cut off. The pressure meant nothing. Ricardo fell, letting his head snap back from under the bar, and his weight dropped him out of Diego's grip. Another demonic movement. But he would not survive this fight as a human.

Esteban came at him with his spear, ready to pin him to the ground. Ricardo rolled, and did not stop when he was clear. *I am mist, I am speed.* He spun and wrenched the spear from Esteban's grip. He was charging one way and couldn't resist the force of Ricardo's movement in another direction. Even then, Ricardo didn't stop. He slipped behind Esteban, who had pivoted with equal speed and grace to face him. But he had no weapon, and Ricardo did. He speared the third of the demons through his dead heart. Another desiccated corpse collapsed at his feet.

Ricardo stared at Diego, who stood by, watching.

"I was right to want you as one of Fray Juan's caballeros," Diego said. "You are very strong. You have the heart to control the power."

"Fray Juan is a monster."

"But Ricardo. New Spain is filled with monsters. We both know that."

Screaming, Ricardo charged him. Diego let him run against him, and they both toppled to the ground, wrestling.

How did one defeat a man who was already dead? Who moved by demonic forces of blood? Ricardo closed his hands around the man's throat, but Diego only laughed silently. He did not breathe—choking did no good. He tried to beat the man, pound his head into the ground, but Diego's strength was effortless, unyielding. He might as well wrestle a bear.

Diego must have grown tired of Ricardo's flailing, because he finally hit him, and Ricardo flew, tumbling down the hill, away from his dropped weapons. Diego loomed over him now, with the advantage of high ground.

Ricardo made himself keep rolling. Time slowed, and he knew what would happen—at least what might happen. So he slid all the way to the bottom of the hill and waited. He wasn't breathing hard—he wasn't breathing at all. He hadn't broken a sweat. He was as calm as still water. But Diego didn't have to know that.

The smart thing for Diego to do would be to drive a spear through his chest. But Ricardo thought Diego would gloat. He'd pick Ricardo up, laugh in his face one more time, before tossing him aside and stabbing him. Ricardo waited for this to happen, ready for it.

But he'd also be ready to dodge if Diego surprised him and went for a quick kill.

"Ricardo! You're more than a fool. You're an idealist," Diego said, making his way down the hill, sauntering like a man with an annoying chore at hand.

God, give me strength, Ricardo prayed, not knowing if God would listen to one such as him. Not caring. The prayer focused him.

He struggled to get up, as if he were weak, powerless, starving. Let Diego think he had all the power. He flailed like a beetle trapped on his back, while Diego leaned down, twisted his hands in the fabric of his doublet and hauled him to his feet.

Then Ricardo took hold of the man's wrists and dragged him toward the hole that had swallowed Octavio.

Diego seemed not to realize what was happening at first. His eyes went wide, and he actually let go of Ricardo, which was more than Ricardo had hoped for. Using Diego's own arms for leverage, he swung the man and let go. Diego was already at the edge of the pit, and like Octavio he made an effort to avoid the fall. But with the grace of a drifting leaf, he sank.

Ricardo stood on the edge and watched the body, stuck onto the stakes on top of Octavio, turn to a dried husk.

He gathered up their horses and rode back to the church, torn between wanting to move and worrying about breaking them down. They had already made this trip once, and they were mortal. He rode both as quickly and slowly as he dared, and when he reached the village, the sky had paled. He could feel the rising sun within his bones.

Rushing, he unsaddled the horses and set them loose in the pasture. He would need resources, when he started his new life, and they were worth something, even in the dark of night.

He had only moments left to find Juan. Striding through the chapel, he hid a spear along the length of his leg.

"Juan! Bastard! Come show yourself!"

The friar was waiting in the back room where Ricardo had first spoken with him, a respectable if bedraggled servant of God hunched over his desk, watching the world with a furtive gaze.

"I felt it when you killed them," the friar said in a husky voice. "They were my children, part of me—I felt the light of their minds go out."

Don't let him speak. Ricardo's own power recognized the force behind the words, the connection that bound them together. His power flowed from the other.

Ricardo started to lunge, but the friar held up a hand and said, "No!" The younger man stopped, spear upraised, face in a snarl, an allegorical picture of war.

Fray Juan smiled. "Understand, you are mine. You will serve me as my caballeros served me. You cannot stop it." The Master had a toothy, wicked smile.

Ricardo closed his eyes. He'd fought for nothing, all these years and nothing to show for it but a curse. He was not even master of his fate.

Free will was part of God's plan. What better way to damn the sinful than to let them choose sin over righteousness? But he had not chosen this. Had he? Had something in his past directed him to this moment? To this curse?

Then couldn't he choose to walk away from this path?

He started to pray out loud, all the prayers he knew. Pater Noster, Ave Maria, even passages of Psalms, what he could remember.

The friar stared back at him. His lips trembled. "You should not be able to speak those words," Juan said. "You are a demon. One of Satan's pawns. He is our father. The holy words should burn your tongue."

"Then you believe the tales of the Inquisition? I don't think I do. Come, Juan, pray with me." Louder now, he spoke again, and still Juan trembled at the words.

"They're only words, Padre! Why can't you speak them?" Ricardo shouted, then started the prayers again.

The hold on his body broke. He had been balanced, poised for the strike, and now he plunged forward, his spear leading, and drove it into the friar's chest. Juan tumbled back in his chair, Ricardo standing over him, still leaning on the spear though it wouldn't go further. Juan didn't make a sound.

Juan's skin turned gray. It didn't simply dry into hard leather; it turned to dust, crumbling away, his cassock collapsing around him. A corpse decayed by decades or centuries.

Ricardo backed away from the dust. He dropped the spear. His knees gave out then, and he folded to the floor, where he curled up on his side and let the sleep of daylight overcome him.

Rumor said that the small estancia had once been a mission, but that the friar who ran it went mad and fled to the hills, never to be seen again. A young hidalgo now occupied the place, turning it into a quiet manor that bred and raised sheep for wool and mutton. The peasants who lived and worked there were quiet and seemed happy. The Governor said that the place was a model which all estancias ought to learn from.

The hidalgo himself was a strange, mysterious man, seldom seen in society. Of course all the lords in New Spain with daughters had an interest in getting to know him, for he was not only successful, but unmarried. But the man refused all such overtures.

It was said that Don Ricardo had ridden north with Coronado. Of course that rumor had to be false, because everyone knew Ricardo was a man in the prime of his life, and Coronado's expedition to find Cíbola rode out fifty years ago.

But such wild rumors will grow up around a gentleman who only leaves his house at night.

Endless Night
Barbara Roden

Barbara Roden is a World Fantasy Award-winning editor and publisher, whose short stories have appeared in numerous publications, including Year's Best Fantasy and Horror: Nineteenth Annual Collection, Horror: Best of the Year 2005, Bound for Evil, Strange Tales 2, Gaslight Grimoire, Gaslight Grotesque, The Year's Best Dark Fantasy and Horror: 2010, Best New Horror 21, *and* Poe: 19 New Tales Inspired by Edgar Allan Poe. *Her first collection,* Northwest Passages, *was published in 2009; the title story was nominated for the Stoker, International Horror Guild, and World Fantasy awards, while the book received a World Fantasy Award nomination for Best Collection. She writes, "'Endless Night' was always going to be set in Antarctica during the 'Golden Age' of Antarctic exploration, but it didn't start out as a vampire story; initially it was about a close-knit group having to deal with the sudden arrival of an outsider. However, as the story developed I saw the possibilities of introducing a vampire into a setting where, for several months of the year, there is no daylight. What if this 'endless night' proved to be a curse rather than a blessing? And when you have fled to the most remote place on Earth in order to escape who and what you are, where do you go when you realize that even in Antarctica there is no escape?" Good questions result in a good story.*

"THANK YOU so much for speaking with me. And for these journals, which have never seen the light of day. I'm honoured that you'd entrust them to me."

"That's quite all right." Emily Edwards smiled; a delighted smile, like a child surveying an unexpected and particularly wonderful present. "I don't receive very many visitors; and old people do like speaking about the past. No"—she held up a hand to stop him—"I *am* old; not elderly, not 'getting on,' nor any of the other euphemisms people use these days. When one has passed one's centenary, 'old' is the only word which applies."

"Well, your stories were fascinating, Miss Edwards. As I said, there are so few people alive now who remember these men."

Another smile, gentle this time. "One of the unfortunate things about living to my age is that all the people one knew in any meaningful or intimate way have died; there is no one left with whom I can share these things. Perhaps that is why I have so enjoyed this talk. It brings them all back to me. Sir Ernest; such a charismatic man, even when he was obviously in ill-health and worried about money. I used to thrill to his stories; to hear him talk of that desperate crossing of South Georgia Island to Stromness, of how they heard the whistle at the whaling station and knew that they were so very close to being saved, and then deciding to take a treacherous route down the slope to save themselves a five-mile hike when they were near exhaustion. He would drop his voice then, and say to me 'Miss Emily'—he always called me Miss Emily, which was the name of his wife, as you know; it made me feel very grown-up, even though I was only eleven—'Miss Emily, I do not know how we did it. Yet afterwards we all said the same thing, those three of us who made that crossing: that there had been another with us, a secret one, who guided our steps and brought us to safety.' I used to think it a very comforting story, when I was a child, but now—I am not as sure."

"Why not?"

For a moment he thought that she had not heard. Her eyes, which until that moment had been sharp and blue as Antarctic ice, dimmed, reflecting each of her hundred-and-one years as she gazed at her father's photograph on the wall opposite. He had an idea that she was not even with him in her comfortable room, that she was instead back in the parlour of her parents' home in north London, ninety years earlier, listening to Ernest Shackleton talk of his miraculous escape after the sinking of the *Endurance*, or her father's no less amazing tales of his own Antarctic travels. He was about to get up and start putting away his recording equipment when she spoke.

"As I told you, my father would gladly speak about his time in Antarctica with the Mawson and Shackleton expeditions, but of the James Wentworth expedition aboard the *Fortitude* in 1910 he rarely talked. He used to become quite angry with me if I mentioned it, and I learned not to raise the subject. I will always remember one thing he *did* say of it: 'It was hard to know how many people were there. I sometimes felt that there were too many of us.' And it would be frightening to think, in that place where so few people are, that there was another with you who should not be."

The statement did not appear to require an answer, for which the thin man in jeans and rumpled sweater was glad. Instead he said, "If you remember anything else, or if, by chance, you should come across those journals from the 1910 expedition, please do contact me, Miss Edwards."

"Yes, I have your card." Emily nodded towards the small table beside her, where a crisp white card lay beside a small ceramic tabby cat, crouched as if eyeing a mouse in its hole. Her gaze rested on it for a moment before she picked it up.

"I had this when I was a child; I carried it with me everywhere. It's really a wonder that it has survived this long." She gazed at it for a moment, a half-smile on her lips. "Sir Ernest said that it put him in mind of Mrs. Chippy, the ship's cat." Her smile faded. "He was always very sorry, you know, about what he had to do, and sorry that it caused an estrangement between him and Mr. McNish; he felt that the carpenter never forgave him for having Mrs. Chippy and the pups shot before they embarked on their journey in the boats."

"It was rather cruel, though, wasn't it? A cat, after all; what harm could there have been in taking it with them?"

"Ah, well." Emily set it carefully back down on the table. "I thought that, too, when I was young; but now I see that Sir Ernest was quite right. There was no room for sentimentality, or personal feeling; his task was to ensure that his men survived. Sometimes, to achieve that, hard decisions must be made. One must put one's own feelings and inclinations aside, and act for the greater good."

He sensed a closing, as of something else she might have said but had decided against. No matter; it had been a most productive afternoon. At the door Emily smiled as she shook his hand.

"I look forward to reading your book when it comes out."

"Well"—he paused, somewhat embarrassed—"it won't be out for a couple of years yet. These things take time, and I'm still at an early stage in my researches."

Emily laughed; a lovely sound, like bells chiming. "Oh, I do not plan on going anywhere just yet. You must bring me a copy when it is published, and let me read again about those long ago days. The past, where everything has already happened and there can be no surprises, can be a very comforting place when one is old."

It was past six o'clock when the writer left, but Emily was not hungry. She made a pot of tea, then took her cup and saucer into the main room and placed it on the table by her chair, beside the ceramic cat. She looked at it for a moment, and ran a finger down its back as if stroking it; then she picked up the card and considered it for a few moments.

"I think that I was right not to show him," she said, as if speaking to someone else present in the room. "I doubt that he would have understood. It is for the best."

Thus reminded, however, she could not easily forget. She crossed the room to a small rosewood writing desk in one corner, unlocked it, and pulled down the front panel, revealing tidily arranged cubbyholes and drawers of various sizes. With another key she unlocked the largest of the drawers, and withdrew from it a notebook bound in leather, much battered and weathered, as with long use in difficult conditions. She returned with it to her armchair, but it was some minutes before she opened it, and when she did it was with an air almost of sadness. She ran her fingers over the faded ink of the words on the first page.

Robert James Edwards
Science Officer
H.M.S. *Fortitude*
1910–11

"No," she said aloud, as if continuing her last conversation, "there can be no surprises about the past; everything there has happened. One would like to think it happened for the best; but we can never be sure. And *that* is not comforting at all." Then she opened the journal and began to read from it, even though the story was an old one which she knew by heart.

⚬══✦══⚬

20 November 1910: A relief to be here in Hobart, on the brink of starting the final leg of our sea voyage. The endless days of fundraising, organisation, and meetings in London are well behind us, and the Guvnor is in high spirits, and as usual has infected everyone with his enthusiasm. He called us all together this morning, and said that of the hundreds upon hundreds of men who had applied to take part in the expedition when it was announced in England, we had been hand-picked, and that everything he has seen on the journey thus far has reinforced the rightness of his choices; but that the true test is still to come—in the journey across the great Southern Ocean and along the uncharted coast of Antarctica. We will be seeing sights that no human has yet viewed and will, if all goes to plan, be in a position to furnish exact information which will be of inestimable value to those who come after us. Chief among this information will be noting locations where future parties can establish camps, so that they might use these as bases for exploring the great heart of this unknown land, and perhaps even establishing a preliminary base for Mawson's push, rumoured to be taking place in a year's time. We are not tasked with doing much in the way of exploring ourselves, save in the vicinity of any base we do establish, but we have the dogs and sledges to enable us at least to make brief sorties into that mysterious continent, and I think that all the men are as eager as I to set foot where no man has ever trodden.

Of course, we all realize the dangers inherent in this voyage; none more so than the Guvnor, who today enjoined anyone who had the least doubt to say so now, while there was still an opportunity to leave. Needless to say, no one spoke, until Richards gave a cry of "Three cheers for the *Fortitude*, and all who sail in her!"; a cheer which echoed to the very skies, and set the dogs barking on the deck, so furiously that the Guvnor singled out Castleton and called good-naturedly, "Castleton, quiet your dogs down, there's a good chap, or we shall have the neighbours complaining!" which elicited a hearty laugh from all.

22 November: Such a tumultuous forty-eight hours we have not seen on this voyage, and I earnestly hope that the worst is now behind us. Two days ago the Guvnor was praising his hand-picked crew, and I, too, was thinking how our party had pulled together on the trip from Plymouth, which boded well, I thought, for the trials which surely face us; and now we have said farewell to one of our number, and made room for another. Chadwick, whose excellent meals brightened the early part of our voyage, is to be left in Hobart following a freakish accident which none could have foreseen, he having been knocked down in the street by a runaway horse and cart. His injuries are not, thank Heaven, life threatening, but are sufficient to make it impossible for him to continue as part of the expedition.

It is undoubtedly a very serious blow to the fabric of our party; but help has arrived in the form of Charles De Vere, who was actually present when the accident occurred, and was apparently instrumental in removing the injured man to a place of safety following the incident. He came by the ship the next day, to enquire after Chadwick, and was invited aboard; upon meeting with the Guvnor he disclosed that he has, himself, worked as a ship's cook, having reached Hobart in that capacity. The long and the short of it is that after a long discussion, the Guvnor has offered him Chadwick's place on the expedition, and De Vere has accepted.

"Needs must when the devil drives," the Guvnor said to me, somewhat ruefully, when De Vere had left to collect his things. "We can't do without a cook. Ah well, we have a few days more here in Hobart, and shall see how this De Vere works out."

What the Guvnor did not add—but was, I know, uppermost in his mind—is that a few days on board a ship at dockside is a very different proposition to what we shall be facing once we depart. We must all hope for the best.

28 November: We are set to leave tomorrow; the last of the supplies have been loaded, the last visiting dignitary has toured the ship and departed—glad, no doubt, to be going home safe to down pillows and a comfortable bed—and the men have written their last letters home, to be posted when the *Fortitude* has left. They are the final words we shall be able to send our loved ones before our return, whenever that will be, and a thin thread of melancholy pervades the ship tonight. I have written to Mary, and enclosed a message for sweet little Emily; by the time I return home she will have changed greatly from the little girl—scarcely more than a babe in arms—whom I left. She will not remember her father; but she and Mary are never far from my mind, and their photographs gaze down at me from the tiny shelf in my cabin, keeping watch over me as I sleep.

I said that the men had written their last letters home; but there was one exception. De Vere had no letters to give me, and while I made no comment he obviously noted my surprise, for he gave a wintry smile. "I said my goodbyes long ago," was all he said, and I did not press him, for there is something about his manner that discourages chatter. Not that he is standoffish, or unfriendly; rather, there is an air about him, as of a person who has spent a good deal of time alone, and has thus become a solitude unto himself. The Guvnor is pleased with him, though, and I must say that the man's cooking is superb. He spends most of his time in the tiny galley; to acquaint himself with his new domain, he told me. The results coming from it indicate that he is putting his time to good use, although I hope he will not have many occasions to favour us with seal consommé or Penguin *à la* Emperor.

Castleton had the largest batch of letters to send. I found him on the deck as usual, near the kennels of his charges. He is as protective of his dogs as a mother is of her children, and with good cause, for on these half-wild creatures the sledge teams shall depend. His control over them is quite wonderful. Some of the men are inclined to distrust the animals, which seem as akin to the domesticated dogs we all know as tigers are to tabby cats; none more so than De Vere who, I notice, gives them a wide berth on the rare occasions when he is on the deck. This wariness appears to be mutual; Castleton says that it is because the dogs scent food on De Vere's clothing.

29 November: At last we are under way, and all crowded to the ship's rail as the *Fortitude* departed from Hobart, to take a last look at civilisation. Even De Vere emerged into the sunlight, sheltering his sage eyes with his hand as we watched the shore recede into the distance. I think it fair to say that despite the mingled wonder and excitement we all share about the expedition, the feelings of the men at thus seeing the known world slip away from us were mixed; all save De Vere, whose expression was one of relief before he retreated once more to his sanctum. I know that the Guvnor—whose judgement of character is second to none—is satisfied with the man, and with what he was able to find out about him at such short notice, but I cannot help but wonder if there is something which makes De Vere anxious to be away from Hobart.

20 December: The Southern Ocean has not been kind to us; the storms of the last three weeks have left us longing for the occasional glimpse of blue sky. We had some idea of what to expect, but as the Guvnor reminds us, we are charting new territory every day, and must be prepared for any eventuality. We have repaired most of the damage done to the bridge and superstructure by the heavy seas of a fortnight ago, taking advantage of a rare spell of relative calm yesterday to accomplish the task and working well into the night, so as to be ready should the wind and water resume their attack.

The strain is showing on all the men, and I am thankful that the cessation of the tumultuous seas has enabled De Vere to provide hot food once more; the days of cold rations, when the pitching of the ship made the galley unusable, told on all of us. The cook's complexion, which has always been pale, has assumed a truly startling pallor, and his face looks lined and haggard. He spent most of yesterday supplying hot food and a seemingly endless stream of strong coffee for all of us, and then came and helped with the work on deck, which continued well into the long Antarctic summer night. I had wondered if he was in a fit state to do such heavy labour, but he set to with a will, and proved he was the equal of any aboard.

22 December: Yet another accident has claimed one of our party; but this one with graver consequences than the one which injured Chadwick. The spell of calmer weather which enabled us to carry out the much-needed repairs to the ship was all too short, and it was not long after we had completed our work that the storm resumed with even more fury than before, and there was a very real possibility that the sea waves would breach our supply of fresh water, which would very seriously endanger the fate of the expedition. As it was, those of us who had managed to drop off into some kind of sleep awoke to find several inches of icy water around our feet; and the dogs were in a general state of uproar, having been deluged by waves. I stumbled on to the deck and began helping Castleton and one or two others who were removing the dogs to a more sheltered location—a difficult task given the rolling of the ship and the state of the frantic animals. I was busy concentrating on the task at hand, and thus did not see one of the kennels come loose from its moorings on the deck; but we all heard the terrible cry of agony which followed.

When we rushed to investigate we found young Walker crushed between the heavy wooden kennel and the rail. De Vere had reached the spot before us and, in a fit of energy which can only be described as superhuman, managed single-handedly to shift the kennel out of the way and free Walker, who was writhing and moaning in pain. Beddoes was instantly summoned, and a quick look at the doctor's face showed the gravity of the situation. Walker was taken below, and it was some time before Beddoes emerged, looking graver than before, an equally grim-faced Guvnor with him. The report is that Walker's leg is badly broken, and there is a possibility of internal injuries. The best that can be done is to make the injured man as comfortable as possible, and hope that the injuries are not as severe as they appear.

25 December: A sombre Christmas Day. De Vere, in an attempt to lighten the mood, produced a truly sumptuous Christmas dinner for us all, which did go some way towards brightening our spirits, and afterwards the Guvnor conducted a short but moving Christmas Day service for all the men save Walker, who cannot be moved, and De Vere, who volunteered to sit with the injured man. One thing for which we give thanks is that the storms which have dogged our journey thus far seem to have abated; we have had no further blasts such as the one which did so much damage, and the Guvnor is hopeful that it will not be very much longer before we may hope to see the coast of Antarctica.

28 December: De Vere has been spending a great deal of time with Walker, who is, alas, no better; Beddoes's worried face tells us all that we need know on that score. He has sunk into a restless, feverish sleep which does nothing to refresh him, and seems to have wasted away to a mere shell of his former self in a shockingly brief period of time. De Vere, conversely, appears to have shaken off the adverse effects which the rough weather had on him; I had occasion to visit the galley earlier in the day, and was pleased to see that our cook's visage has assumed a ruddy hue, and the haggard look has disappeared.

De Vere's attendance on the injured man has gone some way to mitigating his standing as the expedition's "odd man out." Several of the men have worked with others here on various voyages, and are old Antarctic hands, while the others were all selected by the Guvnor after careful consideration: not only of their own qualities, but with an eye to how they would work as part of the larger group. He did not, of course, have this luxury with De Vere, whose air of solitude has gone some way to making others keep their distance. Add to this the fact that he spends most of his time in the galley, and is thus excused from taking part in much of the daily routine of the ship, and it is perhaps not surprising that he remains something of a cipher.

31 December: A melancholy farewell to the old year. Walker is no better, and Beddoes merely shakes his head when asked about him. Our progress is slower than we anticipated, for we are plagued with a never-dissipating fog which wreathes the ship, reducing visibility to almost nothing. Brash ice chokes the sea: millions of pieces of it, which grind against the ship in a never-ceasing cacophony. We are making little more than three knots, for we dare not go any faster, and risk running the *Fortitude* against a larger piece which could pierce the hull; on the other hand, we must maintain speed, lest we become mired in a fast-freezing mass. It is delicate work, and Mr. Andrews is maintaining a near-constant watch, for as captain he bears ultimate responsibility for the ship and her crew, and is determined to keep us safe.

I hope that 1911 begins more happily than 1910 looks set to end.

3 January 1911: Sad news today. Walker succumbed to his injuries in the middle of last night. The Guvnor gathered us all together this morning to inform us. De Vere was with Walker at the end, so the man did not die alone, a fact for which we are all grateful. I think we all knew that there was little hope of recovery; I was with him briefly only yesterday, and was shocked by how pale and gaunt he looked.

There was a brief discussion as to whether or not we should bury Walker at sea, or wait until we made land and bury him ashore. However, we do not know when—or even if—we shall make landfall, and it was decided by us all to wait until the water around the ship is sufficiently clear of ice and bury him at sea.

5 January: A welcome break in the fog today, enabling us to obtain a clear view of our surroundings for the first time in many days. We all knew that we were sailing into these waters at the most treacherous time of the southern summer, when the ice breaking up in the Ross Sea would be swept across our path, but we could not wait until later when the way would be clearer, or we would risk being frozen in the ice before we completed our work. As it is, the prospect which greeted us was not heartening; the way south is choked, as far as the eye can see, with vast bergs of ice; one, which was directly in front of us, stretched more than a mile in length, and was pitted along its base by caves, in which the water boomed and echoed.

Though the icebergs separate us from our goal, it must be admitted that they are beautiful. When I tell people at home of them, they are always surprised to hear that the bergs and massive floes are not pure white, but rather contain a multitude of colours: shades of lilac and mauve and blue and green, while pieces which have turned over display the brilliant hues of the algae which live in these waters. Their majesty, however, is every bit as awesome as has been depicted, in words and in art; Coleridge's inspired vision in his "Ancient Mariner" being a case in point.

I was standing at the rail this evening, listening to the ice as it prowled restlessly about the hull, gazing out upon the larger floes and bergs surrounding us and thinking along these lines, when I became aware of someone standing at my elbow. It was De Vere, who had come up beside me as soundlessly as a cat. We stood in not uncompanionable silence for some moments; then, as if he were reading my thoughts, he said quietly, "Coleridge was correct, was he not? How does he put it:

'The ice was here, the ice was there
The ice was all around:
It cracked and growled, and roared and howled,
Like noises in a swound!'

"Quite extraordinary, for a man who was never here. And Doré's illustrations for the work are likewise inspired. Of course, he made a rather dreadful *faux pas* with his polar bears climbing up the floes, although it does make a fine illustration. He was not at all apologetic when his mistake was pointed out to him. 'If I wish to place polar bears on the southern ice I shall.' Well, we must allow as great an artist as Doré some licence."

I admitted that I had been thinking much the same thing, at least about Coleridge. De Vere smiled.

"Truly one of our greatest and most inspired poets. We must forever deplore that visitor from Porlock who disturbed him in the midst of 'Kubla Khan'. And 'Christabel'; what might that poem have become had Coleridge finished it? That is the common cry; yet Coleridge's fate was always to have a vision so vast that in writing of it he could never truly 'finish,' in the conventional sense. In that he must surely echo life. Nothing is ever 'finished,' not really, save in death, and it is this last point which plays such a central role in 'Christabel'. Is the Lady

Geraldine truly alive, or is she undead? He would never confirm it, but I always suspected that Coleridge was inspired, in part, to write 'Christabel' because of his earlier creation, the Nightmare Life-in-Death, who 'thicks men's blood with cold.' When she wins the Mariner in her game of dice with Death, does he join her in a deathless state, to roam the world forever? It is a terrible fate to contemplate."

"Surely not," I replied; "only imagine all that one could see and do were one given eternal life. More than one man has sought it."

De Vere, whose eyes had focussed on the ice around us, turned and fixed me with a steady gaze. The summer night was upon us, and it was sufficiently dark that I could not see his face distinctly; yet his grey eyes were dark pools, which displayed a grief without a pang, one so old that the original sting had turned to dull, unvarying sorrow.

"Eternal life," he repeated, and I heard bitterness underlying his words. "I do not think that those who seek it have truly considered it in all its consequences."

I did not know how to respond to this statement. Instead I remarked on his apparent familiarity with the works of Doré and Coleridge. De Vere nodded.

"I have made something of a study of the literature of the undead, if literature it is. *Varney the Vampyre*; certainly not literature, yet possessed of a certain crude power, although not to be mentioned in the same breath as works such as Mr. Poe's 'Berenice' or the Irishman Le Fanu's sublime 'Carmilla'."

I consider myself to be a well-read man, but not in this field, as I have never had an inclination for bogey stories. I made a reference to the only work with which I was familiar that seemed relevant, and my companion shook his head.

"Stoker's novel is certainly powerful; but he makes of the central character too romantic a figure. Lord Byron has much for which to answer. And such a jumble of legends and traditions and lore, picked up here and there and then adapted to suit the needs of the novelist! Stoker never seems to consider the logical results of the depredations of the Count; if he were as bloodthirsty as depicted, and leaving behind such a trail of victims who become, in time, like him, then our world would be overrun." He shook his head. "One thing that the author depicted well was the essential isolation of his creation. Stoker does not tell us how long it was before the Count realized how alone he was, even in the midst of bustling London. Not long, I suspect."

It was an odd conversation to be having at such a time, and in such a place. De Vere must have realized this, for he gave an apologetic smile.

"I am sorry for leading the conversation in such melancholy channels, especially in light of what has happened. Did you know Walker very well?"

"No," I replied; "I did not meet him until shortly before we sailed from England. This was his first Antarctic voyage. He hoped, if the Guvnor gave him a good report at the end of it, to sign on with Mawson's next expedition, or even with Shackleton or Scott. Good Antarctic hands are in short supply. I know that the Guvnor, who has never lost a man on any of his expeditions, appreciates the time that you spent with Walker, so that he did not die alone. We all do."

"Being alone is a terrible thing," said De Vere, in so soft a voice that I could scarce hear him. "I only wish that . . . " He stopped. "I wish that it could have been avoided, that I could have prevented it. I had hoped . . . " He stopped once more.

"But what could you have done?" I asked in some surprise, when he showed no sign, this time, of breaking the silence. "You did more than enough. As I said, we are all grateful."

He appeared not to hear my last words. "More than enough," he repeated, in a voice of such emptiness that I could make no reply; and before long the cook excused himself to tend his duties before retiring for the night. I stayed on deck for a little time after, smoking a pipe and reflecting on our strange conversation. That De Vere is a man of education and intelligence I had already guessed, from his voice and manner and speech; he is clearly not a common sailor or sea-cook. What had brought him to Australia, however, and in such a capacity, I do not know. Perhaps he is one of those men, ill-suited to the rank and expectations of his birth, who seeks to test himself in places and situations which he would not otherwise encounter; or one of the restless souls who finds himself constrained by the demands of society.

It was, by this time, quite late; the only souls stirring on deck were the men of the watch, whom it was easy to identify: Richards with his yellow scarf, about which he has taken some good-natured ribbing; Wellington, the shortest man in our crew but with the strength and tenacity of a bulldog; and McAllister, with his ferocious red beard. All eyes would, I knew, be on the ice, for an accident here would mean the end.

The dogs were agitated; I could hear whining and a few low growls from their kennels. I glanced in that direction, and was startled to see a man, or so I thought, standing in the shadows beside them. There was no one on the watch near that spot, I knew, and while it was not unthinkable that some insomniac had come up on deck, what startled me was the resemblance the figure bore to Walker: the thin, eager face, the manner in which he held himself, even the clothing called to mind our fallen comrade. I shook my head, to clear it, and when I looked again the figure was gone.

This is, I fear, what comes of talks such as the one which I had with De Vere earlier. I must banish such thoughts from my head, as having no place on this voyage.

7 January: There was a sufficient clearing of the ice around the ship today to enable us to commit Walker's body to the deep. The service was brief, but very moving, and the faces of the men were solemn; none more so than De Vere, who still seems somewhat distraught, and who lingered at the rail's edge for some time, watching the spot where Walker's remains slipped beneath the water.

The ice which is keeping us from the coastline is as thick as ever; yet we are noting that many of the massive chunks around us are embedded with rocky debris, which would seem to indicate the presence of land nearby. We all hope this is a sign that, before long, we will sight that elusive coastline which hovers just outside our view.

17 January: We have reached our El Dorado at last! Early this morning the watch wakened the Guvnor and Mr. Andrews to announce that they had sighted a rocky beach which looked suitable for a base camp. This news, coming as it does on the heels of all that we have seen and charted in the last few days, has inspired a celebration amongst the expedition members that equals that which we displayed when leaving Plymouth to begin our voyage. The glad news spread quickly, and within minutes everyone was on deck—some of the men only half-dressed—to catch a glimpse of the spot, on a sheltered bay where the *Fortitude* will be able to anchor safely. There was an excited babble of voices, and even some impromptu dancing, as the prospect of setting foot in this unknown land took hold; I suspect that we will be broaching some of the twenty or so cases of champagne which we have brought with us.

And yet I found myself scanning the faces on deck, and counting, for ever since the evening of that conversation with De Vere I have half-convinced myself that there are more men on board the ship than there should be. Quite how and why this idea has taken hold I cannot say, and it is not something which I can discuss with anyone else aboard; but I cannot shake the conviction that this shadowy other is Walker. If I believed in ghosts I could think that our late crew mate has returned to haunt the scene of his hopes and dreams; but I do not believe, and even to mention the idea would lead to serious concerns regarding my sanity. De Vere's talk has obviously played on my mind. Bogeys indeed!

The man himself seems to have regretted his speech that night. He spends most of his time in the galley, only venturing out on deck in the late evening, but he has restricted his comments to commonplaces about the weather, or the day's discoveries. The dogs are as uncomfortable with him as ever, but De Vere appears to be trying to accustom them to his presence, for he is often near them, speaking with Castleton. The dog master spends most of his time when not on watch, or asleep, with his charges, ensuring that they are kept healthy for when we need them for the sledging parties, a task which we are all well content to leave him to. "If he doesn't stop spending so much time alone with those brutes he'll soon forget how to talk, and start barking instead," said Richards one evening.

The dogs may be robust, but Castleton himself is not looking well; he appears pale, and more tired than usual. It cannot be attributed to anything lacking in our diet, for the Guvnor has ensured that our provisions are excellent, and should the need arise we can augment our supplies with seal meat, which has proven such an excellent staple for travellers in the north polar regions. It could be that some illness is doing the rounds, for De Vere was once again looking pale some days ago, but seems to have improved. I saw him only a few minutes ago on the deck, looking the picture of health. While the rest of us have focussed our gazes landward, the cook was looking back the way we had come, as if keeping watch for something he expected to see behind us.

20 January: It has been a Herculean task, landing all the supplies, but at last it is finished. The men who have remained on the beach, constructing the hut, have done yeomans' work and, when the *Fortitude* departs tomorrow to continue along the coast on its charting mission, we shall have a secure roof over our heads. That it shall also be warm is thanks to the work of De Vere. When we went to assemble the stove we found that a box of vital parts was missing. McAllister recalled seeing a box fall from the motor launch during one of its landings, and when we crowded to the water's edge we did indeed see the box lying approximately seven feet down, in a bed of the kelp which grows along the coast. As we debated how best to grapple it to the surface, De Vere quietly and calmly removed his outer clothing and boots and plunged into the icy water. He had to surface three times for great gulps of air before diving down once more to tear the kelp away from the box and then carry it to the surface. It was a heroic act, but he deflected all attempts at praise. "It needed to be done," he said simply.

I have erected a small shed for my scientific equipment, at a little distance from the main hut. The dogs are tethered at about the same distance in the other direction, and we are anticipating making some sledging runs soon, although Castleton advises that the animals will be difficult to handle at first, which means that only those with some previous skill in that area will go on the initial journeys. It is debatable whether Castleton himself will be in a fit state to be one of these men, for he is still suffering from some illness which is leaving him in a weakened state; it is all he can do to manage his tasks with the dogs, and De Vere has had to help him.

And still—I hesitate to confess it—I cannot shake myself of this feeling of someone with us who should not be here. With all the bustle of transferring the supplies and erecting the camp it has been impossible for me to keep track of everyone, but I am sure that I have seen movement beyond the science hut when there should be no one there. If these delusions—for such they must be—continue, then I shall have to consider treatment when we return to England, or risk being unable to take part in future expeditions. I am conscious it is hallucination, but it is a phantasm frozen in place, at once too fixed to dislodge and too damaging to confess to another. We have but seven weeks—eight at most—before the ship returns to take us back to Hobart, in advance of the Antarctic winter; I pray that all will be well until then.

24 January: Our first sledging mission has been a success; two parties of three men each ascended the pathway that we have carved from the beach to the plateau above and behind us, and from there we travelled about four miles inland, attaining an altitude of 1500 feet. The feelings of us all as we topped the final rise and saw inland across that vast featureless plateau are indescribable. We were all conscious that we were gazing upon land that no human eye has ever seen, as we gazed southwards to where the ice seemed to dissolve into a white, impenetrable haze. The enormity of the landscape, and our own insignificance within it, struck us all, for it was a subdued party that made its way back to the camp before the night began to draw in to make travel impossible; there are crevasses—some hidden, some not—all about, which will make travel in anything other than daylight impossible. We were prepared to spend the night on the plateau should the need arise, but we were all glad to be back in the icicled hut with our fellows.

The mood there was subdued also. Castleton assisted, this morning, in harnessing the dogs to the sledges, but a task of which he would have made short work only a month ago seemed almost beyond him; and the look in his eyes as he watched us leave, on a mission of which he was to have been a part, tore at the soul. De Vere's health contrasted starkly with the wan face of the man beside him, yet the cook had looked almost as stricken as the dog master as we left the camp.

1 February: I did not think that I would find myself writing these words, but the *Fortitude* cannot return too quickly. It is not only Castleton's health that is worrisome; it is the growing conviction that there is something wrong with *me*. The fancy that someone else abides here grows stronger by the day and, despite my best efforts, I cannot rid myself of it. I have tried, as delicately as possible, to raise the question with some of the others, but their laughter indicates that no one else is suffering. "Get better snow goggles, old man," was Richards's response. The only person who did not laugh was De Vere, whose look of concern told me that he, too, senses my anxiety.

6 February: The end has come, and while it is difficult to write this, I feel I must; as if setting it down on paper will go some way to exorcising it from my mind. I know, however, that the scenes of the last two days will be with me until the grave.

Two nights ago I saw Walker again, as plainly as could be. It was shortly before dark, and I was returning from the hut which shelters my scientific equipment. The wind, which howls down from the icy plateau above us, had ceased for a time, and I took advantage of the relative calm to light my pipe.

All was quiet, save for a subdued noise from the men in the hut, and the growling of one or two of the dogs. I stood for a moment, gazing about me, marvelling at the sheer immensity of where I was. Save for the *Fortitude* and her crew, and Scott's party—wherever they may be—there are no people within 1200 miles of us, and we are as isolated from the rest of the world and her bustle as if we were on the moon. Once again the notion of our own insignificance in this uninhabited land struck me, and I shivered, knocked the ashes out of my pipe, and prepared to go to the main hut.

A movement caught my eye, behind the shed containing my equipment; it appeared to be the figure of a man, thrown into relief against the backdrop of ice. I called out sharply "Who's there?" and, not receiving an answer, took a few steps in the direction of the movement; but moments later stopped short when the other figure in turn took a step towards me, and I saw that it was Walker.

And yet that does not convey the extra horror of what I saw. It was not Walker as I remembered him, either from the early part of the voyage or in the period just before his death; then he had looked ghastly enough, but it was nothing as to how he appeared before me now. He was painfully thin, the colour of the ice and snow behind him, and in his eyes was a terrible light; they seemed to glow like twin lucifers. His nose was eaten away, and his lips, purple and swollen, were drawn back from his gleaming teeth in a terrible parody of a smile; yet there was nothing of mirth in the look which was directed towards me. I felt that I was frozen where I stood, unable to move, and I wondered what I would do if the figure advanced any further towards me.

It was De Vere who saved me. A cry must have escaped my lips, and the cook heard it, for I was aware that he was standing beside me. He said something in a low voice, words that I was unable to distinguish, and then he was helping me—not towards the main hut, thank God, for I was in no state to present myself before the others, but to the science hut. He pulled open the door and we stumbled inside, and De Vere lit the lantern which was hanging from the ceiling. For a moment, as the match flared, his own eyes seemed to glow; then the lamp was sending its comforting light, and all was as it should be.

He was obviously concerned; I could see that in his drawn brow, in the anxious expression of his eyes. I found myself telling him what I had seen, but if I thought that he would immediately laugh and tell me that I was imagining things I was much mistaken. He again said some words in a low voice; guttural and harsh, in a language I did not understand. When he looked at me his grey eyes were filled with such pain that I recoiled slightly. He shook his head.

"I am sorry," he said in a quiet voice. "Sorry that you have seen what you did, and . . . for other things. I had hoped . . . "

His voice trailed off. When he spoke again it was more to himself than to me; he seemed almost to have forgotten my presence.

"I have lived a long time, Mr. Edwards, and travelled a great deal; all my years, in fact, from place to place, never staying long in one location. At length I arrived in Australia, travelling ever further south, away from civilisation, until I found myself in Hobart, and believed it was the end. Then the *Fortitude* arrived, bound on its mission even further south, to a land where for several months of the year it is always night. Paradise indeed, I thought." His smile was twisted. "I should have remembered the words of Blake: 'Some are born to sweet delight / Some are born to endless night.' It is not a Paradise at all."

I tried to speak, but he silenced me with a gesture of his hand and a look from those haunted eyes. "If I needed something from you, would you help me?" he asked abruptly. I nodded, and he thought for a moment. "There are no sledge trips tomorrow; am I correct?"

"Yes," I replied, somewhat bewildered by the sudden change in the direction of the conversation. "The Guvnor feels that the men need a day of rest, so no trips are planned. Why?"

"Can you arrange that a single trip should be made, and that it shall be only you and I who travel?"

"It would be highly irregular; usually there are three men to a sledge, because of the difficulty of . . . "

"Yes, yes, I understand that. But it is important that it should be just the two of us. Can it be managed?"

"If it is important enough, then yes, I should think so."

"It is more important than you know." He gave a small smile, and some of the pain seemed gone from his eyes. "Far more important. Tomorrow night this will be over. I promise you."

I had little sleep that night, and next day was up far earlier than necessary, preparing the sled and ensuring that all was in order. There had been some surprise when I announced that De Vere and I would be off, taking one of the sledges ourselves, but I explained it by saying that the cook merely wanted an opportunity to obtain a glimpse of that vast land for himself, and that we would not be travelling far. When De Vere came out to the sledge he was carrying a small bag. It was surprisingly heavy, but I found a place for it, and moments later the dogs strained into their harnesses, and we were away.

The journey up to the plateau passed uneventfully under the leaden sun, and we made good time on the trail, which was by now well established. When we topped the final rise I stopped the sledge, so that we could both look out across that vast wasteland of ice and snow, stretching away to the South Pole hundreds and hundreds of miles distant. De Vere meditated upon it for some minutes, then turned to me.

"Thank you for bringing me here," he said in his quiet voice. "We are about four miles from camp, I think you said?" When I concurred, he continued, "That is a distance which you can travel by yourself, is it not?"

"Yes, of course," I replied, somewhat puzzled.

"I thought as much, or I would not have brought you all this way. And I did want to see this"—he gestured at the silent heart of the continent behind us—"just once. Such a terrible beauty on the surface, and underneath, treachery. You say here there are crevasses?"

"Yes," I said. "We must be careful when breaking new trails, lest a snow bridge collapse under us. Three days ago a large crevasse opened up to our right"—I pointed—"and there was a very real fear that one of the sledges was going to be carried down into it. It was only some quick work on the part of McAllister that kept it from plunging through."

"Could you find the spot again?"

"Easily. We are not far."

"Good." He turned to the sledge, ignoring the movement and barking of the dogs; they had not been much trouble when there had been work to do, but now, stopped, they appeared restless, even nervous. De Vere rustled around among the items stowed on the sledge, and pulled out the bag he had given me.

He hesitated for a moment; then he walked to where I stood waiting and passed it to me.

"I would like you to open that," he said, and when I did so I found a small, ornate box made of mahogany, secured with a stout brass hasp. "Open the box, and remove what is inside."

I had no idea what to expect; but any words I might have said failed me when I undid the hasp, opened the lid, and found inside the box a revolver. I looked up at De Vere, who wore a mirthless smile.

"It belonged to a man who thought to use it on me, some years ago," he said simply. "That man died. I think you will find, if you look, that it is loaded."

I opened the chamber, and saw that it was so. I am by no means an expert with firearms, but the bullets seemed to be almost tarnished, as with great age. I closed the chamber, and glanced at De Vere.

"Now we are going to go over to the edge of the crevasse, and you are going to shoot me." The words were said matter-of-factly, and what followed was in the same dispassionate tone, as if he were speaking of the weather, or what he planned to serve for dinner that evening. "Stand close, so as not to miss. When you return to camp you will tell them that we came too near to the edge of the crevasse, that a mass of snow collapsed under me, and that there was nothing you could do. I doubt that any blame or stigma will attach to you—not with your reputation—and while it may be difficult for you for a time, you will perhaps take solace in the fact that you will not see Walker again, and that Castleton's health will soon improve." He paused. "I am sorry about them both; more than I can say." Then he added some words in an undertone, which I did not quite catch; one word sounded like "hungry," and another like "tired," but in truth I was so overwhelmed that I was barely in a position to make sense of anything. One monstrous fact alone stood out hard and clear, and I struggled to accept it.

"Are you . . . are you ill, then?" I asked at last, trying to find some explanation at which my mind did not rebel. "Some disease that will claim you?"

"If you want to put it that way, yes; a disease. If that makes it easier for you." He reached out and put a hand on my arm. "You have been friendly, and I have not had many that I could call a friend. I thank you, and ask you to do this one thing for me; and, in the end, for all of you."

I looked into his eyes, dark as thunderclouds, and recalled our conversation on board the ship following Walker's death, and for a moment had a vision of something dark and terrible. I thought of the look on Walker's face—or the thing that I had thought was Walker—when I had seen it the night before. "Will you end up like him?" I asked suddenly, and De Vere seemed to know to what I referred, for he shook his head.

"No, but if you do not do this then others will," he said simply. I knew then how I must act. He obviously saw the look of resolution in my face, for he said again, quietly, "Thank you," then turned and began walking towards the crevasse in the ice.

I cannot write in detail of what followed in the next few minutes. I remained beside the crevasse, staring blankly down into the depths which now held him, and it was only with considerable effort that I finally roused myself enough to stumble back to the dogs, which had at last quietened. The trip back to camp was a blur of white, and I have no doubt that, when I stumbled down the final stretch of the path, I appeared sufficiently wild-eyed and distraught that my story was accepted without question.

The Guvnor had a long talk with me this morning when I woke, unrefreshed, from a troubled sleep. He appears satisfied with my answers, and while he did upbraid me slightly for failing to take a third person with us—as that might have helped avert the tragedy—he agreed that the presence of another would probably have done nothing to help save De Vere.

Pray God he never finds out the truth.

15 February: More than a week since De Vere's death, and I have not seen Walker in that time. Castleton, too, is much improved, and appears well on the way to regaining his full health.

Subsequent sledge parties have inspected the crevasse, and agree that it was a terrible accident, but one that could not have been avoided. I have not been up on the plateau since my trip with De Vere. My thoughts continually turn to the man whom I left there, and I recall what Cook wrote more than one hundred years ago. He was speaking of this place; but the words could, I think, equally be applied to De Vere: "Doomed by nature never once to feel the warmth of the sun's rays, but to be buried in everlasting snow and ice."

⚬━━╋━━⚬

A soft flutter of leaves whispered like a sigh as Emily finished reading. The last traces of day had vanished, leaving behind shadows which pooled at the corners of the room. She sat in silence for some time, her eyes far away; then she closed the journal gently, almost with reverence, and placed it on the table beside her. The writer's card stared up at her, and she considered it.

"He would not understand," she said at last. "And they are all dead; they can neither explain nor defend themselves or their actions." She looked at her father's photograph, now blurred in the gathering darkness. "Yet you did not destroy this." She touched the journal with fingers delicate as a snowflake. "You left it for me to decide, keeping this a secret even from my mother. You must have thought that I would know what to do."

Pray God he never finds out the truth.

She remained in her chair for some moments longer. Then, with some effort, Emily rose from her chair and, picking up the journal, crossed once more to the rosewood desk and its shadows. She placed the journal in its drawer, where it rested beside a pipe which had lain unsmoked for decades. The ceramic cat watched with blank eyes as she turned out the light. In so doing she knocked the card to the floor, where it lay undisturbed.

Dahlia Underground
Charlaine Harris

Charlaine Harris is a New York Times *best-selling author who has been writing for thirty years. After publishing two stand-alone mysteries, she published eight books featuring Aurora Teagarden, a mystery-solving Georgia librarian. In 1996, she released the first in the much darker Shakespeare mysteries that featured amateur sleuth Lily Bard. The fifth (and last) of the series was published in 2001. Harris, had, by then, created the Southern Vampire Mystery series about a telepathic waitress named Sookie Stackhouse who works in a bar in the fictional Northern Louisiana town of Bon Temps. The first book,* Dead Until Dark, *won the Anthony Award for Best Paperback Mystery in 2001. The twelfth novel,* Dead Reckoning, *will be released May 2011. There's also a collection of Sookie short stories and* The Sookie Stackhouse Companion *will be published in 2011. Harris has co-edited four anthologies with Toni L.P. Kelner; a fifth is slated for 2011. Alan Ball produced the HBO series based on the Sookie books,* True Blood, *which premiered in September of 2008. It was an instant success and is now filming its fourth season. Personally, Harris is married and the mother of three. She lives in a small town in Southern Arkansas and when she is not writing her own books, she reads omnivorously. Her house is full of rescue dogs.*

"Dahlia Underground" features Dahlia Lynley-Chivers, who was introduced in Sookieverse short story "Tacky" in anthology My Big, Fat Supernatural Wedding *(2006). She appears in the seventh novel* All Together Dead *and "Dahlia Underground" takes place during the period of that book. Dahlia made a recent appearance in "A Very Vampires Christmas," a short story published in the December 2010 issue of* Glamour *and Harris has mentioned there are other Dahlia stories to come. Dahlia's also "starring" soon in an interactive PC game.*

DAHLIA LYNLEY-CHIVERS woke up as soon as the sun went down. But this awakening was like none she'd experienced in her long second life: on her back, pinned down, and injured.

Badly injured.

Dahlia cursed in a language that had not been spoken for centuries. She'd lost a lot of blood. Though the air was filled with smoke and dust, she could smell a body close to her. The blood of the dead person was repellent, but it would help.

She carefully extended her right arm to discover it was free and unbroken, unlike her left. Her left leg was immovable, though her right leg wasn't, because the beam trapping her lay at a slant.

While she was evaluating her situation, Dahlia wondered what the hell had happened when she was in her day sleep. She heard distant screams and sirens, while around and above her lay destruction. A huge pane of glass, intact, had landed upright on a vampire, shearing him in half. Though he was beginning to flake away, he looked familiar.

Her memory began filling in the blanks.

The Pyramid. She'd suddenly decided to spend the day at the Pyramid, the vampire hotel in Rhodes. The disintegrating vampire had been a handsome male in the service of the Queen of Indiana, and she'd accepted an invitation to dally with him rather than return to her room in the mansion of the Sheriff of Rhodes.

Though the night had been notable, the day must have been more so.

High above her, Dahlia could see a bit of night sky lit by flashes of artificial light. Every now and then there was an ominous creak or groan from the heap of twisted metal, shattered glass, and concrete. Dahlia wondered how long it would be before it shifted. She might yet end up in the same condition as her bedmate. Dahlia had not been afraid in a long time, but she was almost afraid now. She wasn't so afraid she was going to yell for human help, though.

A smaller beam was lying crossways on the one that pinned her, very close to her right hand. Dahlia figured if she could grip the smaller beam, she'd get enough purchase to drag herself out. Then she could work her way over to the dead human, feed, and begin the perilous climb upward.

She had a plan.

Dahlia's right hand gripped the crossbeam, and she pulled. But she realized instantly that her left leg would rip off unless the heavier beam was lifted at least another inch.

"Well," said Dahlia. "Crap."

Dahlia was extremely strong, but extricating herself cost another hour. By the time her leg slid free, she was close to exhaustion. As she rested, she looked down at herself. Ugh! She was naked and streaked with dirt, soot, blood, and pale, powdery dust. She held up a strand of her long, wavy hair, normally coal black. In the dim light, it looked white. She'd been there awhile. How much time before dawn? She made herself move.

The corpse was that of a uniformed hotel maid. Her neck had been broken in the explosion. Since she hadn't bled much, Dahlia was able to tank up. The blood of the dead was even worse than the bottled blood substitute that had enabled vampires to become legal citizens of the United States. The vampires could truthfully say they no longer needed to feed from live humans. Of course, they still enjoyed it much more.

Dahlia lay across the maid's body, gathering strength for the climb up through the rubble. For a black moment, her normal confidence wavered, and she wasn't sure she could manage it.

"Hello!" called a hoarse voice from above. "This is Captain Ted Fortescue, Rhodes Fire Department! Anyone alive down there?"

She thought about remaining silent. Then she bit her lip. Dahlia was very proud, but she was also a survivor of no mean skill. "I'm here," Dahlia called up out of the darkness.

"Human or vamp?"

"Vampire," she said defiantly, even though she feared he'd leave her where she was when he found out she wasn't a breather.

"Ma'am, how hungry are you?"

He'd been coached. Good. "I've had the blood of a corpse. I will not attack you."

"'Cause we can have Red Stuff O-Positive ready when we raise you . . . "

"Not necessary."

"There's a corpse?"

"Two, Ted Fortescue. A vampire, though he's mostly gone. A human woman dead before I found her."

"We gotta take her word for it," said a lighter voice.

"Can you grip a rope if we send it down?" Fortescue called.

"Yes," Dahlia said. "If I try to climb, the ruins will shift." Humans were going to save her. Humans. Though Dahlia hadn't wanted to build her character, after all these hundreds of years it was apparently going to be built.

"Okay, here comes the rope."

The lifeline uncoiled about a yard from Dahlia. She pulled herself to it with her right arm. Gripping the pieces of wreckage that looked most firmly lodged, Dahlia pushed herself erect. Luckily, she was a very small woman. She seized the rope with her right hand. Gritting her teeth, she wrapped her right leg around the rope and called, "Pull!"

After a swaying, painful ascent, Dahlia Lynley-Chivers emerged into a night-time landscape of horror.

One glance at Dahlia had Ted Fortescue bellowing for a blanket. The captain looked almost as battered as she did. His brown face was as dirty as hers, his close-shaved hair white from the powdery dust. Above his mask, his wide brown eyes were shocked.

Dahlia found his smell enticing. She needed some blood very soon. But her need was drowned by the humiliation of having to stand with the man's support until her blanket was passed up. When he'd wrapped her in it with impersonal hands, Fortescue handed Dahlia down to the next human in line until she reached the base of the mountain of debris. The last person in the chain directed Dahlia to a line of humans waiting on the nearest clear sidewalk. She said, "Those are people willing to give you a drink, ma'am. Please try not to go overboard."

"They volunteered?" Dahlia tried not to sound disbelieving.

"Yes, ma'am. A lot of people are upset that the Fellowship of the Sun took such an extreme action against your people."

"The Fellowship is taking responsibility?"

"Yes. I guess they figured a vampire conference would be a prime target. Some of their own people hired onto the hotel staff. But they didn't feel the necessity to tell their fellow humans to get out before it blew. In fact, their news release says it served the staff right for serving vampires. Not too many people are happy with the Fellowship."

"My home is here in Rhodes. Is there a way I can get a ride to my house?"

"Get your drink, if you want it, and then head over to that other line over there. They'll help you out."

"Thank you for your courtesy," Dahlia said stiffly. "Can you help me over to the donors? My arm and leg are broken."

Captain Ted Fortescue had descended from the mountain of rubble by that time, and he overheard Dahlia's words.

"Jesus Christ, why didn't you tell me?" Ted Fortescue took Dahlia in his arms and carried her to the donor line on the sidewalk.

"Thanks so much," Dahlia said through clenched teeth. "Where do you serve?"

"We're the Thirty-four Company from the station at the corner of Almond and Lincoln. You gonna be okay, now?"

She assured him she could stand on one leg while she fed. He needed to get back to his work, so he left her there. Dahlia watched him walk away.

For a short time, she'd loved a werewolf. He hadn't been exactly human, of course, though close enough to cause her qualms. Dahlia had always felt the same kind of contempt for humans that most humans feel for Brussels sprouts. They were good for her health, but she didn't like their proximity.

The donor was a short woman with long white hair. Her name was Sue, she told Dahlia, and Sue held Dahlia's hand during the feeding. If Dahlia had been herself, she would have been put off by the woman's prattle about "we're all one family." She didn't like her food to talk. But tonight was different.

Having fed, Dahlia was able to hobble to the impromptu cab rank, where a free voucher got her a ride to her home. The vampires who lived in Cedric's mansion, already beside themselves with grief and rage, were glad to see a survivor come through the door. All Dahlia wanted to do was shower and crawl into her own bed in her own room in the windowless basement.

The next night, all the Rhodes vampires met in the mansion's common room. At least fifty vampires from the central United States had died in the bombing, the newspapers said. Their deaths were not the worst part of the attack, to this assemblage. The worst part was the loss of face. Their city had been targeted, and the attack obviously had been planned well in advance—but they had not detected it or forestalled it, though the plan had been devised and carried out by *humans.*

"We have been dishonored," Cedric, Sheriff of Rhodes, said. Every vampire in the city had been present at the meeting, from those who had their own homes to those who lived in the nest. Even Dahlia's friend Taffy, married to a werewolf, had been present.

Cedric turned his large blue eyes on Dahlia. Pink tears glistened in their corners. "Our sister Dahlia nearly met her final death and had to be rescued by humans."

"I accepted human help because it cut short the time I was trapped," Dahlia said, her back absolutely straight and her face utterly composed, though it was an effort.

"We must meet this challenge directly," said Cedric. "This is our city. Now we are at war."

The vamps of Rhodes had not been at war since Prohibition, when some bloodsuckers from Chicago, frightened away by the aggression of Al Capone's henchmen, had tried to move into the tunnels below Rhodes. They'd survived one night.

"Tell us what to do," Taffy said. Taffy was tall and buxom, her physique emphasized by the slut-biker outfit her husband, Don, favored.

"Taffy, you and Dahlia must visit the headquarters of the Fellowship. Get in by whatever means necessary. Look for membership lists. We want to know their leaders."

"This will have been done by the police," Taffy said.

"And will the police share with us what they found?" Cedric had a point.

"I'll do whatever I can to bring the whoresons to justice," Dahlia said carefully, "but the lists will be on computers, and Taffy and I are not conversant with these machines."

"One of the Arkansas vampires is adept with computers, but he was burned so badly he'll take time to heal," Cedric said. "Wait! I know someone." He whipped out his cell phone again. It was the one piece of modern technology that thoroughly entranced the sheriff. "His name is Melponeus, he's a half demon, and his services do not come cheap." Cedric, who was cheapness personified except when it came to maintaining his pride, grasped the financial nettle firmly.

The half demon was at the mansion within thirty minutes. He was a short man with reddish skin, a head of thickly curling chestnut hair, and pale eyes the color of snowmelt. When Dahlia greeted him at the door, those pale eyes showed instant admiration. Dahlia, though used to this, was nevertheless pleased. She was glad she'd worn her pink three-piece suit with the pencil skirt.

"I hope you're as good with modern technology as your reputation has it," she said tartly and beckoned him to follow her to the common room.

"I love a good, strong vampire woman," Melponeus said. "Such a woman, if she is willing, can take a lot of . . . energetic activity."

"I am several hundred years old," Dahlia said. "I assure you, I can take anything you could imagine handing out." She didn't turn to look at the half demon, but her lips curled in a little smile.

"You're older than Cedric," Melponeus observed. "But you're not the sheriff."

"I don't want to be," Dahlia said. "And some think I'm not diplomatic enough."

"I remember your name, now. It was you who broke the newscaster's arm?"

"She wouldn't stop asking me questions, after I'd warned her," Dahlia said reasonably. "I told her I would break her arm if she didn't leave me alone."

"Foolish woman," Melponeus said.

"Deserved what she got," Dahlia agreed. She was thinking that after the honor of the nest had been restored, she might find out what it felt like to kiss lips as full and hot as the half demon's. Since hers were always cold, the sensation might be interesting.

Cedric greeted Melponeus with appropriate dignity, mentioned a price, and Melponeus agreed to accompany Dahlia and Taffy. When the three were setting out, Dahlia realized no one knew the location of the Fellowship's organizational offices. Taffy had to look it up in the phone book. "This is the kind of thing detective novels don't cover," Taffy complained.

"You haven't read a detective novel since Agatha Christie quit writing," Dahlia said. "Don't whine."

"She's quit writing?" Taffy was really put out. "When did that happen?"

"She died. Probably fifty years ago."

"And why should I know that?"

"There have been plenty of novels since then. You should read some of them," said Dahlia, who seldom read herself . "We've got the address. Let's pay them a visit." In Taffy's Trans Am, they drove west into the old part of Rhodes.

They left the Trans Am on Trask, which ran a block south of Field Street, the location of the modest storefront housing the Fellowship headquarters. The small businesses in the area had already closed for the night. The occasional pedestrian hurried along, since the evening was chilly. The three approached Field through a filthy alley two blocks west of their goal. Since they could all remember times when filth and debris were the norm, this didn't bother them. The two vampires and the half demon hung in the shadows of a trash bin while they evaluated the Fellowship headquarters.

"Cameras," Melponeus murmured.

"I see them," Dahlia said. There were cameras all around the building. After a low-voiced discussion, Dahlia returned to Trask Street and ran silently east until she was pretty sure she was in line with the Fellowship building. She slid into the next alleyway and headed north. About halfway down the alley, Dahlia found a nice dark patch she didn't believe human eyes could penetrate. She crouched and gathered herself She launched herself upward, landing neatly on the roof. Dahlia was confident that even the Fellowship wouldn't think of pointing a camera upward. She was right.

After a quick smile of self-congratulation, she took off her designer heels and made a great leap, landing across the street on the roof of the two-story building housing the Fellowship. She swung her legs over. Her fingers and toes clamped into the little spaces between the lines of brick, and she worked her way to the first camera. With a quick twist, she removed it from its mounting. She pitched the camera onto the roof, then did the same with all the others. Then she put on her shoes again.

She waved at Taffy and Melponeus, who began trotting toward the Fellowship. Dahlia leaped down from the roof to join them, landing on the sidewalk as lightly as a feather, though she was wearing three-inch heels.

"Good job," said Taffy, and Dahlia inclined her head.

"I'm impressed," Melponeus said, looking at Dahlia's legs. "Taffy, let's see who's minding the store."

Taffy knocked on the door, which bore the distinctive Fellowship symbol—a sun, represented by a circle with wavy rays leading outward. Within the circle was a pyramid.

"What does the pyramid mean?" Taffy asked.

"Earth for Humans, Eradication of Vampires, Eternal Victory," Melponeus said. "Kind of ironic that the hotel was the same shape. Maybe that sparked the plan."

A young man came to the door. Through the thick glass (bulletproof?) the three could see he was a reedy Asian guy in his twenties with a soul patch.

Taffy gave him her best smile and said, "Young man, I want to come in."

If she hadn't called him "young man," he might have unlocked the door, because Taffy had a great no-fangs smile, and her tight leather pants added a powerful incentive. But the "young" roused his suspicion, since Taffy looked (at most) twenty-five. He began punching numbers on a cell phone.

"Look at me," Dahlia said in a voice that managed to compel, even through the glass. And he did, no matter what he'd been taught.

"Open the door," she said. And her voice was so reasonable that the young man did just that.

Melponeus immediately set to work looking at the Fellowship computers. Dahlia sat opposite Asian Soul Patch at a table covered with coffee stains and notepads.

She said, "What is your name?"

"Jeffrey Tan."

"You're Fellowship?"

"I hate vampires. I killed one myself."

"Did you really?"

"Yes, I did."

While Taffy searched the office building and Melponeus began copying files onto a disc, Dahlia asked a few more questions. Jeffrey Tan had been dating a vampire, a girl he'd known before she went over. They'd been going at it hot and heavy one night, and she'd bitten him. Terrified, he'd stabbed her with a handy wooden chopstick. (Unfortunately for the young vampire, Jeffrey's mother had brought him a traditional meal that day.)

In a flash, Jeffrey's lover had been shriveling and flaking on his bed.

He had to live with himself, and the easiest way to do that was to find other people who thought he'd been perfectly justified.

Dahlia, who'd heard this sort of story many times before, had a fleeting moment of sympathy for Jeffrey, since she'd become reacquainted with panic the night before. But she squelched the moment ruthlessly. She asked, "Did you help bomb the Pyramid?"

"No, but I applaud the courage and determination of our soldiers," he said unconvincingly.

"Yes, slaughtering people who are asleep is brave. Do you know who planned and executed this action?"

"They're hiding, getting ready," he said, his eyelids flickering furiously. "The vamp lovers in the police department and the fire department who rescued vampires, they'll die next."

"Where are these heroes hiding?" Dahlia asked.

Melponeus, who'd been looking at the screen of one of the office computers, said, "I think I may have the membership list," at nearly the same moment as Taffy pulled a large file out of the filing cabinet.

"Here's a list of the properties they lease or own," Taffy said, as Melponeus began downloading the list. "Oh, I checked out the basement. No one there."

A phone began ringing. Jeffrey Tan reached for it, but Dahlia stayed his hand. "What does the phone call mean?" she asked.

"I told them the cameras went out. They're calling to check on me," he said, and he seemed to be coming out of his trance. His gaze began flickering from Taffy to Dahlia to Melponeus.

"You said the Fellowship was going after firefighters?" Dahlia had a sudden misgiving.

"We have pictures of every traitor who worked the rescue at the Pyramid."

Melponeus said, "We'd better hustle."

"Shall I kill him?" Taffy asked.

"No, that would be too much of a red flag," Dahlia said. "Though I'd enjoy it very much. Look at me, Jeffrey!"

He couldn't disobey, but he was struggling.

"We were here to check for your leaders," Dahlia said, gripping his chin to force his attention on her. "They weren't here, so we left full of frustration."

"Yes," he said, his face slack again.

The three left the building as quickly and quietly as they'd entered. In silent accord, Dahlia and Taffy flanked Melponeus and held him, leaping to the top of the building. The three made their getaway across the roofs. By the time they'd gone two blocks, cars were parking in front of the Fellowship office.

"That was almost too easy," Dahlia said, on their return to the mansion. She and Taffy were drinking Red Stuff, and Melponeus was sipping coffee, very strong and very black. Cedric had come to the common room to listen to their report. "They left one human, and such a puppy, to guard the office? When they'd have to figure we'd be looking?"

"Humans do underestimate us," Taffy said. "Their thinking's limited."

"And we underestimate them," Dahlia snapped. "Look who wiped out over fifty vampires at once. Even that puppy killed his girlfriend with a chopstick."

"I'm half-human," Melponeus said. "Some of us are honorable."

Though Taffy and Cedric looked in another direction, embarrassed, Dahlia met his snowmelt eyes and inclined her head regally.

Cedric said, "What do you suggest we do, Dahlia?"

"This list of properties has to be checked out, as does the membership list," Dahlia said. "We'll be spread very thin, but I think we can do it. After all . . . " She didn't have to emphasize their responsibility.

"You're in charge, Dahlia," Cedric said. "Melponeus, if you will come with me, Lakeisha will write a check."

"How will we do this?" Taffy asked when they had left.

"Divide into teams. Give each team a short list of properties to search," Dahlia said. "Each place must be searched very thoroughly but very discreetly. One special team has to kidnap a Fellowship officer, a person without family. This team can't be averse to forceful persuasion. We need to know if there's some place not on this list, perhaps a place belonging to one member, that's large enough to hide ten to fifteen people. The newspaper said that's roughly how many Fellowship fanatics are missing. We'll check the people we can find against the list to get a better count."

Cedric returned in time to hear. He nodded. "This seems sound," he said. "Especially the torture part." He smiled.

"Thank you, Sheriff." Dahlia braced herself. "Someone must be detailed to warn the humans involved in the rescue. They saved lives that night; not just human lives."

"Some of them were not pleased to rescue vampires," Cedric said. "I read that in the newspapers, too."

"However they felt, they did it. We can't abandon those who've done us a service."

"Are you telling me my duty, Dahlia?"

"Sorry, Sheriff." Dahlia looked away to compose her face.

"This is very unlike you."

"I've never been hauled out of a pit before."

"The half demon—the half human—would take no money for his service," Cedric said. "He told me we were on the same side." Dahlia tried not to look self-conscious. She mostly succeeded.

Cedric nodded to Dahlia. "All right, go."

That was how Dahlia came to be walking into the firehouse of the Thirty-four Company at the corner of Almond and Lincoln. Though the night was chilly, the door to the firehouse was open. The men and women inside were washing the fire trucks under floodlights. None of them whistled when Dahlia approached, though she was the center of attention in her black belted coat and black high heels.

"A cold one," said the biggest firefighter of all, a burly guy over six feet tall. "Whatcha want, vampie?"

To rip your impudent throat out, Dahlia thought. But she recognized his high voice; he had helped the captain haul her up out of hell. "I need to speak to Captain Fortescue," she said.

That brought a chorus of whistles and comments about Ted's wife and her reaction to his extracurricular pastimes.

If Dahlia had been a breather, she'd have sighed.

Ted Fortescue came out, wiping his hands on a towel. His men and women fell silent when the captain looked around to meet their eyes. He recognized Dahlia immediately, somewhat to her surprise. "Evening. Have you recovered from your broken leg?"

"I have," Dahlia replied. Her back was stiff as a poker. "I have come to warn you. The people of the Fellowship of the Sun have said they'll take vengeance on those who rescued vampires."

"They're going to target first responders?" Fortescue was appalled.

"Yes," Dahlia said.

"They'll lose all public sympathy for their cause," he said slowly, "aside from the obvious point, they believe in killing vampires and recruiting humans."

"I don't pretend to make sense of what humans do," she said. "You saved my life. Now I am doing my best to save yours."

"Well . . . thanks," he said. The firefighters looked from the captain to the vampire, obviously thinking he should say something else. "You were human, once," Fortescue said.

Dahlia was taken aback. She fumbled for a response. "I was a human for eighteen years. I have been a vampire for . . ." She shook her head. "Nine hundred years, perhaps."

There was a little moment of total silence.

"Good luck to you, Ted Fortescue, and to all of you who helped us," Dahlia said. She looked at each face around her. She would remember each one. "I'll dispose of them all if I can," she promised the firefighters, and then she walked away.

"Commando Barbie," one of the women muttered, but Dahlia heard her. In fact, she smiled a little, all to herself.

Worry was not a familiar pastime for Dahlia, who was more of a direct action person. During the bit of dark remaining, Dahlia and Taffy visited two Fellowship locations, a "church" on the south side and a "meeting hall" on the east. Both buildings were easy to break into, and the two vampires searched both very thoroughly. They were straightforward modern constructions: no hidden passages, secret rooms, or false floors.

The next night similar results were reported by the other search teams.

The Rhodes vampires felt the pressure. By the time they had to retreat to day sleep lairs, they'd only learned where the Fellowship plotters weren't. Their shame was mounting.

Even the abduction-and-torture team reported failure. True, they managed to find a family-free Fellowship official, and true, they managed to snatch her unobserved, but to their immense irritation, the woman had a weak heart. She died too early in the proceedings to offer any useful information. In fact, the team simply restored her body to her house, and no one was the wiser.

Taffy arrived at the mansion the next night radiating excitement. She made a beeline for the common room. Dahlia was sitting at the table, lost in unhappy thought. "Don says we should look in the tunnels!" Taffy said, seizing her friend.

Dahlia said, "If you shake me again, I'll break both your arms."

Taffy let her go with alacrity. "Sorry! I'm just so excited!"

"That's a very good idea," Dahlia said. "We should have thought of the tunnels earlier."

The tunnel system lying below the original city center of Rhodes was extensive, and it had once connected all the major buildings in the area. The tunnels had seen much use in the years before and during Prohibition. In the decades since, some passages had been blocked up as part of new construction. Vampires seldom used the tunnels anymore . . . but they had in years past, along with all kinds of other creatures, including regular humans.

"Do the tunnels run under Field Street?" Dahlia asked Taffy.

"Don's faxing us a map."

Don, Taffy's werewolf husband, had a friend who was a historian at Rhodes's City University. Don's friend faxed the map to the little office where Lakeisha took care of Cedric's correspondence. Lakeisha had been an executive assistant in life, and Cedric had brought her over expressly to be his executive assistant in death. Lakeisha knew her office machinery and had a thorough grounding in modern communications, skills most of the older vampires found baffling.

Lakeisha had had the advantage of knowing she was going to be brought over, so she'd had her hair washed, cut, and styled before her death. She was perpetually cute. "I don't think you've ever gotten a fax before, Dahlia," Lakeisha said.

"I hope I never get another one."

"Grumpy, grumpy!" Lakeisha chided. Dahlia snarled at her.

"Did we get up on the wrong side of the coffin tonight?" Lakeisha said.

"It's annoying that you're not frightened of me, and it's a mistake."

"You don't want to make Cedric mad," the young vampire said calmly.

Dahlia snatched up the tunnel map, and she and Taffy retreated to the common room to study it.

"Yes! We gotcha, assholes!" Taffy said, after the two had found Field Street and examined it.

"I'll give Don something nice," Dahlia said.

"Not a groomer's brush, like you sent last time? That shit gets old," Taffy said.

"No, something really nice."

"Not another bag of doggie treats!"

"I'm serious; it'll be very appropriate. Lakeisha, we need you," Dahlia called. Normally, Lakeisha would have insisted the request come through Cedric, but circumstances were hardly ordinary.

Lakeisha used the copying machine and then the intercom. When everyone had assembled in the common room, she passed out copies of the map.

Dahlia stood up on the hearth, so they could all see her. She was wearing her black leather jumpsuit and was happily aware she was being admired. Melponeus was there; she could see his curls and reddish face in the corner. Good.

"Thanks to Taffy, we've gotten a map of the tunnels," Dahlia said when the silence was complete. "They run under the Fellowship headquarters, and if the leaders entered the tunnels after their attack against us, they may still be there. Has anyone here been down below the city in the last twenty years?"

"I have," said Melponeus. "I was in the tunnels five years ago, chasing an imp because . . . well, it's not relevant. There are more dead ends in the tunnels now than your map shows. The Fullmore Street tunnel is blocked with rubble at the intersection with Gill." Pens moved over paper. "The Banner Street tunnel is divided in the middle. Someone built a bank aboveground, and in the process they made the tunnel impassable—though I've heard someone's cut a hole in that wall." Melponeus went on to list two more closed or abbreviated tunnels.

"Thanks, Melponeus," Dahlia said. "We owe you."

"Oh, I'll collect," he said, a gleam in his eye.

It was a measure of Dahlia's reputation that no one sniggered.

Cedric strolled through, carrying a pipe and wearing a smoking jacket. Taffy rolled her eyes at Dahlia.

"Do you have a plan of action, then?" he said.

"Yes, my sheriff."

"Good luck. Oh, by the way."

Every vampire froze.

"You must bring them back alive," Cedric said. "I know you want to have fun with them. In fact, I'd planned to ask you to bring me one to play with. But I've gotten a phone call from the chief of police, who said . . . and I think this is interesting . . . that some of his officers told him they'd been running across vampires in unexpected places, asking unexpected questions, and he certainly hoped we weren't taking any vigilante action of our own, since the whole Rhodes police department is anxious to bring the Fellowship terrorists to justice."

None of the vampires cast guilty looks at each other—they were all much too seasoned for that.

"Of course we were planning to kill them," Dahlia said. "What else?"

"I'm afraid you must alter your plan," Cedric told her, using his "sympathetic but firm" voice that carried so well. "Think of how wonderful it will look, a picture of you handing over the culprits to the police. Think of how people will say that we've honored our commitment to refrain from taking human blood— even the blood of our enemies."

Dahlia looked mutinous. "Cedric, we'd anticipated . . . "

"Having a good old-fashioned party," he said. "I regret that, too. But when you find these murderers, they go to police headquarters. Undrained and intact."

And, in turn, every head nodded.

Five teams of two vamps each had been dispatched to the five tunnel accesses closest to Fellowship headquarters. Dahlia thought it possible the bombers had blasted or cut through some of the more recent walls. She would have done so if she'd been planning on using the tunnels as a refuge.

These teams were armed with shotguns. None of them were happy about it. Most vampires (especially the older ones) thought carrying a gun implied a certain lack of confidence in one's own lethality.

Dahlia divided the rest of the Rhodes vamps into two parties. Each would enter the tunnels about a mile away from Fellowship headquarters, one from the east and one from the west. That way, the hunting party could descend without alerting their prey. A couple of cars took Dahlia's party (Taffy headed the other one) to the east entrance she'd selected. This access happened to lie below a restaurant that had opened before World War I.

The Cappelini's Ristorante staff was used to parties trailing through on the "Old Rhodes" tour, but they were taken aback when the eight o'clock tour party consisted wholly of bloodsuckers. Dahlia hung back. Though she was tiny and pretty, she was also unmistakably menacing. Lakeisha beamed her perky smile, tipped heavily, and the atmosphere relaxed.

The party, which consisted of Dahlia, Lakeisha, and three male vamps (Roscoe, Parnell, and Jonathan) all passed through a door the teenage tour guide had unlocked. They descended the stairs into the Cappelini basement. The very nervous young woman pointed out how various things were stored, talked about when the building had been erected, and revealed how many pounds of pasta the restaurant had served since it had opened its doors. Though the vampires gave her polite attention, she was visibly nervous as she prepared to enter the old tunnels.

She unlocked yet another door, this one a very old wooden slab. Greeted by a rush of cool air, the party descended a very narrow flight of stairs, then a steep and twisting ramp, and came to yet another door, much lower than modern doors and heavily locked. Their guide unlocked the last door, keeping up her patter the whole time, though with an effort. She flipped a light switch, and the tunnel appeared, running straight for about ten yards before turning to veer right.

Lakeisha said, "Let me ask you a question." Relieved, the girl looked at the cute dark-skinned vampire inquiringly. Lakeisha said, "See how big my eyes are?" The next minute, the girl was under. "Sit on the floor here and wait until we come back," Lakeisha said, and the girl smiled and nodded agreeably.

The vampires were all used to enclosed spaces, and they all had excellent vision. Dahlia barely seemed to touch the ground as she began to move forward. At first, two of them could walk abreast. After the jog to the right, the old tunnel narrowed.

The walls were brick, plastered here and there. Every now and then the narrow space widened into a storeroom, littered with old signs, broken chairs, all sorts of debris discarded from the businesses above. From time to time a ghostly door, sometimes with glass panels still intact, offered access to an underground saloon or whorehouse that hadn't seen a customer in seventy years.

"This is great," Roscoe said. Though Dahlia didn't reply, she agreed completely.

They didn't meet any other tours, because Cedric had booked them all. For two hours, the vampires owned the tunnels below old Rhodes.

Dahlia brought the party to a halt when she figured they were two blocks away from Field Street. She whispered: "You heard Cedric. No killing. If they resist, you can break a bone." Despite the embargo, they were all tense with anticipation. It had been a long time since a worthy battle had come their way. This was a good moment to be a vampire. With a sharp nod, Dahlia turned and raced down the last section of tunnel.

In the end, the conquering of the Fellowship bombers was almost anticlimactic. There were only seven conspirators below the Fellowship headquarters. Of those, two had been too close to their own handiwork and had been injured by flying debris from the Pyramid. Only three men resisted with any determination, and Taffy, who got to the group seconds before Dahlia, had subdued the largest of these with no trouble at all by kicking him in the ribs. Jonathan and Roscoe took care of the others.

Rather than herd their hostages back to Cappelini's, Dahlia decided to surface at the closest access point. Lakeisha used her cell phone to call the two vampires guarding that spot, their signal to alert the police that there were prisoners to deliver.

Instead of feeling triumphant, Dahlia found herself doubtful. Surely there should have been more Fellowship people in hiding?

"Wait!" she called at the first flight of stairs. She turned. Taffy, right behind her, was carrying the man whose ribs she'd broken. He was groaning, the noise irritating her. To make sure a rib didn't puncture the human's lung, Taffy was carrying the man in front of her. Dahlia looked into his unshaven face.

"What's your name?" she asked, and the man began to recite some membership number the Fellowship had allotted him.

"That's even more irritating than the pain noises," she said. "Shut up, asshole."

He cut himself off in mid-number.

The practical Lakeisha extracted a wallet from his pants. "This particular asshole is named Nick DeLeo."

"Ever talked to a vampire before, Nick?"

"I don't deal with hell spawn," the man said.

"I was not spawned by hell. I met with something much older than myself in Crete, more years ago than you can imagine. I will still be here when your children are dust, if anyone deigns to breed with you." That seemed doubtful to Dahlia. "Where are the others?"

"I'm not supposed to tell you that," he said. It was hard for him to look formidable when a woman was carrying him, and he gave up the attempt when Dahlia came even closer. He flinched.

"Yes," Dahlia said with some satisfaction. "I'm truly frightening. You can hardly imagine the pain I'll cause you, if you don't tell me what I want to know."

"Don't tell him, Ni-*aaargh*!" A scream effectively ended another hostage's exhortation.

"Oh, Roscoe, is he hurt?" Dahlia asked with patently false concern.

"Hard to lend his buddy moral support with a broken jaw," Roscoe said. "Oops."

Dahlia smiled down at Nick. "I have ripped people apart with my bare hands. And I enjoyed it, too."

Nick believed Dahlia. "The others have gone to get the firefighters who fished the vamps out of the Pyramid," he said. "It's easier to get the firefighters; they're not armed. Three of us are going to each station around here that responded. They're going to shoot until their weapons are empty except for one bullet, and then they'll kill themselves. Holy martyrs to the cause."

"That's a terrible plan," Lakeisha said. "You think this will discourage people from helping vampires? Make them want to join your stupid Fellowship? The slaughter of public servants?"

"We have a new goal," Dahlia said. "We deposit these losers with the police. We go to the places they're going to attack. They have a head start on us, so let's be quick."

Up the stairs they swarmed, to be met by media galore. The police knew a good photo op, too. As soon as possible, Dahlia and her nest mates faded away into the shadows. The others had their own assignments, but Dahlia herself ran full tilt toward the corner of Almond and Lincoln.

Four of the Pyramid conspirators were converging on the Thirty-four Company.

At least the big doors were shut. The firefighters inside were cooking, sleeping, playing video games—until the first rifle shot whistled through the upstairs window, missing one of their drivers by a hair. Then shots were pouring into the station from all directions. There was screaming and cursing and panic.

Until, one by one, the rifles stopped firing.

The newspaper photographers would have liked to take a picture of the four Fellowship members piled in a heap on the concrete in front of the station with

Dahlia standing on top of them. But Dahlia was too clever for that. Instead, the next day's paper had a wonderful picture of tiny Dahlia in her black leather jumpsuit in the center of a huddle of firefighters, hoisted up on the shoulder of Captain Ted Fortescue.

Any tendency the fire company might have to rhapsodize sentimentally over Dahlia's one-woman antiterrorist action was dampened when they got a good look at the broken bones and bloody injuries the five foot nothing vampire had inflicted-though all four gunmen were alive, at least for a while.

The newspapers were happy with their pictures, the firefighters were happy to be alive and mostly uninjured, the Fellowship fanatics were secretly glad to be out of the tunnels and to anticipate reiterating their inane credo at their trials, Cedric was happy that his vampires had obeyed his direction, and the vampires felt they had at least made a beginning on their revenge for the Pyramid bombing.

Happiest of all was Melponeus the half demon, because he and Dahlia celebrated the victory until Melponeus had to crawl back to his demon brethren with weak knees and a silly grin.

As for Dahlia, she developed a strange new habit. She felt she had established a relationship with the men and women of Company Number Thirty-four.

She began to drop in from time to time. By her third visit, the humans were matter-of-fact about her presence. Ted Fortescue absentmindedly offered her some chili instead of the Red Stuff they'd started keeping at the back of the refrigerator.

When the city council of Rhodes voted to give Dahlia a special commendation for her defense of the firehouse, everyone from the Thirty-four Company attended.

"I feel like they're my pets," Dahlia confided to Taffy.

Taffy wisely hid her smile.

And when one of the shooters was released on a technicality, and every firefighter in the Thirty-four sounded off about it while Dahlia was there learning how to play *Grand Theft Auto*, none of the firefighters were surprised when the shooter vanished twenty-four hours later.

"Dahlia's like, our mascot," said one firefighter to Ted Fortescue.

"She'll be around a lot longer than we are," Ted Fortescue said. "Especially if you ever say anything like that where she can hear you."

But no one was foolish enough for that.

The Belated Burial
Caitlín R. Kiernan

Caitlín R. Kiernan has published eight novels, including Daughter of Hounds *and* The Red Tree. *She is a prolific author of short fiction, and her stories have been collected in* Tales of Pain and Wonder; From Weird and Distant Shores; Alabaster; To Charles Fort, With Love; A is for Alien; *and, most recently,* The Ammonite Violin & Others. *Since 2004, she has also published the monthly ezine,* Sirenia Digest, *which features her erotica. Kiernan is currently working on her next novel,* The Wolf Who Cried Girl. *She lives in Providence, Rhode Island, with her partner Kathryn and two cats. Kiernan has written several stories that deal with vampires in a nontraditional way. (She also wrote a vampire novel,* The Five of Cups, *which she has described as an "overly-ambitious jumble of competing ideas and subplots, trying to unite vampirism, the grail myth, the tarot, T.S. Eliot's* The Waste Land, *and the Arthuriad into a single, coherent storyline." An early effort, Kiernan later allowed it to be published only in a limited edition.) Her "Ode to Edvard Munch," a story about immortality and time, is a notable example of her recent short fiction that* might *be termed vampiric. Originally published in* Sirenia Digest #6, *May 2006, it has already been republished in vampire anthologies in 2008 and 2009. I recommend it, but instead chose "The Belated Burial." It is unique, both in perspective and subject matter—although if you are well acquainted with the author's work you've already met Miss Josephine and visited the yellow house on Benefit Street in Providence mentioned here.*

> *Mere puppets they, who come and go*
> *At bidding of vast formless things . . .*
> —Edgar Allan Poe

BRYLEE DID object to the casket, and also to the hole in the frozen earth. She did object, in a hesitant, deferential sort of way. But, as they say, her protestations fell upon deaf ears, even though Miss Josephine fully acknowledged that none of it was necessary.

"It will do you good," the vampire said, and, too, she said, "One day you'll understand, when you are older." And, she added, "There is far too little respect for tradition these days." Brylee came near to begging, at the end, but she's not a stupid girl, and she knew that, likely as not, begging would only annoy the vampire and make the whole affair that much more unpleasant.

Being buried when one is fully conscious and keenly aware of the confines of her narrow house and the stink of cemetery soil, these things are terrible, but, as she has learned, there is always something incalculably worse than the very worst thing that she can imagine. Miss Josephine has had centuries to perfect the stepwise procession from Paradise to Purgatory to the lowest levels of an infinitely descending Hell, and she wears her acumen and expertise where it may be seen by all, and especially where it may be seen by her lovers (whether they are living, dead, or somewhere in between). So, yes, Brylee objected, but only the halfhearted, token objection permitted by her station. And then she did as she was bidden. She dressed in the funerary gown from one of her mistress's steamer trunks, the dress, all indecent, immaculate white lace and silk taffeta; it smells of cedar and moth balls. Amid the palest chrysanthemums and lilies, baby's breath and albino roses, she lay down in the black-lacquered casket, which is hardly more than a simple pine box, and she did not move. She did not make a sound. Not breathing was, of course, the simplest part. Miss Josephine laid a heavy gold coin on each of her eyelids before the mourners began to arrive, that she would have something to give the ferryman.

"She was so young," one of the vampires said, the one named Addie Goodwin.

"Your sorrow must be inconsolable," said another, the man whom they all call simply Signor Garzarek, who came all the way from New York for the mock-somber ceremony in the ancient yellow house on Benefit Street.

"It was an easy death," Miss Josephine told him, struggling to hold back tears her atrophied ducts could never actually manufacture. "She went in her sleep, the poor dear." And there was the sound of weeping, so Brylee knew that not all the mourners gathered by Miss Josephine were dead. An antique gramophone played "Be Thou My Vision" again and again and again, and there was a eulogy, delivered by an unfamiliar, stuttering voice. And then, before the lid was finally placed on the black casket and nailed firmly down, Miss Josephine laid a single *red* rose across Brylee's folded hands. The vampire leaned close, and she whispered, "You are exquisite, my dear. You are superb. Sleep tight."

When the casket was lifted off its marble pedestal by the pallbearers, Brylee fought back a sudden wave of panic that threatened to get the better of her.

She came very near to screaming, and that would have ruined everything. That would have undone all her mistress' painstaking theater and pretense, and only the knowledge that there is always something worse kept her silent as she was carried out to the waiting hearse.

No harm can come to me, she reminded herself again and again and again. *I am dead, and what harm can possibly come from these silly games. I am dead almost a month now, and the grave can surely hold no horror for me anymore.* "One night and one day," her mistress had promised, "and not an hour longer. You can do that, sweetheart. The time will fly by, you'll see." Brylee had not been told to which cemetery she would be delivered, so it might be the Old North Burial Ground in Providence, or some place as far away as Westerly, or even Stonington Cemetery in Connecticut. The hearse ride was longer than she expected, but maybe it circled blocks and doubled back, so maybe it didn't go very far at all from the yellow house on Benefit Street. She lay still with the gold coins on her eyes and the rose gripped now in her hands, and the words to "Be Thou My Vision" repeating again and again behind her eyelids, which Miss Josephine had sewn shut for the occasion, just in case. *Be Thou my battle Shield, Sword for the fight; Be Thou my Dignity, Thou my Delight; Thou my soul's Shelter, Thou my high Tower: Raise Thou me heavenward, O Power of my power.* Neither death nor undeath had done very much to shatter Brylee's atheistic convictions, so these words held within them no possible comfort. They seemed, at best, a cruel, mocking chorus, childish taunts she would carry with her down into the cold dirt. *Riches I heed not, nor man's empty praise, Thou mine Inheritance, now and always: Thou and Thou only, first in my heart, High King of Heaven, my Treasure Thou art.* "You are fortunate," Miss Josephine told her when Brylee made the aforementioned objections. "When it was my time to go into the ground, I was wrapped in only a cotton winding cloth, with a little myrrh and frankincense, then buried beneath a dozen feet of Egyptian sand. I was forbidden to rise for a full month, and could always hear the jackals and vultures close at hand, pawing and pecking for a scrap of carrion. There was a sandstorm, and a dozen feet became almost a hundred overnight. And when my time below had passed, no one came for me. I was left to dig myself free." Which is to say, again, that the most appalling situation can always become so much more appalling, and the lesson has not been lost on Brylee.

She suffered the ride to the unknown cemetery in perfect silence. She made no utterance as the pine casket was lowered into the waiting grave, nor when the raw wound in the January landscape was filled in again by men with shovels and the more efficient bucket of a noisy, chugging skid loader. She was silent as silent ever dared to be, while the earth rained loudly down upon the lid of her casket. But she did flinch, and her sharp teeth pierced her lower lip, half expecting the lid to collapse at any moment, splintered by the weight of all that dirt (though she knew well enough there are steel reinforcements to prevent such a mishap). In the darkness, she grew almost as taut as any genuine corpse bound by the shackles of *rigor mortis*, and she tasted her own blood. Or, rather, the stolen blood that she pretended was her own. In the hour of twilight, before the funeral service, when she was still half awake at best, Miss Josephine had brought a gift to her. "Because it is such a special day," the vampire said, then gently laid the banquet on the bed next to Brylee. The girl's hair was almost the same color as the black-lacquered casket, and Miss Josephine had only taken the smallest sip from her, just enough that she wouldn't struggle and ruin Brylee's last meal before the grave.

"It's very kind of you," she told her mistress and pantomimed a grateful smile, though, in truth she was much too nervous to be very hungry; she would not be so impolite as to say so. "Do you know her name," Brylee asked. Miss Josephine made a sour sort of face, and asked her what possible difference a name would make, one way or the other. Brylee did not ask the question a second time. Instead, her tongue flicked across the wound that had already been made in the girl's throat. Brylee's incisors and eye teeth made a wider insult of Miss Josephine's kiss, parting skin and fascia, the protective sheets of platysma and sternocleidomastoid muscle, to reveal the pulsing ecstasy of the carotid artery. She'd paid close attention to the anatomy lessons that she'd been sent down to the Hounds to learn, and she knew well enough to avoid the less-healthful, deoxygenated blood of the jugular. And for a short time, to Brylee's surprise, the joy of the nameless girl's fading life rushing into her was enough to take her mind off everything that was to come.

When she was finished, when the heart had ceased pumping and little remained but a pale husk, Miss Josephine made her sit up, and she cleaned Brylee's blood-smeared face with a black silk handkerchief imported from France more than a hundred years before. Then her mistress kissed her, licking the last few stains from her face, and they lay together for a time, with the dead girl's body growing cold between them. Miss Josephine's delicate hands wandered lazily across Brylee's body, the vampire's fingernails dancing like animated shards of glass; she spoke of other funerals, other burials, and she spoke of resurrection, too. "There is not a surrender to the clay," she said, "without a concomitant rebirth. We do not lie down, but that we rise when our sleep is done." And these were pretty words, to be sure, as were the prayers she muttered to forgotten deities while her sharp fingers strayed and wandered and found their way inside Brylee.

But when the last clod of frozen soil has been shoved rudely back into place, and she can no longer discern the noise of either men or their machines, when all that has *passed* in the preceding few hours dissolves into a seemingly timeless *present*, the beauty of words is overthrown. Here there is a growing silence, and an absence of light that she knows would not be the least bit lessened if stitches did not prevent the opening of her eyelids. This is the truth lurking in back of all the ceremony. This is the simple and inviolable negation of the tomb. Brylee laughs very softly, for no ears but her own, and then she whispers, more quietly still, "Out—out are the lights—out all! And over each quivering form, the curtain, a funeral pall, comes down with the rush of a storm . . . " But she trails off, leaving the stanza unfinished. It would be a grand joke, if uttered by Miss Josephine, or Signor Garzarek, but from Brylee's lips, in this box and in this hole, the words tumble senselessly back upon themselves. She stops before they choke her. They lie like ashes and mold upon her tongue. And so she is quiet, and very, very still, because she has been assured it will be only one night and one day before the hour of her exhumation. She can do that much, surely, and when it is over and she's once again safe in the arms of her mistress, even the suggestion that her current situation held some minor species of dread will seem patently absurd. There is nothing here to fear, and even the bitter cold is not a hardship to one such as herself. She is safe inside her shell, and has but to wait, and waiting is the only genuine trial here to be endured. She thinks to speed the end of her interment by busying her mind, because, as Miss Josephine has said, it is *only* an undisciplined mind that can pose any possible threat while she is below.

Brylee licks her dry lips, and she begins counting backwards from one-hundred thousand, for she can not conceive any more mundane task. With luck, she will bore herself to sleep, and not wake until the men return with their shovels. She says the numbers aloud, laying each one with the same meticulous care a brick mason might go about his work. And in this manner, time passes, even if she is not precisely aware of its passage. She stops thinking about the underside of the casket's lid, mere inches from her face, and all the weight bearing down upon the wood. She does not dwell on how little unfilled space there is to her left or her right. It hardly matters that she is unable to sit up, or roll over on her side, or bend her knees, and she does not succumb to morbid, irrational fears of suffocation. Dead lungs have no need of air. She counts, and counts, and, soon enough, her voice becomes a calming metronome.

"And when you return," Miss Josephine said the night before, "when you are given back to me, delivered from that underworld like Proserpine or, more appropriately, like cruel and wanton Ishtar—when we are so soon reunited, you will never again be called upon to prove yourself. There will only be the long red sea of eternity." And recalling these words, Brylee loses count somewhere after forty-five thousand, and, full in the knowledge of her own recklessness, she listens. Her lips are stilled, and there is no longer the distraction of her voice. There is the sound of the wild January wind, but muffled by her tomb into the most indistinct threnody. Here would be the living hammer of her heartbeat, if her heart still beat. If she still lived. Here would be her hitching breath, perhaps. But her body has been rendered all but inert by the ministrations of her ravenous lover. So, the silence is profound, and for some period of time that passes without being measured, Brylee lies listening to almost nothing at all.

In this slumberous white month, even the worms and beetles do not stir, and the moles and voles and millipedes are as monstrously serene as the surface of the moon. With no forethought, no intention to do anything of the sort, Brylee raises her right hand, the pads of her fingers brushing the lid above her, wood sanded almost completely smooth. Having found that barrier, touching it, she immediately withdraws her hand. And then, as she begins to feel the dry folds of that alarm she promised her mistress and promised herself would not overtake her, she hears a *new* sound. Very far away, at first, or so it seems, and she is reminded of a discarded life, standing on a subway platform station as a train rumbled towards the terminal. Though, whatever thing is the author of *this* approaching tumult would put any subway train to shame. Over minutes or hours, the distant rumble becomes a not-so-distant boom, as of summer thunder, and, at last, a roar. And it cannot be so very far below her, this passing demon, which seems to roll on forever, dragging itself through an unsuspected burrow gnawed in the rotten bedrock below the cemetery. But even now, Brylee does not scream. If she screams, it might hear, and she imagines it moving restlessly, never-sleeping, a labyrinthine circuit running from one graveyard to the next in, listening for anything that is, by some accident, not yet dead. In times past, it must have been more often sated than in this faultless age of embalming. She squeezes her eyes shut as tightly as she may (though the stitches forbid any chance of them opening), and remembers something Miss Josephine said when they lay together in bed with the devoured girl's cadaver in between. Brylee was lost in the bliss that follows feeding, and the bliss of her mistress's hands upon her, upon her and within her. "Perhaps, down there, you will even be so fortunate as to hear his coming and going about his incessant, immemorial rounds," and in the haze of pleasure she'd not thought to ask the identity of this possible august visitor, a name nor any other manner of appellation. Around her pine box, the world shudders, and all the prayers she offers up in the all-but-endless pandemonium are shameless, bald-faced lies. But, it passes her by, this innomi-nate leviathan, and either she was unnoticed or nothing it desired. Or, possibly, Brylee was only meant to bear blind witness to its coming and going. No offering trussed up pretty and left helpless within an inverted altar. Some time that she can only mark as later, the ground around and below her is silent and still again, and whatever came so awfully near would seem only a dream, if she did not, by heretofore unsuspected instincts, know otherwise. Brylee lies in the black-lacquered casket, and she is silent, and she is still, and she waits, permitting no thoughts now but her mistress's beloved face and recollections of wide and star-dappled skies stretched out forever above them.

Twilight States
Albert Cowdrey

Albert E. Cowdrey was born and grew up in New Orleans, and became a historian after going through the academic mill at Tulane and Johns Hopkins. He served in the army, wrote a historical novel which did not feed him, and found work that did in the Department of Defense as a writer of official history. Most of his professional life was spent in the Northeast; he lived in Baltimore, in Annapolis, and for the last fifteen years of his employed life in Washington, D.C., writing for the army's Center of Military History. After retirement he returned to New Orleans, only to be uprooted again by Hurricane Katrina, and today lives in Natchez, Mississippi, a town of conspicuous oddity and charm that has served him as the background of several stories. "Twilight States," a story in which he offers a completely different idea of what a vampire might be, is set, however in New Orleans.

As a writer of imaginative fiction, he has produced one recent novel, Crux, *and fifty or so stories that have appeared in* The Magazine of Fantasy and Science Fiction. *His varied output has been reprinted in English—British English, that is—and in German, Russian, Polish, Czech, Romanian, Hebrew, and Chinese. He has received awards from both the American Historical Association and the World Fantasy Convention. A loner by choice or by DNA (sometimes it's hard to tell the difference) he lives with a border collie named Lagniappe, a Creole word meaning something you get for nothing. Of the two, she is much the cleverer—that's in the nature of the breed.*

A DUSTY shop window, a darkening street outside. Streetlights winking on at three o'clock. A summer storm brewing. Milton's reflection—dim, bent, somehow older than his fifty-two years-stared at him through backward lettering that said *Sun & Moon Metaphysical Books.*

He sighed and flipped the pages of his desk calendar. June 1979 was drawing to an end. Could he afford to close for the day? A customer might yet be driven in by the threat of rain. . . .

As if summoned, the doorbell jangled and a fat old man carrying a furled umbrella erupted into the shop. He strode to a bookcase, browsed for a moment, then snatched down a faded red volume.

"Why d'you stock a fool like Montague Summers?" he boomed.

"Because he s-sells," Milton answered.

Why the stutter? He hadn't stuttered for years. Decades, maybe. Then he knew why: he'd heard that voice before.

"A superstitious Jesuit who thought vampires were real," the intruder was grumbling. "I'm a scientist myself . . . Somebody told me you stock old science fiction."

Milton took a deep breath. "Like *Weird Tales, Astounding, Arcana*?"

"That's it. *Arcana*."

He drew out a ring of keys and unlocked a cabinet. "You're a collector?"

"No. I read for pleasure. And professional interest."

Milton explained that *Arcana* lasted only twenty issues, from mid-1941 until wartime scarcities of paper and ink shut it down. Yet in its brief lifespan it published everybody—big names, promising unknowns.

"Do you have the January '42 issue?"

Milton took another deep breath and offered a flawless copy in its plastic jacket.

"Of course it's pricey. But very rare."

"I'll take it," said the fat man, paying two hundred dollars for a pulp magazine thirty-seven years old. The check he wrote identified him as Erasmus Bloch, M.D., and gave his address and phone number.

The name too rang a bell. An alarm bell, maybe? Yet this was a customer Milton wanted to keep.

"This issue's got a bit of history attached to it," he said, wrapping the package. "My brother Ned was a World War Two hero—Navy Cross—and he got this *Arcana* just about the time of Pearl Harbor. He volunteered so quickly that he never had a chance to read it."

Actually, Milton had bought the copy (and a dozen others) at a newsstand on Royal Street. But people liked pricey purchases to come with a legend.

"Your brother," came that loud, abrupt voice. "Is he still alive?"

Instantly Milton's stutter resurfaced. "No. He was m-murdered. After the war. T-terribly."

Even Bloch seemed to realize he'd put a heavy thumb on an old wound. He touched Milton's bony shoulder with a hand like a flipper.

"This copy will be treasured," he said.

An instant later, the bell jangled, his umbrella deployed with a snap, and the door clicked shut behind him.

Milton folded his arms tight against his concave chest. How could you? He silently berated himself How could you say so much to a stranger? Worse yet, to somebody who may not be a stranger at all?

By now the French Quarter was adrift in rain. Gutters spouted like whales and ankle-deep water washed the streets clean of tourists. No more customers today.

Milton locked the shop and climbed a circular staircase to his living quarters on the second floor. At the top he paused, wheezing. The hall was deep in shadow and rain streamed down the only window. Four closed doors stood in a row: his parents' bedroom, Ned's, his own, and the bath. Something scratched at Ned's door with a sound like a wire brush.

"It's all right,' said Milton. "Don't you be worried. I'm not."

In his room he took off his shoes, stretched out on the bed, and flicked on an old brass lamp. Erasmus, Erasmus. Odd name. Now where—?

In search of an elusive memory, his eyes traveled over the yellow walls, the scarred plaster, the heavy purple furniture, the wall clock missing its pendulum. But no memory came.

Rain drummed on the balcony and rattled the wooden shutters. Gradually Milton's breathing became regular, and sleep fell on him like a coverlet.

He began to dream. Ralph O'Meagan, aged ten, lay in bed listening to his mother curse his father. She was out of the hospital again, and as usual the drying-out treatment hadn't worked for long. She was drinking, and the drunker she got the more she tried to fight with her silent husband, and the more he ignored her the sorrier she felt for herself and the more she drank.

Ralph suffered from nightmares and his parents allowed him to keep a night-light burning. He lay on his side staring at the wall, at the scars and bumps in the old yellow plaster. *"Why don't you SAY something?"* He concentrated, doing magic, knowing that when his eyes grew tired the wall would seem to move. *"You miserable BASTARD!"*

It was stirring now. Wavering, rippling like a broad flag stirred by a light wind. Then it bellied out like a sail.

Startled, he closed his eyes. Looked again through his lashes. The wall was swollen and straining. When he tried to will it back, it burst in a soundless explosion, flinging sparks in every direction.

The dazzle faded. Ralph was lying on a wet field of grass and reeds. He felt the damp and the cold through his PJs. His breath came quickly and he could hear the beating of his heart.

Bewildered, he sat up, shivering in a raw wind. The sky was blue dusk except for one smear of red in the west and a dim moon rising in the east. Far away, he saw a roller coaster's snaky form outlined in lights. A calliope hooted a popular tune of 1948, "The Anniversary Waltz."

Something scratched and snorted and he turned his head. No more than ten yards away, a giant wild boar was digging at the grass. Its flat bristly nostrils blew puffs of smoke, it braced its thick legs, pulled with orange tusks, and a human arm lifted into view. The fingers moved feebly—

Milton sat up, sweating.

He was safe in his own bed, in his own room where he'd slept all his life. Rain pattered against the shutters. And Ralph O'Meagan was back where and when he belonged, in the January '42 issue of *Arcana*, his name forever attached to an intense and disturbing transdimensional story called "Borderland."

The wire-brush sound came again from Ned's room next door, and Milton muttered, "I told you it's all right."

He got up stiffly, put his shoes on and shuffled downstairs. In a small kitchen behind the bookshop he made green tea on a hot plate and inserted a frozen dinner into a dirty microwave oven.

He sat down at a metal-topped table, sipping the tea, and listened to the fan droning in the microwave. He had no way to avoid thinking about Ned, and about himself.

They'd shared Mama's fair coloring, sharp nose, and prominent chin, but not much else.

The product of an earlier marriage, Ned was a bully and a braggart, a fanatic athlete with an appetite for contact sports. Feared in grade school, worshipped in high school. Milton lived in terror of him, never knowing from day to day whether Ned would use him as a playmate or a punching bag.

Early on, Ned demanded and got a separate room so he wouldn't have to live with The Drip. He warned Milton not to talk to him at school, because he didn't want anybody to know they were related. Ned's door sported a poster of a soldier in a tin helmet and a gas mask. A hand-lettered sign said *POISON! KEEP OUT!*

"I ever catch you in my stuff," Ned warned him, "I'll fix you a knuckle sandwich. You hear that, Drip?"

What was Ned hiding? On December 1, 1941—Milton was an obscure freshman in Jesuit High School, Ned a prominent senior—thinking Ned was out, he filled a skeleton key into the old-fashioned lock and went exploring.

The yellow walls were exactly like those in his own room, only stuck all over with movie posters of Humphrey Bogart and Edward G. Robinson looking tough. On Ned's desk, athletic trophies towered over a litter of papers and schoolbooks. Magazines—fantasy, sport, muscle, mystery—lay scattered over the rumpled bed.

Not knowing what he wanted to find, Milton began pawing through papers, opening desk drawers. He was still at work when the door crashed against the wall and Ned erupted into the room.

The memory lingered after almost forty years. Milton stopped sipping his tea and ran his fingertips over his ribs, touching the little lumps where cracked bones had healed. He shivered, reliving his terror as Ned's big hands pounded him.

"God damn you, you fucking punk," he bawled, "keep outta here! Keep outta here!"

The boy Milton had hunkered down, trying to shield his face—that was when his ribs took the pounding—and waited for death. But Ned was fighting himself, too. His face and whole body twisted as he tried to regain control.

Milton slipped under his arm and ran away and locked himself in his room, sobbing with rage and shame. Little by little the sparks of acute pain died out and a slow dull throbbing began in his chest, shoulders, arms, face. Blood soaked his undershirt and he tore it off and threw it away.

Later, when Daddy asked him what had happened to him—most of his injuries were hidden by his clothes, but Milton was walking stiffly and sporting a plum-sized black eye and a swollen jaw—he said he'd fallen downstairs at school.

"Clumsy goddamn kid," said Daddy.

By then Pearl Harbor had happened and Daddy was signing papers so that Ned could volunteer for the Navy. "One less mouth to feed," remarked Mr. Warmth.

Ned vanished into the alternate dimension that people called The Service, and Mama locked up his room, saying it must be kept just as he left it or he'd never return alive.

"Crazy bitch," said Daddy, whose comments were usually terse and always predictable.

Night after night for weeks afterward, Milton opened his window, slipped out onto the cold balcony that connected the three bedrooms, lifted the latch on Ned's shutters with a kitchen knife, and silently raised the sash.

One at a time he took Ned's trophies, wrapped them in old newspapers, and put them out with the trash. He threw away Ned's magazines, books, and posters.

He was hoping that Mama was right and Ned would never return. He hoped the Japs would capture him and torture him. He hoped Ned would fall into the ocean and be eaten by sharks. The depth of his loathing surprised even him, and he treasured it as a lover savors his love.

Then he received Ned's first letter. "Hi, Bro!" it started breezily.

Ned told about the weird people he was meeting in the Navy, about the icy wind blowing off the Great Lakes, about learning to operate a burp gun. Milton read the letter dozens, maybe hundreds of times.

More letters came on tissue-paper V-Mail, the APOs migrating westward to San Diego, then to Hawaii. Ned told about the great fleets gathering in Pearl Harbor for the counterpunch against Japan, about the deafening bombardment of Tarawa before the Marines went in. Gifts began arriving for Milton, handfuls of Japanese paper money, a rising-sun flag, a Samurai short sword.

Why had Ned turned from a domestic monster to a brother? Milton never knew. Maybe the war, maybe the presence of death. As the fighting darkened and lengthened, he could see something of the same spirit touching them all.

Mama went to work for the Red Cross and stayed sober until evening. Daddy took the Samurai short sword and hung it over the fireplace in the living room, where everybody could see it. When Ned sent Mama the Navy Cross he'd won, Daddy sat beside her on the sofa, staring at the medal in its little leather box as if a star had fallen from heaven. That was when he stopped calling Ned "my wife's kid" and started calling him "my son."

In the summer of 1945 Ned himself arrived at the naval air station on Lake Pontchartrain. Broad-shouldered and burned mahogany, he burst upon their lives like a bomb blowing down a wall and letting sunlight pour in.

He ordered Mama to stop drinking, and she put her bottles out with the trash. He ordered Daddy to stop insulting her, and he obeyed. At the first sign of backsliding, Ned would fly into one of his patented rages and his parents would hurry back into line. He was still a bully—only now he controlled his chronic abiding fury and used it for good.

Did hatred really lie so close to love? Could God and the devil swap places so easily? Apparently so.

Now Milton loved him and wanted desperately to be like him. An impossible job, of course. But he tried. Out of sheer hero-worship he decided to volunteer for the peacetime Navy and began going to the Y, trying to get in shape for boot camp. The new Ned didn't laugh at his belated efforts to be athletic. Instead, he went running with him at six in the morning, down the Public Belt railroad tracks along the wharves, among the wild daisies, while a great incandescent sun rose and a rank, fresh wind blew off the Father of Waters.

Life seemed to be brightening for all of them. Who could have guessed it would all go so terribly wrong?

Next day Dr. Bloch dropped by the shop to tell Milton how much he's enjoyed reading *Arcana*.

"I love pulp," he confessed. "I like the energy, the violence, the fact that there's always a resolution. The one thing in *The New Yorker* I never read is the fiction."

They chatted cautiously, like strange dogs sniffing each other. Bloch explained he'd retired from practice but still did a little consulting at St. Vincent's, the mental hospital where both of Milton's parents had been patients.

"You're a psychiatrist?" asked Milton, astonished. Bloch was so noisy and intrusive that he wondered how the man got anyone to confide in him.

"The technical term is shrink," Bloch boomed. "I suppose it's all right to say this now. Your brother was a patient of mine long ago. Somebody who knows I'm a fan of old sf told me about your shop, and as soon as I saw your face it all came back. You're very like him, you know."

Milton sat open-mouthed, while—like some cinematic effect—the lines of a younger face emerged from the old man's spots, creases and wattles. How could he have missed it? Dr. Erasmus Bloch was *Dr. Erasmus Bloch*.

"When did you treat Ned?" he asked, his voice unsteady.

"In forty-eight, I think. Gave him a checkup first, naturally. Well set-up young fellow. Athletic. No physical problems at all."

"Was he . . . ah . . . "

"Psychotic? No. But he was hallucinating, and of course he was scared. We ruled out a brain tumor, drug use, and alcoholism—I don't think he drank at all—"

"No. Because of our mother. I'm the same way. So what was wrong?"

"He was terribly unhappy. He'd grown up isolated, with a drunken mother and a rigid, cold, possibly schizoid father. He had violent impulses that he found hard to control. Frankly, he scared me a bit. These borderline cases can be much more dangerous than the certified screwballs. And he was *strong*, you know?"

"Yes," said Milton, "I remember. . . . You said he was hallucinating?"

"Yes. Quite an interesting case. He believed his frustration and rage had turned him into a god or demon that had created a world. He'd written a story about it, and he loaned me a copy of *Arcana* so I could read it. Matter of fact, I read it again just last night."

Milton nodded. "I've known for years that Ned wrote the story. But I never imagined he thought the—what did he call it? the Alternate Dimension—was real. I mean . . . it's hard to believe he was serious."

"Oh, he was serious, all right. I knew that when I saw the name he'd signed to his story."

"Ralph O'Meagan?"

"It's the closest Ned could come to Alpha Omega. You know, as in Revelations: 'I am the Alpha and Omega, the beginning and the end.' Yes, he actually believed he was a god and he'd made a world."

That was a riveting insight. Milton wondered wily he'd never seen it himself. His breath came quicker, this was turning out to be the most involving conversation he'd had in decades.

"How do you treat something like that?"

"One technique for dissolving a delusional system is to move into it with the patient. It's such a private thing, it disintegrates when he finds another person inside it. So I told Ned, "I want to hear more about this world of yours. Perhaps I can go there with you.'

"Something about that scared him. He skipped our next appointment. My nurse tried to call him, but it turned out he'd given her a wrong number. When she looked him up in the phone book, he claimed he'd never heard of me. Sounded as if he really hadn't. Might have been stress-induced amnesia—rather a radical form of denial."

"Yes," murmured Milton. "That does sound radical."

Bloch glanced at his watch, said he was due at the hospital and took his leave. Milton sat for a few minutes hugging his midsection, then got up and locked the door.

This wasn't his regular day to dust Ned's bedroom, but he went upstairs anyway, for the terrible past had taken him in its grip.

His key chain jangled and he sensed something beyond the door as the key turned silently in the well-oiled lock. But the shadowy room held only a faintly sour organic smell.

He opened the window, unbolted the shutters and flung them wide. Light flooded in. The room looked just as it had the week before Christmas 1945, when Ned had thrown his second-to-last tantrum and stormed out of the house.

Milton hadn't actually witnessed it, but he heard about it later. Ned went into a fury because Mama, possibly in honor of the season, had disobeyed his orders and started drinking again. After he walked out, of course, she drank more. Milton came home carrying an armful of presents to find her staggering, and Ned forever gone.

God, how he'd hated him that day. Tearing out the underpinnings of his life just when he'd begun to be happy.

On the dresser stood a mirror where Ned had combed his hair, and a tarnished silver frame with a faded picture of him as a young sailor wearing a jaunty white cap. Ned was smiling a fake photographic smile, but his eyes didn't smile. Neither did Milton's as he approached and stared at him.

His face hovered in the mirror, Ned's in the picture. Youth and decay: Dorian Gray in reverse. Suddenly feeling an intolerable upsurge of rage, he growled at the picture, "You were such a lousy stinking bastard."

That was only the beginning. Grinding his teeth, he cursed the picture with every word he'd ever learned from chief petty officers and drunks brawling on Bourbon Street and his own unforgiving heart.

Exhausted by the eruption, trembling, clutching his ribs, Milton staggered back and sat down suddenly on the bed. Little by little he calmed down. After ten minutes he stood up and carefully smoothed the bedspread.

"Time to open the shop again," he said in a quiet voice.

He closed Ned's room and locked it, knowing it would be here when he came again, exactly as it was, never changing, never to be changed. The love and hate of his life, shut up in one timeless capsule.

The afternoon brought few customers, the following morning fewer still.

Milton filled the empty hours as he always did, sitting at his desk with his hollow chest collapsed in upon itself, taking rare and slow and shallow breaths, like a hibernating hear. Musing, dreaming, rearranging the pieces of his life like a chess player with no opponent, pushing wood idly on the same old squares.

How much he wanted to put his family into a gothic novel. How often he'd tried to write it, but never could. He smiled ruefully, thinking: Where are you, Ralph O'Meagan, when I need you?

All around him, stacked shelf on shelf, stood haunted books full of demons and starships, the horrors of Dunwich and Poe's Conqueror Worm. But none held the story he longed to tell. He smiled wearily at a dusty print hanging on the wall Dali's *The Persistence of Memory*, with its limp watches.

He knew now why people talked to noisy Dr. Bloch. It was quite simple: they needed to talk, and he was willing to listen. Shortly after eleven o'clock, Milton dug out his customer file and called Bloch's number. It turned out to belong to a posh retirement home called Serena House.

"This is God's waiting room," the loud voice explained, and Milton moved the phone an inch away from his ear. "God's *first-class* waiting room. Want to join me for lunch?"

Milton found himself stuttering again as he accepted. He locked up, fetched his old Toyota from a garage he rented and drove up St. Charles Avenue to Marengo Street. The block turned out to be one of those odd corners of the city where time had stopped around 1890. The houses were old paintless wooden barns, most wearing thick mats of cat's claw vine like dusty habits.

But in their midst sat a new and massive square structure of faux stone with narrow lancet windows. Serena House was a thoroughly up-to-date antechamber to the tomb. After speaking to the concierge—a cool young blonde—Milton waited in a patio that was pure Motel Modern: cobalt pool, palms in large plastic pots, metal lawn furniture, concrete frogs and bunnies and a nymph eternally emptying water from an urn.

"You see what you have to look forward to," boomed Bloch, and they shook hands.

"I can't afford Serena House. Don't you think my shop's a nice place for an old guy to dream away his days?"

"Yes, provided a wall doesn't blow in on you!"

Bloch, that impressively tactless man, laughed loudly at his own wit while leading the way to the dining room. The chairs were ivory enameled with rose upholstery and the walls were festive with French paper. By tacit agreement, they said nothing about Ned until the crème brûlée had been polished off.

Instead they talked sci-fi and fantasy. Milton found Bloch a man of wide reading. He knew the classics by Cyrano and Voltaire, Poe and Carroll and Stoker and Wells. He'd read Huxley's and Forster's ventures into the field. He declared that *Faust* and the *Divine Comedy* were also fantasy masterpieces—epic attempts to make ideas real.

"Because that's what fantasy is, isn't it?" he demanded. "Not just making things up, but taking ideas and giving them hands and feet and claws and teeth!"

After lunch they moved to poolside. Bloch lit a cigar that smelled expensive and resumed grilling Milton. "Your brother—did he die in the room where the story was set?"

He had a gift for asking unexpected questions. Milton cleared his throat, hesitated, then evaded—neatly, he thought—saying where Ned actually did die.

"No. He was found in the marshland out near the lake, about a quarter of a mile from that old amusement park on the shore."

"Any idea what he was doing there?"

"The police thought he'd been killed elsewhere and dumped. I wasn't much help to them—hadn't seen Ned in years. Actually, we'd been on bad terms, and that was sad."

"And your parents . . . what happened to them?"

"Mama drank herself to death. Daddy went senile. Alzheimer's, they'd call it today. He died in St. Vincent's. I got a call one night, and this very firm Negro voice said, 'Your dad, he ain't got no life signs.' I said, 'You mean he's dead?' 'We ain't 'lowed to use that word,' said the voice. 'He ain't got no life signs is all.'

" 'That's okay,' I said. "He never did.' "

Bloch smiled a bit grimly, exhaled a puff of blue smoke. "Tell me . . . exactly what killed Ned?"

Milton took a deep breath. He'd left himself open to such probing, and now had no way to evade an answer.

"Hard to say. He was such a mess by the time they found him. It was November, nineteen-forty-eight. The—the damage to his face and body was devastating. There was a nick in one thoracic vertebra that possibly indicated a knife thrust through the chest. But the coroner couldn't be sure—so much of him had been eaten—there were toothmarks on a lot of the bones. . . .

"Eaten by what?"

Milton squinted at the cobalt pool. Sunstarts on the ripples burned his eyes. He said, "The c-coroner said wild pigs. Razorbacks. The m-marshes were full of them."

Bloch's little pouchy eyes gleamed with interest.

"Amazing. The monster in his story was a wild boar. You're saying he wrote the story in nineteen-forty-one, and seven years later actual wild pigs mutilated his body?"

When Milton didn't answer, Bloch said soberly, "You seem to have lived a Gothic novel, my friend."

"I was thinking the same thing this morning," Milton said, getting up to go. "You know, you're filling your own prescription, Dr. Bloch. You're moving into the fantasy."

"Good Lord," said he, knocking the ash off his cigar as he rose. "I hope not."

By the time he reached the shop, Milton was finding his own behavior incredible. After decades of silence, he couldn't believe the things he'd been saying—to Bloch, of all people.

He was confused as well, angry and fearful yet not sure exactly what he was afraid of. Sitting slumped at his desk, he worked it out.

There was the practical danger, of course. But beyond that lay a metaphysical peril: that he might somehow lose his world. *It's such a private thing,* Bloch had said, *it disintegrates when another person moves into it.*

Rising, Milton unlocked his cabinet and took out a second copy of the January '42 *Arcana.* Six others reposed in the same place, awaiting buyers. He put on white cotton gloves to protect the old brittle pages, and began leafing through them. The words of Ralph O'Meagan were an echo of long ago.

For many long weeks I lived in trembling fear of the night, when I would have to go to my room and see the lamplight on that wall. For now I knew that the world called real is an illusion of lighted surfaces and the resonances of touch, while underneath surges immortal and impalpable Energy, ever ready to create or kill.

There was no possible way of explaining to my father why I should sleep anywhere else, and no way of explaining anything to my mother at all. I tried to sleep without the nightlight, only to find that I feared the demons of the dark even more than those of the light.

Yet I grew tired of waiting and watching for something that never happened, and as time went by I began to persuade myself that what I'd seen that one time was, after all, a mere nightmare, such as I often had.

I was sound asleep, some three or four weeks after my first visit to the Alternate Dimension, when something tickling my face caused me to awaken. At first I had absolutely no sense of fear or dread. Then I felt a prickling on my face and hands like the "pins and needles" sensation when a foot has been asleep—and a memory stirred.

Reluctantly I opened my eyes. I was lying as before in that field of dying grass. One coarse stem was rubbing against my nose, other stems probed my hands and bare feet.

I raised my head and saw the great beast once again. This time I waited until it had finished its horrible meal and had turned away, like an animal well satisfied and ready for sleep.

Trembling, I stood up. I was soaked and shivering and felt as cold and empty as the boar was warm and full. I approached the body it had been mutilating, and it was that of a grown man, with something intolerably familiar about its face—for the face remained: remained, frozen into its last rictus of agony: and I knew that the face one day would be mine.

Milton closed the magazine. Poor Ralph O'Meagan. Poor Alpha Omega. Caught in an eddy of the time process, condemned to return again and again to the same place to undergo the same death and mutilation.

The Alternate Dimension was not the past and not the future. Ralph was encountering Forever.

How extraordinary, Milton thought, that a fourteen-year-old boy should have such ideas and write them so well and then live mute forever afterward. But fourteen, that's the age of discovery, isn't it? Of sexual awakening? Of sudden insights into your fate that you spend the rest of your life trying to understand?

And that rhetoric about immortal and impalpable Energy-was it mere adolescent rubbish? An early symptom of madness? Or a revelation of truth?

That night his sleep was restless. Bloch kept intruding into his dreams, with spotty face thrust forward and eyes staring. Their dialogue resumed, and soon the dream Bloch was breaking into areas the real one hadn't yet imagined.

—*That's what happened, isn't it?* accused the loud metallic voice. *You killed Ned, didn't you?*

—*Christ. Well, yes. I didn't mean to.*

—*No, of course not.*

—*I didn't!*

—*Oh, I think there was a lot of hatred there, plus a lot of rather unbrotherly love. And I don't think you're a forgiving type . . . How'd you do it, anyway?*

—*With a samurai short sword he'd sent me from the Pacific. When he came at me I snatched it off the living room wall and ran it into his chest. Or he did. I mean, he was the one in motion. I was just holding the sword, trying to fend him off. Really.*

—*Why'd he attack you?*

—*He was in one of his rages. It was late at night. Mama was dead and Daddy was in the hospital. I was out of the Navy and living here alone when Ned came bursting into the house, roaring. He'd found out I'd been going to a shrink and using his name instead of my own.*

—*Why'd you do a thing like that?*

—*I was afraid. It was 1948 and people could be committed a lot more easily than they can today. I was afraid I was going crazy and you'd have me put away. It was a dumb trick, but I thought I could find out what was happening to me without running such a risk.*

—*Ah. Now we're getting at it. So you and Ned had your second big fight and—*

—*Just like the first time, he won.*

—*How could he, if you killed him?*

—*He only died. I died but went on living. He became one of the dead but I became one of the undead.*

—*Oh, Lord. Not Montague Summers again.*

—*Yes. Montague Summers again.*

Milton woke up. The clock said 4:20. He got up anyway, and made tea. Except for one light the shop was dark, the books in shadow, all their tales of horror and discovery in suspended animation, like a freeze frame in a movie.

Milton drank green tea, and slowly two images, the dream Bloch and the real one, overlapped in his mind and fused together. What he'd discover in the dream, the real fat noisy old Bloch would discover in time—the pushy devil.

So, Milton thought. I'll have to get rid of him, too.

He added too because over the last three decades there had been other people who seemed to threaten him. He no longer remembered just how many.

Bathed, breakfasted, his long strands of sparse hair neatly combed across his skull, Milton opened his shop as usual at ten. Just before noon Bloch came in, puffing, intruding with his big belly, shaking his veinous wattles.

"Welcome to my house!" Milton quoted, smiling. "Enter freely, and of your own will!"

Bloch chuckled appreciatively. "Thank you, Count."

"That was a fine lunch yesterday," Milton went on warmly, "and the talk was even better than the food."

As usual, they chatted about books. Bloch had been reading an old text from the early days of psychoanalysis, Schwarzwalder's *Somnarrzbulisinus und Däminerzustände*—somnambulism and twilight states. To doctors of the Viennese school, he explained, somnambulism didn't mean literal sleepwalking but rather dissociated consciousness, a transient doubling of the personality.

"Those old boys had something to say," Bloch boomed. "They believed in the reality of the mind. Modern psychiatrists don't. Today it's all drugs, drugs, drugs."

So thought Milton, Bloch had been analyzing him. He said, "As long as you're here, would you like to see Ned's room? I've kept it exactly as it was when he was alive."

Bloch was enthusiastic. "Indeed I would. I wasn't able to help him, and I seem to remember my failures more than my successes."

"Success always moves on to the next thing," Milton agreed, as Bloch trailed him up the circular stair. "But failure's timeless, isn't it? Failure is forever."

Upstairs the hall was clean and bright, with the sun reflecting through the patio window. There was no sound behind Ned's door.

Bloch stopped to catch his breath, then asked, "I'm invited in here too? Otherwise I wouldn't intrude, you know"—carrying on the Dracula bit in his heavy-handed way.

Smiling, Milton unlocked the door and bowed him in. He opened the window and the shutters, and suddenly the room was full of light. The young sailor's face grinned fixedly from the picture frame, and Bloch approached it, eager as a collector catching sight of a moth he'd missed the last time.

"Ah," he said. "Yes, I remember. He looked a lot like this thirty years ago, when I treated him. Or—"

He paused, confused. Milton had come up behind him and looked over his shoulder. Frowning, Bloch stared at the picture, then at the reflection, then at the picture again. It was the first time he'd seen the brothers together.

"You never really knew Ned, did you?" Milton asked.

"But the man I saw—the one who came for treatment—he was built like an athlete—"

"I spent more than two years in the Navy before they Section-Eighted me. It was the only time in my life I was ever in shape."

That was another bit of news for Bloch to absorb, and for the first time Milton heard him stutter a little.

"And the, ah, r-reason for your d-discharge—"

"Oh, the usual. 'Psychotic.' As far as I could see, the word meant only that they didn't know what they were dealing with. At that time, neither did I."

"The story . . . you wrote it?"

"Have you ever known an athlete who could write, or a bookworm who didn't want to?"

"And the things you told me about Ned—"

"Were true. But of course about me. Hasn't it occurred to you that Ned discharged his rage while I buried mine deep? That if there was a maniac in the family, it was far more likely to be me? What kind of a lousy doctor are you, anyway?"

Despite the harsh words his voice was eerily tranquil, and he smiled when Bloch turned his head to see how far he was from the door.

Then he turned back, staring at Milton's bent and narrow frame, and his thoughts might as well have been written on his face. *This bag of bones—what do I have to fear from him?*

Suddenly his voice boomed out. "Ralph O'Meagan, I'm delighted to make your acquaintance at last!"

He stretched out his fat hand and as he did the yellow wall bellied out and burst, blowing away the room and the whole illusion of the world called real.

Gaping, letting his hand drop nervelessly, Bloch stared now at the smudge of fire in the west, now at the rising moon in the east.

A raw wind blew; delighted shrieks echoed from the roller coaster; the calliope was hooting, and Milton hummed along: *Oh, how we danced on the night we were wed—*

"Welcome to my world," he said, standing back.

Swift trotters were drumming on the earth and splashing in the pools and Bloch whirled as the huge humpbacked beast came at him out of the sunset, smoke jetting from its nostrils, small red eyes glinting like sardonyx.

"What did I do?" Bloch cried, waving his fat hands. "I wanted to help! What did I do?"

The boar struck his fat belly with lethal impact and his lungs exploded like balloons. He lived for a few minutes, writhing, while it delved into his guts. Milton leaned forward, hugging himself, breathlessly watching.

The scene was elemental. Timeless. The beast rooting and grunting, the sunset light unchanging, cries of joy from the roller coaster, and the calliope hooting on: *Could we but relive that sweet moment divine/We'd find that our love is unaltered by time.*

"Now you're really part of the fantasy," he assured Dr. Bloch.

Not that Bloch heard him. Or anything else.

Life returned to normal in Sun & Moon Metaphysical Books where, of course, things were never totally normal.

Milton's days went by as before, opening the shop, chatting with the occasional customer, closing it again. Drowsy days spent amid the smell of old books, a smell whose color, if it had a color, would be brownish gray.

Serena House called to inquire about their lodger—Dr. Bloch had left Milton's number when he went out. Milton expressed astonishment over the disappearance, offered any help he could give. Next day a bored policewoman from Missing Persons arrived to take a statement. Milton described how Bloch had visited the shop, chatted, and left.

"He was one of my best customers," he said. "Any idea what might have happened to him?"

"Nothing yet," said the cop, closing her notebook. "It's kind of like Judge Crater."

More than you know, thought Milton. Where Bloch's bones lay it was always 1948, and whole neighborhoods had been built over the spot, a palimpsest of fill and tarmac and buildings raised, razed and raised again. Milton's voice was confident and strong and totally without a stutter as he chatted with the policewoman, and he could see she believed what he told her.

After she left, the afternoon was dull as usual. Around four Milton got up from his desk and took down his copy of Montague Summers's *The Vampire in Europe.*

He hefted it, did not open it, put it back on the shelf and addressed its author aloud.

"Reverend Summers, you're a fool. Thinking the undead drink blood. No, we suck such life as we have from rage and memories. It must be a nourishing diet, because we live on. And on. And on. And on. I knew that when I wrote my story."

An hour later, after closing the shop, he entered Ned's room and for a time stood gazing into the mirror. The sun was going down. As the room darkened, he heard the unseen beast rubbing its nap of stiff hair against the wall and smelled the morning-breath odor of unfresh blood that always attended it.

Was it something or somebody? Was it his creature, or himself? Did he dream its world, or did it dream his? Milton brooded, asking himself unanswerable questions while his image faded slowly into the brown shadows, until the glass held nothing, nothing at all.

To the Moment
Nisi Shawl

Nisi Shawl packs a lot into this very short story: an intriguing and original concept of the vampire plus sex, death, procreation, and a dollop of horror.

Shawl's story collection Filter House, *lauded by Ursula K. Le Guin as "superb," and by Samuel R. Delany as "simply amazing," won the 2008 James Tiptree, Jr. Award and was nominated for a 2009 World Fantasy Award. Shawl is the coauthor of* Writing the Other, *a guide to developing characters of varying racial, religious, and sexual backgrounds, and one of the founding members of the Carl Brandon Society, a nonprofit dedicated to supporting the representation of people of color in the fantastic genres. She is the editor of Aqueduct Press's* WisCon Chronicles 5: Writing and Racial Identity, *and a coeditor of* Strange Matings: Octavia E. Butler, Feminism, Science Fiction, and African American Voices, *forthcoming from Seven Stories. Her speaking engagements include presentations at Duke University, Stanford University, and Smith College. In May 2011 she will be the Guest of Honor for the feminist science fiction convention WisCon. She blogs at nisi-la.livejournal.com.*

WE ARE not extinct. There are sixteen of us, and I'm pregnant. I only just found out.

I like to travel. Not by plane, because on long flights I get restless, and the changes in air pressure hurt. My cavities ache terribly with every ascent and landing, unless I've managed to fill them completely in the last few minutes before boarding. This is difficult to do at almost any airport.

Usually I take a train wherever I want to go. But at times there are oceans in my way.

So I am on a ship, a big white cruiser headed south through the Atlantic. Prior to sailing, I glutted myself with blood enough to last the entire voyage, under normal circumstances.

The circumstances are not normal.

The sun is bright, but winter-thin. I'm wearing a coat of ivory wool and large, hexagonal sunglasses with honey-colored frames. They make me think of bees. The wind does what it wants with my long, dark hair; nothing pretty or symmetrical. I don't care. I've been told I resemble Jackie Onassis since 1971. Monkeys always assume I'm beautiful, no matter how I look.

There's one sitting next to me where I stand on deck. I've been considering him casually since we started out from Lisbon two days ago. Balding—lots of testosterone. From England—skin that lovely rose-flooded milkiness they get in these Northern latitudes. Wife weak with sea-sickness before we left the harbor.

Now I'm afraid. I'm pregnant, and this monkey is far, far too tempting. He reaches up with a long, possessive arm and pulls me down beside him. He doesn't care who sees. He wants them to see.

I do care. I ought to leave, to come for him later, when he's alone.

He leans over to nuzzle my ear, masking the sound of the wind and the waves with his noisy breath and blood. Canvas snaps, flapping loose from the frame of a nearby chair. The gulls come and make their cries, high and wheedling. Strollers on the deck below have brought table scraps to feed them. Little beggars. They snatch what is offered from the air: a crust of someone's sandwich, a crisp, a bit of pink tomato. They feed flying in the light, which reveals the beautiful separateness of all things. While I must go below.

I take him to my cabin. He has his own, since his wife, even on dry land, is a semi-invalid, and they can well afford it. But the two adjoin, so I take him to mine, because there will be noise. I even say that's why I want to go there, and he smiles. He's so sure I'll be the source of that noise.

We take off our clothes in the dark, stuffy room. I could have a better one, if I wanted. But this cabin, so low down, is more isolated. Insulated by emptiness on either side.

I have removed my glasses. My eyes are adjusted now and I can see how self-conscious he is without his clothes. He bumps against the bed and sits down, then fumbles for the light switch. I kneel on the floor in front of him and make him stop. It's easy. I let my tongues relax and wrap around his penis, which is a good size, not too big. Things are going well, considering.

Then, amazingly, he resists. An unusually strong-minded monkey, this one. He pushes me away by my shoulders, slides his hands into my armpits and lifts. He's trying to get me to sit on him, he mumbles how he's always wanted to do it this way. The soft hairs covering his legs brush the backs of my thighs, my calves, as I obediently slide my knees up beside his hips. He rolls his penis against my pubic bone in a practiced move, which might excite me if I had a clitoris. He makes me taste his antiseptic, minty lips, the breath between them laden with the odors of coffee, sugar, flour, eggs. Breakfast. Then he pushes me away again, grappling me into position. He is strong, but I could fight him. I don't. I want this. I need it. I have given up trying to make myself be careful and use my mouth.

He does scream. I do too, and shout Oh God, I'm coming, I'm coming, so if anyone hears us they'll stay away. It lasts a little long for an orgasm, but after a couple of minutes he stops thrashing on the bed and lies still, deflating. I pump and pump. The rosy goodness suffuses me, warming my womb. When I'm done I fall into a dream, sliding slowly off the monkey and curling up next to him on the soiled sheets.

D. is with me and we're on a mountain in Costa Rica, in the seven-sided house he had them build. He tries to tell me why it's better, how the design dissipates the energy of earthquakes, which are common, but I am looking at the green, a green so very green I think my eyes will turn to emeralds before the sun has set. Behind a distant peak it goes, but the green does not go with it. Instead the valleys brim with green darkness, leaf-filled shadows expanding and thickening, clotting up the night with a truer, deeper green.

I realize my companion has been silent for some time. "D.," I say, "it's good to be here, really here. Do you know what I mean?" He nods and touches the back of my neck. His sensitivity to the moment must be, in large part, responsible for the lengthiness of his life. Nine hundred years without even a half-hearted attempt at suicide. That's good, for a male. Soon he will be fully mature.

I find myself kissing him. Our tongues separate, then twine, like lashing vines.

No force is applied on either side, but slowly we grow closer, closer. I am penetrated by the breeze coming through the open window, sharp as citrus; by the fine, probing mouths of flying insects, frustrated in their search for food. By D.'s tongues, too, delicately drawn along my skin, down, down, in, and piercing the membrane over my womb's entrance in an empty, reflexive action. Or I assume the action's emptiness, in the moment. And as I return to the moment, dreaming.

Knowing this assumption is wrong disturbs my sleep.

I wake. The monkey's corpse reeks of feces and the barest beginnings of decay. No blood—that's all mine now, mine and my offspring's.

D.'s offspring, too. Precocious D., fertile a good century before it might have been expected. When my membrane thinned and tore, I should have known. But this is my first pregnancy. Not until I noticed other signs did I fathom the truth of my condition, so rare among us. And by then I had boarded the ship, and it was too late.

I could have consumed the blood of a year's supply of monkeys, if I'd had the cavities to store so much, and still that would be barely enough to satisfy me one month in this state.

Anxiously I examine myself once again, to be sure. Nipples dark and hard. Vaginal dentata pronounced—the normally flat triangular flaps are erect again with hunger, even so soon after my recent, reckless meal.

H. told me many visits ago that the blood volume of an average female monkey increases by fifty percent in the early stages of her pregnancy.

I'm not used to having to work these sorts of things out, but I try to come up with a plan for disposing of the monkey's remains. Although I concentrate, my head is filled with aimless, rootless thoughts. Perfume ads. Nursery rhymes. *Three, six, nine, the goose drank wine. The monkey chewed tobacco on the street car line.* I remember watching one of them, a small one, a female, jumping rope. The glass of shattered bottles glittered in the sun and she sang fiercely, breathlessly, as she leapt and fell, leapt and fell. *The line broke, the monkey got choked.* This is really very bad. *And they all went to heaven in a little rowboat.*

The sad thing is, I have no choice. Even if I managed to escape suspicion in the matter of this monkey's death, the next stop is an island. Madeira. Entirely as problematic as a cruise ship.

So I spend an hour being charming, a few minutes being devious in cramped, unlovely spaces, several more waiting near the lifeboat I've selected. Then everything's all right again.

It's not that I don't care about the monkeys. I'm genuinely sorry that so many have to die, especially when it's such a waste. I manage to salvage quite a few passengers and a handful of the crew. Not the boilermaster, nor his mate, so no one knows I have any idea about the cause of the explosion. Even in memory it's tremendous, the most profound sound; much more ringing and metallic than any volcano. The dark, messy, crowded events preceding it fade in its majestic wake.

A stiff breeze keeps most of the smoke to our south. Rainbows of oil and bobbing detritus surround us, carried here on contrary currents. Each is unique: each random pattern, each odd, useless object brings its own ineffable message to the moment. Removed from context, these fragments of enameled metal, plastic, and wood, charred and reshaped by the forces I have unleashed, are sweetly new.

I wish I could show D. I know how deeply he understands these sorts of things. It is this that makes me sure he will live long, unlike so many other males. So many I have loved. As the coast of Africa comes into view, shorebirds soaring over whitecapped waves, I am buoyed by confidence. He will live many, many more years. Centuries. Long enough to witness the thousand births of each and every child I carry within my womb.

Castle in the Desert:
Anno Dracula 1977
Kim Newman

*What if Dracula defeated Van Helsing, married Queen Victoria, and established a
new world order? Kim Newman invented this alternate history in 1992 with a short
story that was expanded into novel* Anno Dracula *(which brilliantly added Jack the
Ripper, Mycroft Holmes, and other fascinating elements to the mix). He continued
the tale through the first World War in* The Bloody Red Baron *(1995),* Judgment
of Tears: Anno Dracula 1959 *(1998), and in several stories and novellas, including
"Castle in the Desert: Anno Dracula 1977." You'll find the nameless narrator of the
story bears more than a passing resemblance to Raymond Chandler's Philip Marlowe.
The altruistic vampire is Geneviève Dieudonne, who appears (sometimes as a variant
character) in other Newman/Yeovil works.*

Newman's other fiction includes The Night Mayor, Bad Dreams, Jago, The
Quorum, Life's Lottery, Back in the USSA *(with Eugene Byrne), and* The Man
From the Diogenes Club *under his own name. As Jack Yeovil he wrote* The Vampire
Genevieve *and* Orgy of the Blood Parasites. *Newman's nonfiction books include*
Nightmare Movies, Ghastly Beyond Belief *(with Neil Gaiman), and* Horror:
100 Best Books *(with Stephen Jones). He has written and broadcast widely on a
range of topics, and scripted for radio and television. Stories "Week Woman" and
"Ubermensch" have been adapted into an episode of the TV series* The Hunger *and
an Australian short film. His official website, Dr Shade's Laboratory, can be found
at www.johnnyalucard.com. His current publications are expanded reissues of the*
Anno Dracula *series and* The Hound of the d'Urbervilles *and a much-expanded
edition of* Nightmare Movies.

THE MAN who had married my wife cried when he told me how she died.
Junior—Smith Ohlrig, Jr., of the oil and copper Ohlrigs—hadn't held on to

Linda much longer than I had, but their marriage had gone one better than ours by producing a daughter.

Whatever relation you are to a person who was once married to one of your parents, Racquel Loring Ohlrig was to me. In Southern California, it's such a common family tie you'd think there'd be a neat little name for it, pre-father or potential-parent. The last time I'd seen her was at the Poodle Springs bungalow her mother had given me in lieu of alimony. Thirteen or fourteen going on a hundred and eight, with a micro-halter top and frayed jean shorts, stretch of still-chubby tummy in between, honey-colored hair past the small of her back, an underlip that couldn't stop pouting without surgery, binary star sunglasses and a leather headband with Aztec symbols. She looked like a preschooler dressed up as a squaw for a costume party, but had the vocabulary of a sailor in Tijuana and the glittery eyes of a magpie with three convictions for aggravated burglary. She'd asked for money, to gas up her boyfriend's "sickle," and took my television (no great loss) while I was in the atrium telephoning her mother. In parting, she scrawled "fuck you, piggy-dad" in red lipstick on a Spanish mirror. Piggy-dad, that was me. She still had prep-school penmanship, with curly-tails on her *y*s and a star over the *i*.

Last I'd heard, the boyfriend was gone with the rest of the Wild Angels and Racquel was back with Linda, taking penicillin shots and going with someone in a rock band.

Now things were serious.

"My little girl," Junior kept repeating, "my little girl . . . "

He meant Racquel.

"They took her away from me," he said. "The vipers."

All our lives, we've known about the vampires, if only from books and movies. Los Angeles was the last place they were likely to settle. After all, California is famous for sunshine. Vipers would frazzle like burgers on a grill. Now, it was changing. And not just because of affordable prescription sunglasses.

The dam broke in 1959, about the time Linda was serving me papers, when someone in Europe finally destroyed Dracula. Apparently, all vipers remembered who they were biting when they heard the news. It was down to the Count that so many of them lived openly in the world, but his continued unlife—and acknowledged position as King of the Cats—kept them in the coffin, confined to joyless regions of the old world like Transylvania and England. With the wicked old witch dead, they didn't have to stay on the plantation any longer. They spread.

The first vipers in California were elegant European predators, flush with centuried fortunes and keen with red thirsts. In the early '60s, they bought up real estate, movie studios, talent agencies (cue lots of gags), orange groves, restaurant franchises, ocean-front properties, parent companies. Then their get began to appear: American vampires, new-borns with wild streaks. Just as I quit the private detective business for the second time, bled-dry bodies turned up all over town as turf wars erupted and were settled out of court. For some reason, drained corpses were often dumped on golf courses. Vipers made more vipers, but they also made viper-killers—including such noted humanitarians as Charles Manson—and created new segments of the entertainment and produce industries. Vampire dietary requirements opened up whole new possibilities for butchers and hookers.'

As the Vietnam War escalated, things went quiet on the viper front. Word was that the elders of the community began ruthless policing of their own kind. Besides, the cops were more worried about draft dodgers and peace-freak protesters. Now, vampires were just another variety of Los Angeles fruitcake. Hundred-coffin mausolea were opening up along the Strip, peddling shelter from the sun at five bucks a day. A swathe of Bay City, boundaried by dried-up canals, was starting to be called Little Carpathia, a ghetto for the poor suckers who didn't make it up to castles and estates in Beverly Hills. I had nothing real against vipers, apart from a deep-in-the-gut crawly distrust it was impossible for anyone of my generation—the WWII guys—to quell entirely. Linda's death, though, hit me harder than I thought I could be hit, a full-force ulcer-bursting right to the gut. Ten years into my latest retirement, I was at war.

To celebrate the bicentennial year, I'd moved from Poodle Springs back into my old Los Angeles apartment. I was nearer the bartenders and medical practitioners to whom I was sole support. These days, I knocked about, boring youngsters in the profession with the Sternwood case or the Lady in the Lake, doing light sub-contract work for Lew Archer—digging up family records at county courthouses—or Jim Rockford. All the cops I knew were retired, dead or purged by Chief Exley, and I hadn't had any pull with the D.A.'s office since Bernie Ohls's final stroke. I admitted I was a relic, but so long as my lungs and liver behaved at least eight hours a day I was determined not to be a shambling relic.

I was seriously trying to cut down on the Camels, but the damage was done back in the puff-happy '40s when no one outside the cigarette industry knew nicotine was worse for you than heroin. I told people I was drinking less, but never really kept score. There were times, like now, when Scotch was the only soldier that could complete the mission.

Junior, as he talked, drank faster than I did. His light tan suit was the worse for a soaking, and had been worn until dry, wrinkling and staining around the saggy shape of its owner. His shirtfront had ragged tears where he had caught on something.

Since his remarriage to a woman nearer Racquel's age than Linda's, Junior had been a fading presence in the lives of his ex-wife and daughter (ex-daughter?). I couldn't tell how much of his story was from experience and how much filtered through what others had told him. It was no news that Racquel was running with another bad crowd, the Anti-Life Equation. They weren't all vipers, Junior said, but some, the ringleaders, were. Racquel, it appears, got off on being bitten. Not something I wanted to know, but it hardly came as a surprise. With the motorcycle boy, who went by the name of Heavenly Blues but liked his friends to address him as "Mr. President," she was sporting a selection of bruises that didn't look like they'd come from taking a bad spill off the pillion of his hog. For tax purposes, the Anti-Life Equation was somewhere between religious and political. I had never heard of them, but it's impossible to keep up with all the latest cults.

Two days ago, at his office—Junior made a pretense of still running the company, though he had to clear every paper clip purchase with Riyadh and Tokyo—he'd taken a phone call from his daughter. Racquel sounded agitated and terrified, and claimed she'd made a break with the ALE, who wanted to sacrifice her to some elder vampire. She needed money—that same old refrain, haunting me again—to make a dash for Hawaii or, oddly, the Philippines (she thought she'd be safe in a Catholic country, which suggested she'd never been to one). Junior, tower of flab, had written a check, but his new wife, smart doll, talked him out of sending it. Last night, at home, he had gotten another call from Racquel, hysterical this time, with screaming and other background effects. They were coming for her, she said. The call was cut off.

To his credit, Junior ignored his lawfully-married flight attendant and drove over to Linda's place in Poodle Springs, the big house where I'd been uncomfortable. He found the doors open, the house extensively trashed and no sign of Racquel. Linda was at the bottom of the kidney-shaped swimming pool, bitten all over, eyes white. To set a seal on the killing, someone had driven an iron spike through her forehead. A croquet mallet floated above her. I realized he had gone into the pool fully-dressed and hauled Linda out. Strictly speaking, that was violating the crime scene but I would be the last person to complain.

He had called the cops, who were very concerned. Then, he'd driven to the city to see me. It's not up to me to say whether that qualified as a smart move or not.

"This Anti-Life Equation?" I asked Junior, feeling like a shamus again. "Did it come with any names?"

"I'm not even sure it's called that. Racquel mostly used just the initials, ALE. I think it was Anti-Life Element once. Or Anti-Love. Their guru or nabob or whatever he calls himself is some kind of hippie Rasputin. He's one of them, a viper. His name is Khorda. Someone over at one of the studios—Traeger or Mill or one of those kids, maybe Bruckheimer—fed this Khorda some money on an option, but it was never-never stuff. So far as I know, they never killed anyone before."

Junior cried again and put his arms around me. I smelled chlorine on his ragged shirt. I felt all his weight bearing me down, and was afraid I'd break, be no use to him at all. My bones are brittle these days. I patted his back, which made neither of us feel any better. At last, he let me go and wiped his face on a wet handkerchief.

"The police are fine people," he said. He got no argument from me. "Poodle Springs has the lowest crime rate in the state. Every contact I've had with the PSPD has been cordial, and I've always been impressed with their efficiency and courtesy."

The Poodle Springs Police Department were real tigers when it came to finding lost kittens and discreetly removing drunken ex-spouses from floodlit front lawns. You can trust me on this.

"But they aren't good with murder," I said. "Or vipers."

Junior nodded. "That's just it. They aren't. I know you're retired. God, you must be I don't know how old. But you used to be connected. Linda told me how you met, about the Wade-Lennox case. I can't even begin to imagine how you could've figured out that tangle. For her, you've got to help. Racquel is still alive. They didn't kill her when they killed her mother. They just took her. I want my little girl back safe and sound. The police don't know Racquel. Well, they do . . . and that's the problem. They said they were taking the kidnap seriously, but I saw in their eyes that they knew about Racquel and the bikers and the hippies. They think she's run off with another bunch of freaks. It's only my word that Racquel was even at the house. I keep thinking of my little girl, of sands running out. Desert sands. You've got to help us. You've just got to."

I didn't make promises, but I asked questions.

"Racquel said the ALE wanted to sacrifice her? As in tossed into a volcano to appease the Gods?"

"She used a bunch of words. 'Elevate' was one. They all meant 'kill.' Blood sacrifice, that's what she was afraid of. Those vipers want my little girl's blood."

"Junior, I have to ask, so don't explode. You're sure Racquel isn't a part of this?"

Junior made fists, like a big boy about to get whipped by someone half his size. Then it got through to the back of his brain. I wasn't making assumptions like the PSPD, I was asking an important question, forcing him to prove himself to me.

"If you'd heard her on the phone, you'd know. She was terrified. Remember when she wanted to be an actress? Set her heart on it, nagged for lessons and screen tests. She was—what?—eleven or twelve? Cute as a bug, but froze under the lights. She's no actress. She can't fake anything. She can't tell a lie without it being written all over her. You know that as well as anyone else. My daughter isn't a perfect person, but she's a kid. She'll straighten out. She's got her mom's iron in her."

I followed his reasoning. It made sense. The only person Racquel had ever fooled was her father, and him only because he let himself be fooled out of guilt. She'd never have come to me for gas money if Junior were still giving in to his princess's every whim. And he was right— I'd seen Racquel Ohlrig (who had wanted to call herself Amber Valentine) act, and she was on the Sonny Tufts side of plain rotten.

"Khorda," I said, more to myself than Junior. "That's a start. I'll do what I can."

Mojave Wells could hardly claim to come to life after dark, but when the blond viper slid out of the desert dusk, all four living people in the diner—Mom and Pop behind the counter, a trucker and me on stools—turned to look. She smiled as if used to the attention but deeming herself unworthy of it, and walked between the empty tables.

The girl wore a white silk minidress belted on her hips with interlocking steel rings, a blue scarf that kept her hair out of the way, and square black sunglasses. Passing from purple twilight to fizzing blue-white neon, her skin was white to the point of colorlessness, her lips naturally scarlet, her hair pale blond. She might have been Racquel's age or God's.

I had come to the desert to find vampires. Here was one.

She sat at the end of the counter, by herself. I sneaked a look. She was framed against the "No Vipers" sign lettered on the window. Mom and Pop—probably younger than me, I admit—made no move to throw her out on her behind, but also didn't ask for her order.

"Get the little lady whatever she wants and put it on my check," said the trucker. The few square inches of his face not covered by salt-and-pepper beard were worn leather, the texture and color of his cowboy hat.

"Thank you very much, but I'll pay for myself."

Her voice was soft and clear, with a long-ago ghost of an accent. Italian or Spanish or French.

"R.D., you know we don't accommodate vipers," said Mom. "No offense, ma'am, you look nice enough, but we've had bad ones through here. And out at the castle."

Mom nodded at the sign and the girl swivelled on her stool. She genuinely noticed it for the first time and the tiniest flush came to her cheeks.

Almost apologetically, she suggested, "You probably don't have the *fare* I need?"

"No, ma'am, we don't."

She slipped off her stool and stood up. Relief poured out of Mom like sweat.

R.D., the trucker, reached out for the viper's slender, bare arm, for a reason I doubt he could explain. He was a big man, not slow on the draw. However, when his fingers got to where the girl had been when his brain sparked the impulse to touch, she was somewhere else.

"Touchy," commented R.D.

"No offense," she said.

"I've got the fare you need," said the trucker, standing up. He scratched his throat through beard.

"I'm not that thirsty."

"A man might take that unkindly."

"If you know such a man, give him my condolences."

"R.D.," said Mom. "Take this outside. I don't want my place busted up."

"I'm leaving," said R.D., dropping dollars by his coffee cup and cleaned plate. "I'll be honored to see you in the parking lot, Missy Touchy."

"My name is Geneviève," she said, "*accent grave* on the third *e*."

R.D. put on his cowboy hat. The viper darted close to him and lightning-touched his forehead. The effect was something like the Vulcan nerve pinch. The light in his eyes went out. She deftly sat him down at a table, like a floppy rag doll. A yellow toy duck squirted out of the top pocket of his denim jacket and thumped against a plastic ketchup tomato in an unheard-of mating ritual.

"I am sorry," she said to the room. "I have been driving for a long time and could not face having to cripple this man. I hope you will explain this to him when he wakes up. He'll ache for a few days, but an icepack will help."

Mom nodded. Pop had his hands out of sight, presumably on a shotgun or a baseball bat.

"For whatever offense my kind has given you in the past, you have my apologies. One thing, though: your sign—the word 'viper.' I hear it more and more as I travel west, and it strikes me as insulting. 'No Vampire Fare on Offer' will convey your message, without provoking less gentle *vipers* than myself." She looked mock-sternly at the couple, with a hint of fang. Pop pulled his hold-out pacifier and I tensed, expecting fireworks. He raised a gaudy Day of the Dead crucifix on a lamp-flex, a glowing-eyed Christ crowned by thorny lightbulbs.

"Hello, Jesus," said Geneviève, then added, to Pop: "Sorry, sir, but I'm not that kind of girl."

She did the fast-flit thing again and was at the door.

"Aren't you going to take your trophy?" I asked.

She turned, looked at me for the first time, and lowered her glasses. Green-red eyes like neons. I could see why she kept on the lens caps. Otherwise, she'd pick up a train of mesmerized conquests.

I held up the toy and squeezed. It gave a quack.

"Rubber Duck," said Mom, with reverence. "That's his CB handle."

"He'll need new initials," I said.

I flew the duck across the room and Geneviève took it out of the air, an angel in the outfield. She made it quack, experimentally. When she laughed, she looked the way Racquel ought to have looked. Not just innocent, but solemn and funny at the same time.

R.D. began moaning in his sleep.

"May I walk you to your car?" I asked.

She thought a moment, sizing me up as a potential geriatric Duckman, and made a snap decision in my favor, the most encouragement I'd had since Kennedy was in the White House.

I made it across the diner to her without collapsing.

I had never had a conversation with a vampire before. She told me straight off she was over five hundred and fifty years old. She had lived in the human world for hundreds of years before Dracula changed the rules. From her face, I'd have believed her if she said she was born under the shadow of Sputnik and that her ambition was to become one of Roger Vadim's ex-wives.

We stood on Main Street, where her fire-engine-red Plymouth Fury was parked by my Chrysler. The few stores and homes in sight were shuttered up tight, as if an air raid was due. The only place to go in town was the diner and that seemed on the point of closing. I noticed more of those ornamental crucifixes, attached above every door as if it were a religious holiday. Mojave Wells was wary of its new neighbors.

Geneviève was coming from the East and going to the West. Meager as it was, this was the first place she'd hit in hours that wasn't a government proving ground. She knew nothing about the Anti-Life Equation, Manderley, Castle or a viper named Khorda, let alone Racquel Ohlrig.

But she was a vampire and this was all about vampires.

"Why all the questions?" she asked.

I told her I was a detective. I showed my license, kept up so I could at least do the sub-contract work, and she asked to see my gun. I opened my jacket to show the shoulder holster. It was the first time I'd worn it in years, and the weight of the Smith & Wesson .38 special had pulled an ache in my shoulder.

"You are a private eye? Like in the movies."

Everyone said that. She was no different.

"We have movies in Europe, you know," she said. The desert wind was trying to get under her scarf, and she was doing things about it with her hands. "You can't tell me why you're asking questions because you have a client. Is that not so?"

"Not so," I said. "I have a man who might think he's a client, but I'm doing this for myself. And a woman who's dead. Really dead."

I told the whole story, including me and Linda. It was almost confessional. She listened well, asking only the smart questions.

"Why are you here? In . . . what is the name of this village?"

"Mojave Wells. It calls itself a town."

We looked up and down the street and laughed. Even the tumbleweeds were taking it easy.

"Out there in the desert," I explained, "is Manderley Castle, brought over stone by stone from England. Would you believe it's the wrong house? Back in the Twenties, a robber baron named Noah Cross wanted to buy the famous Manderley—the one that later burned down—and sent agents over to Europe to do the deal. They came home with Manderley Castle, another place entirely. Cross still put the jigsaw together, but went into a sulk and sold it back to the original owners, who emigrated to stay out of the War. There was a murder case there in the Forties, nothing to do with me. It was one of those locked-room things, with Borgia poisons and disputed wills. A funny little Chinaman from Hawaii solved it by gathering all the suspects in the library. The place was abandoned until a cult of moon-worshippers squatted it in the sixties, founded a lunatic commune. Now, it's where you go if you want to find the Anti-Life Equation.'"

"I don't believe anyone would call themselves that."

I liked this girl. She had the right attitude. I was also surprised to find myself admitting that. She was a bloodsucking viper, right? Wasn't Racquel worried that she was to be sacrificed to a vampire elder? Someone born in 1416 presumably fit the description. I wanted to trust her, but that could be part of her trick. I've been had before. Ask anyone.

"I've been digging up dirt on the ALE for a few days," I said, "and they aren't that much weirder than the rest of the local kooks. If they have a philosophy, this Khorda makes it all up as he goes along. He cut a folk rock album, *The Death-master*. I found a copy for ninety-nine cents and feel rooked. 'Drinking blood/ Feels so good,' that sort of thing. People say he's from Europe, but no one knows exactly where. The merry band at the ALE includes a Dragon Lady called Diane LeFanu, who may actually own the castle, and L. Keith Winton, who used to be a pulp writer for *Astounding Stories* but has founded a new religion that involves the faithful giving him all their money.'

"That's not a *new* religion."

I believed her.

"What will you do now?" she asked.

"This town's dead as far as leads go. Dead as far as anything else, for that matter. I guess I'll have to fall back on the dull old business of going out to the castle and knocking on the front door, asking if they happen to have my ex-wife's daughter in the dungeon. My guess is they'll be long gone. With a body left back in Poodle Springs, they have to figure the law will snoop for them in the end."

"But we might find something that'll tell us where they are. A clue?"

"'We?'"

"I'm a detective, too. Or have been. Maybe a detective's assistant. I'm in no hurry to get to the Pacific. And you need someone who knows about vampires. You may need someone who knows about other things."

"Are you offering to be my muscle? I'm not that ancient I can't look after myself."

"I *am* that ancient, remember. It's no reflection on you, but a new-born vampire could take you to pieces. And a new-born is more likely to be stupid enough to want to. They're mostly like that Rubber Duck fellow, bursting with impulses and high on their new ability to get what they want. I was like that once myself, but now I'm a wise old lady."

She quacked the duck at me.

"We take your car," I said.

Manderley Castle was just what it sounded like. Crenellated turrets, arrow-slit windows, broken battlements, a drawbridge, even a stagnant artificial moat. It was sinking slowly into the sands and the tower was noticeably several degrees out of the vertical. Noah Cross had skimped on foundation concrete. I wouldn't be surprised if the minion who mistook this pile for the real Manderley was down there somewhere, with a divot out of his skull.

We drove across the bridge into the courtyard, home to a VW bus painted with glow-in-the-dark fanged devils, a couple of pickup trucks with rifle racks, the inevitable Harley-Davidsons, and a fleet of customized dune buggies with batwing trimmings and big red eye-lamps.

There was music playing. I recognized Khorda's composition, "Big Black Bat in a Tall Dark Hat."

The Anti-Life Equation was home.

I tried to get out of the Plymouth. Geneviève was out of her driver's side door and around (over?) the car in a flash, opening the door for me as if I were her great-grandmama.

"There's a trick to the handle," she said, making me feel no better.

"If you try and help me out, I'll shoot you."

She stood back, hands up. Just then, my lungs complained. I coughed a while and red lights went off behind my eyes. I hawked up something glistening and spat it at the ground. There was blood in it.

I looked at Geneviève. Her face was flat, all emotion contained.

It wasn't pity. It was the blood. The smell did things to her personality.

I wiped off my mouth, did my best to shrug, and got out of the car like a champion. I even shut the door behind me, trick handle or no.

To show how fearless I was, how unafraid of hideous death, I lit a Camel and punished my lungs for showing me up in front of a girl. I filled them with the smoke I'd been fanning their way since I was a kid.

Coffin nails, they called them then.

We fought our aesthetic impulses, and went towards the music. I felt I should have brought a mob of Mojave Wells villagers with flaming torches, sharpened stakes and silvered scythes.

"'What a magnificent pair of knockers,'" said Geneviève, nodding at a large square door.

"There's only one," I said.

"Didn't you see *Young Frankenstein*?"

Though she'd said they had movies in Europe, somehow I didn't believe vipers—vampires, I'd have to get used to calling them if I didn't want Geneviève ripping my throat out one fine night—concerned themselves with dates at the local passion pit. Obviously, the undead read magazines, bought underwear, grumbled about taxes, and did crossword puzzles like everyone else. I wondered if she played chess.

She took the knocker and hammered to wake the dead.

Eventually the door was opened by a skinny old bird dressed as an English butler. His hands were knots of arthritis and he could do with a shave.

The music was mercifully interrupted.

"Who is it, George?" boomed a voice from inside the castle.

"Visitors," croaked George the butler. "You are visitors, aren't you?"

I shrugged. Geneviève radiated a smile.

The butler was smitten. He trembled with awe.

"Yes," she said, "I'm a vampire. And I'm very, very old and very, very thirsty. Now, aren't you going to invite me in? Can't cross the threshold unless you do."

I didn't know if she was spoofing him.

George creaked his neck, indicating a sandy mat inside the doorway. It was lettered with the word WELCOME.

"That counts," she admitted. "More people should have those."

She stepped inside. I didn't need the invite to follow.

George showed us into the big hall. Like all decent cults, the ALE had an altar and thrones for the bigwigs and cold flagstones with the occasional mercy rug for the devoted suckers.

In the blockiest throne sat Khorda, a vampire with curly fangs, the full long-hair-and-tangled-beard hippie look, and an electric guitar. He wore a violent purple and orange caftan, and his chest was covered by bead necklaces hung with diamond-eyed skulls, plastic novelty bats, Austro-Hungarian military medals, inverted crucifixes, a "Nixon in '72" button, gold marijuana leaves, and a dried human finger. By his side was a wraith-thin vision in velvet I assumed to be Diane LeFanu, who claimed—like a lot of vipers—to be California's earliest vampire settler. I noticed she wore discreet little ruby earplugs.'

At the feet of these divines was a crowd of kids, of both varieties, all with long hair and fangs. Some wore white shifts, while others were naked. Some wore joke-shop plastic fangs, while others had real ones. I scanned the congregation, and spotted Racquel at once, eyes a red daze, kneeling on stone with her shift tucked under her, swaying her ripe upper body in time to the music Khorda had stopped playing.

I admitted this was too easy. I started looking at the case again, taking it apart in my mind and jamming the pieces together in new ways. Nothing made sense, but that was hardly breaking news at this end of the century.

Hovering like the Wizard of Oz between the throne-dais and the worshipper-space was a fat vampire in a 1950s suit and golf hat. I recognized L. Keith Winton, author of "Robot Rangers of the Gamma Nebula" (1946) and other works of serious literature, including *Plasmatics: The New Communion* (1950), founding text of the Church of Immortology. If ever there were a power-behind-the-throne bird, this was he.

"We've come for Racquel Loring Ohlrig," announced Geneviève. I should probably have said that.

"No one of that name dwells among us," boomed Khorda. He had a big voice.

"I see her there," I said, pointing.

"Sister Red Rose," said Khorda.

He stuck out his arm and gestured. Racquel stood. She did not move like herself. Her teeth were not a joke. She had real fangs. They fit badly in her mouth, making it look like an ill-healed red wound. Her red eyes were puffy.

"You turned her," I said, anger in my gut.

"Sister Red Rose has been elevated to the eternal."

Geneviève's hand was on my shoulder.

I thought of Linda, bled empty in her pool, a spike in her head. I wanted to burn this castle down, and sow the ground with garlic.

"I am Geneviève Dieudonné," she announced, formally.

"Welcome, Lady Elder," said the LeFanu woman. Her eyes held no welcome for Geneviève. She made a gesture, which unfolded membrane-like velvet sleeves. "I am Diane LeFanu. And this is Khorda, the Deathmaster."

Geneviève looked at the guru viper.

"General Iorga, is it not? Late of the Carpathian Guard. We met in 1888, at the palace of Prince Consort Dracula. Do you remember?"

Khorda/Iorga was not happy.

I realized he was wearing a wig and a false beard. He might have immortality, but was well past youth. I saw him as a tubby, ridiculous fraud. He was one of those elders who had been among Dracula's toadies, but was lost in a world without a King Vampire. Even for California, he was a sad soul.

"Racquel," I said. "It's me. Your father wants . . ."

She spat hissing red froth.

"It would be best if this new-born were allowed to leave with us," Geneviève said, not to Khorda but Winton. "There's the small matter of a murder charge."

Winton's plump, bland, pink face wobbled. He looked anger at Khorda. The guru trembled on his throne, and boomed without words.

"Murder, Khorda?" asked Winton. "Murder? Who told you we could afford murder?"

"None was done," said Khorda/Iorga.

I wanted to skewer him with something. But I went beyond anger. He was too afraid of Winton—not a person you'd immediately take as a threat, but clearly the top dog at the ALE—to lie.

"Take the girl," Winton said to me.

Racquel howled in rage and despair. I didn't know if she was the same person we had come for. As I understood it, some vampires changed entirely when they turned, their previous memories burned out, and became sad blanks, reborn with dreadful thirsts and the beginnings of a mad cunning.

"If she's a killer, we don't want her," said Winton. "Not yet."

I approached Racquel. The other cultists shrank away from her. Her face shifted, bloating and smoothing as if flatworms were passing just under her skin. Her teeth were ridiculously expanded, fat pebbles of sharp bone. Her lips were torn and split.

She hissed as I reached out to touch her.

Had this girl, in the throes of turning, battened on her mother, on Linda, and gone too far, taken more than her human mind had intended, glutting herself until her viper thirst was assuaged?

I saw the picture only too well. I tried to fit it with what Junior had told me.

He had sworn Racquel was innocent.

But his daughter had never been innocent, not as a warm person and not now as a new-born vampire.

Geneviève stepped close to Racquel and managed to slip an arm round her. She cooed in the girl's ear, coaxing her to come, replacing the Deathmaster in her mind.

Racquel took her first steps. Geneviève encouraged her. Then Racquel stopped as if she'd hit an invisible wall. She looked to Khorda/Iorga, hurt and betrayal in her eyes, and to Winton, with that pleading *moué* I knew well. Racquel was still herself, still trying to wheedle love from unworthy men, still desperate to survive through her developing wiles.

Her attention was caught by a noise. Her nose wrinkled, quizzically.

Geneviève had taken out her rubber duck and quacked it.

"Come on, Racquel," she said, as if to a happy dog. "Nice quacky-quacky. Do you want it?"

She quacked again.

Racquel attempted a horrendous smile. A baby tear of blood showed on her cheek.

We took our leave of the Anti-Life Equation.

○═╼☓╾═○

Junior was afraid of his daughter. And who wouldn't be?

I was back in Poodle Springs, not a place I much cared to be. Junior's wife had stormed out, enraged that this latest drama didn't revolve around her. Their house was decorated in the expensive-but-ugly mock Spanish manner, and called itself ranch style though there were no cattle or crops on the grounds.

Geneviève sat calmly on Junior's long gray couch. She fit in like a piece of Carrara marble at a Tobacco Road yard sale. I was helping myself to Scotch.

Father and daughter looked at each other.

Racquel wasn't such a fright now. Geneviève had driven her here, following my lead. Somehow, on the journey, the elder vampire had imparted grooming tips to the new-born, helping her through the shock of turning. Racquel had regular-sized fangs, and the red in her eyes was just a tint. Outside, she had been experimenting with her newfound speed, moving her hands so fast they seemed not to be there.

But Junior was terrified. I had to break the spell.

"It's like this," I said, setting it out. "You both killed Linda. The difference is that one of you brought her back."

Junior covered his face and fell to his knees.

Racquel stood over him.

"Racquel has been turning for weeks, joining up with that crowd in the desert. She felt them taking her mind away, making her part of a harem or a slave army. She needed someone strong in her corner, and Daddy didn't cut it. So she went to the strongest person in her life, and made her stronger. She just didn't get to finish the job before the Anti-Life Equation came to her house. She called you, Junior, just before she went under, became part of their family. When you got to the house, it was just as you said. Linda was at the bottom of the swimming pool. She'd gone there to turn. You didn't even lie to me. She was dead. You took a mallet and a spike—what was it from, the tennis net?—and made her truly dead. Did you tell yourself you did it for her, so she could be at peace? Or was it because you didn't want to be in a town—a world—with a *stronger* Linda Loring. She was a fighter. I bet she fought you."

There were deep scratches on his wrists, like the rips in his shirt I had noticed that night. If I were a gather-the-suspects-in-the-library type of dick, I would have spotted that as a clue straight off.

Junior sobbed a while. Then, when nobody killed him, he uncurled and looked about, with the beginnings of an unattractive slyness.

"It's legal, you know," he said. "Linda was dead."

Geneviève's face was cold. I knew California law did not recognize the state of undeath. Yet. There were enough vampire lawyers on the case to get that changed soon.

"That's for the cops," I said. "Fine people. You've always been impressed with their efficiency and courtesy."

Junior was white under the tear-streaks. He might not take a murder fall on this, but Tokyo and Riyadh weren't going to like the attention the story would get. That was going to have a transformative effect on his position in Ohlrig Oil and Copper. And the PSPD would find something to nail him with: making false or incomplete statements, mutilating a corpse for profit (no more alimony), contemptible gutlessness.

Another private eye might have left him with Racquel.

She stood over her father, fists swollen by the sharp new nails extruding inside, dripping her own blood—the blood that she had made her mother drink—onto the mock-Mission-style carpet.

Geneviève was beside her, with the duck.

"Come with me, Racquel," she said. "Away from the dark red places."

Days later, in a bar on Cahuenga just across from the building where my office used to be, I was coughing over a shot and a Camel.

They found me.

Racquel was her new self, flitting everywhere, flirting with men of all ages, sharp eyes fixed on the pulses in their necks and the blue lines in their wrists.

Geneviève ordered bull's blood.

She made a face.

"I'm used to fresh from the bull," she said. "This is rancid."

"We're getting live piglets next week," said the bartender. "The straps are already fitted, and we have the neck-spigots on order."

"See," Geneviève told me. "We're here to stay. We're a market."

I coughed some more.

"You could get something done about that," she said, softly.

I knew what she meant. I could become a vampire. Who knows: if Linda had made it, I might have been tempted. As it was, I was too old to change.

"You remind me of someone," she said. "Another detective. In another country, a century ago."

"Did he catch the killer and save the girl?"

An unreadable look passed over her face. "Yes," she said, "that's exactly what he did."

"Good for him."

I drank. The Scotch tasted of blood. I could never get used to drinking that.

According to the newspapers, there'd been a raid on the castle in the desert. General Iorga and Diane LeFanu were up on a raft of abduction, exploitation, and murder charges; with most of the murder victims undead enough to recite testimony in favor of their killers, they would stay in court forever. No mention was made of L. Keith Winton, though I had noticed a storefront on Hollywood Boulevard displaying nothing but a stack of Immortology tracts. Outside, fresh-faced new-born vampires smiled under black parasols and invited passersby in for "a blood test." Picture this: followers who are going to give you all their money *and* live forever. And they said Dracula was dead.

"Racquel will be all right," Geneviève assured me. "She's so good at this that she frightens me. And she won't make get again in a hurry."

I looked at the girl, surrounded by eager warm bodies. She'd use them up by the dozen. I saw the last of Linda in her, and regretted that there was none of me.

"What about you?" I asked Geneviève.

"I've seen the Pacific. Can't drive much further. I'll stay around for a while, maybe get a job. I used to know a lot about being a doctor. Perhaps I'll try to get into med school, and requalify. I'm tired of jokes about leeches. Then again, I have to unlearn so much. Medieval knowledge is a handicap, you know."

I put my license on the bar.

"You could get one like it," I said.

She took off her glasses. Her eyes were still startling.

"This was my last case, Geneviève. I got the killer and I saved the girl. It's been a long goodbye and it's over. I've met my own killers, in bottles and soft-packs of twenty. Soon, they'll finish me and I'll be sleeping the big sleep. There's not much more I can do for people. There are going to be a lot more like Racquel. Those kids at the castle in the desert. The customers our bartender is expecting next week. The suckers drawn into Winton's nets. Some are going to need you. And some are going to be real vipers, which means other folk are going to need you to protect them from the worst they can do. You're good, sweetheart. You could do good. There, that's my speech. Over."

She dipped a finger-tip in her glass of congealing blood and licked it clean, thinking.

"You might have an idea there, gumshoe."

I drank to her.

Vampires in the Lemon Grove
Karen Russell

Karen Russell, a native of Miami, has been featured in The New Yorker's *debut fiction issue and on* The New Yorker's *20 Under 40 list, and was chosen as one of Granta's Best Young American Novelists. In 2009, she received the 5 Under 35 award from the National Book Foundation. She is the author of* St. Lucy's Home for Girls Raised by Wolves *and* Swamplandia!, *both published by Knopf. Both literary and fantastic, her "Vampires in the Lemon Grove" is one of those stories that different readers will find different meanings in. I suspect that essays have already been written about it, but at its core it is a story about both love and monstrosity—as vampire stories often are.*

IN OCTOBER, the men and women of Sorrento harvest the *primofiore*, or "first fruit," the most succulent lemons; in March, the yellow *bianchetti* ripen, followed in June by the green *verdelli*. In every season you can find me sitting at my bench, watching them fall. Only one or two lemons tumble from the branches each hour, but I've been sitting here so long their falling seems contiguous, close as raindrops. My wife has no patience for this sort of meditation. "Jesus Christ, Clyde," she says. "You need a hobby."

Most people mistake me for a small, kindly Italian grandfather, a nonno. I have an old *nonno*'s coloring, the dark walnut stain peculiar to southern Italians, a tan that won't fade until I die (which I never will). I wear a neat periwinkle shirt, a canvas sunhat, black suspenders that sag at my chest. My loafers are battered but always polished. The few visitors to the lemon grove who notice me smile blankly into my raisin face and catch the whiff of some sort of tragedy; they whisper that I am a widower, or an old man who has survived his children. They never guess that I am a vampire.

Santa Francesca's Lemon Grove, where I spend my days and nights, was part of a Jesuit convent in the 1800s. Now it's privately owned by the Alberti family, the prices are excessive, and the locals know to buy their lemons elsewhere. In summers a teenage girl named Fila mans a wooden stall at the back of the grove. She's pain-fully thin, with heavy, black bangs. I can tell by the careful way she saves the best lemons for me, slyly kicking them under my bench, that she knows I am a monster. Sometimes she'll smile vacantly in my direction, but she never gives me any trouble. And because of her benevolent indifference to me, I feel a swell of love for the girl.

Fila makes the lemonade and monitors the hot dog machine, watching the meat rotate on wire spits. I'm fascinated by this machine. The Italian name for it translates as "carousel of beef." Who would have guessed at such a device two hundred years ago? Back then we were all preoccupied with visions of apocalypse; Santa Francesca, the foundress of this very grove, gouged out her eyes while dictating premonitions of fire. What a shame, I often think, that she foresaw only the end times, never hot dogs.

A sign posted just outside the grove reads:

CIGERETTE PIE

HEAT DOGS

GRANITE DRINKS

Santa Francesca's Limonata—

THE MOST REFRISITING DRANK ON THE PLENET!!

Every day, tourists from Wales and Germany and America are ferried over from cruise ships to the base of these cliffs. They ride the funicular up here to visit the grove, to eat "heat dogs" with speckly brown mustard and sip lemon ices. They snap photographs of the Alberti brothers, Benny and Luciano, teenage twins who cling to the trees' wooden supports and make a grudging show of harvesting lemons, who spear each other with trowels and refer to the tourist women as "vaginas" in Italian slang. "Buena sera, *vaginas*!" they cry from the trees. I think the tourists are getting stupider. None of them speaks Italian anymore, and these new women seem deaf to aggression. Often I fantasize about flashing my fangs at the brothers, just to keep them in line.

As I said, the tourists usually ignore me; perhaps it's the dominoes. A few years back, I bought a battered red set from Benny, a prop piece, and this makes me invisible, sufficiently banal to be hidden in plain sight. I have no real interest in the game; I mostly stack the pieces into little houses and corrals.

At sunset, the tourists all around begin to shout. "Look! Up there!" It's time for the path of *I Pipistrelli Impazziti*—the descent of the bats.

They flow from cliffs that glow like pale chalk, expelled from caves in the seeming billions. Their drop in steep and vertical, a black hail. Sometimes a change in weather sucks a bat beyond the lemon trees and into the turquoise sea. It's three hundred feet to the lemon grove, six hundred feet to the churning foam of the Tyrrhenian. At the precipice, they soar upward and crash around the green tops of the trees.

"Oh!" the tourists shriek, delighted, ducking their heads.

Up close, the bats' spread wings are an alien membrane—fragile, like something internal flipped out. The waning sun washes their bodies a dusky red. They have wrinkled black faces, these bats, tiny, like gargoyles or angry grandfathers. They have teeth like mine.

Tonight, one of the tourists, a Texan lady with a big, strawberry red updo, has successfully captured a bat in her hair, simultaneously crying real tears and howling: "TAKE THE GODDAMN PICTURE, Sarah!"

I stare ahead at a fixed point above the trees and light a cigarette. My bent spine goes rigid. Mortal terror always trips some old wire that, leaves me sad and irritable. It will be whole minutes now before everybody stops screaming.

The moon is a muted shade of orange. Twin discs of light burn in the sky and. the sea. I scan the darker indents in the skyline, the cloudless spots that I know to be caves. I check my watch again. Ifs eight o'clock, and all the bats have disappeared into the interior branches. Where is Magreb? My fangs are throbbing, but I won't start without her.

I once pictured time as d black magnifying glass and myself as a microscopic, flightless insect trapped in that circle of night. But then Magreb came along, and eternity ceased to frighten me. Suddenly each moment followed its antecedent in a neat chain, moments we filled with each other.

I watch a single bat falling from the cliffs, dropping like a stone: headfirst, motionless, dizzying to witness.

Pull up.

I close my eyes. I press my palms flat against the picnic table and tense the muscles of my neck.

Pull UP. I tense until my temples pulse, until little black and red stars flutter behind my eyelids.

"You can look now."

Magreb is sitting on the bench, blinking her bright pumpkin eyes. "You weren't even *watching.* If you saw me coming down, you'd know you have nothing to worry about." I try to smile at her and find I can't. My own eyes feel like ice cubes.

"It's stupid to go so fast." I don't look at her. "That easterly could knock you over the rocks."

"Don't be ridiculous. I'm an excellent flier."

She's right. Magreb can shape-shift midair, much more smoothly than I ever could. Even back in the 1850s when I used to transmute into a bat two, three times a night, my metamorphosis was a shy, halting process.

"Look!" she says, triumphant, mocking, "you're still trembling!"

I look down at my hands, angry to realize it's true.

Magreb roots through the tall, black blades of grass. "It's late, Clyde; where's my lemon?"

I pluck a soft, round lemon from the grass, half a summer moon, and hand it to her. The *verdelli* I have chosen is perfect, flawless. She looks at it with distaste and makes a big show of brushing off a marching ribbon of ants.

"A toast!" I say.

"A toast," Magreb replies, with the rote enthusiasm of a Christian saying grace. We lift the lemons and swing them to our faces. We plunge our fangs, piercing the skin, and emit a long, united hiss: "Aaah!"

Over the years, Magreb and I have tried everything—fangs in apples, fangs in rubber balls. We have lived everywhere: Tunis, Laos, Cincinnati, Salamanca. We spent our honeymoon hopping continents, hunting liquid chimeras: mint tea in Fez, coconut slurries in Oahu, jet black coffee in Bogota, jackal's milk in Dakar, cherry Coke floats in rural Alabama, a thousand beverages that purported to have magical quenching properties. We went thirsty in every region of the globe before finding our oasis here, in the blue boot of Italy, at this dead nun's lemonade stand. It's only these lemons that give us any relief.

When we first landed in Sorrento I was skeptical. The pitcher of lemonade we ordered looked cloudy and adulterated. Sugar clumped at the bottom. I took a gulp, and a whole small lemon lodged in my mouth; there is no word sufficiently lovely for the first taste, the first feeling of my fangs in that lemon. It was bracingly sour, with a delicate hint of ocean salt. After an initial prickling—a sort of chemical effervescence along my gums—a soothing blankness traveled from the tip of each fang to my fevered brain. These lemons are a vampire's analgesic. If you have been thirsty for a long time, if you have been suffering, then the absence of those two feelings—however brief—becomes a kind of heaven. I breathed deeply through my nostrils. My throbbing fangs were still.

By daybreak, the numbness had begun to wear off. The lemons relieve our thirst without ending it, like a drink we can hold in our mouths but never swallow. Eventually the original hunger returns. I have tried to be very good, very correct and conscientious about not confusing this original hunger with the thing I feel for Magreb.

I can't joke about my early years on the blood, can't even think about them without guilt and acidic embarrassment. Unlike Magreb, who has never had a sip of the stuff, I listened to the village gossips and believed every rumor, internalized every report of corrupted bodies and boiled blood. Vampires were the favorite undead of the Enlightenment, and as a young boy I aped the diction and mannerisms I read about in books: Vlad the Impaler, Count Heinrich the Despoiler, Goethe's blood-sucking bride of Corinth. I eavesdropped on the terrified prayers of an old woman in a cemetery, begging God to protect her from . . . me. I felt a dislocation then, a spreading numbness, as if I were invisible or already dead. After that, I did only what the stories suggested, beginning with that old woman's blood. I slept in coffins, in black cedar boxes, and woke every night with a fierce headache. I was famished, perennially dizzy. I had unspeakable dreams about the sun.

In practice I was no suave viscount, just a teenager in a red velvet cape, awkward and voracious. I wanted to touch the edges of my life. The same instinct; I think, that inspires young mortals to flip tractors and enlist in foreign wars. One night I skulked into a late Mass with some vague plan to defeat eternity. At the back of the nave, I tossed my mousy curls, rolled my eyes heavenward, and then plunged my entire arm into the bronze pail of holy water. Death would be painful, probably, but I didn't care about pain. I wanted to overturn my sentence. It was working; I could feel the burn beginning to spread. Actually, it was more like an itch, but I was sure—the burning would start any second. I slid into a pew, snug in my misery, and waited for my body to turn to ash.

By sunrise, I'd developed a rash between my eyebrows, a little late-flowering acne, but was otherwise fine, and I understood I truly was immortal. At that moment I yielded all discrimination; I bit anyone kind or slow enough to let me get close: men, women, even some older boys and girls. The littlest children I left alone, very proud at the time of this one scruple. I'd read stories about Hungarian *vampirs* who drank the blood of orphan girls and mentioned this to Magreb early on, hoping to impress her with my decency. Not *children*! she wept. She wept for a day and a half.

Our first date was in Cementerio de Colon, if I can call a chance meeting between headstones a date. I had been stalking her, following her swishing hips as she took a shortcut through the cemetery grass. She wore her hair in a low, snaky braid that was coming unraveled. When I was near enough to touch her trailing ribbon she whipped around. "Are you following me?" she asked, annoyed, not scared. She regarded my face with the contempt of a woman confronting the town drunk. "Oh," she said, "your teeth."

And then she grinned. Magreb was the first and only other vampire I'd ever met. We bared our fangs over a tombstone and recognized one another. There is a loneliness that must be particular to monsters, I think, the feeling that each is the only child of a species. And now that loneliness was over.

Our first date lasted all night. Magreb's talk seemed to lunge forward, like a train without a conductor; I suspect even she didn't know what she was saying. I certainly wasn't paying attention, staring dopily at her fangs, and then I heard her ask: "So, when did you figure out that the blood does nothing?"

At the time of this conversation, I was edging on 130. 1 had never gone a day since early childhood without drinking several pints of blood. *The blood does nothing?* My forehead burned and burned.

"Didn't you think it suspicious that you had a heartbeat?" she asked me. "That you had a reflection in water?"

When I didn't answer, Magreb went on. "Every time I saw my own face in a mirror, I knew I wasn't any of those ridiculous things, a bloodsucker, a *sanguina*. You know?"

"Sure," I said, nodding. For me, mirrors had the opposite effect: I saw a mouth ringed in black blood! I saw the pale son of the villagers' fears.

Those early days with Magreb nearly undid me. At first my euphoria was sharp and blinding, all my thoughts spooling into a single blue thread of relief—*The blood does nothing!* I don't have to drink the blood!—but when that subsided, I found I had nothing left. If we didn't have to drink the blood, then what on earth were these fangs for?

Sometimes I think she preferred me then: I was like her own child, raw and amazed. We smashed my coffin with an ax and spent the night at a hotel. I lay there wide-eyed in the big bed, my heart thudding like a fish tail against the floor of a boat.

"You're really sure?" I whispered to her. "I don't have to sleep in a coffin? I don't have to sleep through the day?" She had already drifted off.

A few months later, she suggested a picnic.

"But the sun."

Magreb shook her head. "You poor thing, believing all that garbage."

By this time we'd found a dirt cellar in which to live in Western Australia, where the sun burned through the clouds like dining lace. That sun ate lakes, rising out of dead volcanoes at dawn, triple the size of a harvest moon and skull-white, a grass-scorcher. Go ahead, try to walk into that sun when you've been told your bones are tinder.

I stared at the warped planks of the trapdoor above us, the copper ladder that led rung by rung to the bright world beyond. Time fell away from me and I was a child again, afraid, afraid. Magreb rested her hand on the small of my back. "You can do it," she said, nudging me gently. I took a deep breath and hunched my shoulders, my scalp grazing the cellar door, my hair soaked through with sweat. I focused my thoughts to still the tremors, lest my fangs slice the inside of my mouth, and turned my face away from Magreb.

"Go on."

I pushed up and felt the wood give way. Light exploded through the cellar. My pupils shrank to dots.

Outside, the whole world was on fire. Mute explosions rocked the scrubby forest, motes of light burning like silent rockets. The sun fell through the eucalyptus and Australian pines in bright red bars. I pulled myself out onto my belly, balled up in the soil, and screamed for mercy until I'd exhausted myself. Then I opened one watery eye and took a long look around. The sun wasn't fatal! It was just uncomfortable, making my eyes itch and water and inducing a sneezing attack. (Magreb still has not let me forget this scene, and it happened two hundred years ago.)

After that, and for the whole of our next thirty years together, I watched the auroral colors and waited to feel anything but terror. Fingers of light spread across the gray sea toward me, and I couldn't see these colors as beautiful. The sky I lived under was a hideous, lethal mix of orange and pink, a physical deformity. By the 1950s we were living in a Cincinnati suburb; and as a day's first light hit the kitchen windows, I'd press my face against the linoleum and gibber my terror into the cracks.

"So-o," Magreb would say, "I can tell you're not a morning person." Then she'd sit on the porch swing and rock with me, patting my hand.

"What's wrong, Clyde?"

I shook my head. This was a new sadness, difficult to express. My bloodlust was undiminished but now the blood wouldn't fix it.

"It never fixed it," Magreb reminded me, and I wished she would please stop talking.

That cluster of years was a very confusing period. Mostly I felt grateful, aboveground feelings. I was in love. For a vampire, my life was very normal. Instead of stalking prostitutes, I went on long bicycle rides with Magreb. We visited botanical gardens and rowed in boats. In a short time, my face had gone from lithium white to the color of milky coffee. Yet sometimes, especially at high noon, I'd study Magreb's face with a hot, illogical hatred, each pore opening up to swallow me. *You've ruined my life*, I'd think. To correct for her power over my mind I tried to fantasize about mortal women, their wild eyes and bare swan necks; I couldn't do it, not anymore—an eternity of vague female smiles eclipsed by Magreb's tiny razor fangs. Two gray tabs against her lower lip.

But like I said, I was mostly happy. I was making a kind of progress.

One night, children wearing necklaces of garlic bulbs arrived giggling at our door. It was Halloween; they were vampire hunters. The smell of garlic blasted through the mail slot, along with their voices: "Trick or treat!" In the old days, I would have cowered from these children. I would have run downstairs to barricade myself in my coffin. But that night, I pulled on an undershirt and opened the door. I stood in a square of green light in my boxer shorts hefting a bag of Tootsie Roll Pops, a small victory over the old fear.

"Mister, you okay?"

I blinked down at a little blond child and then saw that my two hands were shaking violently, soundlessly, like old friends wishing not to burden me with their troubles. I dropped the candies into the children's bags, thinking: *You small mortals don't realize the power of your stories.*

We were downing strawberry velvet cocktails on the Seine when something inside me changed. Thirty years. Eleven thousand dawns. That's how long it took for me to believe the sun wouldn't kill me.

"Want to go see a museum or something? We're in Paris, after all."

"Okay."

We walked over a busy pedestrian bridge in a flood of light, and my heart was in my throat. Without any discussion, I understood that Magreb was my wife.

Because I love her, my hunger pangs have gradually mellowed into a comfortable despair. Sometimes I think of us as two holes cleaved together, two twin hungers. Our bellies growl at one another like companionable dogs. I love the sound, assuring me we're equals in our thirst. We bump our fangs together and feel like we're coming up against the same hard truth.

Human marriages amuse me: the brevity of the commitment and all the ceremony that surrounds it, the calla lilies, the veiled mothers-in-law like lilac spiders, the tears and earnest toasts. Till death do us part! Easy. These mortal couples need only keep each other in sight for fifty, sixty years.

Often I wonder to what extent a mortal's love grows from the bedrock of his or her foreknowledge of death, love coiling like a green stem out of that blankness in a way I'll never quite understand. And lately I've been having a terrible thought: *Our love affair will end before the world does.*

One day, without any preamble, Magreb flew up to the caves. She called over her furry, muscled shoulder that she just wanted to sleep for a while.

"What? Wait! What's wrong?"

I'd caught her midshift, halfway between a wife and a bat.

"Don't be so sensitive, Clyde! I'm just tired of this century, so very tired, maybe it's the heat? I think I just need a little rest. . . . "

I assumed this was an experiment, like my cape, an old habit to which she was returning; and from the clumsy, ambivalent way she crashed around on the wind I understood I was supposed to follow her. Well, too bad. Magreb likes to say she freed me, disabused me of the old stories; but I gave up more than I intended: I can't shudder myself out of this old man's body. I can't fly anymore.

Fila and I are alone. I press my dry lips together and shove dominoes around the table; they buckle like the cars of a tiny train.

"More lemonade, *nonno?*" she smiles. She leans from her waist and boldly touches my right fang, a thin string of hanging drool. "Looks like you're thirsty."

"Please," I gesture at the bench. "Have a seat."

Fila is seventeen now and has known about me for some time. She's toying with the idea of telling her boss, weighing the sentence within her like a bullet in a gun: *There is a vampire in our grove.*

"You don't believe me, *signore* Alberti?" she'll say, before taking him by the wrist and leading him to this bench, and I'll choose that moment to rise up and bite him in his hog-thick neck. "Right through his stupid tie!" she says with a grin.

But this is just idle fantasy, she assures me. Fila is content to let me alone. "You remind me of my *nonno,*" she says approvingly, "you look very Italian."

In fact, she wants to help me hide here. It gives her a warm feeling to do so, like helping her own fierce *nonno* do up the small buttons of his trousers, now too intricate a maneuver for his palsied hands. She worries about me, too. And she should: lately I've gotten sloppy, incontinent about my secrets. I've stopped polishing my shoes; I let the tip of one fang hang over my pink lip. "You must be more careful," she reprimands. "There are tourists *everywhere.*"

I study her neck as she says this, her head rolling with the natural expressiveness of a girl. She checks to see if I am watching her collarbone, and I let her see that I am. I feel like a threat again.

Last night I went on a rampage. On my seventh lemon I found with a sort of drowsy despair that I couldn't stop. I crawled around on all fours looking for the last *bianchettis* in the dewy grass: soft with rot, mildewed, sun-shriveled, black-ened. Lemon skin bulging with tiny cellophane-green worms. Dirt smells, rain smells, all swirled through with the tart sting of decay.

In the morning, Magreb steps around the wreckage and doesn't say a word.

"I came up with a new name," I say, hoping to distract her. "*Brandolino.* What do you think?"

Magreb and I have spent the last several years trying to choose Italian names, and every day that I remain Clyde feels like a defeat. Our names are relics of the places we've been. "Clyde" is a souvenir from the California Gold Rush. I was callow and blood-crazed back then, and I saw my echo in the freckly youths panning along the Sacramento River. I used the name as a kind of bait. It sounded innocuous, like someone a boy might get a malt beer with or follow into the woods.

Magreb chose her name in the Atlas Mountains for its etymology, the root word *ghuroob*, which means "to set" or "to be hidden." "That's what we're looking for," she tells me. "The setting place. Some final answer." She won't change her name until we find it.

She takes a lemon from her mouth, slides it down the length of her fangs, and places its shriveled core on the picnic table. When she finally speaks, her voice is so low the words are almost unintelligible.

"The lemons aren't working, Clyde."

But the lemons have never worked. At best, they give us eight hours of peace. We aren't talking about the lemons.

"How long?"

"Longer than I've let on. I'm sorry."

"Well, maybe it's this crop. Those Alberti boys haven't been fertilizing prop-erly, maybe the *primofiore* will turn out better."

Magreb fixes me with one fish-bright eye. "Clyde, I think it's time for us to go."

Wind blows the leaves apart. Lemons wink like a firmament of yellow stars, slowly ripening, and I can see the other, truer night behind them.

"Go where?" Our marriage, as I conceive it, is a commitment to starve together.

"We've been resting here for decades. I think it's time . . . what is that thing?"

I have been preparing a present for Magreb, for our anniversary, a "cave" of scavenged materials—newspaper and bottle glass and wooden beams from the lemon tree supports—so that she can sleep down here with me. I've smashed dozens of bottles of fruity beer to make stalactites. Looking at it now, though, I see the cave is very small. It looks like an umbrella mauled by a dog.

"That thing?" I say. "That's nothing. I think it's part of the hot dog machine."

"Jesus. Did it catch on fire?"

"Yes. The girl threw it out yesterday."

"Clyde," Magreb shakes her head. "We never meant to stay here forever, did we? That was never the plan."

"I didn't know we had a plan," I snap. "What if we've outlived our food supply? What if there's nothing left for us to find?"

"You don't really believe that."

"Why can't you just be grateful? Why can't you be happy and admit defeat? Look at what we've found here!" I grab a lemon and wave it in her face.

"Goodnight, Clyde."

I watch my wife fly up into the watery dawn, and again I feel the awful tension. In the flats of my feet, in my knobbed spine. Love has infected me with a muscular superstition that one body can do the work of another.

I consider taking the funicular, the ultimate degradation—worse than the dominoes, worse than an eternity of sucking cut lemons. All day I watch the cars ascend, and I'm reminded of those American fools who accompany their wives to the beach but refuse to wear bathing suits. I've seen them by the harbor, sulking in their trousers, panting through menthol cigarettes and pacing the dock while the women sea-bathe. They pretend they don't mind when sweat darkens the armpits of their suits. When their wives swim out and leave them. When their wives are just a splash in the distance.

Tickets for the funicular are twenty lire I sit at the bench and count as the cars go by.

That evening, I take Magreb on a date. I haven't left the lemon grove in upward of two years, and blood roars in my ears as I stand and clutch at her like an old man. We're going to the Thursday night show, an antique theater in a castle in the center of town. I want her to see that I'm happy to travel with her, so long as our destination is within walking distance.

A teenage usher in a vintage red jacket with puffed sleeves escorts us to our seats, his biceps manacled in clouds, threads loosening from the badge on his chest. I am jealous of the name there: GUGLIELMO.

The movie's title is already scrolling across the black screen: *Something Clandestine Is Happening in the Corn!*

Magreb snorts. "That's a pretty lousy name for a horror movie. It sounds like a student film."

"Here's your ticket," I say. "I didn't make the title up. If you wanted to see something else you should have said so."

It's a vampire movie set in the Dust Bowl. Magreb expects a comedy, but the Dracula actor fills me with the sadness of an old photo album. An Okie has unwittingly fallen in love with the monster, whom she's mistaken for a rich European creditor eager to pay off the mortgage on her family's farm.

"That Okie," says Magreb, "is an idiot."

I turn my head miserably and there's Fila, sitting two rows in front of us with a greasy young man. Benny Alberti. Her white neck is bent to the left, Benny's lips affixed to it as she impassively sips a soda.

"Poor thing," Magreb whispers, indicating the pigtailed actress. "She thinks he's going to save her."

Dracula shows his fangs, and the Okie flees through a cornfield. Corn stalks smack her face. "Help!" she screams to a sky full of crows. "He's not actually from Europe!"

There is no music, only the girl's breath and the *fwap-fwap-fwap* of the off-screen fan blades. Dracula's mouth hangs wide as a sewer grate. His cape is curiously still.

The movie picture is frozen. The *fwap*ing is emanating from the projection booth; it rises to a grinding *r-r-r*, followed by lyrical Italian cussing and silence and finally a tidal sigh. Magreb shifts in her seat.

"Let's wait," I say, seized with an empathy for these two still figures on the movie screen, mutely waiting for repair. "They'll fix it."

People begin to file out of the theater, first in twos and threes and then in droves.

"I'm tired, Clyde."

"Don't you want to know what happens?" My voice is more frantic than I intend it to be.

"I already know what happens."

"Don't you leave now, Magreb. I'm telling you, they're going to fix it. If you leave now, that's it for us, I'll never . . . "

Her voice is beautiful, like gravel underfoot: "I'm going to the caves."

I'm alone in the theater. When I turn to exit, the picture is still frozen, the Okie's blue dress floating over windless corn, Dracula's mouth a hole in his white greasepaint.

Outside I see Fila standing in a clot of her friends, lit by the marquee. These kids wear too much makeup, and clothes that move like colored oils. They all looked rained on. I scowl at them and they scowl back; and then Fila crosses to me.

"Hey, you," she grins, breathless, so very close to my face. "Are you stalking somebody?"

My throat tightens.

"Guys!" Her eyes gleam. "Guys, come over and meet the *vampire*."

But the kids are gone.

"Well! Some friends," she says, then winks. "Leaving me alone, defenseless

"You want the old vampire to bite you, eh?" I hiss. "You want a story for your friends?"

Fila laughs. Her horror is a round, genuine thing, bouncing in both her black eyes. She smells like hard water and glycerin. The hum of her young life all around me makes it difficult to think. A bat filters my thoughts, opens its trembling lampshade wings.

Magreb. She'll want to hear about this. How ridiculous, at my age, to find myself down this alley with a young girl: Fila powdering her neck, doing her hair up with little temptress pins, yanking me behind this Dumpster. "Can you imagine," Magreb will laugh, "a teenager goading you to attack her! You're still a menace, Clyde."

I stare vacantly at a pale mole above the girl's collarbone. *Magreb*, I think again, and I smile; and the smile feels like a muzzle. It seems my hand has tightened on the girl's wrist, and I realize with surprise, as if from a great distance, that she is twisting away.

"Hey, *nonno*, come on now, what are you—"

The girl's head lolls against my shoulder like that of a sleepy child, then swings forward in a rag-doll circle. The starlight is white mercury compared to her blotted-out eyes. There's a dark stain on my periwinkle shirt, and one suspender has snapped. I sit Fila's body against the alley wall, watch it dim and stiffen. Spidery graffiti weaves over the brick behind her, and I scan for some answer contained there: Giovanna & Fabiano. Vaffanculo! Vai in Culo.

A scabby-furred creature, our only witness, arches its orange back against the Dumpster. If not for the lock I would ease the girl inside. I would climb in with her and let the red stench fill my nostrils, let the flies crawl into the red corners of my eyes. I am a monster again.

I ransack Fila's pockets and find the key to the funicular office, careful not to look at her face. Then I'm walking, running for the lemon grove. I jimmy my way into the control room and turn the silver key, relieved to hear the engine roar to life. Locked, locked, every car is locked, but then I find one with thick tape in Xs over a busted door. I dash after it and pull myself onto the cushion, quickly, because the ears are already moving. The box jounces and trembles. The chain pulls me into the heavens link by link.

My lips are soon chapped; I stare through a crack in the glass window. The box swings wildly in the wind. The sky is a deep blue vacuum. I can still smell the girl in the folds of my clothes.

The cave system is vaster than I expected; and with their grandfather faces tucked away, the bats are anonymous as stones. I walk beneath a chandelier of furry bodies, heartbeats wrapped in wings the color of rose petals or corn silk. Breath ripples through each of them, a tiny life in its translucent envelope.

"Magreb?"

Is she up here?

Has she left me?

(I will never find another vampire.)

I double back to the moonlit entrance, the funicular cars. When I find Magreb, I'll beg her to tell me what she dreams up here. I'll tell her my waking dreams in the lemon grove: the mortal men and women floating serenely by in balloons freighted with the ballast of their deaths. Millions of balloons ride over a wide ocean, lives darkening the sky. Death is a dense powder cinched inside tiny sandbags, and in the dream I am given to understand that instead of a sandbag I have Magreb.

I make the bats' descent in a cable car with no wings to spread, knocked around by the wind with a force that feels personal. I struggle to hold the door shut and look for the green speck of our grove.

The box is plunging now, far too quickly. It swings wide, and the igneous surface of the mountain fills the left window. The tufa shines like water, like a black, heatbubbled river. For a disorienting moment I expect the rock to seep through the glass.

Each swing takes me higher than the last, a grinding pendulum that approaches a full revolution around the cable. I'm on my hands and knees on the car floor, seasick in the high air, pressing my face against the floor grate. I can see stars or boats burning there, and also a ribbon of white, a widening fissure. Air gushes through the cracks in the glass box.

What does Magreb see, if she can see? Is she waking from a nightmare to watch the line snap, the glass box plummet? From her inverted vantage, dangling from the roof of the cave, does the car seem to be sucked upward, rushing not toward the sea but to another Sort of sky? To a black mouth open and foaming with stars?

I like to picture my wife like this: Magreb shuts her thin eyelids tighter. She digs her claws into the rock. Little clouds of dust rise around her toes as she swings upside down. She feels something growing inside her, unstoppable as a dreadful suspicion. It is solid, this new thing, it is the opposite of hunger. She's emerging from a dream of distant thunder, rumbling and loose. Something has happened tonight that she thought impossible. In the morning, she will want to tell me about it.

Vampire Anonymous
Nancy Kilpatrick

Award-winning author Nancy Kilpatrick has published eighteen novels, around two hundred short stories, one nonfiction book (The Goth Bible) *and edited ten anthologies. She writes mainly horror, dark fantasy, mysteries, and erotica. She is currently working on two new novels. Some of her recent short fiction appears in:* Blood Lite *and* Blood Lite 2: Overbite, Hellbound Heart, The Bleeding Edge, The Living Dead, Don Juan and Men, Vampires: Dracula and the Undead Legions, By Blood We Live, The Bitten Word, Campus Chills, Chilling Tales, *and* Darkness on the Edge. *She recently co-edited (with David Morrell) the horror/ dark fantasy anthology* Tesseracts Thirteen *and edited (solo) the anthology* Evolve: Vampire Stories of the New Undead. *She has just finished editing a sequel to* Evolve, *to be published in 2011. Her graphic novel* Nancy Kilpatrick's Vampyre Theatre *will be out in early 2011, and a collector's edition of the erotic horror series* The Darker Passions *began in December 2010. Her website is www.nancykilpatrick.com.*

In case you missed it from the above, Kilpatrick—among other things—has written quite a number of vampire stories. In "Vampires Anonymous" she manages to bring the archetype right up to date while still referencing its grand traditions.

Vampire Anonymous

Mortals! Enter freely and of your own free will!
All may post in the section marked
VICTIMS
with absolutely no assurance that
your post will ever receive a written response!
To post on this site:
VICTIMS will only be accepted once personal info is submitted:
Name: _____
Address: _____

Phone number: _____

Email Address: _____

Age: _____ Internet Name: _____

Gender (not optional): M / F

VICTIMS:

Hey man, cool site so far! Cool images. Well, cool fangs, anyway. Looking forward to some chillin' words 'o wisdom from the great Undead!"
Your Boi Georgie

I find the idea of a new vampire blog intoxicating. I just hope you don't resort to the mundane clichés so many pseudo vampires do. In darkness . . . *Lucrezia*

Am SOOOOO lovin' this! Hozit feel ded? LUV 2 B U! xxooxx—*Lisa*

Not too many blogs have a chat function for the general public. WTG!
Your Boi Georgie

This is the stupidest blog I've ever seen. Fuck off! *Nightmare on Elm*

I've yearned to be a vampire. And now you're here! I can tell just from the visuals that my dreams are coming true! *Dark Angel*

Nightmare on Elm, you obviously don't possess the sensibilities for this blog. Perhaps U should go elsewhere for entertainment. Maybe there's a Freddie blog somewhere. *Lucrezia*

Screw U bimbo!" *Nightmare on Elm*

Vampires Anonymous rule! Bitchin'! *Your Boi Georgie*

Testament #1

Those perusing this site will surely wonder if you exist. Out there. In here. You do not wonder where is *here*, meaning this cyber world. It is a place for hiding, a realm of disguises, the realm of the Giaour. Or, as your contemporary Edgar Allan would have put it, a veritable "Masque of the Red Death" virtual ball. Hence no Facebook or My Space but a unique invention where you remain anonymous and yet your VICTIMS reveal all! After all, one who dwells in the land between Heaven and Earth cannot remain surreptitious when forced to expose details, and this is, after all, your blog!

But OTOH, you must reluctantly acknowledge that the world of phosphors isn't exactly foreign terrain. Anyone in doubt can read the poem "Darkness." Reality is a fine weave of the senses, is it not? The five mundane senses, and that elusive sixth. You can frolic in any of those arenas, yet most often you are relegated to what is not seen, heard, felt, touched or tasted. You are the intangible. Others know you exist, but may not admit it. For lack of a better word—which they likely find unpronounceable—they call you *The Vampyre*.

Enough tedious philosophizing. In this, your first blog entry, you must cater to the VICTIMS, who are—your tongue-firmly-in-your-cheek—dying to learn something of you. Here it is, a tidbit. A veritable bloody morsel, gouged from your beatless heart and offered on this microchip plate: You were born in 1788, just five years before the French Revolution, not that you are French, nor have you ever been revolting, as it were, at least not to your own mind. Mileage varies as they say. Some may beg to differ.

There! A British-ism has crept into that previous paragraph, betraying your ancestry. You are not ashamed of your past. Why should you be? All creatures born must adjust to their circumstances, or die. But sometimes they die anyway, when circumstances prove unnatural or, if the VICTIMS prefer, supernatural. Die and revive. As did you. Fate is a bitch.

But you were birthed during the long and diseased reign of the vegetarian king George III, who suffered porphyria. Anyone who has found this blog is a true vampyre, or a wanna be, and in either situation knows about the "vampire disease." For the uninitiated:

The Symptoms: sensitivity to sunlight, receding gums (all the better for the fangs to show!), bloody urine, etc. etc. Oh, and the incessant talking. They say George 3 once chatted non-stop for fifty-eight hours! Half the time reciting "Childe Harold's Pilgrimage" and other assorted poems. But enough of this tedious medical trivia. You are not an encyclopedia. Anyone desiring to know the symptoms of porphyria can bloody well go look them up!

You met George 3 in his dotage. George, with whom you shared a first name. It wasn't long after the turn of the 19th century, years before your "official" death, but not before your death to life as it is generally understood. The monarch, then in his eighties, had been exiled to Windsor Castle where he was more or less left to his own devices. He'd gone both blind and deaf. The first night as you entered the castle at his invitation, it was clear to you that no one looked after the old bastard. Indeed, his eldest son had already been named Regent, anticipating the ancient one's demise. George had gone quite bonkers. He mistook you first for the wind, then a ghostly friend. Only the insane seem to notice the presence of your kind. Isn't it peculiar that the lucid tend to rationalize cold drafts, fleeting shades, barely heard whispers, while those who have lost their marbles see more clearly the shadows? The insane and the bards of this world, and perhaps visual artists, but you digress.

Poor George had stopped shaving for quite some time and sported a scraggly, wiry beard that brushed the middle of his chest, about heart level. Sleepless, he wandered the dank castle halls garbed in a regally purple dressing gown with his Garter star pinned to his chest. You did not believe he knew that his wife Charlotte had died, but then he did not seem to have a clue that his own demise was eminent. At your hands.

Yes, before the unsettling thought enters any mortal heads, you want to make it perfectly clear that back then you still retained vestiges of human emotion and felt sorry for perhaps the kindest, most fair-minded of British monarchs. In your lifetime no one would have called you selfless. In fact, your reputation was the opposite. Still, due no doubt to *Hours of Idleness*, you helped George to his end as a generous if yet selfish act. To this day, you still remember the texture of his parchment skin, and the sour taste of his thin blood, the coppery element common in human vitae all but missing from the liquid weakly spurting from his aorta, replaced by something more acrid. His skinny chicken neck and the prolapsed veins and arteries proved difficult to work with and, back in the day, you found this not esthetically pleasing. Still, these aspects of George to the third power did not prove insurmountable, but the process of piercing him became extended. Oddly, his rummy eyes found yours as you moved in close to bite him. He smiled with his eyes and his lips and murmured something endearing which you've forgotten, though you do recall that he whispered Sarah, a reference no doubt to the lovely Lady Sarah Lennox of whom George was enamored in his youth—before his mother bollixed that romance.

Never mind *The Dream*. Sentiment be damned. Your dagger-sharp incisors sliced through the emaciated flesh to allow what blood he possessed to trickle like hot treacle between your eager lips, quenching the dire thirst which has since become perpetual, that drives your every waking moment. *When We Two Parted* and it was done and his corpse lay crumpled on the floor at your feet, you, who sported the title Lord, who loved and was loved by many including your sister, you who enjoyed early fame if not fortune in the realm of realms literature, you came to a startling discovery: blue blood is not nearly as satisfying as red blood. It was at that moment that you decided you would, once your death had been staged in Greece, move to America.

◦—✦—◦

VICTIMS:

This old one is soooo amazing! I really want to meet YOU. *Lucrezia*

Y R so real, VA! Keep the stories commin' xxooxx—*Lisa*

Man, there's like SO many people on here now. Get a life, folks! *Nightmare*

Why don't YOU get a life, Nightmare! *Lucrezia*

I'm new here. I'm not sure what's going on. *Harry Lewis*

Well, Harry Lewis, you've hit the pit of hell where all these morons are talking about vampires. Get out before the stake swings in your direction! *Nightmare*

Welcome, Harry. You are fortunate to be here and we are fortunate to meet you. We are in the presence of an Old One who has lived many centuries and shares with us his dark history. George Gordon Byron. *Dark Angel*

Lord Byron? The poet? Impressive. *Harry Lewis*

Yeah, right! *Nightmare*

I've waited one entire month for another entry. Please, kind vampire sir, the esteemed Lord Byron, bestow upon us another tale! *Lucrezia*

How come you talk like you're in some Anne Rice book? *Nightmare*

Where's Your Boy Georgie? He hasn't posted lately. *Dark Angel*

No idea. xxooxx—*Lisa*

People come, people go. Only those of us with deeper sensibilities remain. *Dark Angel*

Like you, airhead? *Nightmare*

Honestly, I don't know why you're still here! You think its all crap, so just go somewhere else. *Lucrezia*

Hey, I'm hangin' to see just how stupid you people can get! *Nightmare*

Testament #2

You observe that your list of VICTIMS has grown. Furiously they post between your monthly entries, when *la luna* fills, when you fill. Let them speak with one another! You have no need to respond. That is not your concern, although you will miss Your Boi Georgie who seems to have . . . vanished. *Arrivederci, bello!*

Still, what a strange phenomenon, human beings desperate to befriend a *vampiro*. And after centuries on this Earth, you thought you'd seen it all!

If you are nuovo, you have arrived at *Vampire Anonymous*, where the undead speak and the living listen. Come one, come all! Enter freely, but enter at your own risk (especially you, lovely Lucrezia.)

All have been warned! What more can you do?

One VICTIM in particular you find intriguing, at least the photo—those long dark tresses, eyes obsidian almonds accentuated by black kohl from the Orient, lips as red as virgin blood, skin corpse white. *Si*, Lucrezia, you are a look-alike for she for whom you are named. An homage to the Renaissance beauty Valencian Borgia, famous for her poison rings. Do you own a poison ring? What type of poison does it contain? Would you let me touch your ring, taste your poison?

Ha! Lucrezia Borgia. Her beauty was renowned. Her lips red passion, her breasts fruits for your lips . . . You remember her well. How could you not remember your sister?

Back then, you carried the mortal name of Cesare, bequeathed by your despotic "padre," Pope Alexander VI. Yes, at that time, *Papa* equated with *King*, and this office incorporated a different meaning than it does today. At least you believe so. Be that as it may, ultimately, you were forced to kill your father, an all too common action. Then. Now. Oedipus Rules!

You were fortunate to have been born *vampiro* and did not need to suffer the transition to this eternal existence. Naturally, you were a beautiful child who grew tall and handsome, dark wavy locks swirling down to your shoulders, hypnotic black almond eyes that lured everyone—hair and eyes like your sister's, like the lovely VICTIM Lucrezia.

Your parentage remained somewhat obscure, at least on the paternal side. But full of ambition, you were destined for *grandi cose*. At the tender age of fifteen, you were appointed Bishop of Pamplona, and at eighteen Cardinal. Of course, you were more or less forced to resign that last post, becoming the first Cardinal in history to do so. This, at the "request" of your father, who needed you to head the military when your oh-so-beloved brother Giovanni met his untimely end. An end that involved your teeth at his throat!

Leaving the church for a more mundane if volatile profession had its perks. For a brief time you employed Leonardo da Vinci as an architect and engineer, although that didn't last long. You found the artist, like all artists, annoyingly arrogant. His blood, though, contained a certain heady quality, like a *vino* grown with fat antique Sicilian grapes.

During your military career, you also had occasion to meet and befriend

Niccolò Machiavelli, a brilliant analyst, who resided at court for just over one year until you brought him, too, to an undead state. You wonder how many VICTIMS recognize that his seminal work *The Prince* is largely based on your military and political strategies?

In any event, it was the French King Louis XII aka the Duck of Orleans— he of The Crusades, and the defeated in the four decades of pointless wars with Italy—it was he who dubbed you Duke of Valentinois, hence your nickname Valentino. Is it possible that any VICTIM recalls your reinvention in the early part of the twentieth century as a fabulously famous film star of the silent screen? A mesmeric star, hypnotic, especially the eyes. *Si, bello,* the *vampiro* charm! Yes, you have gotten around.

Suffice it to say that you had always been a Prince of Darkness. Sadly, though, your body "died," at least officially, yet you resurrected and your unnatural state became permanent during a siege at the age of thirty-one. Had you not been so near dissolution of mortality already suffering symptoms of third stage syphilis, you most certainly would have fought courageously to preserve not just the physical body, despite its pathetic condition, but also the anima *immortale*. But mortal death would have happened eventually. And logic was always your strong suit. Better to leave with a pleasing body intact, which is a state you bestow on your food sources. Live fast, die young, leave a corpse you would be proud of! But, as they say nowadays, *ciò è la vita*: such is life. Or, in your case, living death. One cannot predict nor do much to change Fate. You had always found acting out the role of undead to be a humorous enterprise.

But of course the VICTIMS are modern and bored with history and long explanations and want nothing more than to know the connections, for example, to sweet poisonous-ringed Lucrezia, your sister. She became your lover at an early age—relationships like that happened back then. She even birthed your child. And you birthed both of them to a new existence, an eternal life that the church fathers had not envisioned.

VICTIM Lucrezia entertains thoughts of being your lover. Perhaps she is your sister, now living incognito in Kalamazoo, Michigan, as her personal information states. She would like you to taste her blood and compare it with your darling sibling's, trace memories of which still linger within you. Shared DNA. Sharing so much more! Blood is thicker than any important liquid. It travels through the centuries and finds its way to you again. Ah, but fantasy is everything is it not, *il mio amore Lucrezia*? Tantalizing fantasy, meshed with the reality of the *vampiro*. Come! We are *famiglia*. Take my hand, *sorella*! I desire to taste your blood. Again . . .

VICTIMS:

Where's Lucrezia? *Lisa*

She hasn't logged on in weeks! *Morticia*

Maybe she finally got a life! *NoE*

She's probably busy. *Harry Lewis*

Yeah, playing Vampire the Masquerade! *NoE*

Perhaps she's stepped over into the Other Realm? *Dark Angel*

Is that not what you did? Sorry for my English, I'm Swiss. *Nosferatu*

Of course not! I have not yet been called. *Dark Angel*

You mean excuse you being Swiss! *NoE*

That's racist! *Harry Lewis*

You mean nationalist, doofus! *NoE*

Guys, chill! *Lisa*

Hi! I'm new! *Sin-de*

And oh-so-perky! *NoE*

Leave her alone! Don't listen to him, Sin-de. He's our Resident Evil. *Morticia*

Welcome! *Dark Angel*

Welcome. *Harry Lewis*

Wavin'—*Lisa*

I'm new too. *Vampira*

Hiya! *Harry Lewis*

This place is so crowded! *Sin-de*

We are the regular posters but there are others. *Dark Angel*

So, who's this guy posting this vampire stuff? *Vampira*

It is all in the posts. *Dark Angel*

It's all in the Prozac. *NoE*

What's NoE? North of Erie? *Sin-de*

Nightmare on Elm. *Lisa*

Nightmare on Elm. *Harry Lewis*

Nobody Owns Elvira. *Dark Angel*

Wouldn't you like to know? *NoE*

Duh, that's why she asked. *Vampira*

Guys, chill!! *Lisa*

We must be respectful of the blogger's space. Or as Lucrezia would say: Why is it only girls are human? *Dark Angel*

Hi. I'm Elizabeth. But you can call me Black Lily. *Black Lily*

More females, yes! *Nosferatu*

When's the next post? I'm bored. *NoE*

He posts on the full moon, as anyone intelligent could figure out. *Dark Angel*

Hi Black Lily. Welcome to hell! *Vampira*

Testament #3

So many *lány*, so very little time. I am amazed at how the gentler sex finds it way to me, *lepkék-hoz egy láng* or, as the English speakers say, moths to the flame. There! I have already tarnished my reputation as a high-born lady by littering this site with clichés. I am an educated woman, an exceptional creature for the place and time of my birth—Hungary, 1560. Destined to be a Countess or to carry some other high-born title, I learned at my mother's knee to read and write four languages and a smattering of three others at a time when women received little or no education. But this damned English language! It stymies me now, so lacking as it is in innuendo. In any event, I am known to all of you already, I am quite sure. Countess Erzsébet Báthory, aka the Bloody Lady of Čachtice. And now you will hear the truth!

How can I convey my extraordinary life to you VICTIMS who speak with one another electronically and share but an image that may or may not reflect who you are? I can only tell each of you, my precious little ones, that four hundred and fifty years ago life was primitive by today's standards, even for those of us of noble birth. Primitive and dangerous.

Luckily, I was somewhat protected. For the daughter of parents directly related to two distinguished *vivodes*, or warlords, of Transylvania, and niece of the King of Poland, how could it have been otherwise? In fact, I was next in line to be Queen of Poland, a task for which I was eminently suited and one which met my ambitions.

At the tender age of eleven, I was were already betrothed for political reasons to a rather rough soldier named Ferenc Nádasdy who stank of garlic morning, noon and night. My parents sent me to Nádasdy Castle in Sárvár. It was not against my will. Perhaps you cannot grasp the concept of an arranged marriage. Such unions were the practice everywhere among the wealthy and this one spoke to the goals of my parents as well as my own. Betrothal is not marriage, and even as a young girl I was keenly aware of the difference. A charming peasant in the village—a blacksmith as I recall—took my maidenhead—oh did I bleed! My first enrapture with blood! From that union I suffered a stillborn daughter. The gods owed me!

You must indulge me. I love talking about myself. So much has been written about me, and I think you should all know the truth. And where better to hear it than from my own, perfect lips!

Yes, you guessed it, I was an exquisite girl, my beauty legendary, and the times were such that four years later Nadasdy, smitten with me, forgave my indiscretions and married me anyway. Perhaps the best part of the marriage was his wedding gift to me, his home Čachtice Castle, situated in the Carpathian Mountains near Trenčín, together with the Čachtice country house and seventeen adjacent villages.

Ferenc was reasonable for a man, but a soldier to the core, and a beautiful, young, intelligent wife could not hold the attention for long of a man who longed for battle. Three years after the nuptials he was appointed chief commander of the Hungarian troops and off to war for much of the remainder of the marriage. I'll just say that I was not heart-broken.

Managing such a vast estate and being charged with protecting our lands, especially during more than a decade of war, took up much of my time, yes, but not all. There were servants, many, to be managed. The role of Countess is exhausting, yet I fulfilled my responsibilities, even intervening in the causes of peasant women who needed help for one thing or another.

Then, one day, I had a rude awakening. In my silvered hand mirror I found a shocking sight. My flawless porcelain skin, famous in four countries, showed signs of aging. A wrinkle here, a sag there . . . How had I not noticed before? But I did now, and the awareness hit deep in my chest. At that very moment a *szolga* or servant girl had been brushing my hair and allowed the boar's bristles to tangle in my dark tresses, yanking my head back sharply. Instinctively, I slapped her, hard enough that a drop of blood splattered onto my cheek. Mesmerized, I stared in the mirror, watching the vitae drip down my skin. Impulsively, I rubbed the glistening ruby liquid into my cheek. And it seemed to me then that the flesh on that side of my face took on a new hue, a glow of vitality.

This discovery led to musing and long discussions with several of my most trusted and loyal servants, including Dorka who was closer to me than the others. We came to the conclusion that the blood produced an alchemical transformation. Blood was the answer, the elixir guaranteed to stave off the ravages of time.

One thing, as they say, led to another. At first, with Dorka's help, I drew blood from the servants, but the stupid girls resisted my humane methods and quickly we resorted to the whip. Dorka used the hide liberally and I admit that from time to time I took a turn flailing. The blood of the screaming peasant girls who unfortunately often perished in the experiment was gathered and applied to my face and, astonished, I immediately saw the change occur. Suddenly I looked younger, as if I had discovered the Spanish explorer Juan Ponce de León's Fountain of Youth.

I acknowledge to you all now that perhaps I allowed Dorka and the others to go too far. They not only whipped but they burned, froze, starved and bit girls, needles under the fingernails, and mutilation of faces and genitalia, all in an effort to, as they assured me, "excite the vér and render it more potent" which, at the time, seemed a reasonable avenue to pursue.

Several years passed and it occurred to me that what worked magic on the face and the neck would transform just as well skin on the entire body. I knew that in order to achieve the desired effect I needed a constant supply of girls. Too quickly I ran out of expendable servants and was forced to bring in female peasant from the villages, lured to the castle with the promise of well-paid work as maidservants. The job required living at the castle full-time, no days off as you modern workers are offered. Consequently these girls never returned home. No one missed them. They were hung upside down, their veins sliced open, their precious offerings caught in my bath. My skin stayed lovely and fresh as the day I'd wed Ferenc. For a time, all was well.

Then, on another fateful day, I stared in my damned mirror lamenting that I was no longer the fairest in the land, despite daily treatments with the magic potent. I became furious and threw the mirror against the wall, shattering it to bits. Dorka, as always, comforted me. She brought me to the realization that it was some basic coarseness in the blood of these *paraszt* that left my skin unnourished. Dorka insisted that I required refined blood, and the only way to have that would be to acquire refined donors.

Through my many contacts I was able to invite the daughters of nobles to my home, ostensibly to be trained in the ways of the aristocracy. I generously offered to be their mentor, assuring these young women would possess the manners, skills and intelligence needed to function at the level of society to which they aspired—one level up. I was overwhelmed with requests to take in these well-born girls and tutor them. You can see that I had little choice in the matter. Fate called me to preservation.

I procured a house in Bucharest on a small street that has today come to be called Blood Alley. This is where I met these refined girls as they came to the city. With the help of a German clockmaker, I created a design, ingenious if I say so myself, and far ahead of its time. I called it the Iron Virgin—a later design which imitated my own was known as the Iron Maiden. But I named this Virgin for I had realized rather early on the exquisite and dramatic effects of virgin blood which far outweighed that of non-virgins. Anyway, the device allowed me to imprison a girl in a sarcophagus then hoist the apparatus to the ceiling. Within this iron structure with its painted blue eyes, the yellow hair of one of my prettier princesses and the white perfect teeth of another, were long spikes that, as the door slammed shut and automatically locked, pierced the flesh in such a manner and in so many places that the blood was permitted to flow freely down to a tub below in which I was immersed. With a small leap of the imagination I am certain you can envision my ecstasy. Any woman could.

I can still recall the sharp, sweet aroma and the tangy-sweet taste as the vitae engulfed my flesh, the hot blood burning through my skin, altering it with its magical properties, transforming what had become old and tired and revitalizing my body. I reveled in the blood. It filled my mouth, my nose, and I gulped it down greedily, allowing it to burn away from the inside the dross of age and reveal the hidden, nearly lost beauty of my youth. Call it early Botox!

I am certain that each girl VICTIM understands my pursuit, my desire to stay attractive at any price. And if you do not now understand it, you will!

These noble girls performed a service for me. I took possession of their youth gratefully and they gave up their lives in the same way, gratefully, at least in their hearts. A symbiosis. A sacrifice. For the greater good. Isn't that obvious?

In any event, I continued in this way for many years, retaining my beauty to the amazement of those in my social circle. During this time, at age forty-four, I became a widow, barely noticing. Ferenc had been absent for some years. He died at the hand of a general, or having been killed in battle, or murdered by a prostitute in

Bucharest whom he refused to pay—take your pick. I had little interest in his fate. And upon his demise I inherited his wealth and consequently had no shortage of suitors lured as much by my youthful beauty as by the hope of marrying my money and power. But I barely tolerated these leeches. Especially now that I was in direct line for the throne. I was, you see, on the verge of becoming the Queen of Poland! And now, sweet VICTIMS, you understand the greater good, do you not?

Alas, nothing continues forever. Mine was a political era and rumors abounded about illicit practices involving witchcraft at my estate and at my house in Bucharest. While the deaths of peasant girls were tolerated or ignored, the offspring of nobles was duly noted. Eventually, in 1610, I was brought to trial, found guilty of twenty-five years of abuses. Three of my most trusted servants were burned alive as witches, including Dorka. From my window I watch her body blacken, her dark hair catch fire and all the while I listened as her screams filled my ears.

I was charged with bringing about the deaths through sadistic torture of 650 girls, an absurd number. Although I kept no written records, I did compile a tally in my head and the numbers had been triple that, at least!

During this sham trial I refused to respond with the regret or remorse expected. After all, I was a Countess and did not deign to address their ridiculous accusations. Consequently, without being found guilty because of my station, I received the harshest punishment—I were walled up alive in the tower of my own castle where I remained for the next three years, being fed through a slot like an animal. Were the powers-that-be concerned with the deaths? Of course not! The entire charade of a trial was a strategic move on the part of the then heads of state to usurp my land and my wealth, which they did, and to keep me from ascending to the throne. A woman then had few legal recourses.

Ah, but did I not have the last laugh? You see, the blood not only changed my skin but it altered every aspect of my being, body and soul. Not only did I return to youth, but that youth became eternal, and my taste for blood infinite.

When I stopped eating, they finally opened the tower door. But I was not there! My body, you see, has never been found. The pathetic *paraszt* who resided near Nádasdy Castle have insisted for centuries, to this day in fact, that they can hear the wail of girls being tortured to death, and my sparkling laugh as I delight in the voluptuous richness of their young blood. Me, whom these cretins call *vámpír*!

So many young and pretty girls here! And of course you understand. There are far more important concerns that those of a petty nature, what might be deemed "personal' problems. The greater good must prevail! You are not VICTIMS but lovers of history, of tradition, of fate. Surely, my pretties, you would like to meet me? Ah, to surrender to a larger fate, what better destiny . . . ?

VICTIMS:

Awesome! *Harry Lewis*

That story chills my bones, man. *Nosferatu*

Where's all the chicks? How come they aren't posting anymore? *NoElm*

Maybe they got tired of your stupidity! *Harry Lewis*

Hey, how's it going? Thought I'd check this out. *Vampire of Dusseldorf*

Hey V of D. Good to meet you! *Harry Lewis*

Yeah, man, it's getting lonely here without chicks. *NoElm*

Doesn't matter to me. I'm gay. And German. *Vampire of Dusseldorf*

That's a problem. *NoElm*

Being gay? *Vampire of Dusseldorf*

Being German! *NoElm*

Groan! *Nosferatu*

Don't you think it's weird that every time this guy tells a story, VICTIMS disappear? I mean, the missing people are like the people in the stories! *Nosferatu*

It's coincidental, man. Do I have to remind you we're on the Net. There aren't any vampires here! *NoElm*

Testament #4

Landsmann! A Deutsch amongst the VICTIMS! Vampire of Düsseldorf. Düsseldorf. Northwest of Köln, *ja*? I am familiar with your small city. *Und* your reputation!

Have you not heard of me? My name is Fritz. Fritz Haarmann. Like you, I have been identified for eternity. They call me The Hanover Vampire, The Butcher of Hanover, oh, so many names! We are alike, you and I, but different. But you have a taste for girls while my predilection is for boys. Not for you but for me, there are many now here amongst the VICTIMS . . .

THE WIDE, CARNIVOROUS SKY

John Langan

*Our final story, "The Wide, Canivorous Sky," was re-published (as was our first)
in* The Year's Best Dark Fantasy and Horror: 2010. *I'm pleased to present this
novella again because—like Holly Black's tale—it is not only an outstanding
vampire story, it's simply an outstanding story. And, pragmatically, I suspect there
will be many readers to whom the story will be new. It's another answer to those
who think the vampire is no longer seen as a monster, that the icon appears so often
these days as the desirable anti-hero, or the outright hero, or a sexy butt-kicking
babe, or a kid's chum, or a pin-up for tweens to swoon over . . . and so on . . . that
there's nothing left to fear. It's also more proof that although the "dreaded fiend"
trope may suffer from the "same old story too often retold" syndrome, that there's
still such a thing as a highly effective, thoroughly relevant, completely twenty-first
century scary vampire story.*

John Langan is the author of novel House of Windows *(2009) and collection*
Mr. Gaunt and Other Uneasy Encounters *(2008).* Creatures, *an anthology he
is editing with Paul Tremblay will be published this fall. He lives in Upstate New
York with his wife, son, dog, and two cats.*

I

9:13 PM

FROM THE other side of the campfire, Lee said, "So it's a vampire."

"I did not say vampire," Davis said. "Did you hear me say vampire?"

It was exactly the kind of thing Lee would say, the gross generalization that
obscured more than it clarified. Not for the first time since they'd set out up
the mountain, Davis wondered at their decision to include Lee in their plans.

Lee held up his right hand, index finger extended. "It has the fangs."

"A mouthful of them."

Lee raised his middle finger. "It turns into a bat."

"No—its wings are like a bat's."

"Does it walk around with them?"

"They—it extrudes them from its arms and sides."

"'Extrudes'?" Lee said.

Han chimed in: "College."

Not this shit again, Davis thought. He rolled his eyes to the sky, dark blue studded by early stars. Although the sun's last light had drained from the air, his stomach clenched. He dropped his gaze to the fire.

The Lieutenant spoke. "He means the thing extends them out of its body."

"Oh," Lee said. "Sounds like it turns into a bat to me."

"Uh-huh," Han said.

"Whatever," Davis said. "It doesn't—"

Lee extended his ring finger and spoke over him. "It sleeps in a coffin."

"Not a coffin—"

"I know, a flying coffin."

"It isn't—it's in low-Earth orbit, like a satellite."

"What was it you said it looked like?" the Lieutenant asked. "A cocoon?"

"A chrysalis," Davis said.

"Same thing," the Lieutenant said.

"More or less," Davis said, unwilling to insist on the distinction because, even a year and three-quarters removed from Iraq, the Lieutenant was still the Lieutenant and you did not argue the small shit with him.

"Coffin, cocoon, chrysalis," Lee said, "it has to be in it before sunset or it's in trouble."

"Wait," Han said. "Sunset."

"Yes," Davis began.

"The principle's the same," the Lieutenant said. "There's a place it has to be and a time it has to be there by."

"Thank you, sir," Lee said. He raised his pinky. "And, it drinks blood."

"Yeah," Davis said, "it does."

"Lots," Han said.

"Yeah," the Lieutenant said.

For a moment, the only sounds were the fire popping and, somewhere out in the woods, an owl prolonging its question. Davis thought of Fallujah.

"Okay," Lee said, "how do we kill it?"

II

2004

There had been rumors, stories, legends of the things you might see in combat. Talk to any of the older guys, the ones who'd done tours in Vietnam, and you heard about a jungle in which you might meet the ghosts of Chinese invaders from five centuries before; or serve beside a grunt whose heart had been shot out a week earlier but who wouldn't die; or find yourself stalked by what you thought was a tiger but had a tail like a snake and a woman's voice. The guys who'd been part of the first war in Iraq—"The good one," a sailor Davis knew called it—told their own tales about the desert, about coming across a raised tomb, its black stone worn free of markings, and listening to someone laughing inside it all the time it took you to walk around it; about the dark shapes you might see stalking through a sandstorm, their arms and legs a child's stick-figures; about the sergeant who swore his reflection had been killed so that, when he looked in a mirror now, a corpse stared back at him. Even the soldiers who'd returned from Afghanistan talked about vast forms they'd seen hunched at the crests of mountains; the street in Kabul that usually ended in a blank wall, except when it didn't; the pale shapes you might glimpse darting into the mouth of the cave you were about to search. A lot of what you heard was bullshit, of course, the plot of a familiar movie or TV show adapted to new location and cast of characters, and a lot of it started off sounding as if it were headed somewhere interesting then ran out of gas halfway through. But there were some stories about which, even if he couldn't quite credit their having happened, some quality in the teller's voice, or phrasing, caused him to suspend judgment.

During the course of his Associate's Degree, Davis had taken a number of courses in psychology—preparation for a possible career as a psychologist— and in one of these, he had learned that, after several hours of uninterrupted combat (he couldn't remember how many, had never been any good with numbers), you would hallucinate. You couldn't help it; it was your brain's response to continuous unbearable stress. He supposed that at least some of the stories he'd listened to in barracks and bars might owe themselves to such cause, although he was unwilling to categorize them all as symptoms. This was not due to any overriding belief in either organized religion or disorganized superstition; it derived more from principle, specifically, a conclusion that an open mind was the best way to meet what continually impressed him as an enormous world packed full of many things.

By Fallujah, Davis had had no experiences of the strange, the bizarre, no stories to compare with those he'd accumulated over the course of basic and his deployment. He hadn't been thinking about that much as they took up their positions south of the city; all of his available attention had been directed at the coming engagement. Davis had walked patrol, had felt the crawl of the skin at the back of your neck as you made your way down streets crowded with men and women who'd been happy enough to see Saddam pulled down from his pedestal but had long since lost their patience with those who'd operated the crane. He'd ridden in convoys, his head light, his heart throbbing at the base of his throat as they passed potential danger after potential danger, a metal can on the right shoulder, what might be a shell on the left, and while they'd done their best to reinforce their Hummers with whatever junk they could scavenge, Davis was acutely aware that it wasn't enough, a consequence of galloping across the Kuwaiti desert with The Army You Had. Davis had stood checkpoint, his mouth dry as he sighted his M-16 on an approaching car that appeared full of women in black burkas who weren't responding to the signs to slow down, and he'd wondered if they were suicide bombers, or just afraid, and how much closer he could allow them before squeezing the trigger. However much danger he'd imagined himself in, inevitably, he'd arrived after the sniper had opened fire and fled, or passed the exact spot an IED would erupt two hours later, or been on the verge of aiming for the car's engine when it screeched to a halt. It wasn't that Davis hadn't discharged his weapon; he'd served support for several nighttime raids on suspected insurgent strongholds, and he'd sent his own bullets in pursuit of the tracers that scored the darkness. But support wasn't the same thing as kicking in doors, trying to kill the guy down the hall who was trying to kill you. It was not the same as being part of the Anvil.

That was how the Lieutenant had described their role. "Our friends in the United States Marine Corps are going to play the Hammer," he had said the day before. "They will sweep into Fallujah from east and west and they will drive what hostiles they do not kill outright south, where we will be waiting to act as the Anvil. The poet Goëthe said that you must be either hammer or anvil. We will be both, and we are going to crush the hostiles between us."

After the Lieutenant's presentation, Han had said, "Great—so the jarheads have all the fun," with what Davis judged a passable imitation of regret, a false sentiment fairly widely held. Davis had been sure, however, the certainty a ball of lead weighting his gut, that this time was going to be different. Part of it was that the Lieutenant had known one of the contractors who'd been killed, incinerated, and strung up at the Saddam Bridge last April. Davis wasn't clear exactly how the men had been acquainted, or how well, but the Lieutenant had made no secret of his displeasure at not being part of the first effort to (re)take the city in the weeks following the men's deaths. He had been—you couldn't say happy, exactly, at the failure of that campaign—but he was eager for what was shaping up to be a larger-scale operation. Though seven months gone, the deaths and dishonorings of his acquaintances had left the Lieutenant an appetite for this mission. Enough to cause him to disobey his orders and charge into Fallujah's southern section? Davis didn't think so, but there was a reason the man still held the rank of Lieutenant when his classmates and colleagues were well into their Captaincies.

The other reason for Davis's conviction that, this time, something was on its way to him was a simple matter of odds. It wasn't possible—it was not possible that you could rack up this much good luck and not have a shitload of the bad bearing down on you like a SCUD on an anthill. A former altar boy, he was surprised at the variety of prayers he remembered—not just the Our Father and the Hail Mary, but the Apostles' Creed, the Memorare, and the Hail, Holy Queen. As he disembarked the Bradley and ran for the shelter of a desert-colored house, the sky an enormous, pale blue dome above him, Davis mumbled his way through his prayers with a fervency that would have pleased his mother and father no end. But even as his lips shaped the words, he had the strong sense that this was out of God's hands, under the control of one of those medieval demi-goddesses, Dame Fortune or something.

Later, recovering first in Germany, then at Walter Reed, Davis had thought that walking patrol, riding convoy, standing checkpoint, he must have been saved from something truly awful each and every time, for the balance to be this steep.

III

10:01 PM

"I take it stakes are out," the Lieutenant said.

"Sir," Lee said, "I unloaded half a clip easy into that sonovabitch, and I was as close to him as I am to you."

"Closer," Han said.

"The point is, he took a half-step backwards—maybe—before he tore my weapon out of my hands and fractured my skull with it."

"That's what I'm saying," the Lieutenant said. "I figure it has to be . . . what? Did you get your hands on some kind of major ordnance, Davis? An rpg? A

Stinger? I'll love you like a son—hell, I'll adopt you as my own if you tell me you have a case of Stingers concealed under a bush somewhere. Those'll give the fucker a welcome he won't soon forget."

"Fucking-A," Han said.

"Nah," Lee said. "A crate of Willy Pete oughta just about do it. Serve his ass crispy-fried!"

Davis shook his head. "No Stingers and no white phosphorous. Fire isn't going to do us any good."

"How come?" Lee said.

"Yeah," Han said.

"If I'm right about this thing spending its nights in low-Earth orbit—in its 'coffin'—and then leaving that refuge to descend into the atmosphere so it can hunt, its skin has to be able to withstand considerable extremes of temperature."

"Like the Space Shuttle," the Lieutenant said. "Huh. For all intents and purposes, it's fireproof."

"Oh," Lee said.

"Given that it spends some of its time in the upper atmosphere, as well as actual outer space, I'm guessing substantial cold wouldn't have much effect, either."

"We can't shoot it, can't burn it, can't freeze it," Lee said. "Tell me why we're here, again?" He waved at the trees fringing the clearing. "Aside from the scenery, of course."

"Pipe down," the Lieutenant said.

"When we shot at it," Davis said, "I'm betting half our fire missed it." He held up his hand to the beginning of Lee's protest. "That's no reflection on anyone. The thing was fast, cheetah-taking-down-a-gazelle fast. Not to mention, it's so goddamned *thin* . . . Anyway, of the shots that connected with it, most of them were flesh wounds." He raised his hand to Lee, again. "Those who connected with it," a nod to Lee, "were so close their fire passed clean through it."

"Which is what I was saying," Lee said.

"There's a lot of crazy shit floating around space," Davis said, "little particles of sand, rock, ice, metal. Some of them get to moving pretty fast. If you're doing repairs to the Space Station and one of those things hits you, it could ruin your whole day. Anything that's going to survive up there is going to have to be able to deal with something that can punch a hole right through you."

"It's got a self-sealing mechanism," the Lieutenant said. "When Lee fired into it, its body treated the bullets as so many dust-particles."

"And closed right up," Davis said. "Like some kind of super-clotting-factor. Maybe that's what it uses the blood for."

"You're saying it's bulletproof, too?" Lee said.

"Shit," Han said.

"Not—more like, bullet-resistant."

"Think of it as a mutant healing ability," the Lieutenant said, "like Wolverine."

"Oh," Han said.

"Those claws it has," Lee said, "I guess Wolverine isn't too far off the mark."

"No," Han said. "Sabertooth."

"What?" Lee said. "The fuck're you going on about?"

"Sabertooth's claws." Han held up his right hand, fingers splayed. He curled his fingers into a fist. "Wolverine's claws."

"Man has a point," the Lieutenant said.

"Whatever," Lee said.

"Here's the thing," Davis said, "it's bullet-resistant, but it can still feel pain. Think about how it reacted when Lee shot it. It didn't tear his throat open: it took the instrument that had hurt it and used that to hurt Lee. You see what I'm saying?"

"Kind of," Lee said.

"Think about what drove it off," Davis said. "Remember?"

"Of course," the Lieutenant said. He nodded at Han. "It was Han sticking his bayonet in the thing's side."

For which it crushed his skull, Davis could not stop himself from thinking. He added his nod to the Lieutenant's. "Yes he did."

"How is that different from shooting it?" Lee said.

"Your bullets went in one side and out the other," Davis said. "Han's bayonet stuck there. The thing's healing ability could deal with an in-and-out wound no problem; something like this, though: I think it panicked."

"Panicked?" Lee said. "It didn't look like it was panicking to me."

"Then why did it take off right away?" Davis said.

"It was full; it heard more backup on the way; it had an appointment in fucking Samara. How the fuck should I know?"

"What's your theory?" the Lieutenant said.

"The type of injury Han gave it would be very bad if you're in a vacuum. Something opening you up like that and leaving you exposed . . . "

"You could vent some or even all of the blood you worked so hard to collect," the Lieutenant said. "You'd want to get out of a situation like that with all due haste."

"Even if your healing factor could seal the wound's perimeter," Davis said, "there's still this piece of steel in you that has to come out and, when it does, will reopen the injury."

"Costing you still more blood," the Lieutenant said.

"Most of the time," Davis said, "I mean, like, nine hundred and ninety-nine thousand, nine hundred and ninety-nine times out of a million, the thing would identify any such threats long before they came that close. You saw its ears, its eyes."

"Black on black," Lee said. "Or, no—black over black, like the corneas had some kind of heavy tint and what was underneath was all pupil."

"Han got lucky," Davis said. "The space we were in really wasn't that big. There was a lot of movement, a lot of noise—"

"Not to mention," Lee said, "all the shooting and screaming."

"The right set of circumstances," the Lieutenant said.

"Saved our asses," Lee said, reaching over to pound Han's shoulder. Han ducked to the side, grinning his hideous smile.

"If I can cut to the chase," the Lieutenant said. "You're saying we need to find a way to open up this fucker and keep him open so that we can wreak merry havoc on his insides."

Davis nodded. "To cut to the chase, yes, exactly."

"How do you propose we do this?"

"With these." Davis reached into the duffel bag to his left and withdrew what appeared to be a three foot piece of white wood, tapered to a point sharp enough to prick your eye looking at it. He passed the first one to the Lieutenant, brought out one for Lee and one for Han.

"A baseball bat?" Lee said, gripping near the point and swinging his like a Louisville Slugger. "We gonna club it to death?"

Neither Davis nor the Lieutenant replied; they were busy watching Han, who'd located the grips at the other end of his and was jabbing it, first underhand, then overhand.

"The people you meet working at Home Depot," Davis said. "They're made out of an industrial resin, inch-for-inch, stronger than steel. Each one has a high-explosive core."

"Whoa," Lee said, setting his on the ground with exaggerated care.

"The detonators are linked to this," Davis said, fishing a cell phone from his shirt pocket. "Turn it on." Pointing to the Lieutenant, Han, Lee, and himself, he counted, "One-two-three-four. Send. That's it."

"I was mistaken," the Lieutenant said. "It appears we will be using stakes, after all."

IV

2004

At Landstuhl, briefly, and then at Walter Reed, at length, an impressive array of doctors, nurses, chaplains, and other soldiers whose job it was encouraged Davis to discuss Fallujah. He was reasonably sure that, while under the influence of one of the meds that kept his body at a safe distance, he had let slip some detail, maybe more. How else to account for the change in his nurse's demeanor? Likely, she judged he was a psych case, a diagnosis he half-inclined to accept. Even when the Lieutenant forced his way into Davis's room, banging around in the wheelchair he claimed he could use well enough, goddamnit, Davis was reluctant to speak of anything except the conditions of the other survivors. Of whom he had been shocked—truly shocked, profoundly shocked, almost more so than by what had torn through them—to learn there were only two, Lee and Han, Manfred bled out on the way to be evac'd, everyone else long gone by the time the reinforcements had stormed into the courtyard. According to the Lieutenant, Han was clinging to life by a thread so fine you couldn't see it. He'd lost his helmet in the fracas, and the bones in his skull had been crushed like an eggshell. Davis, who had witnessed that crushing, nodded. Lee had suffered his own head trauma, although, compared to Han's, it wasn't anything a steel plate couldn't fix. The real problem with Lee was that, if he wasn't flooded with some heavy-duty happy pills, he went fetal, thumb in his mouth, the works.

"What about you?" the Lieutenant said, indicating the armature of casts, wires, weights, and counterweights that kept Davis suspended like some overly-ambitious kid's science project.

"Believe it or not, sir," Davis said, "it really is worse than it looks. My pack and my helmet absorbed most of the impact. Still left me with a broken back, scapula, and ribs—but my spinal cord's basically intact. Not that it doesn't hurt like a motherfucker, sir. Yourself?"

"The taxpayers of the United States of America have seen fit to gift me with a new right leg, since I so carelessly misplaced the original." He knocked on his pajama leg, which gave a hollow, plastic sound.

"Sir, I am so sorry—"

"Shut it," the Lieutenant said. "It's a paper cut." Using his left foot, he rolled himself back to the door, which he eased almost shut. Through the gap, he surveilled the hallway outside long enough for Davis to start counting, *One*

Mississippi, Two Mississippi, then wheeled himself to Davis's head. He leaned close and said, "Davis."

"Sir?"

"Let's leave out the rank thing for five minutes, okay? Can we do that?"

"Sir—yes, yes we can."

"Because ever since the docs have reduced my drugs to the point I could string one sentence after another, I've been having these memories—dreams—I don't know what the fuck to call them. Nightmares. And I can't decide if I'm losing it, or if this is why Lee needs a palm full of M&Ms to leave his bed. So I need you to talk to me straight, no bullshit, no telling the officer what you think he wants to hear. I would genuinely fucking appreciate it if we could do that."

Davis looked away when he saw the Lieutenant's eyes shimmering. Keeping his own focused on the ceiling, he said, "It came out of the sky. That's where it went, after Han stuck it, so I figure it must have dropped out of there, too. It explains why, one minute we're across the courtyard from a bunch of hostiles, the next, that thing's standing between us."

"Did you see it take off?"

"I did. After it had stepped on Han's head, it spread its arms—it kind of staggered back from Han, caught itself, then opened its arms and these huge wings snapped open. They were like a bat's, skin stretched over bone—they appeared so fast I'm not sure, but they shot out of its body. It tilted its head, jumped up, high, ten feet easy, flapped the wings, which raised it another ten feet, and turned—the way a swimmer turns in the water, you know? Another flap, two, and it was gone."

"Huh."

Davis glanced at the Lieutenant, whose face was smooth, his eyes gazing across some interior distance. He said, "Do you—"

"Back up," the Lieutenant said. "The ten of us are in the courtyard. How big's the place?"

"I'm not very good with—"

"At a guess."

"Twenty-five feet wide, maybe fifty long. With all of those jars in the way—what were they?"

"Planters."

"Three-foot-tall stone planters?"

"For trees. They were full of dirt. Haven't you ever seen those little decorative trees inside office buildings?"

"Oh. All right. What I was going to say was, With the row of planters at either end, the place might have been larger."

"Noted. How tall were the walls?"

"Taller than any of us—eight feet, easy. They were thick, too, a foot and a half, two feet." Davis said, "It really was a good spot to attack from. Open fire from the walls, then drop behind them when they can't maintain that position. The tall buildings are behind it, and we don't hold any of them, so they don't have to worry about anyone firing down on them. I'm guessing they figured we didn't know where we were well enough to call in any artillery on them. No, if we want them, we have to run a hundred feet of open space to a doorway that's an easy trap. They've got the planters for cover near and far, not to mention the doorway in the opposite wall as an exit."

"Agreed."

"To be honest, now that we're talking about it, I can't imagine how we made it into the place without losing anyone. By all rights, they should have tagged a couple of us crossing from our position to theirs. And that doorway: they should have massacred us."

"We were lucky. When we returned fire, they must have panicked. Could be they didn't see all of us behind the wall, thought they were ambushing three or four targets, instead of ten. Charging them may have given the impression there were even more of us. It took them until they were across the courtyard to get a grip and regroup."

"By which time we were at the doorway."

"So it was Lee all the way on the left—"

"With Han beside him."

"Right, and Bay and Remsnyder. Then you and Petit—"

"No—it was me and Lugo, then Petit, then you."

"Yes, yes. Manfred was to my right, and Weymouth was all the way on the other end."

"I'm not sure how many—"

"Six. There may have been a seventh in the opposite doorway, but he wasn't around very long. Either he went down, or he decided to season his valor with a little discretion."

"It was loud—everybody firing in a confined space. I had powder all over me from their shots hitting the wall behind us. I want to say we traded bullets for about five minutes, but it was what? Half that?"

"Less. A minute."

"And . . . "

"Our guest arrived."

"At first—at first it was like, I couldn't figure out what I was seeing. I'm trying to line up the guy who's directly across from me—all I need is for him to stick up his head again—and all of a sudden, there's a shadow in the way. That was my first thought: *It's a shadow.* Only, who's casting it? And why is it hanging in the air like that? And why is it fucking eight feet tall?"

"None of us understood what was in front of us. I thought it was a woman in a burka, someone I'd missed when we'd entered the courtyard. As you say, though, you don't meet a lot of eight-foot-tall women, in or out of Iraq."

"Next thing . . . no, that isn't what happened."

"What?"

"I was going to say the thing—the Shadow—was in among the hostiles, which is true, it went for them first, but before it did, there was a moment . . . "

"You saw something—something else."

"Yeah," Davis said. "This pain shot straight through my head. We're talking instant migraine, so intense I practically puked. That wasn't all: this chill . . . I was freezing, colder than I've ever been, like you read about in Polar expeditions. I couldn't—the courtyard—"

"What?"

"The courtyard wasn't—I was somewhere high, like, a hundred miles high, so far up I could see the curve of the Earth below me. Clouds, continents, the ocean: what you see in the pictures they take from orbit. Stars, space, all around me. Directly, overhead, a little farther away than you are from me, there was this thing. I don't know what the fuck it was. Big—long, maybe long as a house. It bulged in the middle, tapered at the ends. The surface was dark, shiny—does that make any sense? The thing was covered in—it looked like some kind of lacquer. Maybe it was made out of the lacquer.

"Anyway, one moment, my head's about to crack open, my teeth are chattering and my skin's blue, and I'm in outer space. The next, all of that's gone, I'm back in the courtyard, and the Shadow—the thing is ripping the hostiles to shreds."

"And then," the Lieutenant said, "it was our turn."

V

November 11, 2004, 11:13 AM

In the six hundred twenty-five days since that afternoon in the hospital, how many times had Davis recited the order of events in the courtyard, whether with the Lieutenant, or with Lee once his meds had been stabilized, or with Han once he'd regained the ability to speak (though not especially well)? At some point a couple of months on, he'd realized he'd been keeping count—*That's the thirty-eighth time; that's the forty-third*—and then, a couple of months after that, he'd realized that he'd lost track. The narrative of their encounter with what Davis continued to think of as the Shadow had become daily catechism, to be reviewed morning, noon, and night, and whenever else he happened to think of it.

None of them had even tried to run, which there were times Davis judged a sign of courage, and times he deemed an index of their collective shock at the speed and ferocity of the thing's assault on the insurgents. Heads, arms, legs were separated from bodies as if by a pair of razored blades, and wherever a wound opened red, there was the thing's splintered maw, drinking the blood like a kid stooping to a water fountain. The smells of blood, piss, and shit mixed with those of gunpowder and hot metal. While Davis knew they had been the next course on the Shadow's menu, he found it difficult not to wonder how the situation might have played out had Lee—followed immediately by Lugo and Weymouth—not opened up on the thing. Of course, the instant that narrow head with its spotlight eyes, its scarlet mouth, turned in their direction, everyone else's guns erupted, and the scene concluded the way it had to. But if Lee had been able to restrain himself . . .

Lugo was first to die. In a single leap, the Shadow closed the distance between them and drove one of its sharpened hands into his throat, venting his carotid over Davis, whom it caught with its other hand and flung into one of the side walls with such force his spine and ribs lit up like the Fourth of July. As he was dropping onto his back, turtling on his pack, the thing was raising its head from Lugo's neck, spearing Petit through his armor and hauling him towards it. Remsnyder ran at it from behind; the thing's hand lashed out and struck his head from his shoulders. It was done with Petit in time to catch Remsnyder's body on the fall and jam its mouth onto the bubbling neck. It had shoved Petit's body against the Lieutenant, whose feet tangled with Petit's and sent the pair of them down. This put him out of the way of Manfred and Weymouth, who screamed for everyone to get clear and fired full automatic. Impossible as it seemed, they missed, and for their troubles, the Shadow lopped Manfred's right arm off at the elbow and opened Weymouth like a Christmas present. From the ground, the Lieutenant shot at it; the thing sliced through his weapon and the leg underneath it. Now Bay, Han, and Lee tried full auto, which brought the thing to Bay, whose face it bit off. It swatted Han to the ground, but Lee somehow ducked the swipe it aimed at him and tagged it at close range. The Shadow threw Bay's body across the courtyard, yanked Lee's rifle from his hands, and swung it against his head like a ballplayer aiming for the stands. He crumpled, the thing reaching out for him, and Han leapt up, his bayonet ridiculously small in his hand. He drove it into the thing's side—what would be the floating ribs on a man—to the hilt. The Shadow, whose only sound thus far had been its feeding, opened its jaws and shrieked, a high scream more like the cry of a bat, or a hawk, than anything human. It caught Han with an elbow to the temple that tumbled him to the dirt, set its foot on his head, and pressed down. Han's scream competed with the sound of his skull cracking in multiple spots. Davis was certain the thing meant to grind Han's head to paste, but it staggered off him, one claw reaching for the weapon buried in its skin. Blood so dark it was purple was oozing around the hilt. The Shadow spread its arms, its wings cracked open, and it was gone, fled into the blue sky that Davis would spend the next quarter-hour staring at, as the Lieutenant called for help and tried to tourniquet first his leg then Manfred's arm.

Davis had stared at the sky before—who has not?—but, helpless on his back, his spine a length of molten steel, his ears full of Manfred whimpering that he was gonna die, oh sweet Jesus, he was gonna fucking die, the Lieutenant talking over him, insisting no he wasn't, he was gonna be fine, it was just a little paper cut, the washed blue bowl overhead seemed less sheltering canopy and more endless depth, a gullet over which he had the sickening sensation of dangling. As Manfred's cries diminished and the Lieutenant told—ordered him to stay with him, Davis flailed his arms at the ground to either side of him in an effort to grip onto an anchor, something that would keep him from hurtling into that blue abyss.

The weeks and months to come would bring the inevitable nightmares, the majority of them the Shadow's attack replayed at half-, full-, or double-speed, with a gruesome fate for himself edited in. Sometimes repeating the events on his own or with a combination of the others led to a less-disturbed sleep; sometimes it did not. There was one dream, though, that no amount of discussion could help, and that was the one in which Davis was plummeting through the sky, lost in an appetite that would never be sated.

VI

12:26 AM
Once he was done setting the next log on the fire, Davis leaned back and said, "I figure it's some kind of stun effect."

"How so?" Lee said.

"The thing lands in between two groups of heavily-armed men: it has to do something to even the odds. It hits us with a psychic blast, shorts out our brains so that we're easier prey."

"Didn't seem to do much to Lee," the Lieutenant said.

"No brain!" Han shouted.

"Ha-fucking-ha," Lee said.

"Maybe there were too many of us," Davis said. "Maybe it miscalculated. Maybe Lee's a mutant and this is his special gift. Had the thing zigged instead of zagged, gone for us instead of the insurgents, I don't think any of us would be sitting here, regardless of our super powers."

"Speak for yourself," Lee said.

"For a theory," the Lieutenant said, "it's not bad. But there's a sizable hole in it. You," he pointed at Davis, "saw the thing's coffin or whatever. Lee," a nod to him, "was privy to a bat's-eye view of the thing's approach to one of its hunts in—did we ever decide if it was Laos or Cambodia?"

"No sir," Lee said. "It looked an awful lot like some of the scenery from the first *Tomb Raider* movie, which I'm pretty sure was filmed in Cambodia, but I'm not positive."

"You didn't see Angelina Jolie running around?" Davis said.

"If only," Lee said.

"So with Lee, we're in Southeast Asia," the Lieutenant said, "with or without the lovely Ms. Jolie. From what Han's been able to tell me, he was standing on the moon or someplace very similar to it. I don't believe he could see the Earth from where he was, but I'm not enough of an astronomer to know what that means.

"As for myself, I had a confused glimpse of the thing tearing its way through the interior of an airplane—what I'm reasonably certain was a B-17, probably during the Second World War.

"You see what I mean? None of us witnessed the same scene—none of us witnessed the same time, which you would imagine we would have if we'd been subject to a deliberate attack. You would expect the thing to hit us all with the same image. It's more efficient."

"Maybe that isn't how this works," Davis said. "Suppose what it does is more like a cluster bomb, a host of memories it packs around a psychic charge? If each of us thinks he's someplace different from everybody else, doesn't that maximize confusion, create optimal conditions for an attack?"

The Lieutenant frowned. Lee said, "What's your theory, sir?"

"I don't have one," the Lieutenant said. "Regardless of its intent, the thing got in our heads."

"And stayed there," Lee said.

"Stuck," Han said, tapping his right temple.

"Yes," the Lieutenant said. "Whatever their precise function, our exposure to the thing's memories appears to have established a link between us and it."

Davis said, "Which is what's going to bring it right here."

VII

2004-2005

When Davis was on board the plane to Germany, he could permit himself to hope that he was, however temporarily, out of immediate danger of death—not from the injury to his back, which, though painful in the extreme, he had known from the start would not claim his life, but from the reappearance of the Shadow. Until their backup arrived in a hurry of bootsteps and rattle of armor, he had been waiting for the sky to vomit the figure it had swallowed minutes (moments?) prior, for his blood to leap into the thing's jagged mouth. The mature course of action had seemed to prepare for his imminent end, which he had attempted, only to find the effort beyond him. Whenever word of some acquaintance's failure to return from the latest patrol had prompted Davis to picture his final seconds, he had envisioned his face growing calm, even peaceful, his lips shaping the syllables of a heartfelt Act of Contrition. However, between the channel of fire that had replaced his spine and the vertiginous sensation that he might plunge into the sky—not to mention, the Lieutenant's continuing monologue to Manfred, the pungence of gunpowder mixed with the bloody reek of meat, the low moans coming from Han—Davis was unable to concentrate. Rather than any gesture of reconciliation towards the God with Whom he had not been concerned since his discovery of what lay beneath his prom date's panties junior year, Davis's attention had been snarled in the sound of the Shadow's claws puncturing Lugo's neck, the fountain of Weymouth's blood over its arm and chest, the wet slap of his entrails hitting the ground, the stretch of the thing's mouth as it released its scream. Despite his back, which had drawn his vocal chords taut, once the reinforcements had arrived and a red-faced medic peppered him with questions while performing a quick assessment of him, Davis had strained to warn them of their danger. But all his insistence that they had to watch the sky had brought him was a sedative that pulled him into a vague, gray place.

Nor had his time at the Battalion Aid Station, then some larger facility (Camp Victory? with whatever they gave him, most of the details a variety of medical staff poured into his ears sluiced right back out again) caused him to feel any more secure. As the gray place loosened its hold on him and he stared up at the canvas roof of the BAS, Davis had wanted to demand what the fuck everyone was thinking. Didn't they know the Shadow could slice through this material like it was cling film? Didn't they understand it was waiting to descend on them right now, this very fucking minute? It would rip them to shreds; it would drink their fucking *blood*. At the presence of a corpsman beside him, he'd realized he was shouting—or as close to shouting as his voice could manage—but he'd been unable to restrain himself, which had led to calming banalities and more vague grayness. He had returned to something like consciousness inside a larger space in the CSH, where the sight of the nearest wall trembling from the wind had drawn his stomach tight and sped a fresh round of protests from his mouth. When he struggled up out of the shot that outburst occasioned, Davis had found himself in a dim cavern whose curving sides rang with the din of enormous engines. His momentary impression that he was dead and this some unexpected, bare-bones afterlife was replaced by the recognition that he was on a transport out of Iraq—who knew to where? It didn't matter. A flood of tears had rolled from his eyes as the dread coiling his guts had, if not fled, at least calmed.

At Landstuhl, in a solidly-built hospital with drab but sturdy walls and a firm ceiling, Davis was calmer. (As long as he did not dwell on the way the Shadow's claws had split Petit's armor, sliced the Lieutenant's rifle in two.) That, and the surgeries required to relieve the pressure on his spine left him, to quote a song he'd never liked that much, comfortably numb.

Not until he was back in America, though, reclining in the late-Medieval luxury of Walter Reed, the width of an ocean and a continent separating him from Fallujah, did Davis feel anything like a sense of security. Even after his first round of conversations with the Lieutenant had offered him the dubious reassurance that, if he were delusional, he was in good company, a cold comfort made chillier still by Lee, his meds approaching the proper levels, corroborating their narrative, Davis found it less difficult than he would have anticipated to persuade himself that Remsnyder's head leaping from his body on a jet of blood was seven thousand miles away. And while his pulse still quickened whenever his vision strayed to the rectangle of sky framed by the room's lone window, he could almost pretend that this was a different sky. After all, hadn't that been the subtext of all the stories he'd heard from other vets about earlier wars? Weird shit happened, yes—sometimes, very bad weird shit happened—but it took place over there, In Country, in another place where things didn't work the same way they did in the good old U.S. of A. If you could keep that in mind, Davis judged, front-and-center in your consciousness, you might be able to live with the impossible.

Everything went—you couldn't call it swimmingly—it went, anyway, until Davis began his rehabilitation, which consisted of: a) learning how to walk again and b) strength training for his newly-(re)educated legs. Of course, he had been in pain after the initial injury—though shock and fear had kept the hurt from overwhelming him—and his nerves had flared throughout his hospital stay—especially following his surgery—though a pharmacopeia had damped those sensations down to smoldering. Rehab was different. Rehab was a long, low-ceilinged room that smelled of sweat and industrial antiseptic, one end of which grazed a small herd of the kind of exercise machines you saw faded celebrities hawking on late-night TV, the center of which held a trio of parallel bars set too low, and the near end of which was home to a series of overlapping blue mats whose extensive cracks suggested an aerial view of a river basin. Rehab was slow stretches on the mats, then gripping onto the parallel bars while you tried to coax your right leg into moving forward; once you could lurch along the bars and back, rehab was time on one of the exercise machines, flat on your back, your legs bent, your feet pressed against a pair of pedals connected to a series of weights you raised by extending your legs. Rehab was about confronting pain, inviting it in, asking it to sit down and have a beer so the two of you could talk for a while. Rehab was not leaning on the heavy-duty opiates and their synthetic friends; it was remaining content with the over-the-counter options and ice-packs. It was the promise of a walk outside—an enticement that made Davis's palms sweat and his mouth go dry.

When the surgeon had told Davis the operation had been a success, there appeared to be no permanent damage to his spinal cord, Davis had imagined himself, freed of his cast and its coterie of pulleys and counterweights, sitting up on his own and strolling out the front door. Actually, he'd been running in his fantasy. The reality, he quickly discovered, was that merely raising himself to a sitting position was an enterprise far more involved than he ever had appreciated, as was a range of action so automatic it existed below his being able to admit he'd never given it much thought. He supposed the therapists here were as good as you were going to find, but that didn't make the routines they subjected him to—he subjected himself to—any easier or less painful.

It was during one of these sessions, his back feeling as if it had been scraped raw and the exposed tissue generously salted, that Davis had his first inkling that Fallujah was not a self-contained narrative, a short, grisly tale; rather, it was the opening chapter of a novel, one of those eight-hundred-page, Stephen-King specials. Lucy, Davis's primary therapist, had him on what he had christened the Rack. His target was twenty leg presses; in a fit of bravado, he had promised her thirty. No doubt, Davis had known instances of greater pain, but those had been spikes on the graph. Though set at a lower level, this hurt was constant, and while Lucy had assured him that he would become used to it, so far, he hadn't. The pain glared like the sun flaring off a window; it flooded his mind white, made focusing on anything else impossible. That Lucy was encouraging him, he knew from the tone of her voice, but he could not distinguish individual words. Already, his vision was blurred from the sweat streaming out of him, so when the blur fractured, became a kaleidoscope-jumble of color and geometry, he thought little of it, and raised his fingers to clear his eyes.

According to Lucy, Davis removed his hand from his face, paused, then fell off the machine on his right side, trembling and jerking. For what she called his seizure's duration, which she clocked at three minutes fifteen seconds, Davis uttered no sound except for a gulping noise that made his therapist fear he was about to swallow his tongue.

To the Lieutenant, then to Lee and eventually Han, Davis would compare what he saw when the rehab room went far away to a wide-screen movie, one of those panoramic deals that was supposed to impart the sensation of flying over the Rockies, or holding on for dear life as a roller coaster whipped up and down its course. A surplus of detail crowded his vision. He was in the middle of a sandy street bordered by short buildings whose walls appeared to consist of sheets of long, dried grass framed with slender sticks. A dozen, two dozen women and children dressed in pastel robes and turbans ran frantically from one side of the street to the other as men wearing dark brown shirts and pants aimed Kalashnikovs at them. Some of the men were riding brown and white horses; some were stalking the street; some were emerging from alleys between the buildings, several of whose walls were releasing thick smoke. Davis estimated ten men. The sounds—it was as if the soundtrack to this film had been set to record the slightest vibration of air, which it played back at twice the normal level. Screams raked his eardrums. Sandals scraped the ground. Guns cracked; bullets thudded into skin. Horses whickered. Fire snapped. An immense thirst, worse than any he had known, possessed him. His throat was not dry; it was arid, as if it—as if he were composed of dust from which the last eyedropper of moisture had long been squeezed.

One of the men—not the nearest, who was walking the opposite direction from Davis's position, but the next closest, whose horse had shied from the flames sprouting from a grass wall and so turned its rider in Davis's direction—caught sight of Davis, his face contracting in confusion at what he saw. The man, who might have been in his early twenties, started to raise his rifle, and everything sped up, the movie fast-forwarded. There was—his vision wavered, and the man's gun dipped, his eyes widening. Davis was next to him—he had half-scaled the horse and speared the hollow of the man's throat with his right hand, whose fingers, he saw, were twice as long as they had been, tapered to a set of blades. He felt the man's tissue part, the ends of his fingers (talons?) scrape bone. Blood washed over his palm, his wrist, and the sensation jolted him. His talons flicked to the left, and the man's head tipped back like a tree falling away from its base. Blood misted the air, and before he realized what was happening, his mouth was clamped to the wound, full of hot, copper liquid. The taste was rain falling in the desert; in three mighty gulps, he had emptied the corpse and was springing over its fellows, into the midst of the brightly-robed women and children.

The immediate result of Davis's three-minute hallucination was the suspension of his physical therapy and an MRI of his brain. Asked by Lucy what he recalled of the experience, Davis had shaken his head and answered, "Nothing." It was the same response he gave to the new doctor who stopped into his room a week later and, without identifying himself as a psychiatrist, told Davis he was interested in the nightmares that had brought him screaming out of sleep six of the last seven nights. This was a rather substantial change in his nightly routine; taken together with his recent seizure, it seemed like cause for concern. Perhaps Davis could relate what he remembered of his nightmares?

How to tell this doctor that closing his eyes—an act he resisted for as long as could each night—brought him to that yellow-brown street; the lime, saffron, and orange cloth stretching as mothers hauled their children behind them; the dull muzzles of the Kalashnikovs coughing fire? How to describe the sensations that still lived in his skin, his muscles: the tearing of skin for his too-long fingers; the bounce of a heart in his hand the instant before he tore it from its setting; the eggshell crunch of bone between his jaws? Most of all, how to convey to this doctor, this shrink who was either an unskilled actor or not trying very hard, the concentrate of pleasure that was the rush of blood into his mouth, down his throat, the satisfaction of his terrific thirst so momentary it made the thirst that much worse? Although Davis had repeated his earlier disavowal and maintained it in the face of the doctor's extended—and, to be fair, sympathetic—questions until the man left, a week's worth of poor sleep made the wisdom of his decision appear less a foregone conclusion. What he

had seen—what he had been part of the other week was too similar to the
vision he'd had in the courtyard not to be related; the question was, how? Were
Davis to summarize his personal horror ride to the psychiatrist—he would
have to tell him about Fallujah first, of course—might the doctor have more
success at understanding the connections between his driver's-seat views of the
Shadow's activities?

Sure, Davis thought, *right after he's had you fitted for your straightjacket.*
The ironic thing was, how often had he argued the benefits of the Army's
psychiatric care with Lugo? It had been their running gag. Lugo would return
from reading his e-mail with news of some guy stateside who'd lost it, shot his
wife, himself, which would prompt Davis to say that it was a shame the guy
hadn't gotten help before it came to that. Help, Lugo would say, from who?
The Army? Man, you must be joking. The Army don't want nothing to do with
no grunt can't keep his shit together. No, no, Davis would say, sure, they still
had a ways to go, but the Army was changing. The kinds of combat-induced
pathologies it used to pretend didn't exist were much more likely to be treated
early and effectively. (If Lee and Han were present, and/or Remsnyder, they'd
ooh and aah over Davis's vocabulary.) Oh yeah, Lugo would reply, if they don't
discharge your ass right outta here, they'll stick you at some bullshit post where
you won't hurt anyone. No, no, Davis would say, that was a rumor. Oh yeah,
Lugo would say, like the rumor about the guys who went to the doctor for help
with their PTSD and were told they were suffering from a fucking pre-existing
condition, so it wasn't the Army's problem? No, no, Davis would say, that was
a few bad guys. Oh yeah, Lugo would say.

Before he and the Lieutenant—who had been abducted by a platoon of
siblings, their spouses, and their kids for ten days in Florida—discussed the
matter, Davis passed his nightly struggles to stay awake wondering if the
psychiatric ward was the worst place he might wind up. His only images of
such places came from films like *One Flew Over the Cuckoo's Nest, Awakenings,*
and *K-PAX,* but based on those examples, he could expect to spend his days
robed and slippered, possibly medicated, free to read what he wanted except
during individual and group therapy sessions. If it wasn't quite the career as a
psychologist he'd envisioned, he'd at least be in some kind of proximity to the
mental health field. Sure, it would be a scam, but didn't the taxpayers of the
U.S. of A. owe him recompense for shipping him to a place where the Shadow
could just drop in and shred his life? The windows would be barred or meshed,
the doors reinforced—you could almost fool yourself such a location would
be safe.

However, with his second episode, it became clear that safe was one of those words that had been bayoneted, its meaning spilled on the floor. Davis had been approved to resume therapy with Lucy, who had been honestly happy to see him again. It was late in the day; what with the complete breakdown in his sleeping patterns, he wasn't in optimal condition for another go-around on the Rack, but after so much time stuck in his head, terrified at what was in there with him, the prospect of a vigorous workout was something he was actually looking forward to. As before, gentle stretching preceded the main event, which Lucy told Davis he didn't have to do but for which he had cavalierly assured her he was, if not completely able, at least ready and willing. With the second push of his feet against the pedals, pain ignited up his back, and his lack of sleep did not aid in his tolerating it. Each subsequent retraction and extension of his legs ratcheted the hurt up one more degree, until he was lying on a bed of fire.

This time.

VIII

2:15 AM

"My vision didn't blur—it cracked, as if my knees levering up and down were an image on a TV screen and something smacked the glass. Everything spider-webbed and fell away. What replaced it was movement—I was moving up, my arms beating down; there was this feeling that they were bigger, much bigger, that when I swept them down, they were gathering the air and piling it beneath them. I looked below me, and there were bodies—parts of bodies, organs—all over the place. There was less blood than there should have been. Seeing them scattered across the ground—it was like having a bird's- eye view of some kind of bizarre design. Most of them were men, twenties and thirties; although there were two women and a couple-three kids. Almost everybody was wearing jeans and workboots, sweatshirts, baseball caps, except for a pair of guys dressed in khaki and I'm pretty sure cowboy hats."

"What the fuck?" Lee said.

"Cowboys," Han said.

"Texas Border Patrol," the Lieutenant said.

"So those other people were like, illegal immigrants?" Lee said.

The Lieutenant nodded.

Davis said, "I've never been to Texas, but the spot looked like what you see on TV. Sandy, full of rocks, some scrub brush and short trees. There was a muddy stream—you might call it a river, I guess, if that was what you were used to—in the near distance, and a group of hills further off. The sun was perched on top of the hills, setting, and that red ball made me beat me arms again and again, shrinking the scene below, raising me higher into the sky. There was—I felt full— more than full, gorged, but thirsty, still thirsty, that same, overpowering dryness I'd experienced the previous . . . time. The thirst was so strong, so compelling, I was a little surprised when I kept climbing. My flight was connected to the sun balanced on that hill, a kind of—not panic, exactly: it was more like urgency. I was moving, now. The air was thinning; my arms stretched even larger to scoop enough of it to keep me moving. The temperature had dropped—was dropping, plunging down. Something happened—my mouth was already closed, but it was as if it sealed somehow. Same thing with my nostrils; I mean, they closed themselves off. My eyes misted, then cleared. I pumped my arms harder than I had before. This time, I didn't lose speed; I kept moving forward.

"Ahead, I saw the thing I'd seen in the courtyard—a huge shape, big as a house. Pointed at the ends, fat in the middle. Dark—maybe dark purple, maybe not—and shiny. The moment it came into view, this surge of . . . I don't know what to call it. Honestly, I want to say it was a cross between the way you feel when you put your bag down on your old bed and, 'Mommy,' that little kid feeling, except that neither of those is completely right. My arms were condensing, growing substantial. I was heading towards the middle. As I drew closer, its surface rippled, like water moving out from where a stone strikes it. At the center of the ripple, a kind of pucker opened into the thing. That was my destination."

"And?" Lee said.

"Lucy emptied her Gatorade on me and brought me out of it."

"You have got to be fucking kidding me," Lee said.

"Afraid not," Davis said.

"How long was this one?" the Lieutenant asked.

"Almost five minutes."

"It took her that long to toss her Gatorade on you?" Lee said.

"There was some kind of commotion at the same time, a couple of guys got into a fight. She tried to find help; when she couldn't, she doused me."

Lee shook his head.

"And you have since confirmed the existence of this object," the Lieutenant said.

"Yes, sir," Davis said. "It took some doing. The thing's damned near impossible to see, and while no one would come out and say so to me, I'm pretty sure it doesn't show up on radar, either. The couple of pictures we got were more dumb luck than anything."

"'We'?" Lee said.

"I . . . "

The Lieutenant said, "I put Mr. Davis in touch with a friend of mine in Intelligence."

"Oh," Lee said. "Wait—shit: you mean the CIA's involved?"

"Relax," Davis said.

"Because I swear to God," Lee said, "those stupid motherfuckers would fuck up getting toast out of the toaster and blame us for their burned fingers."

"It's under control," the Lieutenant said. "This is our party. No one else has been invited."

"Doesn't mean they won't show up," Lee said. "Stupid assholes with their fucking sunglasses and their, 'We're so scary.' Oooh." He turned his head and spat.

Davis stole a look at the sky. Stars were winking out and in as something passed in front of them. His heart jumped, his hand was on his stake before he identified the shape as some kind of bird. The Lieutenant had noticed his movement; his hand over his stake, he said, "Everything all right, Davis?"

"Fine," Davis said. "Bird."

"What?" Lee said.

"Bird," Han said.

"Oh," Lee said. "So. I have a question."

"Go ahead," the Lieutenant said.

"The whole daylight thing," Lee said, "the having to be back in its coffin before sunset—what's up with that?"

"It does seem . . . atypical, doesn't it?" the Lieutenant said. "Vampires are traditionally creatures of the night."

"Actually, sir," Lee said, "that's not exactly true. The original Dracula—you know, in the book—he could go out in daylight; he just lost his powers."

"Lee," the Lieutenant said, "you are a font of information. Is this what our monster is trying to avoid?"

"I don't know," Lee said. "Could be."

"I don't think so," Davis said. "It's not as if daylight makes its teeth any sharper."

"Then what is it?" Lee said.

"Beats me," Davis said. "Don't we need daylight to make Vitamin D? Maybe it's the same, uses the sun to manufacture some kind of vital substance."

"Not bad," the Lieutenant said.

"For something you pulled out of your ass," Lee said.

"Hey—you asked," Davis said.

"Perhaps it's time for some review," the Lieutenant said. "Can we agree on that? Good.

"We have this thing—this vampire," holding up a hand to Davis, "that spends its nights in an orbiting coffin. At dawn or thereabouts, it departs said refuge in search of blood, which it apparently obtains from a single source."

"Us," Han said.

"Us," the Lieutenant said. "It glides down into the atmosphere on the lookout for likely victims—of likely groups of victims, since it prefers to feed on large numbers of people at the same time. Possibly, it burns through its food quickly."

"It's always thirsty," Davis said. "No matter how much it drinks, it's never enough."

"Yeah," Lee said, "I felt it, too."

"So did we all," the Lieutenant said. "It looks to satisfy its thirst at locations where its actions will draw little to no attention. These include remote areas such as the U.S.-Mexico border, the Sahara and Gobi, and the Andes. It also likes conflict zones, whether Iraq, Darfur, or the Congo. How it locates these sites is unknown. We estimate that it visits between four and seven of them per day. That we have been able to determine, there does not appear to be an underlying pattern to its selection of either target areas or individuals within those areas. The vampire's exact level of intelligence is another unknown. It possesses considerable abilities as a predator, not least of them its speed, reaction time, and strength. Nor should we forget its teeth and," a rap of the artificial leg, "claws."

"Not to mention that mind thing," Lee said.

"Yes," the Lieutenant said. "Whether by accident or design, the vampire's appearance is accompanied by a telepathic jolt that momentarily disorients its intended victims, rendering them easier prey. For those who survive the meeting," a nod at them, "a link remains that may be activated by persistent, pronounced stress, whether physical or mental. The result of this activation is a period of clairvoyance, during which the lucky individual rides along for the vampire's current activities. Whether the vampire usually has equal access to our perceptions during this time is unclear; our combined accounts suggest it does not.

"However, there are exceptions."

IX

2005

"I know how we can kill it," Davis said. "At least, I think I do—how we can get it to come to a place where we can kill it."

Lee put his Big Mac on his tray and looked out the restaurant window. The Lieutenant paused in the act of dipping his fries into a tub of barbecue sauce. Han continued chewing his McNugget but nodded twice.

"The other day—two days ago, Wednesday—I got to it."

"What do you mean?" the Lieutenant said.

"It was coming in for a landing, and I made it mess up."

"Bullshit," Lee said. He did not shift his gaze from the window. His face was flushed.

"How?" the Lieutenant said.

"I was having a bad day, worse than the usual bad day. Things at Home Depot—the manager's okay, but the assistant manager's a raging asshole. Anyway, I decided a workout might help. I'd bought these Kung Fu DVDs—"

"Kung Fu," the Lieutenant said.

Davis shrugged. "Seemed more interesting than running a treadmill."

Through a mouthful of McNugget, Han said, "Bruce Lee."

"Yeah," Davis said. "I put the first disc on. To start with, everything's fine. I'm taking it easy, staying well below the danger level. My back's starting to ache, the way it always does, but that's okay, I can live with it. As long as I keep the situation in low gear, I can continue with my tiger style."

"Did it help?" the Lieutenant asked.

"My worse-than-bad day? Not really. But it was something to do, you know?"

The Lieutenant nodded. Lee stared at the traffic edging up the road in front of the McDonald's. Han bit another McNugget.

"This time, there was no warning. My back's feeling like someone's stitching it with a hot needle, then I'm dropping out of heavy cloud cover. Below, a squat hill pushes up from dense jungle. A group of men are sitting around the top of the hill. They're wearing fatigues, carrying Kalashnikovs. I think I'm somewhere in South America: maybe these guys are FARQ; maybe they're some of Chavez's boys.

"I've been through the drill enough to know what's on the way: a ringside seat for blood and carnage. It's reached the point, when one of these incidents overtakes me, I don't freak out. The emotion that grips me is dread, sickness at what's coming. But this happens so fast, there isn't time for any of that. Instead, anger—the anger that usually shows up a couple of hours later, when I'm still trying to get the taste of blood out of my mouth, still trying to convince myself that I'm not the one who's so thirsty—for once, that anger arrives on time and loaded for bear. It's like the fire that's crackling on my back finds its way into my veins and ignites me.

"What's funny is, the anger makes my connection to the thing even more intense. The wind is pressing my face, rushing over my arms—my wings— I'm aware of currents in the air, places where it's thicker, thinner, and I twitch my nerves to adjust for it. There's one guy standing off from the rest, closer to the treeline, though not so much I—the thing won't be able to take him. I can practically see the route to him, a steep dive with a sharp turn at the very end that'll let the thing knife through him. He's sporting a bush hat, which he's pushed back on his head. His shirt's open, T-shirt dark with sweat. He's holding his weapon self-consciously, trying to looking like a badass, and it's this, more than the smoothness of his skin, the couple of whiskers on his chin, that makes it clear he isn't even eighteen. It—I—we jackknife into the dive, and thirsty, Christ, thirsty isn't the word: this is dryness that reaches right through to your fucking soul. I've never understood what makes the thing tick—what *drives* it—so well.

"At the same time, the anger's still there. The closer we draw to the kid, the hotter it burns. We've reached the bottom of the dive and pulled up; we're streaking over the underbrush. The kid's completely oblivious to the fact that his bloody dismemberment is fifty feet away and closing fast. I'm so close to the thing, I can feel the way its fangs push against one another as they jut from its mouth. We're on top of the kid; the thing's preparing to retract its wings, slice him open, and drive its face into him. The kid is dead; he's dead and he just doesn't know it, yet.

"Only, it's like—I'm like—I don't even think, *No*, or, *Stop*, or *Pull up*. It's more . . . I push; I shove against the thing I'm inside and its arms move. Its fucking arms jerk up as if someone's passed a current through them. Someone has—I have. I'm the current. The motion throws off the thing's strike, sends it wide. It flails at the kid as it flies past him, but he's out of reach. I can sense—the thing's completely confused. There's a clump of bushes straight ahead—*wham*."

The Lieutenant had adopted his best you'd-better-not-be-bullshitting-me stare. He said, "I take it that severed the connection."

Davis shook his head. "No, sir. You would expect that—It's what would have happened in the past—but this time, it was like, I was so close to the thing, it was going to take something more to shake me loose."

"And?" the Lieutenant said.

Lee shoved his tray back, toppling his super-sized Dr Pepper, whose lid popped off, splashing a wave of soda and ice cubes across the table. While Davis and the Lieutenant grabbed napkins, Lee stood and said, "What the fuck, Davis?"

"What?" Davis said.

"I said: What the fuck, asshole," Lee said. Several diners at nearby tables turned their heads toward him.

"Inside voices," the Lieutenant said. "Sit down."

"I don't think so," Lee said. "I don't have to listen to this shit." With that, he stalked away from the table, through the men and women swiftly returning their attentions to the meals in front of them, and out the side door.

"What the fuck?" Davis said, dropping his wad of soggy napkins on Lee's tray.

"That seems to be the question of the moment," the Lieutenant said.

"Sir—"

"Our friend and fellow is not having the best of months," the Lieutenant said. "In fact, he is not having the best of years. You remember the snafus with his disability checks."

"I thought that was taken care of."

"It was, but it was accompanied by the departure of Lee's wife and their two-year-old. Compared to what he was, Lee is vastly improved. In terms of the nuances of his emotional health, however, he has miles to go. The shit with his disability did not help; nor did spending all day home with a toddler who didn't recognize his father."

"He didn't—"

"No, but I gather it was a close thing. A generous percentage of the wedding flatware paid the price for Lee's inability to manage himself. In short order, the situation became too much for Shari, who called her father to come for her and Douglas."

"Bitch," Han said.

"Since then," the Lieutenant said, "Lee's situation has not improved. A visit to the local bar for a night of drinking alone ended with him in the drunk tank. Shari's been talking separation, possibly divorce, and while Lee tends to be a bit paranoid about the matter, there may be someone else involved, an old boyfriend. Those members of Lee's family who've visited him, called him, he has rebuffed in a fairly direct way. To top it all off, he's been subject to the same, intermittent feast of blood as the rest of us."

"Oh," Davis said. "I had no—Lee doesn't talk to me—"

"Never mind. Finish your story."

"It's not a story."

"Sorry. Poor choice of words. Go on, please."

"All right," Davis said. "Okay. You have to understand, I was as surprised by all of this as—well, as anyone. I couldn't believe I'd affected the thing. If it hadn't been so real, so like all the other times, I would have thought I was hallucinating, on some kind of wish-fulfillment trip. As it was, there I was as the thing picked itself up from the jungle floor. The anger—my anger—I guess it was still there, but . . . on hold.

"The second the thing was upright, someone shouted and the air was hot with bullets. Most of them shredded leaves, chipped bark, but a few of them tagged the thing's arm, its shoulder. Something was wrong—mixing in with its confusion, there was another emotion, something down the block from fear. I wasn't doing anything: I was still stunned by what I'd made happen. The thing jumped, and someone—maybe a couple of guys—tracked it, headed it off, hit it in I can't tell you how many places—it felt as the thing had been punched a dozen times at once. It spun off course, slapped a tree, and went down, snapping branches on its way.

"Now it was pissed. Even before it picked itself up, the place it landed was being subject to intensive defoliation. A shot tore its ear. Its anger—if what I felt was fire, this was lava, thicker, slower-moving, hotter. It retreated, scuttled half a dozen trees deeper into the jungle. Whoever those guys were, they were professionals. They advanced on the spot where the thing fell and, when they saw it wasn't there anymore, they didn't rush in after it. Instead, they fell back to a defensive posture while one of them put in a call—for air support, I'm guessing.

"The thing was angry and hurt and the thirst—" Davis shook his head. He sipped his Coke. "What came next—I'm not sure I can describe it. There was this surge in my head—not the thing's head, this was my brain I'm talking about—and the thing was looking out of my eyes."

"It turned the tables on you," the Lieutenant said.

"Not exactly," Davis said. "I continued watching the soldiers maybe seventy-five feet in front of me, but I was . . . aware of the thing staring at the DVD still playing on the TV. It was as if the scene was on a screen just out of view." He shook his head. "I'm not describing it right.

"Anyway, that was when the connection broke."

Davis watched the Lieutenant evade an immediate response by taking a generous bite of his Double Quarter Pounder with Cheese and chewing it with great care. Han swallowed and said, "Soldiers."

"What?"

"Soldiers," Han said.

Through his mouthful of burger, the Lieutenant said, "He wants to know what happened to the soldiers. Right?"

Han nodded.

"Beats the shit out of me," Davis said. "Maybe their air support showed up and bombed the fucker to hell. Maybe they evac'd out of there."

"But that isn't what you think," the Lieutenant said. "You think it got them."

"Yes sir," Davis said. "The minute it was free of me, I think it had those poor bastards for lunch."

"It seems a bit much to hope otherwise, doesn't it?"

"Yes sir, it does."

When the Lieutenant opted for another bite of his sandwich, Davis said, "Well?"

The Lieutenant answered by lifting his eyebrows. Han switched from McNuggets to fries.

"As I see it," Davis began. He stopped, paused, started again. "We know that the thing fucked with us in Fallujah, linked up with us. So far, this situation has only worked to our disadvantage: whenever one of us is in sufficient discomfort, the connection activates and dumps us behind the thing's eyes for somewhere in the vicinity of three to five minutes. With all due respect to Lee, this has not been beneficial to anyone's mental health.

"But what if—suppose we could duplicate what happened to me? Not just once, but over and over—even if only for ten or fifteen seconds at a time—interfere with whatever it's doing, seriously fuck with it."

"Then what?" the Lieutenant said. "We're a thorn in its side. So?"

"Sir," Davis said, "those soldiers hit it. Okay, yes, their fire wasn't any more effective than ours was, but I'm willing to bet their percentages were significantly higher. That's what me being on board in an—enhanced way did to the thing. We wouldn't be a thorn—we'd be the goddamned bayonet Han jammed in its ribs.

"Not that we should wait for someone else to take it down. I'm proposing something more ambitious."

"All right."

"If we can disrupt the thing's routine—especially if we cut into its feeding—it won't take very long for it to want to find us. Assuming the second part of my experience—the thing has a look through our eyes—if that happens again, we can arrange it so that we let it know where we're going to be. We pick a location with a clearing where the thing can land and surrounding tree cover where we can wait to ambush it. Before any of us goes to ruin the thing's day, he puts pictures, maps, satellite photos of the spot on display, so that when the thing's staring out of his eyes, that's what it sees. If the same images keep showing up in front of it, it should get the point."

The Lieutenant took the rest of his meal to reply. Han offered no comment. When the Lieutenant had settled into his chair after tilting his tray into the garbage and stacking it on top of the can, he said, "I don't know, Davis. There are an awful lot more ifs than I prefer to hear in a plan. *If* we can access the thing the same way you did; *if* that wasn't a fluke. *If* the thing does the reverse-vision stuff; *if* it understands what we're showing it. *If* we can find a way to kill it." He shook his head.

"Granted," Davis said, "there's a lot we'd have to figure out, not least how to put it down and keep it down. I have some ideas about that, but nothing developed. It would be nice if we could control our connection to the thing, too. I'm wondering if what activates the jump is some chemical our bodies are releasing when they're under stress—maybe adrenaline. If we had access to a supply of adrenaline, we could experiment with doses—"

"You're really serious about this."

"What's the alternative?" Davis said. "Lee isn't the only one whose life is fucked, is he? How many more operations are you scheduled for, Han? Four? Five?"

"Four," Han said.

"And how're things in the meantime?"

Han did not answer.

"What about you, sir?" Davis said. "Oh sure, your wife and kids stuck around, but how do they act after you've had one of your fits, or spells, or whatever the fuck you call them? Do they rush right up to give Daddy a hug, or do they keep away from you, in case you might do something even worse? Weren't you coaching your son's soccer team? How's that working out for you? I bet it's a lot of fun every time the ref makes a lousy call."

"Enough, Davis."

"It isn't as if I'm in any better shape. I have to make sure I remember to swallow a couple of tranquilizers before I go to work so I don't collapse in the middle of trying to help some customer load his fertilizer into his car. Okay, Rochelle had dumped me while I was away, but let me tell you how the dating scene is for a vet who's prone to seizures should things get a little too exciting. As for returning to college, earning my BS—maybe if I could have stopped worrying about how goddamned exposed I was walking from building to building, I could've focused on some of what the professors were saying and not fucking had to withdraw.

"This isn't the magic bullet," Davis said. "It isn't going to make all the bad things go away. It's . . . it is what it fucking is."

"All right," the Lieutenant said. "I'm listening. Han—you listening?"

"Listening," Han said.

X

4:11 AM

"So where do you think it came from?" Lee said.

"What do you mean?" Davis said. "We know where it comes from."

"No," Lee said, "I mean, before."

"Its secret origin," the Lieutenant said.

"Yeah," Lee said.

"How should I know?" Davis said.

"You're the man with the plan," Lee said. "Mr. Idea."

The Lieutenant said, "I take it you have a theory, Lee."

Lee glanced at the heap of coals that had been the fire. "Nah, not really."

"That sounds like a yes to me," the Lieutenant said.

"Yeah," Han said.

"Come on," Davis said. "What do you think?"

"Well," Lee said, then broke off, laughing. "No, no."

"Talk!" Davis said.

"You tell us your theory," the Lieutenant said, "I'll tell you mine."

"Okay, okay," Lee said, laughing. "All right. The way I see it, this vampire is like, the advance for an invasion. It flies around in its pod, looking for suitable planets, and when it finds one, it parks itself above the surface, calls its buddies, and waits for them to arrive."

"Not bad," the Lieutenant said.

"Hang on," Davis said. "What does it do for blood while it's Boldly Going Where No Vampire Has Gone Before?"

"I don't know," Lee said. "Maybe it has some stored in its coffin."

"That's an awful lot of blood," Davis said.

"Even in MRE form," the Lieutenant said.

"Maybe it has something in the coffin that makes blood for it."

"Then why would it leave to go hunting?" Davis said.

"It's in suspended animation," Lee said. "That's it. It doesn't wake up till it's arrived at a habitable planet."

"How does it know it's located one?" Davis said.

"Obviously," the Lieutenant said, "the coffin's equipped with some sophisticated tech."

"Thank you, sir," Lee said.

"Not at all," the Lieutenant said.

"I don't know," Davis said.

"What do you know?" Lee said.

"I told you—"

"Be real," Lee said. "You're telling me you haven't given five minutes to wondering how the vampire got to where it is?"

"I—"

"Yeah," Han said.

"I'm more concerned with the thing's future than I am with its past," Davis said, "but yes, I have wondered about where it came from. There's a lot of science I don't know, but I'm not sure about an alien being able to survive on human blood—about an alien needing human blood. It could be, I guess; it just seems a bit of a stretch."

"You're saying it came from here," the Lieutenant said.

"That's bullshit," Lee said.

"Why shouldn't it?" Davis said. "There's been life on Earth for something like three point seven *billion* years. Are you telling me this couldn't have developed?"

"Your logic's shaky," the Lieutenant said. "Just because something hasn't been disproved doesn't mean it's true."

"All I'm saying is, we don't know everything that's ever been alive on the planet."

"Point taken," the Lieutenant said, "but this thing lives above—well above the surface of the planet. How do you explain that?"

"Some kind of escape pod," Davis said. "I mean, you guys know about the asteroid, right? The one that's supposed to have wiped out the dinosaurs? Suppose this guy and his friends—suppose their city was directly in this asteroid's path? Maybe our thing was the only one who made it to the rockets on time? Or maybe it built this itself."

"Like Superman," Lee said, "only, he's a vampire, and he doesn't leave Krypton, he just floats around it so he can snack on the other survivors."

"Sun," Han said.

"What?" Lee said.

"Yellow sun," Han said.

Davis said, "He means Superman needs a yellow sun for his powers. Krypton had a red sun, so he wouldn't have been able to do much snacking."

"Yeah, well, we have a yellow sun," Lee said, "so what's the problem?"

"Never mind."

"Or maybe you've figured out the real reason the dinosaurs went extinct," Lee said. "Vampires got them all."

"That's clever," Davis said. "You're very clever, Lee."

"What about you, sir?" Lee said.

"Me?" the Lieutenant said. "I'm afraid the scenario I've invented is much more lurid than either of yours. I incline to the view that the vampire is here as a punishment."

"For what?" Davis said.

"I haven't the faintest clue," the Lieutenant said. "What kind of crime does a monster commit? Maybe it stole someone else's victims. Maybe it killed another vampire. Whatever it did, it was placed in that coffin and sent out into space. Whether its fellows intended us as its final destination, or planned for it to drift endlessly, I can't say. But I wonder if its blood-drinking—that craving—might not be part of its punishment."

"How?" Lee said.

"Say the vampire's used to feeding on a substance like blood, only better, more nutritious, more satisfying. Part of the reason for sending it here is that all that will be available to it is this poor substitute that leaves it perpetually thirsty. Not only does it have to cross significant distances, expose itself to potential harm to feed, the best it can do will never be good enough."

"That," Lee said, "is fucked up."

"There's a reason they made me an officer," the Lieutenant said. He turned to Han. "What about you, Han? Any thoughts concerning the nature of our imminent guest?"

"Devil," Han said.

"Ah," the Lieutenant said.

"Which?" Lee asked. "A devil, or the Devil?"

Han shrugged.

XI

2005-2006

To start with, the Lieutenant called once a week, on a Saturday night. Davis could not help reflecting on what this said about the state of the man's life, his marriage, that he spent the peak hours of his weekend in a long-distance conversation with a former subordinate—as well as the commentary their calls offered on his own state of affairs, that not only was he always in his apartment for the Lieutenant's call, but that starting late Thursday, up to a day earlier if his week was especially shitty, he looked forward to it.

There was a rhythm, almost a ritual, to each call. The Lieutenant asked Davis how he'd been; he answered, "Fine, sir," and offered a précis of the last seven days at Home Depot, which tended to consist of a summary of his assistant manager's most egregious offenses. If he'd steered clear of Adams, he might list the titles of whatever movies he'd rented, along with one- or two-sentence reviews of each. Occasionally, he would narrate his latest failed date, recasting stilted frustration as comic misadventure. At the conclusion of his recitation, Davis would swat the Lieutenant's question back to him. The Lieutenant would answer, "Can't complain," and follow with a distillation of his week that focused on his dissatisfaction with his position at Stillwater, a defense contractor who had promised him a career as exciting as the one he'd left but delivered little more than lunches, dinners, and cocktail parties at which the Lieutenant was trotted out, he said, so everyone could admire his goddamned plastic leg and congratulate his employers on hiring him. At least the money was decent, and Barbara enjoyed the opportunity to dress up and go out to nicer places than he'd ever been able to afford. The Lieutenant did not speak about his children; although if asked, he would say that they were hanging in there. From time to time, he shared news of Lee, whom he called on Sunday and whose situation never seemed to improve that much, and Han, whose sister he e-mailed every Monday and who reported that her brother was making progress with his injuries; in fact, Han was starting to e-mail the Lieutenant, himself.

This portion of their conversation, which Davis thought of as the Prelude, over, the real reason for the call—what Davis thought of as the SITREP—ensued. The Lieutenant, whose sentences hitherto had been loose, lazy, tightened his syntax as he quizzed Davis about the status of the Plan. In response, Davis kept his replies short, to the point. Have we settled on a location? The Lieutenant would ask. Yes sir, Davis would say, Thompson's Grove. That was the spot in the Catskills, the Lieutenant would say, south slope of Winger Mountain, about a half mile east of the principle trail to the summit. Exactly, sir, Davis would say. Research indicates the Mountain itself is among the least visited in the Catskill Preserve, and Thompson's Grove about the most obscure spot on it. The location is sufficiently removed from civilian populations not to place them in immediate jeopardy, yet still readily accessible by us. Good, good, the Lieutenant would say. I'll notify Lee and Han.

The SITREP finished, Davis and the Lieutenant would move to Coming Attractions: review their priorities for the week ahead, wish one another well, and hang up. As the months slid by and the Plan's more elaborate elements came into play—especially once Davis commenced his experiments dosing himself with adrenaline—the Lieutenant began adding the odd Wednesday night to his call schedule. After Davis had determined the proper amount for inducing a look through the Shadow's eyes—and after he'd succeeded in affecting the thing a second time, causing it to release its hold on a man Davis was reasonably sure was a Somali pirate—the Wednesday exchanges became part of their routine. Certainly, they helped Davis and the Lieutenant to coordinate their experiences interrupting the Shadow's routine with the reports coming in from Lee and Han, which arrived with increasing frequency once Lee and Han had found their adrenaline doses and were mastering the trick of interfering with the Shadow. However, in the moment immediately preceding their setting their respective phones down, Davis would be struck by the impression that the Lieutenant and he were on the verge of saying something else, something more—he couldn't say what, exactly, only that it would be significant in a way—in a different way from their usual conversation. It was how he'd felt in the days leading up to Fallujah, as if, with such momentous events roiling on the horizon, he should be speaking about important matters, meaningful things.

Twice, they came close to such an exchange. The first time followed a discussion of the armaments the Lieutenant had purchased at a recent gun show across the border in Pennsylvania. "God love the NRA," he'd said and listed the four Glock 21s's, sixteen extra clips, ten boxes of .45 ammunition, four AR-15's, sixteen extra high-capacity magazines for them, thirty boxes of 223 Remington ammo, and four USGI M7 bayonets.

"Jesus, sir," Davis had said when the Lieutenant was done. "That's a shitload of ordnance."

"I stopped at the grenade launcher," the Lieutenant said. "It seemed excessive."

"You do remember how much effect our guns had on the thing the last time . . . "

"Think of this as a supplement to the Plan. Even with one of us on board, once the thing shows up, it's going to be a threat. We know it's easier to hit when someone's messing with its controls, so let's exploit that. The more we can tag it, the more we can slow it down, improve our chances of using your secret weapon on it."

"Fair enough."

"Good. I'm glad you agree."

Davis was opening his mouth to suggest possible positions the four of them might take around the clearing when the Lieutenant said, "Davis."

"Sir?"

"Would you say you've had a good life? Scratch that—would you say you've had a satisfactory life?"

"I . . . I don't know. I guess so."

"I've been thinking about my father these past few days. It's the anniversary of his death, twenty-one years ago this Monday. He came here from Mexico City when he was sixteen, worked as a fruit picker for a couple of years, then fell into a job at a diner. He started busing tables, talked his way into the kitchen, and became the principle cook for the night shift. That was how he met my mother: she was a waitress there. She was from Mexico, too, although the country—apparently, she thought my old man was some kind of city-slicker, not to be trusted by a virtuous girl. I guess she was right, because my older brother was born seven months after their wedding. But I came along two years after that, so I don't think that was the only reason for them tying the knot.

"He died when I was five, my father. An embolism burst in his brain. He was at work, just getting into the swing of things. The coroner said he was dead before he reached the floor. He was twenty-seven. What I wonder is, when he looked at his life, at everything he'd done, was it what he wanted? Even if it was different, was it enough?

"How many people do you suppose exit this world satisfied with what they've managed to accomplish in it, Davis? How many of our fellows slipped their mortal coils content with what their eighteen or twenty-one or twenty-seven years had meant?"

"There was the Mission," Davis said. "Ask them in public, and they'd laugh, offer some smartass remark, but talk to them one-on-one, and they'd tell you they believed in what we were doing, even if things could get pretty fucked-up.

I'm not sure if that would've been enough for Lugo, or Manfred—for anyone—but it would've counted for something."

"True," the Lieutenant said. "The question is, will something do?"

"I guess it has to."

Their second such conversation came two weeks before the weekend the four of them were scheduled to travel to Upstate New York. They were reviewing the final draft of the Plan, which Davis thought must be something like the Plan version 22.0—although little had changed in the way of the principles since they'd finalized them a month earlier. Ten minutes before dawn, they would take up their positions in the trees around the clearing. If north was twelve o'clock, then Lee and Han would be at twelve—necessary because Han would be injecting himself at t-minus one minute and would require protection—the Lieutenant would take two, and Davis three. The woods were reasonably thick: if they positioned themselves about ten feet in, then the Shadow would be unable to come in on top of them. If it wanted them, it would have to land, shift to foot, and that would be the cue for the three of them aiming their AR-15's to fire. In the meantime, Han would have snuck on board the Shadow and be preparing to jam it. As soon as he saw the opportunity, he would do his utmost to take the thing's legs out from under it, a maneuver he had been rehearsing for several weeks and become reasonably proficient at. The average time Han guesstimated he'd been able to knock the Shadow's legs out was fifteen seconds, though he had reached the vicinity of thirty once. This would be their window: the instant the thing's legs crumpled, two of them had to be up and on it, probably Davis and Lee since the Lieutenant wasn't placing any bets on his sprinter's start. One of them would draw the Shadow's notice, the other hit it with the secret weapon. If for any reason the first attacker failed, the second could engage if he saw the opportunity; otherwise, he would have to return to the woods, because Han's hold on the thing would be wearing off. Once the Lieutenant observed this, he would inject himself and they would begin round two. Round two was the same as round one except for the presumed lack of one man, just as round three counted on two of them being gone. Round four, the Lieutenant said, was him eating a bullet. By that point, there might not be anything he could do to stop the ugly son of a bitch drinking his blood, but that didn't mean he had to stay around for the event.

Davis knew they would recite the Plan again on Saturday, and then next Wednesday, and then the Saturday after that, and then the Wednesday two weeks from now. At the Quality Inn in Kingston, they would recite the Plan, and again as they drove into the Catskills, and yet again as they hiked up Winger Mountain. "Preparation" the Lieutenant had said in Iraq, "is what ensures you will fuck up only eighty percent of what you are trying to do." If the exact numbers sounded overly optimistic to Davis, he agreed with the general sentiment.

Without preamble, the Lieutenant said, "You know, Davis, when my older brother was twenty-four, he left his girlfriend for a married Russian émigré six years his senior—whom he had met, ironically enough, through his ex, who had been tutoring Margarita, her husband, Sergei, and their four-year-old, Stasu, in English."

"No sir," Davis said, "I'm pretty sure you never told me this."

"You have to understand," the Lieutenant went on, "until this point, my brother, Alberto, had led a reasonably sedate and unimpressive life. Prior to this, the most daring thing he'd done was go out with Alexandra, the tutor, who was Jewish, which made our very Catholic mother very nervous. Yet here he was, packing his clothes and his books, emptying his meager bank account, and driving out of town with Margarita in the passenger's seat and Stasu in the back with all the stuff they couldn't squeeze in the trunk. They headed west, first to St. Louis for a couple of months, next to New Mexico for three years, and finally to Portland—actually, it's just outside Portland, but I can never remember the name of the town.

"She was a veterinarian, Margarita. With Alberto's help, she succeeded in having her credentials transferred over here. Has her own practice, these days, treats horses, cows, farm animals. Alberto helps her; he's her assistant and office manager. Sergei gave them custody of Stasu; they have two more kids, girls, Helena and Catherine. Beautiful kids, my nieces.

"You have any brothers or sisters, Davis?"

"A younger brother, sir. He wants to be a priest."

"Really?"

"Yes, sir."

"Isn't that funny."

XII

5:53 AM

Lying on the ground he'd swept clear of rocks and branches, his rifle propped on a small log, the sky a red bowl overhead, Davis experienced a moment of complete and utter doubt. Not only did the course of action on which they had set out appear wildly implausible, but everything from the courtyard in Fallujah on acquired the sheen of the unreal, the delusional. An eight-foot-tall space vampire? Visions of soaring through the sky, of savaging scores of men, women, and children around the globe? Injecting himself with adrenaline, for Christ's sake? What was any of this but the world's biggest symptom, a massive fantasy his mind had conjured to escape a reality it couldn't bear? What had happened— what scene was the Shadow substituting for? Had they in fact found a trap in the courtyard, an IED that had shredded them in its fiery teeth? Was he lying in a hospital bed somewhere, his body ruined, his mind hopelessly crippled?

When the Shadow was standing in the clearing, swinging its narrow head from side to side, Davis felt something like relief. If this dark thing and its depravities were a hallucination, he could be true to it. The Shadow parted its fangs as if tasting the dawn. Davis tensed, prepared to find himself someplace else, subject to a clip from the thing's history, but the worst he felt was a sudden buzzing in his skull that reminded him of nothing so much as the old fuse box in his parents' basement. He adjusted his rifle and squeezed the trigger.

The air rang with gunfire. Davis thought his first burst caught the thing in the belly: he saw it step back, though that might have been due to either Lee or the Lieutenant, who had fired along with him. Almost too fast to follow, the Shadow jumped, a black scribble against the sky, but someone anticipated its leap and aimed ahead of it. At least one of the bullets connected; Davis saw the Shadow's right eye pucker. Stick-arms jerking, it fell at the edge of the treeline, ten feet in front of him. He shot at its head, its shoulders. Geysers of dirt marked his misses. The Shadow threw itself backwards, but collapsed where it landed.

"NOW!" the Lieutenant screamed.

Davis grabbed for his stake with his left hand as he dropped the rifle from his right. Almost before his fingers had closed on the weapon, he was on his feet and rushing into the clearing. To the right, Lee burst out of the trees, his stake held overhead in both hands, his mouth open in a bellow. In front of them, the Shadow was thrashing from side to side like the world's largest insect pinned through the middle. Its claws scythed grass, bushes. Davis saw that its right eye had indeed been hit, and partially collapsed. Lee was not slowing his charge. Davis sprinted to reach the Shadow at the same time.

Although the thing's legs were motionless, its claws were fast as ever. As Davis came abreast of it, jabbing at its head, its arm snapped in his direction. Pain razored up his left arm. Blood spattered the grass, the Shadow's head jerked towards him, and the momentary distraction this offered was, perhaps, what allowed Lee to tumble into a forward roll that dropped him under the Shadow's other claw and up again to drive his stake down into the base of its throat. Reaching for the cell phone in his shirt pocket, Davis backpedaled. The thing's maw gaped as Lee held on to shove the weapon as far as it would go. The Shadow twisted and thrust its claws into Lee's collarbone and ribs. His eyes bulged and he released the stake. Davis had the cell phone in his hand. The Shadow tore its claw from Lee's chest and ripped him open. Davis pressed the three and hit SEND.

In the woods, there was a white flash and the CRUMP of explosives detonating. A cloud of debris rushed between the trunks. The Shadow jolted as if a bolt of lightning had speared it.

"SHIT!" the Lieutenant was screaming. "SHIT!"

The Shadow was on its feet, Lee dangling from its left claw like a child's bedraggled plaything. Davis backpedaled. With its right claw, the Shadow reached for the stake jutting from its throat. Davis pressed the two and SEND.

He was knocked from his feet by the force of the blast, which shoved the air from his lungs and pushed sight and sound away from him. He was aware of the ground pressing against his back, a fine rain of particles pattering his skin, but his body was contracted around his chest, which could not bring in any air. Suffocating, he was suffocating. He tried to move his hands, his feet, but his extremities did not appear to be receiving his brain's instructions. Perhaps his hand-crafted bomb had accomplished what the Shadow could not.

What he could feel of the world was bleeding away.

XIII

2006

Although Lee wanted to wait for sunset, if not total darkness, a preference Davis shared, the Lieutenant insisted they shoulder their packs and start the trail up Winger Mountain while the sun would be broadcasting its light for another couple of hours. At the expressions on Lee and Davis's faces, he said, "Relax. The thing sweeps the Grove first thing in the morning. It's long gone, off feeding someplace."

The trail was not unpleasant. Had they been so inclined, its lower reaches were wide enough that they could have walked them two abreast. (They opted for single file, Lee taking point, Han next, the Lieutenant third, and Davis bringing up the rear. It spread the targets out.) The ground was matted with the leaves of the trees that flanked the trail and stationed the gradual slopes to either side. (While he had never been any good at keeping the names of such things straight, Davis had an idea the trees were a mix of maple and oak, the occasional white one a birch.) With their crowns full of leaves, the trees almost obscured the sky's blue emptiness. (All the same, Davis didn't look up any more than he could help.)

They reached the path to Thompson's Grove sooner than Davis had anticipated. A piece of wood weathered gray and nailed to a tree chest-high pointed right, to a narrower route that appeared overgrown a hundred yards or so in the distance. Lee withdrew the machete he had sheathed on his belt and struck the sign once, twice, until it flew off the tree into the forest.

"Hey," Davis said, "that's vandalism."

"Sue me," Lee said.

Once they were well into the greenery, the mosquitoes, which had ventured only the occasional scout so long as they kept to the trail, descended in clouds. "Damnit!" the Lieutenant said, slapping his cheek. "I used bug spray."

"Probably tastes like dessert topping to them, sir," Lee called. "Although, damn! at this rate, there won't be any blood left in us for Count Dracula."

Thompson's Grove was an irregular circle, forty feet across. Grass stood thigh-high. A few bushes punctuated the terrain. Davis could feel the sky hungry above them. Lee and Han walked the perimeter while he and the Lieutenant stayed near the trees. All of their rifles were out. Lee and Han declared the area secure, but the four of them waited until the sun was finally down to clear the center of the Grove and build their fire.

Lee had been, Davis supposed the word was *off*, since they'd met in Kingston that morning. His eyes shone in his face, whose flesh seemed drawn around the bones. When Davis embraced him in the lobby of the Quality Inn, it had been like putting his arms around one of the support cables on a suspension bridge, something bracing an enormous weight. It might be the prospect of their upcoming encounter, although Davis suspected there was more to it. The Lieutenant's most recent report had been that Lee was continuing to struggle: Shari had won custody of Douglas, with whom Lee was permitted supervised visits every other Saturday. He'd enrolled at his local community college, but stopped attending classes after the first week. The Lieutenant wasn't sure he'd go so far as to call Lee an alcoholic, but there was no doubt the man liked his beer a good deal more than was healthy. After the wood was gathered and stacked, the fire kindled, the sandwiches Davis had prepared distributed, Lee cleared his throat and said, "I know the Lieutenant has an order he wants us to follow, but there's something I need to know about."

"All right," the Lieutenant said through a mouthful of turkey on rye, "ask away."

"It's the connection we have to the thing," Lee said. "Okay, so: we've got a direct line into its central nervous system. The right amount of adrenaline, and we can hijack it. Problem is, the link works both ways. At least, we know that, when the thing's angry, it can look out of our eyes. What if it can do more? What if it can do to us what we've done to it, take us over?"

"There's been no evidence of that," Davis said. "Don't you think, if it could do that, it would have by now?"

"Not necessarily," Lee said.

"Oh? Why not?"

"Why would it need to? We're trying to get its attention; it doesn't need to do anything to get ours."

"It's an unknown," the Lieutenant said. "It's conceivable the thing could assume control of whoever's hooked up to it and try to use him for support. I have to say, though, that even if it could possess one of us, I have a hard time imagining it doing so while the rest of us are trying to shorten its lifespan. To tell you the truth, should we succeed in killing it, I'd be more worried about it using the connection as a means of escape."

"Escape?" Davis said.

Lee said, "The Lieutenant means it leaves its body behind for one of ours."

"Could it do that?"

"I don't know," the Lieutenant said, "I only mention it as a worst-case scenario. Our ability to share its perceptions, to affect its actions, seems to suggest some degree of congruity between the thing and us. On the other hand, it is a considerable leap from there to its being able to inhabit us."

"Maybe that's how it makes more of itself," Lee said. "One dies, one's born."

"Phoenix," Han said.

"This is all pretty speculative," Davis said.

"Yes it is," the Lieutenant said. "Should the thing seize any of us, however, it will have been speculation well-spent."

"What do you propose, then, sir?" Davis said.

"Assuming any of us survives the morning," the Lieutenant said, "we will have to proceed with great caution." He held up his pistol.

XIV

6:42 AM

Davis opened his eyes to a hole in the sky. Round, black—for a moment, he had the impression the earth had gained a strange new satellite, or that some unimaginable catastrophe had blown an opening in the atmosphere, and then his vision adjusted and he realized that he was looking up into the barrel of the Lieutenant's Glock. The man himself half-crouched beside Davis, his eyes narrowed. His lips moved, and Davis struggled to pick his words out of the white noise ringing in his ears.

"Davis," he said. "You there?"

"Yeah," Davis said. Something was burning; a charcoal reek stung his nostrils. His mouth tasted like ashes. He pushed himself up on his elbows. "Is it—"

"Whoa," the Lieutenant said, holding his free hand up like a traffic cop. "Take it easy, soldier. That was some blast."

"Did we—"

"We did."

"Yeah?"

"We blew it to Kingdom Come," the Lieutenant said. "No doubt, there are pieces of it scattered here and there, but the majority of it is so much dust."

"Lee—"

"You saw what the thing did to him—although, stupid motherfucker, it serves him right, grabbing the wrong goddamned stake. Of all the stupid fucking . . . "

Davis swallowed. "Han?"

The Lieutenant shook his head.

Davis lay back. "Fuck."

"Never mind," the Lieutenant said. His pistol had not moved. "Shit happens. The question before us now is, Did it work? Are we well and truly rid of that thing, that fucking blood-drinking monster, or are we fooling ourselves? What do you say, Davis?"

"I . . . " His throat was dry. "Lee grabbed the wrong one?"

"He did."

"How is that possible?" "I don't know," the Lieutenant said. "I do not fucking know."

"I specifically gave each of us—"

"I know; I watched you. In the excitement of the moment, Lee and Han must have mixed them up."

"Mixed . . . " Davis raised his hands to his forehead. Behind the Lieutenant, the sky was a blue chasm.

"Or could be, the confusion was deliberate."

"What?"

"Maybe they switched stakes on purpose."

"No."

"I don't think so, either, but we all know it wasn't much of a life for Han."

"That doesn't mean—"

"It doesn't."

"Jesus." Davis sat up.

The Lieutenant steadied his gun. "So?"

"I take it you're fine."

"As far as I've been able to determine, yes."

"Could the thing have had something to do with it?"

"The mix-up?"

"Made Han switch the stakes or something?"

"That presumes it knew what they were, which supposes it had been spying on us through Han's eyes for not a few hours, which assumes it comprehended us—our language, our technology—in excess of prior evidence."

"Yeah," Davis said. "Still."

"It was an accident," the Lieutenant said. "Let it go."

"What makes you so sure you're all right?"

"I've had no indications to the contrary. I appear in control of my own thoughts and actions. I'm aware of no alien presence crowding my mind. While I am thirsty, I have to desire to quench that thirst from one of your arteries."

"Would you be, though? Aware of the thing hiding in you?"

The Lieutenant shrugged. "Possibly not. You're taking a long time to answer my question; you know that."

"I don't know how I am," Davis said. "No, I can't feel the thing either, and no, I don't want to drink your blood. Is that enough?"

"Davis," the Lieutenant said, "I will do this. You need to understand that. You are as close to me as anyone, these days, and I will shoot you in the head if I deem it necessary. If I believed the thing were in me, I would turn this gun on myself without a second thought. Am I making myself clear? Let me know it's over, or let me finish it."

The Lieutenant's face was flushed. "All right," Davis said. He closed his eyes. "All right." He took a deep breath. Another.

When he opened his eyes, he said, "It's gone."

"You're positive."

"Yes, sir."

"You cannot be lying to me."

"I know. I'm not."

The end of the pistol wavered, and for a moment, Davis was certain that the Lieutenant was unconvinced, that he was going to squeeze the trigger, anyway. He wondered if he'd see the muzzle flash.

Then the pistol lowered and the Lieutenant said, "Good man." He holstered the gun and extended his hand. "Come on. There's a lot we have to do."

Davis caught the Lieutenant's hand and hauled himself to his feet. Behind the Lieutenant, he saw the charred place that had been the Shadow, Lee's torn and blackened form to one side of it. Further back, smoke continued to drift out of the spot in the trees where Han had lain. The Lieutenant turned and started walking towards the trees. He did not ask, and Davis did not tell him, what he had seen with his eyes closed. He wasn't sure how he could have said that the image behind his eyelids was the same as the image in front of them: the unending sky, blue, ravenous.

Selected Vampire Anthologies 2000-2010

There were numerous anthologies of romance novellas (usually four authors) as well as original-fiction anthologies with fantasy, horror, or mixed-genre themes that often included vampire stories but were not exclusive to them. These are not listed. Neither are tie-ins to games or television series, retrospectives of earlier eras of vampire fiction/classics (with one exception), ebook- or erotica-only anthologies. Anthologies listed (with one exception) contained at least some original fiction. (YA=Young Adult.)

2000

Kaye, Marvin, ed. *Vampire Sextette* (Science Fiction Book Club)

2001

Elrod, P.N. & Greenberg, Martin, eds., *Dracula In London* (Ace)

Jones, Stephen, ed., *The Mammoth Book of Vampire Stories By Women* (Carrol & Graf) About half original; half reprint

2002

Anonymous, ed., *Vampires* (Dark Horse) Graphic Anthology; YA

2003

Greenberg, Martin, ed., *Vampire Slayers* (Gramercy)

2004

Allen, Angela, ed., *Dark Thirst* (Pocket)

Cavelos, Jeanne, ed., *The Many Faces of Van Helsing* (Ace)

Jones, Stephen, ed., *The Mammoth Book of Vampires* (Robinson) Expanded from 1992 edition, primarily reprints with some originals added

2007

Greenberg, Martin & Darrell Schweitzer, eds. *The Secret History of Vampires* (Daw)

Harris, Charlaine & Toni L. P. Kelner, eds. *Many Bloody Returns* (Ace)

2008

Cast, P.C., ed. *Immortal: Love Stories With Bite* (BenBella) YA

Trelep, Trisha, ed., *The Eternal Kiss: 13 Vampire Tales of Blood and Desire* (Running Press Kids) YA

Trelep, Trisha, ed., *The Mammoth Book of Vampire Romance* (Running Press)

2009

Adams, John Joseph, ed. *By Blood We Live* (Night Shade) Primarily reprints, but some originals

Kuznia, Yanni, ed. *A Fantasy Medley* (Subterranean Press)

Penzler, Otto, ed. *The Vampire Archive* (Quercus) All reprints, but probably the most comprehensive compilation ever assembled

Trelep, Trisha, ed., *The Eternal Kiss: 13 Vampire Tales of Blood and Desire* (Running Press Kids) YA

Trelep, Trisha, ed., *The Mammoth Book of Vampire Romance 2* (Running Press)

Trelep, Trisha, ed., *The Eternal Kiss: 12 Vampire Tales Of Blood And Desire* (Perseus) YA

Ulanski, Gave & Garrett Anderson, eds., *Vampires: Dracula and the Undead Legions* (Moonstone)

2010

Cast, P.C., ed., *Eternal: More Love Stories with Bite* (Smart Pop) YA

Friesner, Esther, ed., *Fangs for the Mammaries* (Baen)

Kilpatrick, Nancy, ed., *Evolve: Vampire Stories of the New Undead* (Edge)

Whates, Ian, ed. *The Bitten Word* (NewCon Press)

Publication History

Holly Black, "The Coldest Girl in Coldtown" © 2009. *The Eternal Kiss: 13 Vampire Tales of Blood and Desire*, ed. Trisha Telep (Running Press Kids). Reprinted by permission of the author.

Rachel Caine, "Dead Man Stalking" © 2009. Originally published in *Immortal: Stories With Bite*, edited by P.C. Cast (Ben Bella Books). Reprinted by permission of the author.

Albert Cowdrey, "Twilight States" © 2005. Originally published in *The Magazine of Fantasy & Science Fiction*, July 2005. Reprinted by permission of the author.

Stephen Dedman, "Waste Land" © 2002. Originally published in *Agog! Fantastic Fiction*, ed. Cat Sparks, (Agog! Press). Reprinted by permission of the author.

Charles de Lint, "Sisters" © 2002. Originally published in *Waifs and Strays* (Viking). Reprinted by permission of the author.

Charlaine Harris, "Dahlia Underground" © 2010. Originally published in *Crimes by Moonlight: Mysteries from the Dark Side,* ed. Charlaine Harris (Berkley). Reprinted by permission of the author.

Tanya Huff, "No Matter Where You Go" © 2010. Originally published in *A Girl's Guide to Guns and Monsters*, ed. Martin H. Greenberg and Kerrie Hughes (Daw). Reprinted by permission of the author.

Caitlín R. Kiernan, "The Belated Burial" © 2009. First published in *Sirenia Digest #38*, January 2009. Reprinted by permission of the author.

Nancy Kilpatrick, "Vampires Anonymous" © 2009. Originally published in *Vampires: Dracula and the Undead Legions*, ed. Dave Ulanski, Garrett Anderson (Moonstone Books). Reprinted by permission of the author.

J.A. Konrath, "The Screaming" © 2004. Originally published in *The Many Faces of Van Helsing*, ed. Jeanne Cavelos (Ace). Reprinted by permission of the author.

John Langan, "The Wide, Carnivorous Sky" © 2009. *By Blood We Live*, ed. John Joseph Adams (Night Shade). Reprinted by permission of the author.

Tanith Lee, "La Vampiresse" © 2000. Originally published in *Interzone, Number 154*, April 2000. Reprinted by permission of the author.

Kim Newman, "Castle in the Desert: Anno Dracula 1977" © 2001. Originally published in *SCIFI.com*, March 2001. Reprinted by permission of the author.

Tina Rath, "A Trick of the Dark" © 2001. Originally published in *The Mammoth Book of Vampire Stories by Women*, ed. Stephen Jones (Constable & Robinson). Reprinted by permission of the author.

Barbara Roden, "Endless Night" © 2008. Originally published in *Exotic Gothic 2,* ed. Danel Olson (Ash-Tree Press). Reprinted by permission of the author.

Karen Russell, "Vampires in the Lemon Grove" © 2007. Originally published in *Zoetrope: All-Story, Vol. 11 No 4.,* Winter 2007. Reprinted by permission of the author and Denise Shannon Literary Agency, Inc.

Nisi Shawl, "To the Moment" © 2007. Originally published in *Reflection's Edge*, November 2007. Reprinted by permission of the author.

Susan Sizemore, "Dancing With the Star" © 2008. Originally published in *The Mammoth Book of Vampire Romance*, ed. Trisha Telep (Constable & Robinson). Reprinted by permission of the author.

Michael Marshall Smith, "This Is Now" © 2004. Originally published in *BBC Cult Vampire Magazine*, March 2004. Reprinted by permission of the author.

Jeanne C. Stein, "The Ghost of Leadville" © 2009. Originally published in *The Mammoth Book of Vampire Romance 2*, ed. Trisha Telep (Constable & Robinson). Reprinted by permission of the author.

Mary Turzillo, "When Gretchen Was Human" © 2001. Originally published in *The Mammoth Book of Vampire Stories by Women*, ed. Stephen Jones (Constable & Robinson). Reprinted by permission of the author.

Carrie Vaughn, "Conquistador de la Noche" © 2009 by Carrie Vaughn, LLC. Originally published in *Subterranean Online,* Spring 2009. Reprinted by permission of the author.

Conrad Williams, "Outfangthief" © 2001. Originally published in *The Mammoth Book of Vampire Stories by Women*, ed. Stephen Jones (Constable & Robinson). Reprinted by permission of the author.

Chelsea Quinn Yarbro, "Gentleman of the Old School" © 2005. Originally published in *Dark Delicacies: Original Stores of the Macabre from Today's Greatest Horror Writers*, ed. Del Howison & Jeff Gelb (Carroll & Graf). Reprinted by permission of the author.

About the Editor

Paula Guran is the editor of Pocket Book's Juno fantasy imprint and nonfiction editor for *Weird Tales*. In an earlier life, she produced weekly e-mail newsletter *DarkEcho* (winning two Bram Stoker Awards, an International Horror Guild Award award, and a World Fantasy Award nomination) and edited *Horror Garage* magazine (earning another IHG and a second World Fantasy nomination). Guran has contributed reviews, interviews, and articles to numerous professional publications. She's also done a great deal of other various and sundry work in sf/f/h publishing. Earlier anthologies Guran has edited include *Embraces, Best New Paranormal Romance, Best New Romantic Fantasy, The Year's Best Dark Fantasy and Horror: 2010*, and *Zombies: The Recent Dead. The Year's Best Dark Fantasy and Horror, 2011* and *Halloween!* are forthcoming this year.